REBEL AND THE PROMISE

By

Delores M. Dahl

ISBN-13:

978-1502783134

ISBN-10:

1502783134

Copyright © 2014
by Delores M. Dahl
All rights reserved.

Cover Design Copyright © 2014
by Delores M. Dahl
Front cover photo by Injee Unshin

First Kindle Edition

This book is a work of fiction. Any resemblance to actual events or persons living or dead is purely coincidental, with the exception of known historical characters.

All rights reserved. No part of this book may be reproduced, distributed, scanned or transmitted in any printed or electronic form without written permission from the authors.

Dedicated to the loving memory of Conrad and Axelina Nelson

Acknowledgements

I wish to thank friends and fellow writers, DeVera Marcus and Beverly Devoret for being my first, and happily, encouraging readers. A special thanks to my granddaughter Dr Arianna Molloy, who read the first version when she was in the 6th grade and offered great support and wonderful advice.

I am especially grateful to my daughter, Devorah Cutler Rubenstein, for her ongoing encouragement, editing and design help. Special thanks to daughters Wendy Cutler and Johanna Molloy, and granddaughter Romy Cutler/Lengyel who were always there to lend an ear and make helpful critiques. Thanks to my sister Tira Latt and her husband Rein who kept asking for "more chapters, please."

In addition, I am indebted to Frances Dayee and her amazing writer's group, especially Violet Wentland and Michael Soreng. Special thanks to Bill Taylor for patient computer help. I appreciate the many friends who kept faith in the story and my long process. Lastly, I'm grateful to have had time with my courageous young characters and their "Can Do Spirit." They revived me, and I hope they will do the same for you.

REBEL AND THE PROMISE

by

Delores M. Dahl

CHAPTER ONE

July 11, 1860 - Kansas Territory – The wagon train

Gray and still in the early morning light, the prairie sprawled in every direction, dwarfing the tiny band of travelers. As if reluctant to face the harshness of the day, the caravan of twelve prairie schooners remained quietly yoked in its nightly circle. Only a few early risers gathered around the fire pits to prepare for the morning breakfast. Folks nodded their greetings and spoke in hushed tones, so as not to wake others or those still recovering from the plague.

Seventeen-year-old Sara Robbins glanced anxiously about the compound as she finished tightening down the last canopy rope. She paused a moment to check the water barrel at the side of her prairie schooner. The barrel was damp. Good. Her brother had remembered to take care of it. Now everything was ready. But where was Aaron? She watched several men leading livestock down to the river, but she didn't see her brother or old man Tanner. They should've been back with the teams by now. "Oh, please don't let there be a problem," she murmured, feeling the familiar jabs of pain begin across her brow. She pressed little circles on her forehead and reminded herself, "only a little longer."

Across the way, she noticed Ida Mae Thompson sitting on the ground in front of her fire pit. Poor Ida looked so weak and thin. Sara wondered if she'd decided to move on with the wagon train or return east. Ida didn't look strong enough to do either, really, but she'd have to make a choice, by day's end. Hopefully, she'd move on to Salt Lake as her husband had planned.

Sara bit her lower lip and tried to swallow the lump in her throat as she watched Ida's three young boys carry buckets of dried buffalo chips around to the other pits. Ten-year-old Holden stayed to build a fire for his mother. But Ida just sat staring into the pit, rocking and cradling a dirty, rag doll to her chest. Sara turned away, unable to watch.

A wave of dizziness forced Sara to lean against the side of the wagon. She clung to a canopy rope. "No, I won't give way," she insisted, resisting the urge to run screaming into the prairie. She took a deep breath and waited as the wooziness and panic eased. A moment later, she saw her fifteen-year-old brother running up toward their wagon, but without Rufus Tanner.

Aaron stopped abruptly in front of her, frowned and whispered. "I thought you'd be ready."

"I am!" Sara defended, self-consciously running her hand through her uncombed tangle of auburn hair. "Where's Tanner? You were supposed to find him. You know we can't leave without him."

"He'll he'd be here soon. Better settle down, Sara," Aaron said, eying her. Aaron began taking a length of rope and coiling it, then placed it on two pegs beside the water barrel. "By the way, I stopped to say goodbye to Mark. He said to be sure you didn't leave without seeing him. He was pretty sore about last night."

"Sore?" Sara shook her head. "Well, I've already said my goodbyes. We don't have time, now."

"That's stupid, Sara. He's your best friend. You shouldn't leave on a sour note."

"I don't want to discuss it, Aaron. We're already late." The truth was she couldn't bear another scene. Last night had been hard enough. Mark meant well, but he didn't understand. She couldn't change her plans. Even if her "state of mind was questionable," she had to carry on as her parents had hoped. They just had to get to San Francisco by September 30 for the court date, or they'd lose everything. Catching the Overland Stagecoach would make up the lost time.

Sara quickly took a small, silver-handled brush from her yellow-checked apron pocket and began vigorously brushing her long hair. She could feel Aaron watching her and quickly grabbed a wad of hair, pulled it back and tied a blue ribbon around it. "There!" she stated firmly, "I'm ready!"

"You look pale. You fit to travel?"

"I'm fine," she snapped, avoiding her brother's piercing look and determinedly pressed her hands against the skirt of her green, cotton dress. The last thing she needed was for Aaron to worry or show doubt around the caravan. There was enough concern over her "fitness" to travel. Folks might try to detain them, especially the wagon master. Sven Hanson could decide she wasn't up to journeying back to Leavenworth, Kansas Territory, even though it was only two days. And the longer it took to leave, the more likely someone would find an excuse to stop them. Nature's hand was enough caution: the heat of the day was coming on fast.

Sara watched in alarm as sunlight spread quickly across the prairie, revealing the endless miles of ripe summer grass, and at the horizon, an ominous band of red. "It's going to be a scorcher. We'll be lucky to make ten miles."

Instead of answering, Aaron rushed to the front of the wagon, grabbed his new 1860 Henry off the front seat and aimed at the top of a nearby knoll. "Look. Up there!" He pointed. "An Indian!"

"What?" Sara scowled at the hill. "I don't see anything." She squinted against the first rays of sun. "It's just morning shadows. Now put that down, or you'll wake the whole camp."

"I tell you. I saw an Indian. I saw him and his pony. He was staring down at the wagon train; raised his fist, too. Like this." Aaron gestured, punching the sky. "No mistaking that!"

"Well, he's not there now." Sara cupped her hand to her forehead and stood watching the light work its way along the knoll and through the eight crosses. The weathered wood planks seemed unreal and innocent as a garden fence.

"I'm going to warn the others." Aaron leveled the rifle against his shoulder.

"Aaron, no!" Sara reached and pulled Aaron's arm down.

"What are you doing, Sara?" He spun about and quickly re-aimed. "There could be more--might attack any minute."

"Stop! Calm down. Think! The guards would've spotted him, and one Indian isn't a threat." Sara watched her brother back up a few feet. "Don't be foolish, Aaron. Remember Hanson said there hadn't been any Indian trouble in this part of Kansas Territory."

"He can't be sure. Never can be--the grass being so tall and all. Likely, Indians wouldn't come close with the Cholera flag up, but it came down last night." Clutching his rifle, Aaron ran a few feet. "I'm going to see if he took anything."

"Aaron! No! The wagon master warned us to stay away. Don't do anything to rile him. He'll be mad and stop us."

Aaron paused, took off his gray felt hat, slapped it against his brown trousers and glared at the knoll. "Ya, I guess, you're right." Reluctantly, he set the rifle back and took a small knife from his brown, leather belt, lifted a round piece of wood from his trouser pocket and began whittling. "Folks say it's a bad omen, an Indian near a grave-site."

"Please, Aaron, no more talk of omens and Indians." Sara bent and pulled Aaron's bedroll from under the wagon. "Sure hope we can find a place to wash our linen. People will smell us before they see us."

Aaron shook his head. "Some folks claim it was God's punishment for our sins--'God's wrath,' some say."

"How stupid! God's wrath had nothing to do with it." Sara took a faded blue quilt from the bedroll and shook it angrily against the side of the wagon, then quickly folded it. "And it's cruel to say such things. Mom and Dad were the most loving, kind people in the whole world. They'd never done anything wrong to anyone." Sara placed the blanket on the driver's seat and turned to glance again at the top of the knoll. She couldn't take her eyes away. The image, she knew would stay forever.

"Are you all right, Sara?"

"Yes, yes," she murmured. "Just one of my headaches. I'll be fine soon's we leave." She turned abruptly and forced her eyes from the hill. But no amount of time or looking away would ever remove the memories, the horrible images—-the violent sickness, the terrible sounds, the putrid smells, the pain. The unspeakable pictures of death—-her mother, lying helpless, fighting for breath, her father too ill to move--all of that assaulted her again. Her knees weakened and began to give way.

"Sara, you'd better sit down." Aaron rushed to get the folded quilt and spread it on the ground. "Here," he said, "just sit here, rest. You're white as a ghost."

"No, I'm fine," she protested, but did as suggested.

"No wonder. You've hardly slept in three weeks."

"Please don't fuss, Aaron." Sara glanced about. "We don't want folks nosing about."

"You're just wore out, what with nursing the sick and all. You'll be good as new, once we're on our way."

"Yes." Sara nodded wearily.

Aaron whirled about. "Where's Tarney?"

"I don't know." Sara looked beneath the underbelly of nearby wagons, but she didn't see their little black and white border collie anywhere. "Maybe she's with Tanner's dog; probably at the river. You know how she loves dashing about with George. She'll come around, once she sees Danny and Reeves hitched."

"I'm going to find her! I don't want any ol' Indian grabbing her." Aaron took off, waving his hat in the air as he ran.

"No! Aaron, wait! Aaron!!" Sara stood and watched her brother race through the tall grass, his head bobbing and weaving like a moth in a dried corn field, until he was out of sight in the cottonwood trees lining the river bank. Darn Kid! He knows better than to run off. Besides, Tarney always comes back. Aaron was way too headstrong these days—-dashing off, not listening to her. That could be dangerous on the trail. She was in charge now. He'd best remember that.

Sara closed her eyes a moment, rubbed her forehead and slowly drew in a breath. I guess I'll just have to be more patient. After all, they were both doing the best they could. Poor kid. She knew Aaron was hurting and trying hard not to give way. Things will be better once we're gone from all this. And later, much later, we'll both have time to cry. But for now, we have to be strong, push ahead and keep our minds set on getting the Overland Stage Coach. Determinedly, Sara grabbed the quilt, folded it and reset it on the driver's seat.

A moment later, a sound startled her. "What's that?"

Someone or something was moving about near the back of the wagon. "Who's there?" Caravan folks didn't usually go around in back, without calling out, but someone was there. A chill plunged down her spine. She quickly grabbed Aaron's rifle and crept along the side of the wagon, her heart pounding, her mouth dry.

CHAPTER TWO

"Help me!" a girl's voice whimpered.

"Peggy? Is that you?" Sara rushed to the back of the wagon. "Good heavens, Peggy! What happened?" Sara saw her friend stumbling toward the wagon, clutching a dirty, gray shawl over her torn, blue dress.

"Did you see him?" Peggy whispered, glancing about, her eyes wide with terror.

Sara quickly set the rifle against the back wheel and rushed to keep her friend from falling. "Here," she said, placing her arm about Peggy's shoulders and helping her around to the side of the wagon.

"Don't let him find me!" Peggy pleaded, frantically looking about.

"Who?" Sara asked, momentarily confused and thinking of the Indian Aaron mentioned.

"My stepfather." Peggy cried and winced.

"Oh, Peggy, you're hurt!" Peggy looked like she'd been dragged through brambles or maybe even beaten. A small cut on her cheek beneath her right eye had begun to swell. "I'd better get you into the wagon. Can you climb up?"

"I don't know. I'll try."

"Grab hold of the back wheel if you can. I'll give you a boost." Sara bent and lifted Peggy's right boot and helped her up and over the side, then looked about.

"Do you see him?" Peggy whispered from inside the wagon.

Sara stood below, watching and listening for any sign of Donald Colwell. "No, I don't see him." Thankfully, no one appeared to be looking their way. Sara picked up the rifle, Peggy's torn shawl and climbed into the wagon.

Peggy sat on a small barrel, her hands clutching the torn top of her dress. "I'm so sorry to bother you, but I didn't know where else to go," she murmured. "When I got back to camp, I was too scared to go to my wagon, so I hid under Tommy Larson's wagon until it was light. He was on guard duty near the horses."

"You did the right thing, coming here." Sara knelt beside Peggy. "You're safe now." Sara insisted, gingerly touching Peggy's forehead. "Now, let's get this hair off your face--see how deep the cut is." Sara gingerly lifted the dirty, matted, blond hair aside. "It's going to need a couple of stitches."

"You won't tell my stepfather where I am, will you? Promise?"

"Of course, I won't." Sara frowned. "I thought he was gone for a few days, hunting or something."

"He came back late last night--caught up with me by the river. He was so drunk. I never saw him so bad off. He kept talking about how he'd come upon two Indians and that they'd attacked. He bragged about how he killed one and took all their weapons and horses." Peggy shuddered. "And he laughed. Said 'Ain't a one goin' ta make trouble fer us.' Claims he got lucky and sold their ponies." Peggy cringed and covered her eyes.

"Good heavens!" Sara knew that Donald Colwell was a rough and hard sort of man, but now his actions might have created a danger for the whole wagon train. "Did he say where it happened?"

"Only that it was two days ago." Peggy shook her head. "I said we should tell Hanson. But he says we'd be thrown off the wagon train, and that if I tell anyone, he'll kill me." Peggy covered her mouth. "What should I do, Sara?"

"I'm not sure yet, but we'll figure it out." Sara decided not to mention that Aaron had spotted an Indian close by. Could there be a connection to Colwell? "Right now, you'd better hold still and let me clean this cut or it'll fester." Reaching to the side of the canvas dome, Sara removed a small, burlap-sack hanging from a hook. She pulled out a silver flask, then turned around and grabbed a clean rag, needle and thread from her sewing basket. "This will do." She poured an ample amount of whiskey on the rag, thread and needle. "It's going to sting and hurt some, but I'll hurry."

Peggy flinched and took a deep breath as Sara worked on the wound. "Oh, Sara, it was so awful—-my stepfather. He gets crazy mean when he drinks."

"Didn't anyone see or hear you?"

"No…I…I didn't want anyone to know. You see, I'd gone down to the river before. Oh, I knew we're not supposed to, but I felt all hemmed in--couldn't breathe. I needed to be alone, say my prayers and…" Peggy hesitated, shook her head. "Ya see, Momma loved the river. Sometimes, I imagine she's down there, and I talk to her, away from everybody--from my stepfather." Peggy shivered and drew her knees up. "I heard Donald calling, and I tried to hide behind some cotton wood trees. But he found me. He…he says now that my Momma is dead, I belong to him, legal like, and that I have to do what he wants." Peggy covered her face.

"What he wants?"

"He says he wants…" Peggy could barely whisper the words. "He says I have to take my Momma's place. And now that I'm fifteen, I can marry him!"

"Marry!" Sara was furious and fought to control her feelings. She steeled herself against the awful question. "Did he…did he touch you?"

"He tried--threw me against the ground and put his dirty hand over my mouth. But he was too drunk, and I kept hitting him with a rock, and then I bit him and escaped in the brambles." Peggy recoiled.

"Good for you, Peggy!"

"He says he'll lock me up, kill anyone who'd try to take me away."

Sara waited as Peggy choked back tears. Strangled sobs came in small, uneven bursts as she clapped her hands over her mouth. "Oh, Sara, I'm so ashamed."

"Nonsense! Nothing for you to be ashamed of." Sara's voice hardened. "Donald Colwell will be horse-whipped or worse! Don't worry. Hanson will take care of him!" Sara thought the wagon master was one of the few men on the wagon train bigger and stronger than Colwell. "Hanson will…"

"No! You mustn't tell him--mustn't tell anyone!"

"But Peggy, you need help--protection!"

"No! I'll leave. I'll get up and go. I'll…" Grimacing, Peggy struggled to get to her feet. Too weak, she sank back and began to cry.

Sara thought she heard someone calling her name.

"Peggy, hurry and get out of that dress. Here," Sara reached for her quilting basket and pulled out a pink and green striped dress with a pink ruffle at the neck. "You can put this on, but hurry."

Peggy pressed the dress against her. She frowned.

"Yes, I know. Unfortunately, the neck's a bit low. I used the dickey for something else, and was about to cut the dress up for quilting. "

"Oh, Sara, this is so sweet of you."

Sara shook her head. "It's going to be way too big for you,

but..." she suddenly put her finger to her lip and listened. She shook her head and ran to the front and peered through the flap. "Oh, no," Sara whispered. "It's Mark Davis. I have to talk to him, or he'll know something's wrong. You just stay quiet. I won't be long."

Sara grabbed a small jug of water off a little barrel. "Here, it's been boiled. Put some on a rag and douse yourself. It'll get awfully hot in here, once I close the flaps. And oh, there's my Derringer." She pointed to a satchel. "It's cleaned and loaded." Peggy warily eyed the satchel as Sara climbed down.

Sara stood at the front, her mind suddenly in a whirl. Had word gotten out that Peggy was missing? Did Colwell have folks searching? Of course, this would be the first place anyone would look. Oh, heavens! Now what? Her stomach felt all queasy, her legs wobbly. She stiffened her back like a shield, clutched her skirt and stood waiting.

As Mark came closer, Sara noticed how much he'd changed in the last three months. Though only nineteen, he looked and acted older--a head taller than her, now. He'd gotten so thin and let his hair grow to his shoulders in a careless manner. And his face had a scruffy little beard, not like Mark at all, who was always so particular about everything. But the biggest changes were inside. The death of his little brother had left a permanent sadness in his grey eyes, even when he smiled. Sara's heart melted at the sight of him, and she longed to rush into his arms, give him a big "sisterly" hug. But that wouldn't be right now, and could be misunderstood.

Poor Mark. His family had lost so much. Only two weeks ago, the cholera had taken Mark's seven-year-old brother. Oh, how Sara had loved Hamil--such an adorable little imp. She couldn't believe that he wouldn't be chasing the camp dogs or running around the wagons. It's all so...so unreal. But of course, it is real, she reminded herself. She felt light-headed and grabbed hold of the front wheel.

Mark stopped a few feet in front of her. "I saw Aaron. He said you're really going."

"Yes," Sara answered, her lips trembling.

"I'm so sorry about last evening—our quarrel."

"Me, too," Sara said softly..

"I understand." Mark's eyes filled with affection. "You've been worried about your Uncle. Has there been any news?"

"No! The last we heard was what Clara wrote nearly three months ago." Sara shook her head. "Poor kid, she's only ten, you know and she's frightened. She begged us to hurry. Said her father sleeps most of the time. And that their friend, Jessica, is away. Sara's eyes narrowed. It seems the lawyer, Mr. Locke, changed the doctor and hired a new housekeeper. Clara says she's scared of the woman and feels like a prisoner."

"Young girls tend to exaggerate."

"Maybe, but it sounds suspicious. That lawyer is the same one who's trying to steal our inheritance. I wouldn't put anything past him. If Aaron and I don't get there by the end of September, I'm afraid something terrible might happen."

"I know," Mark said softly. I'm sorry I gave you an argument. I hoped you'd change your mind about leaving right now." He sighed. "I thought maybe Dad and Mom would be better soon and I could go with you. "But," he shook his head. "That's unrealistic."

"I know, but they will get better."

"Oh, Sara, I don't know what I'll do without you and Aaron. You're family to me and Mom, too. She said that watching you grow up, running in and out of our house, made her feel she had a daughter." He bit his lip and Sara knew he was trying hard not to give way.

"Just remember," Sara encouraged, "we promised to get together later this year, and I'll write. There'll be letters waiting in Denver or Salt Lake, wherever the Overland Stage goes and there's a post." She saw Mark's doubtful look. Trying to cheer him, she said brightly, "Once you get your parents settled, you'll come to San Francisco. Uncle Jacob and Clara would love to see you. We'll have plenty of time then, to talk about our future."

Mark nodded, tears brimming. "I'll be praying for you, Sara."

I know," she whispered, reaching for his hand.

Fervently, Mark clutched her hand, placed it over his heart. "Oh, Sara, I need you. I don't know what I'll do without you. This whole trip seems so--so futile now. We've lost so much--both of us. Oh, Sara--Sara, I love you. I know we talked about getting married someday, after you helped your Uncle with the Hardware store. But everything's changed. It's all changed. Oh, please say you'll marry me. Now, today! Hanson will do it."

Sara pulled her hand from his chest. "Mark, please, wait."

Mark moved closer, putting his arms around her.

"No, Mark, please--please don't." She pushed against his chest. She had to get away!

"Let me take care of you." He tried to kiss her.
"No! Mark!" She turned her head away.
Mark seemed stunned and surprised.

Suddenly, there were shouts, people running. Sara heard the noise before Mark. "Something is happening!" She turned and ran a few feet towards the center of the compound.

Several women ran past. Someone screamed. People started shouting about a fight. "It's a kid and Colwell," someone yelled as they ran toward the fight.

"Mark!" Sara exclaimed. "I hear Tarney. Something's wrong! Something's happening to Aaron!"

CHAPTER THREE

Sara and Mark ran toward the commotion.

"Aaron!" Sara shouted, trying to be heard over the uproar, but there was too much noise and confusion. Folks seemed to be dashing in every direction.

"Over there!" someone hollered, pointing to the other side of the caravan. "It's Colwell and Nordby!"

"There's Aaron!" Sara pointed to the edge of the crowd where her brother hurtled around the corner of the wagon, as though chased by hornets.

"Colwell's gone crazy," Aaron said between gulps of air. "He's attacking Ed Nordby--thinks Ed's hidden Peggy somewhere."

Sara gasped as she saw Peggy's stepfather stagger forward from between two wagons, chasing a tall, thin, young man.

"It weren't me! I swear!" Ed protested, backing up and trying to get more than an arm's reach away.

Sara watched in alarm as Donald Colwell wielding an axe handle, swung his arm in a murderous arch. He weaved unsteadily as he pursued Ed who began scampering and running in circles.

Colwell came closer, brandishing the axe handle.

Sara watched Ed bolt and run for the center of the caravan. "Help me!" he yelled. "Colwell's going to kill me!"

Folks scrambled out of Ed's way as he rushed into the gathering crowd, then tripped and fell. Terrified, Ed rolled into a ball and put his hands over his face.

"Somebody do something!" Sara yelled, as Colwell swaggered forward, bent on striking Ed.

Just then, three men rushed Colwell from behind. One of them was the wagon master, Sven Hanson. He got a head lock on Colwell, wrenched the axe handle from his right hand and pulled his arm around in back. The other two men wrestled Colwell's other arm around his back while another came running up with a rope.

Sara watched in relief as Colwell's wrists were quickly bound and the three men shoved Colwell ahead of them. Belligerent and unbowed, Colwell yelled "Ya touch her 'n I'll kill ya!"

In shock, Sara watched him led away and out of sight. "Wonder what they'll do with him," she muttered.

"I saw it start!" Aaron eagerly explained. "Ed was minding his own business, just sitting on a barrel when Colwell came up and started accusing him of meeting Peggy. He had that mean ol' axe handle--you could tell he was going to clobber Ed. He pushed Ed against a wagon and was about to shove the axe handle against Ed's throat." He paused a moment. "You see, I was the only one around, but I knew I couldn't stop him, so I ran up, trying to distract him. I yelled at him to stop, but he didn't." Aaron shook his head. "He looked--crazy."

"You should've run away, Aaron!"

Aaron ignored Sara's comment. "I kept hitting him on his back, but he didn't notice me more than a fly. I started yanking the back of his vest, so then he swings around with his other arm. I jumped back and ducked. That's when Ed got away. Tarney helped too--running about and barking, even ran up, nipped at his pant leg, trying to keep Colwell from coming after me. Colwell didn't pay any mind--just turned and chased after Ed. I got away!"

Sara felt nauseous and dizzy. "You could've been hurt!"

"I know." Aaron said, glancing about. "Where's Tarney? He squatted down to look under wagons and called, "Tarney! Oh, there she is." Aaron pointed. "Come here, Tarney," he coaxed. "She's still scared. Come here, girl!"

Finally, Tarney dashed to Aaron.

"You crazy mutt," Aaron said affectionately, squatting to hug her.

"Probably saved your life," Mark added.

"You saved my life!" Aaron heartedly agreed and scratched between Tarney's black ears. He looked up at Mark. "If it weren't for Tarney getting in Colwell's way, he would've cracked my skull, for sure!" He grinned up at Sara. "She's sure brave, ain't she?"

Sara suddenly angry, snapped. "You should've called for help, Aaron. It was stupid to take on Colwell."

"I knew you'd say that! You weren't there!"

"You could've been killed," Sara insisted.

"He's sure crazy," Aaron said, ignoring Sara and turning to Mark.

"Yep, he's a mean one, all right." Mark said, quietly. "I wouldn't want to tangle with him. You were lucky, Aaron. That man's strong as an ox. Better keep out of his way."

"Oh, I will," said Aaron, fervently. "I'd sure hate to have him for a stepfather. Poor Peggy."

"Peggy!" Sara exclaimed, biting her lip to keep from saying anything more. What would they do now?

"Has anyone seen her?" Mark asked.

"I haven't," Aaron answered.

Sara frowned. She had no intention of mentioning anything about Peggy to Mark, but she'd need to talk to her brother right away. "Aaron, I have to talk to you. Now!"

"In a minute," Aaron answered, as he watched the crowd of onlookers surrounding Ed Nordby.

As Sara waited for Aaron, she heard Ed Nordby explain what had happened.

"Well," Ed said, raising his voice for all to hear. "I guess there ain't no real harm done--case of mistaken identity, I warrant. I ain't one ta hold a grudge." His face beamed as several young women giggled and looked coyly at him.

"Guess a man's entitled to protect his daughter, especially one as purdy as Peggy."

The crowd of onlookers continued to talk and whisper among themselves, some agreeing that Colwell probably had cause.

Sara heard a woman say, "I'd lock her up at night if she were my daughter!" Sara suddenly felt weak.

"You all right, Sara?" Mark asked. "You look white as a China plate."

"I'm fine!" she answered curtly, trying not to show her feelings. "It's just these people. They don't even know Peggy."

"Well, that may be." Mark sighed. "But I think you'd better stay clear of the Colwells. I'd keep away from Peggy, if I were you. She'll be trouble now."

"Mark!" Sara turned angrily, "Peggy's my friend!"

"All the same," he said, distractedly, watching the crowd disperse, "I'd stay clear."

Sara felt her face flush with anger, but she knew this was not the time or place to vent her feelings. Mark's attitude was disappointing. She clutched her skirt and kept her voice even. "I have some chores to do. I'll see you at the wagon, Aaron—-soon!"

"Call out if you need any help," Mark offered, though his attention was still on the crowd.

"Aaron, please!" Sara watched as Aaron rushed forward to stand next to Mark.

"Be there in a minute," he said, waving her away.

"Don't forget!" Sara said, biting back the increasing anxiety. But she sauntered away, not wanting to call attention to the urgency she felt.

Sara raced back to the wagon, climbed up and found Peggy cowering under a sheet. "Thank goodness, you're all right. I was so worried about you."

"I heard all the shouting," Peggy said, shaking her head. "I was so scared. I thought he was coming for me."

"Don't worry, Peggy. Your stepfather doesn't know where you are. Besides," she reassured, sounding more confident than she felt. "Hanson has him tied up. He won't get loose. But we'd best leave as soon as possible."

"What did Aaron say about my coming with you?"

Sara hesitated. "He doesn't know yet, but I'm in charge, and I've decided you're coming with us!" Sara raised her chin defiantly. She could only hope that Rufus Tanner wouldn't object, but she'd handle that.

"Oh, Sara!" Peggy cried, jumping up and hugging Sara. "I don't know how to thank you."

"Never mind. You'd do the same for me." Sara smiled reassuringly. "Try to relax, for now, till Aaron comes. I'm sure it won't be long." Sara turned and started for the front flap of the wagon. "I'll stay outside and keep an eye on things. You just rest, Peggy."

Sara climbed down and stood at the side of the wagon, watching the morning activities. She'd have to appear busy. Hopefully, folks would leave her alone. But what would she do if they discovered Peggy? Would Hanson keep them from leaving? Good Heavens! What would she do then? She hadn't decided yet to tell the wagon master about Colwell and the Indian. She wanted to talk to Aaron about that first.

Trying to dispel her growing fears, Sara walked around the outside of the wagon, forcing herself to slow down and appear as though she was looking for rips in the canvas dome. From time to time, she glanced at the center of the wagon train. Most folks had gathered around the campfires--some undoubtedly talking about Colwell, and others visiting openly for the first time in weeks. Now that the quarantine had been lifted, there was a sense of purpose again, but without the usual vitality. Folks would have to make a choice today to either move forward in two days or travel back. Though the caravan would move on in two days—-not fast enough for her and Aaron and it would be a long, hard and sad journey for all of them.

Sara bit back tears. So many had become close friends in the last three months. They'd shared their stories, hopes and dreams. Sara's stomach knotted. She'd never see them again.

Now children ran in and out between the wagons with an assortment of dogs scampering after them. Several women lugged baskets of wet laundry up from the river and hung clothes on ropes strung between wagons.

Sara sighed, shook her head and turned back to check the three-foot water barrel. Fortunately, the wood was still damp. They'd make sure to keep it that way so the slats wouldn't dry out and crack open. They couldn't afford to lose a drop of water. Good boiled water would save their lives. Many waterholes were polluted and it was often hard to tell which ones were safe. They'd found out how to save themselves from the Cholera only days ago. Many folks considered it a miracle when a Captain Johnson, a Mormon, had seen their contagion flag as he passed by eight days ago--said he'd felt led to tell the gentiles about how boiling the water would rid them of the plague. At first folks didn't believe him, but finally they were so desperate they were willing to try anything. And it worked. "God's mercy," folks had claimed. But for Sara, it seemed a bitter and cruel irony—-just days after her parent's death.

Sara saw Aaron and Tarney running towards her.

"Tanner's on his way," he shouted, not bothering to stop.

"Aaron, I have to tell you something--it's about Peg…"

"I'll be back soon! I'm going to get Danny and Reeves." He kept running. "We're going—-we're really going!"

"Yes, but I need to tell you…" She watched her brother dash away. "Oh, Aaron!" Sara fumed, biting back the urge to shout at him. Instead, she kicked her boot heel into the ground, and then quickly turned to see if anyone noticed. The last thing she wanted was to call attention to their leaving.

Sara walked around to the backside of the wagon where she could have a bit of privacy. She looked up at the gravesite. This is the last time I'll stand here, she reminded herself. She straightened her shoulders, determined not to look away or faint. "Well,"   she whispered, "Mom, Dad, we're really going. I'm so sorry you won't be with us. I miss you so much, I can hardly breathe sometimes. But I promise you, I'll take care of Aaron, and I'll get us to San Francisco. I'll do everything I can to save what you and Uncle Jacob worked so hard for. I'll make you proud, I promise." She paused a moment, gathering strength. "It's so awful to leave you in this place. I...I love you both so much." Sara pressed her hands against her mouth, choking back the sobs. No! She wouldn't cry--mustn't make a sound. She stood, willing her feelings against a wall somewhere inside her.

Finally she took a last look at the knoll. But when she did, she noticed that someone was up there. Someone was crouching in the grass, near the crosses. Aaron was right. "It's an Indian."

CHAPTER FOUR

White Hawk crouched in the tall grass and watched as men led livestock back and forth to the river. He counted sixty horses, but did not see the three ponies that had been stolen from his camp, nor did he see the man who had killed his brother. But he was there, somewhere.

"We are close," White Hawk whispered, scowling down at the caravan. WalksThrough, his brown and white-spotted pony, sensed the boy's excitement and cantered forward a few steps, bent her head low and nibbled at the top of White Hawk's head.

"Not now!" White Hawk said, moving aside. "I have no time to play. But WalksThrough pawed the ground, determined. "No!" White Hawk warned, afraid the movement of the horse could be seen from below.

Quickly, he stood and grabbed the pony's mane, then led her to the opposite side of the knoll, away from view.

It was cooler there in the shadow. He could wait unnoticed, rest awhile. White Hawk squatted in the tall grass, breathing in the ripe, morning freshness. This will be a good place to stop and pray to the four corners of the land.

He glanced up and saw a hawk circling in the sky and stood watching how the air eased the bird ever closer to its purpose. White Hawk's spirit rose in kinship, and he closed his eyes, willing the hawk's quiet strength and purpose into the marrow of his bones.

He had followed the man who killed his brother. For two days he followed. Last night he had found him along the river, heard the cries of a girl as the man attacked her. He had been too far away, but saw the girl escape. He'd waited for the clouds to move from the moon, and then he saw what the man looked like, where he was. Soon, he would take his revenge.

A dark fury threatened to overwhelm him, and he grabbed the sides of his leather leggings, willing back control. Slowly, White Hawk opened his brown leather shirt, took a small leather pouch from around his neck, and carefully removed a few strands of sage. He bent down, dug his fingers into the ground, forming a small, brown hole in front of him to set the herb. He took his hand, crushed dirt and herb together into his fist. Then he stood, raising his fists to the sky. He cried, "Keewah Kaaa," making the sound of a hawk circling high in the sky, and then he waited as the sound took wings. He raised his head for a silent prayer. Oh, Hemmawhihio, I call to you, Oh Great One Above. I ask for strength that I may avenge my brother's death before the end of the Dying Grass Moon."

White Hawk's body stiffened as he thrust his arms to the sky. He must hold the image of that night—-burn it into the center of his being, paint it on the skin of his tepee. His parents must see all. He stood tall, pounded his chest and made a sacred vow to keep his promise of revenge.

He remembered how he and his older brother, Red Moon, and Walking Bear, his cousin, had camped along the Kaw River. Red Moon and Walking Bear wanted to trade with the white man and arranged to meet. He would sell ponies to the Pony Express Company near Leavenworth.

White Hawk did not believe they should trade with the evildoers. White men were not to be trusted. He had quarrelled with his brother and cousin.

Red Moon and his cousin had been given promises. Red Moon had called the white men "brothers." He as deceived!

"White Men!" He sneered, glaring at the crosses a few feet away. "Bring only sickness and death!" A tight band of bitterness pulled across his chest until he could no longer bear it. His fists plunged skyward and, once again, he made the piercing sound. "Keewa Kaaaaa," he cried, feeling the sound move through him. His knees buckled and he fell to the ground. He stayed there, his fists hammering the ground, until rage gave way to helplessness and useless tears.

He must face the truth. He was to blame for Red Moon's death. He'd left his brother alone, ridden away in anger, and Standing Bear, had followed on his horse. They were away from camp, arguing, when they heard the shot.

The killer had come in darkness, shot Red Moon in the chest, took two guns and three ponies. White Hawk and Standing Bear rode back to camp, but were too late.

The image of his brother's blood-red chest seared through White Hawk, and filled his spirit with revenge.

He convinced Standing Bear to carry his brother home, explain what happened, and he, White Hawk, would hunt the killer, take revenge before the end of the dying grass moon.

Now he must pray to the Great Spirit Above and to the four corners of the land. The Gods and his ancestors would quicken his spirit and give him strength.

And then, he would steal a gun.

CHAPTER FIVE

Much to Sara's relief, Aaron and Rufus agreed to help Peggy escape. Everyone understood the risk. They thought Colwell would likely follow, but they'd have the advantage of a head start.

"We'll keep an eye out fer him," Rufus declared.

"And," Aaron added, "Rufus is a crack shot." He grinned at Peggy, "Don't worry. I'll take care of you. You just stay hidden in the wagon until we're safely away." He glanced at Sara for confirmation.

He was glad that Peggy was coming with them. She was the prettiest girl on the wagon train, and now he'd have her all to himself.

By late afternoon, the two wagons were slowly plodding their way across the prairie. They followed along a well-worn trail that appeared etched into the ground, like two brown lines, drawing them forever onward for as far as the eye could see. All around, the honey colors of the sun-ripened grass rolled and churned like a huge caramel sea.

The air was hot, reed-dry, and hard to breathe. Whatever moisture existed along the nearby river was greedily sucked dry by miles of grass. At times, the grass seemed to rise up against the sides of the wagons, demanding any spare moisture from the intruders.

The Tanner wagon, pulled by two oxen, moved much slower than the Robbins' sturdy Morgans. Rufus constantly lagged behind, forcing Sara to hold back her team. Danny and Reeves wanted to pull ahead. It was very annoying. By late afternoon Sara was having difficulty keeping the horses and her temper in check.

"We'll lose a whole day, at this rate," she grumbled.

Aaron sat on the driver's seat next to Sara. "Rufus is doing the best he can," he defended, doffing his hat to wipe his forehead. "It sure is hot—-hotter than Hades. Maybe just as well we don't push." He glanced at Sara. Sweat poured down her face. Aaron frowned. "Better let me take over for awhile; you go rest!"

"I'm fine," Sara said testily, scowling into the distance. "Thought I saw something back over there, just to your right." Sara motioned with her head, keeping her hands on the reins.

"Don't see anything." Aaron shielded his eyes. "Where? You mean that swirl of dust, back there?"

"What is it? A rider?"

"Could be." Aaron frowned and whispered. "Do you think it's Colwell? Maybe just a burned out place--wind kicking up dust. Don't say anything to Peggy. I'll tell Rufus."

Aaron signaled for Rufus to pull up. When he did, Aaron ran to his wagon. "Did you notice that?" Aaron pointed.

The old man turned around in his seat and glanced back. "I kin see somethin' all right." Rufus squinted toward a small column of dust, pulled out a spyglass from under his seat and held it up to his good eye. "Could be a rider, all right."

"Should we stop and wait?"

"Nope! Reckon they'll find us." Rufus put the small telescope down and picked up his rifle. "This will let 'em know we spotted 'em." He fired a shot in the air.

"Aaron!" Sara called sharply. "Come here!"

"Now, what's wrong?" Aaron grumbled, catching her tone, and walking back to their wagon.

"Why did you let him do that?" Sara snapped.

"He was just trying to let the person know."

"Obviously, but he should have checked with our wagon first."

"Meaning you," Aaron said, shaking his head.

"Well," Sara retorted, "the fewer folks who know where we are, the better."

"That's crazy. Folks signal each other all the time. And you know it. You just don't like giving him a say."

"We're a team," Sara retorted, refusing to back down. "He needs to check with me before doing something like that."

"It's too hot to argue, but I'll say this--you don't like him because he teases you. Just remember, he's helping us. He may look scruffy and act kind of rude around folks. It's understandable. He's been on his own, without kin for a long time--worked as a trapper and prospector. But he's a very kind old man and he's my friend, so…so just get over yourself."

"Aaron, it's important…" Sara began, but was interrupted as Peggy came through the canopy.

"What's happening?" Peggy looked startled, still half asleep.

"Nothing to worry about. Just signaling a rider," Aaron offered, sounding unconcerned. He climbed back up into the wagon and sat in the driver's seat.

"Do you think it's my stepfather?" Peggy looked stricken.

"Don't worry. We're ready for him." Aaron stated, and turned to his sister. "I'll take over for now. Besides, we'll be stopping soon, anyway." He didn't wait for her answer. "Looks like a good place, over there." He pointed to a bend in the river where a stand of cottonwood trees jutted out on either side. I figure it's less than a mile. Looks like it might offer some shade."

They proceeded towards the river, all the time keeping a sharp eye out for the person who might be following.

"I haven't seen anything for the last twenty minutes. Have you?" Sara asked, untying her floppy straw hat and setting it aside. "Sure is hot." She turned to glance off to the side. "Don't see anything much, just endless prairie. Everything looks so dry," she said, taking a small jar of almond oil from a little basket beside her. She poured some into her palm and rubbed the oil on her face. "See anything?" she called to Peggy who was watching from the rear of the wagon.

"Nothing right now," Peggy answered, anxiously.

Tarney barked, ready to be taken up into the wagon. She'd been running for a while with Tanner's big, yellow dog, George, and appeared worn out. Aaron slowed the wagon and helped Tarney up. She was panting and her little tongue hung out.

"Tarney needs some water, Peggy," Sara called. "Would you bring the jug and Tarney's dish?"

"Be right there," Peggy said, quickly bringing a small crock of water and a little dish. "Here," she said, handing it to Sara. "Poor Tarney. She's nearly parched to death."

Peggy watched Tarney a moment. "I can't really see much of what's happening in back 'cause of our dust. I'm afraid I'm not much help." She looked down and then up at Sara's hands. "Oh, Sara, your hands are all red and sore. Here, let me hold the jug." She quickly reached for it.

"No!" Sara pulled the jug away. But as she did, it slipped out of her oily hands and fell on her foot. "Ouch!" she exclaimed, as pain shot through her big toe. "Oh, no!" she cried, seeing the precious water pour over her boots. "Now look what you've made me do!"

"Oh, Sara, I'm so clumsy. I'm sorry." Nearly in tears, Peggy rushed to the back of the canopy.

"Sara! What in blazes is wrong with you? Peggy was just trying to help."

Sara shook her head and picked up the jug. It hadn't broken, thank goodness. "I'm sorry, Peggy," she called. "It wasn't your fault. Please don't cry. I'm just cross and tired." She heard Peggy trying to choke down tears.

Aaron gave his sister a disgusted look. "You better take the reins. I'll talk to Peggy. What's gotten into you, anyway?" He handed Sara the reins, stood up and went back into the wagon. Tarney jumped off the seat and followed.

Sara heard her brother trying to soothe Peggy. Of course her behavior was wrong, and she felt bad. But she was tired--too tired, to face Peggy's tears. She'd about reached her own limit. Too many things were crowding in at her. Between her worry about being late for the stagecoach, Colwell following them, Tanner's slow oxen team, the heat, and her own feelings bunching up, she was about to explode. After all, there were limits! Her brother would just have to understand. It was unfair the way he always considered everyone else's feelings, but hers. Aggravating! She grabbed her straw hat and began fanning her face. Soon her anger slipped away. It was too hot to nurse a grievance. Besides, she knew things would ease some after they set up camp and rested.

Before long, Peggy stopped crying and came forward. She had dried her tears. "Aaron's awful sweet. You're so lucky to have a brother like him."

"Yes!" Sara smiled, "though sometimes--". Sara shook her head. "You look better, Peggy." Peggy had washed her face and combed her hair.

"Thanks. I'm so grateful to you, Sara. I…I never want to be a burden."

"I know, and you aren't. You'll be a wonderful help, Peggy. I'm the one who's grateful." Sara returned Peggy's smile, grateful for Peggy's sweet and generous nature. Apparently, she'd already forgiven her the out-burst.

"Oh, look, Sara!" Peggy pointed at the setting sun. "Isn't that the prettiest picture ya ever saw?"

They turned to watch a large tomato-ripe sun play its late afternoon hues against the sky, blending mellow gold and pinks on the river's smooth surface.

"I can hardly wait to get settled," Peggy said. "Will it be all right to go swimming? I really need to wash up a bit."

"Good idea." Sara smiled. "You can take my special soap."

Peggy hesitated. "Are you sure? I know it's precious."

"It'll be a treat for you."

Aaron came through the canopy and stood observing the river. "Just don't go wandering off," he said, glancing over at Rufus's wagon. Tanner was following closely now and Aaron directed Rufus' attention to the spot up ahead.

They selected a campsite about twenty feet from the river and sheltered under some cottonwood trees. Aaron and Rufus quickly unhitched the teams and led them down to the river, as Sara and Peggy prepared the campsite.

They cleared a spot under the trees and unrolled the tents. "It feels good to stretch," Sara admitted, bending to fasten a tarp rope around the trunk of a tree. "You better let me hammer those stakes," she said, watching Peggy struggle to pound a metal stake into the hard ground.

"I'm kinda weak, yet," Peggy admitted, but added, "I can gather firewood." She noticed a number of dry limbs within easy reach. "We won't have to use many cow paddies."

Before long, Sara and Peggy had the campsite ready and gathered rocks from the river to make a protective circle for the fire.

"It feels good to be on solid ground, and out from the dusty old canvas, doesn't it?" Sara said, stretching her back. "Wonder what's keeping Aaron? They should have tended to Danny and Reeves by now." Sara glanced uneasily through the trees. It was nearly impossible to see much of the river because of the undergrowth, and she didn't like the idea of Aaron and Tanner being gone so long.

"Is something wrong?" Peggy asked.

"No, nothing," Sara said, thoughtfully. But a moment later, she saw Peggy's concerned look and smiled. "I guess I'm just a little on edge, what with the heat and all." She didn't want to increase Peggy's fears with her own doubts about Tanner. What did they really know about him? Why, she wondered had Tanner claimed that the rider who'd been following them was an old man on a mule. 'Not Colwell,' he'd assured everyone. But Sara had seen what she thought was a tall man on a horse. Perhaps, she reassured herself, that Tanner's eyesight wasn't really very good, even with a spy glass. Maybe, she countered, Tanner just didn't want to worry them. Sara sighed. It's only for two days, she reminded herself.

"Sounds like Tarney and George are having a good time dashing along the river bank," Peggy offered.

Sara nodded. "Yes, but you'd better get your swim before it's too dark. The sun's going down fast, and the men will want supper. I'll start it, and join you in a bit."

Peggy glanced around the camp at the unfinished chores. "Are you sure?"

"Go ahead," Sara nodded. "There's not much left to do. I'll be along soon."

Reassured, Peggy hurried toward the river. She followed a deer path to the water's edge. It was a peaceful place. Here and there, trees bent over the river, reflecting their graceful branches in the water. She stood a while, watching the sun move lower against the horizon. It dipped like a beautiful bird, settling into its nightly nest, and leaving a delicate glow of orange and pinks all along the river. She walked a little ways and came to a thick arbor of trees. She quickly undressed down to her chemise, hung her dress, petticoat and shoes on a lower tree limb. Taking the bar of soap in its little cloth sack, she walked to the water's edge and waded in.

Once the river had been wider, but now there were sand bars and a stream in the middle. Maybe it's deeper than it looks, she thought, hoping for enough water to bathe.

She waded in until the water came up to her waist. It felt warm as her feet sank into the sand beneath. Heavenly! Happily removing the soap, she began lathering herself. But suddenly she felt a chill. Then frightening images of her stepfather swamped her mind. She could see his face, the insane rage, smell his breath. No! No! "Please God, help me." It's only a memory, she told herself, fighting panic. He's not here. She concentrated on the moment, only now, seeing the water, feeling it on her arms and legs, the warm sand beneath her feet. She tried to force her mind, but it seemed locked in its own horror chamber. "Aaron." If she could just see Aaron.

She glanced downstream and noticed that Aaron and Rufus had moved further away. "Oh, no!" The panicky feeling moved up her throat. She felt so alone, vulnerable. Not safe. Where was Sara? Why wasn't she here?

When Aaron turned around to look behind him, he saw Peggy standing in the middle of the river. Her wet chemise clung to her, outlining the top of her body.

Rufus turned to look, following Aaron's gaze. "Sure is a purdy little thing, ain't she?" Rufus said, grinning. He'd caught Aaron's appreciative expression and watched him color with embarrassment.

"Make a fine wife fer ya." He grinned.

Aaron's face flushed a red, but he stood watching Peggy as though transfixed. Peggy appeared like an angel rising from the river's mist. The sun was setting behind her and made a golden halo. Her whole body seemed aglow with warm colors in a beautiful hazy apparition. His rapture was broken.

"Look! Look'a thar!" Rufus pointed to some tracks extending across the bank into the river. "They're Injun ponies!"

CHAPTER SIX

Aaron quickly bent and found more impressions. "They went across the river, but came back." Aaron gestured to some tracks along the riverbank about fifteen feet away. "Over there!" He followed them. "Pretty fresh, I'd say."

"Yep, looks like three ponies and three shod." Rufus said.

Aaron continued examining the ground. "We'd better make sure that's all. Come on, Tarney, we've got work to do."

As Aaron and Rufus headed farther down the riverbank, Peggy tried to call out, but her voice seemed locked in her throat. Never mind, she thought, suddenly chilled. I'll hurry and dress. She quickly put the bar of soap in its sack and walked along the sand bars to where she'd left her clothes. She shuddered as an evening mist closed about her wet chemise and darkening tree shadows loomed along the riverbank. She hurried, jumping the sand bars until she found herself stepping into a different kind of sand. It felt coarse and smelt strange. When she tried to pull her feet up, she couldn't. It was as if the sand were clutching her ankles. She tried again to pull her feet up, but the struggle only made it worse. The sand was like a fist grabbing her. Oh, no! Quicksand!

"Help!" Peggy called, her voice barely a whisper. Instinctively, she clawed at the sand bar, hoping for something to grab on to. But there was nothing. And each time she moved her arms or legs, the sand sucked her deeper. She could smell the murky water—-its rotten stench gagging her. It seemed to have a will of its own—-slowly and determinedly moving up her legs, pulling her down. Acrid fumes rose to burn her throat. Some animal had died here! "Help!" she cried again—a strangled whimper. "Sweet Jesus, don't let me die!"

Relentlessly, the sand sucked her deeper. Soon her limbs grew weak--too tired to fight.

The thick, foul smelling ooze moved up her waist, and coiled against her chest like the giant mouth of a snake, swallowing her inch by inch. She could barely breathe. "No, no! I mustn't give up! Please, God, help me!"

"Peggy!" Aaron exclaimed as he turned and saw what was

happening. "Quicksand!" he yelled to Rufus. "Hurry!"

Aaron ran towards Peggy. He ran without thinking, tearing through brambles and leaping over logs. It was only a question of minutes before she'd disappear beneath the sand. "Sara!" he called, "The rope! Quick! Bring the rope!"

Rufus watched in alarm as Aaron plunged headlong into the river. "No! Aaron, wait!"

But Aaron didn't stop.

"Dang kid will get his self stuck!" Rufus rushed along the bank, found a branch on the ground, dragged it toward the river. Rufus' dog, George, ran barking behind him. "No, you stay!" Rufus ordered.

Tarney, however, was already chasing after Aaron. She jumped across sandbars and dove into the middle of the river.

As Aaron swam toward Peggy, the water gave way to sand bars. He couldn't tell whether it was quicksand or not. He struggled forward until Peggy was only a few feet away. He stretched as far as he could. "Grab hold, Peggy, grab hold!" He could see panic swelling in her eyes. "Reach!"

Try as she might, Peggy couldn't touch him. She was pinned in, with only her head and one arm above the sand.

Again and again Aaron reached out.

Now the hideous odor of the quicksand was all around and closing in on Aaron. He heard his sister call.

"Aaron! The rope! It's coming!" Sara lifted the coiled rope above her head, ready to throw.

Suddenly, Rufus was at her side. "Give it here!" He jerked at the rope, trying to pull it out of her hands.

"What are you doing?" Sara cried, fighting to hang on.

"Gimme that!" he ordered, roughly pushing Sara to the ground. Then he quickly tied one end of the rope to a branch. Ignoring Sara, he growled. "I've got to throw it, jist git outta my way!"

Finally understanding, Sara stood back and watched Rufus take the rope and begin whirling it in a circle over his head. Moments later, he tossed it across the water towards Aaron.

"Oh, no!" Sara cried, watching the rope fall short.

"Here!" Rufus ordered, pulling back part of the rope. "Loop the end 'round thet log." He pointed to a fallen tree a few feet from the water's edge. He took the other end and without looking back or waiting, plunged into the water.

Sara quickly wrapped her end of the rope around the log and hung on to it. She watched Rufus work his way into the murky water. "Hurry!" she shouted. "Hurry!"

Tarney thrashed about in the middle of the river, trying to get closer to Aaron, but the thick, sandy water weighed her down and she spun in circles.

George dashed back and forth at the river's edge, barking. Seconds seemed like hours. Sara was about to jump in and help when she noticed that the log holding one end of the rope was moving, and would soon give way. Quickly finding another log, she pushed it in front of the other.

Rufus was getting closer to Peggy. Moments later, he came alongside and wedged his arm under her neck, holding her mouth above the water. He jabbed the branch end of the rope under her arms and wrapped part of the rope about her. Aaron was near enough to grab his other arm. Soon Rufus began pulling the youngsters, inching his way along the rope. Aaron and Peggy were moving, but barely.

Slowly, ever so slowly, the sand gave way.

Finally, reluctantly, the horrible monster of ooze released its prey.

Aaron was closest to Tarney, but couldn't get a grip on her. "Grab on!"

Tarney understood and dug her teeth into Aaron's shirt and clung tightly.

As Rufus Tanner got Peggy and Aaron closer to shore, Sara dashed into the water. She reached Peggy, grabbed her arms, pulled her from the water and dragged her up the bank.

Once safely on shore, Peggy didn't move. She lay limp as wet burlap.

"Peggy!" Sara urged, bending down and trying to wipe the nasty grit from Peggy's eyes and mouth.

Aaron and Rufus stumbled ashore and sprawled exhausted next to Peggy.

After resting a few minutes, Aaron sat up and wiped his face. "Ugh! Tastes awful!" He gagged and spit the gritty stuff out. He shuddered. "Something died in there!"

"It smells awful. I'll get some clean water!" Sara got up and ran to the wagon. In a few minutes, she was back with a ladle and a bucket of fresh water and a blanket. She covered Peggy with the blanket.

Aaron turned to look at Peggy. "How is she?" He watched Sara hold Peggy's head up to give her a sip of water. "She's alive!"

Peggy raised a weary hand, and then lay back down.

"Yer a lucky young lady." Tanner nodded, and shook his head. "Could've been worse. Somethin' died in there for sure. But folks don't usually drown in quicksand. It's want of water or starvation gets 'em. 'Course, folks will claim different." Rufus wiped his mouth and spat. "Yer lucky, all right!"

Peggy tried to speak. "I lost...lost the...soap."

"Don't try to talk now," Aaron said gently.

"Fortunately," Sara smiled, "I have two more bars."

Tarney twisted about, trying to shake off the sand. But when she saw Aaron wiping his overalls, she ran up to him.

"Phew! Tarney, you smell worse than a skunk." Aaron jerked his face away.

"So do you!" Sara retorted. "Just stay where you are. I'll get the soap."

Sara soon came back with soap, towels and some clean clothes. "You best strip off all the wet things and change. Be quick about it, before you catch your death."

"If I didn't die today, I'm never going to," Aaron said. "You just remember that, Aaron Robbins," Sara insisted.

Tanner stood up to stretch, glanced worriedly up and down the river. The evening mist fanned out and spread along the riverbank. It wouldn't be long before nightfall. He remembered the sign of Indians and nodded to Aaron. "Sun's near down. Best git the ladies in to their tent."

"Here, let me help you, Peggy." Aaron rushed forward.

Sara stepped in front. "I'll take care of her. You and Rufus need to get out of those stinky wet things, and wash it all off; only don't waste any of my soap." She tossed him a bar.

Aaron grimaced. "It smells like perfume--roses."

"It's very special, and" she added with a wink at Peggy, "the ladies love it!"

"Well, in that case," he grinned at Peggy, "I'll use it!"

CHAPTER SEVEN

Sara helped Peggy clean up. There wasn't time to heat buckets of water, so they waded in the river, near the bank, where it appeared safe. Sara quickly scrubbed Peggy's hair, rinsed her off, wrapped her in a quilt, and helped her to the campfire. But by then, Peggy was too weary to eat. All she wanted was sleep.

Peggy took the quilt and, like a little bear, crawled into the tent. Moments later, she was asleep.

Rufus and Aaron sat quietly by the campfire, trying to warm themselves. Too tired to talk and barely able to keep their eyes open, they ate a quick supper of hardtack with jam, dried apples and hot coffee.

Aaron glanced at his sister who sat next to the fire, resting her head on her knees, her eyes closed. "Better get some rest. Rufus and I'll take watch."

Sara didn't protest. But when she stood, she turned and looked down at Rufus. Even in the dim light of the campfire, she could see that the day had taken its toll. Rufus seemed to have aged ten years. "Maybe I'd better take your place."

"Na," he waved her away in irritation. "I'm fit n' fierce as a badger. Now go on."

Sara couldn't help smiling. "Mr. Tanner--Rufus," she began, "I want to thank you--thank you and apologize for—"

"Fer nothing! Now, jest git on ta bed. Me and Aaron can handle things." He scowled and motioned her away.

"I want to thank you for saving our lives."

"Aw, go on 'n give a man a little privacy here," he said gruffly.

"Yes, of course." Sara nodded. "Well, then, good night," she said, walking over to her tent. She paused at the opening and turned back to Aaron. "You were very brave today."

"Well, we made it," he acknowledged. "But the strangest thing happened. I looked around at just the right moment to help Peggy. Honestly, it was as if I was told to. A kind of voice came to me---not Peggy's. I think God or an angel was there, Sara. It's a miracle." He nodded.

"Yes," Sara said, not wanting to admit her troubling lack of faith. All she could say was, "It certainly was timely." She sighed. "Well, goodnight, then. Call when you need me."

Aaron and Rufus sat awhile longer, silently gazing into the campfire. They'd come through something together and understood the silence as unspoken appreciation. Aaron knew Rufus had saved his life. There were no words to express such gratitude. The old man knew the boy felt it, and that was enough.

"You best let me take the first watch," Aaron suggested. Even in the moonlight, he could tell the old man had turned pallid. Rufus did not look well. "Go on, get some rest. I can manage," Aaron urged.

"Yep," Rufus groaned, trying to get up. "My ol' bones hardly go together. Best git some shut-eye."

"Are you all right?" Aaron was concerned as Rufus struggled to get up. Before he got to his feet, he staggered, bent over and clutched his chest.

"What is it? Here..." Aaron rushed to keep his friend from falling. He helped Rufus back down. The old man sat still as a stone, his hand on his chest. A few moments later, he waved Aaron away. "Jist gas. I'm all right. Leave be."

"I'll get you some water," Aaron insisted..

"Naw! I'm fine." He rubbed his arm and tried to get a deep breath. "Right as rain, soon's the pain goes. Nuthin' to fret about."

"You shouldn't have exerted--"

"Hush, yer makin' me nervous."

Aaron glanced about uneasily. "Maybe I should get Sara. She's good at--"

"Naw. Jist help me up. I wan'a git ta bed. George and me will come spell ya later. Come on George," he said, allowing Aaron to help him. Leaning heavily on Aaron, Rufus slowly walked over to his wagon. "Give me yer arm, son. Help me up, here."

"You're better off in the tent."

"Naw, jist hoist me up. I ain't in a mind to argue."

Once Aaron had gotten Rufus settled down inside, he walked back to the fire and huddled close. Tarney stayed near, watching his every move.

"Well, Tarney, it's just you and me. You'll keep me awake, won't you, girl?" Tarney managed a tired glance at the woods. "I know you're as wore out as me. You sure were something out there in the river. Don't know what I'd do without you." Aaron's voice clouded with emotion, but he cautioned himself. "We've got to save strength, stay awake." Tarney seemed to understand, and waged her tail, then laid her head back down, resting on her paws. "You're the best guard dog in the whole world." Aaron looked over at the Tanner wagon. "Sure hope he's okay."

Several hours passed and the night darkened. The moon shone through the cottonwood trees. Now and then the hoot of an owl broke the silence. Twice Aaron got up to set wood on the fire. But it became harder to stay awake. He tried recalling stories he'd read.

Shadows flickered around him, adding their own creepy fiction. A couple of times he thought he saw something in the bush, and once Tarney jumped up and chased a sound, but it had only been a possum, creeping through the undergrowth.

Nearby, the horses remained quiet. That was a good sign. They'd blow and fret if an animal came too close, he reassured himself, yawning. "There's nothing to worry about...nothing," he murmured, feeling heavy eyelids close, till at last he gave way to a warm current that carried him gently into darkness.

An hour later, he was startled awake by the cracking of branches.

Tarney sniffed the air, gave a warning growl at the sounds in the nearby undergrowth. Soon the horses grew restless and began pulling on the tether line, setting off a warning bell.

"What is it, Tarney," Aaron whispered, suddenly wide-awake. He grabbed his colt .45

Impatiently, the little black and white terrier waited for Aaron to give the signal.

"All right, go on!" he said, releasing her and reaching for his gun.

Tarney disappeared into the dark undergrowth.

George heard the noise, as well, jumped down from his wagon and came running after Tarney. Branches snapped and crunched in the dry brush as the dogs chased. So far they'd given no warning bark.

Must be an opossum or deer, Aaron thought, swallowing back fear. There were plenty of deer paths leading down to the river. Of course, they could be Indian paths, as well.

In a few minutes, the dogs scampered back to camp. They had found nothing of consequence, but looked contented and tired. George plopped down next to the fire, panting.

"You did good, George," Aaron smiled.

The old dog wagged his tail, but soon got up and returned to his wagon.

Aaron put more wood on the fire and settled back down with Tarney lying at his feet. He thought about all the other times he'd sat guard. On the wagon train there were always two or three guards posted around camp. He'd never really been alone. And even in the dead of night, he would hear human sounds, folks snoring or coughing, even a child whimpering. This was different. Creepy. All about him, dead, cold silence. He was totally alone, totally responsible. A shiver raced up his spine and he drew a deep breath and rubbed his burning eyes. If only he could see more than ten feet into the brush. But he could smell the river nearby and feel its muddy dampness in the night air.

Aaron worked the stiffness from his neck and shoulders. A good night's rest would help, he sighed. Should he wake Sara? No, she needed her sleep. Aaron glanced up at the sky. "Seems like there are millions and millions of stars just hanging over our heads, doesn't it, Tarney? Ever wonder what keeps them there? Oh, look, there's the North Star and the Big Dipper. Sailors use them to go all over the world."

Aaron watched the moon arch across the sky and move shadows through the trees. At times, the moon shone brightly, and made the woods seemed known and friendly. But at other times, clouds passed over and everything turned dark and creepy. He hated to admit it, but he was scared. If only his Father was here. They could tell stories to each other. Aaron coughed back the tightening in his throat. His father would remind him that he was brave and not to imagine the worst. Yet, he knew there could be Indians about. And he wouldn't put it past Colwell to sneak up and try to steal Peggy in the middle of the night, though he thought it unlikely. After all, Colwell and Indians had to sleep, same as us, he told himself. He laid back, his head resting on a log, and pulled the brown blanket snugly up to his neck. He grabbed hold of his Colt .45.

Having it near made him feel more secure. He glanced at Tarney and rolled over to scratch her ears. "I guess as long as you're awake, I could get a few minutes shuteye. Seems quiet enough."

Finally, no longer able to keep his eyes open, he fell asleep.

So quietly did White Hawk steal into camp that not even Tarney looked up.

White Hawk waited, observing the camp from about thirty yards away. He must be quick, he knew, for he had no knife or bow and arrow. His purpose was his only weapon, but he would defeat his enemy with his bare hands. The men who killed his brother broke his bow and arrows, stole his knife and the two rifles. His enemies thought to stop him. Stupid White Men, White Hawk thought, clenching his fists in a silent vow.

He had tracked the man following this wagon, and knew he'd have seen the smoke of the campfire. Soon he would come. And he, White Hawk, would be ready.

White Hawk crept closer. He heard the heavy snoring of someone sleeping in the nearby wagon. A man, he thought. Two more were in the tent. Next, he observed the guard lying near the campfire. Moving cautiously, a few feet at a time, White Hawk skirted the horses and oxen and counted his steps back to the river where waited.

Crouching behind a large bush, White Hawk listened and waited. All he heard was the hoot of an owl and his heart pounding. He tried to swallow away the dryness of his throat, but the bitter taste would not leave.

He had the advantage. Tonight was his time. There would be only one chance to get a gun. The guard would fall asleep. He would take a stone and bash his head or maybe be lucky. But first, he must distract the dogs.

White Hawk clutched three rocks in his right hand, but his palm was sweaty, so he wiped it on the soft skin of his leggings. Finally, the moon darkened and he threw the first rock. It landed in the dense brush beyond the campfire. When he heard the dogs dash off after it, he pitched a second rock, even further into the thicket.

Quickly now, White Hawk threw his last stone, and then sprinted toward the campfire. He found the guard sprawled on the ground sound asleep. He bent down to look. Stupid white boy, to fall asleep. No brave would do that.

Then he saw the barrel of a gun sticking out from under the boy's blanket. It lay inches away on the ground. White Hawk glanced about, then reached down, grabbed the weapon, and deliberately touched the man's head as he dashed off. He was thirty feet away by the time Aaron awoke.

"What? Who's there?" Aaron cried, startled, reaching for the gun. "It's gone!"

"KeeWaa KeeWaaa!" White Hawk cried in triumph, leaping

and bounding over logs, letting the brambles tear at him. Thorns scratched his arms and tore at his leggings. He didn't mind. He had the weapon. "Ahaeeeeee! He cried again, the power racing through him.

"Indians!"

White Hawk heard the shout, the excited barking. Power ran down his legs, propelling him to the river. The great moon spirit was with him, lighting his way to the water's edge.

He saw WalksThrough waiting. His pony bristled with excitement as White Hawk came near and jumped on his back. The pony charged forward, plunging into the river and throwing up great, silvery sprays in the moonlight. White Hawk's long, black hair fanned wide and glistened in the light. Now he was clutching the weapon in one hand and dashing across the river like a mythical warrior on a great steed.

Once on the other side, White Hawk let loose a final triumphant cry. "Keewaaa Keewaa" The chilling sound echoed along the river and ripped through the woods. It was the cry of a Hawk whose talons had found its prey.

CHAPTER EIGHT

Sara and Peggy were startled awake by White Hawk's frightening cries. They bolted out of their tent and rushed to the campfire.

"Aaron! Where are you?" Sara called. She couldn't see him, but heard him thrashing about in the underbrush.

Rufus slowly climbed down from his wagon and stumbled toward the fire-pit with his .36 Navy Colt in hand. "What's all the fuss?"

Aaron soon stomped back to camp. "He got away!"

"Who?" Sara asked.

"What happened?" Rufus demanded, coming close.

"Stupid Indian stole Dad's Colt!"

"How the hell!" Rufus exploded. "What were you doin'? Sleepin'?"

"Yes!" Aaron snapped. "I fell asleep!" It was obvious he was furious with himself.

"Oh, Aaron!" Sara cried, ran to him. "Thank heaven you're safe." She put her hand on his shoulder. "It could've happened to any of us!"

Aaron pulled away.

Peggy stepped forward, holding a blanket about her. "Please don't blame yourself, Aaron!"

"I was on duty!" Aaron scowled.

"But Aaron," Sara argued, "we're all fine. Nobody's been hurt."

"You don't understand!" Aaron was getting worked up.

"Hold on!" Rufus warned. "Did ya see any others?"

"Just the one. I woke up. He was taking off--had my revolver! Damn!" Aaron exploded. "Was Dad's!"

"How did it happen?" Sara asked.

"I told you. I fell asleep!"

"No! You didn't tell me!"

"Oh, forget it!" Aaron stomped away.

"Aaron, please," Sara called. "Please don't run away."

Sara persisted, following after him. "Aaron," she tried, "Calm down. We're all safe."

"Just boil it, Sara! And don't try to coddle me! Leave me alone!"

"Well," Sara huffed, "be that way, then. See if I care!" She watched him march away. "He's so pigheaded," she grumbled, then turned back to the comforting light of the campfire and sat on a log next to Peggy and Rufus. The three hunkered down, not saying anything. Sara soon found herself the subject of Rufus' critical gaze.

"Bad piece o'luck," Rufus commented wearily.

"Well, yes, but I'm more concerned about Aaron. He feels so...responsible."

"Yep...n' that's only right," Rufus returned.

"Poor kid." Sara shook her head.

Rufus looked straight at Sara. "Ya ought'n ta treat him that way," he warned.

"Why, whatever do you mean?"

"Ya treat him like a child 'n he ain't. Ya gotta expect more, else it'll tear 'm down."

"Well, I never!" Sara fumed, "he's my brother, and I guess I know what's good for him."

"Maybe, maybe not. He's more a man now than you think."

"Really, I think...."

Peggy interrupted. "Do you mean, Sara should've gotten angry?"

"Yep! Darn sight more respectful."

"But wouldn't that make him feel worse?" Peggy frowned.

"Maybe, but it sets better than taking away a man's sense of his self," Rufus explained. "He's got to expect things."

"I think kindness and compassion are more to the point," Sara said, annoyed.

"He failed to do the job he set for himself. That's bad enough. But he'd been a darn sight better off if you'd expect as much. Not less of him. A man don't always want sympathy, especially if he's done wrong. Takes away his pride."

"Really, Mr. Tanner," Sara began, trying to hold her temper, "I don't think you understand..."

"Well," Rufus interrupted, "understandin's a fine thing, all right. I figure it's in need--in need by most folks, young or old."

Rufus was being sarcastic, and it made Sara angry. But she decided to keep her temper in check. She glanced at Peggy. The poor girl looked very distressed. This whole conversation was not helping anybody. Sara looked at her friend. She could get a chill. "Peggy! It's late. Maybe you'd better get back to bed."

"Oh, yes...I guess you're right." She glanced at the woods, and saw Aaron sitting on a log, not far away.

"You need your rest," Sara advised, ignoring Rufus.

"You're right, of course," Peggy answered, distractedly. She rose to leave. "Night," she mumbled as she started for the tent, leaving her friends sitting glumly by the campfire.

"Night," Sara returned and continued poking at the burning embers.

The confrontation between Sara and Aaron had unsettled Peggy and she wondered how Aaron was feeling. After walking a little ways into the woods, she found him sitting on a log. The moonlight shone upon his face and she saw that he'd been crying. She sat next to him and waited for him to speak.

"You're liable to catch cold, Peggy. You should get back." He sounded impatient.

"I will," she whispered, clutching the blanket about her. "I just wanted to make sure you were all right."

"I'm fine!"

Peggy sighed. She'd been trying to gather the courage to tell him something. "I'm sorry I'm such a bother to you and Sara---adding to your worries. I know everyone's real jumpy just thinking about how maybe my stepfather's coming...and I..."

Aaron glanced at Peggy and frowned at the unhappy look on her face. "It's all right. You're not a bother. I like having you along. Don't worry about me. I'm just disappointed in myself. I let everybody down."

"Oh, no! You were very brave!" Peggy said with conviction. "Very brave!"

"Hardly," Aaron shook his head. "I was scared to death, especially when I heard that awful sound. I thought a whole bunch of savages were coming down on us."

"Oh, Aaron," Peggy wailed. "It's my fault--my fault," she cried, covering her face as a sob rose from her chest.

"No--no, don't cry, Peggy. It's over now," he placed his arm around her shoulders. At his touch, Peggy turned and buried her face in his shirt.

"Come on, don't worry. It's going to be fine. I know you were scared, too. But it's over, now. I'll take care of you. Don't worry."

"Oh, Aaron, you're so good, so kind. I don't know what I'd do without you."

"We're all going to be fine, Peggy. And you're a big help." Aaron gently and ever so tenderly, took her chin in his hand, lifted her face and brushed away the tears. Peggy's eyes were so soft and shiny in the moonlight, so trusting. He bent down and brushed his lips across hers--so sweet and warm they were.

Peggy placed her hands on his cheeks, returning the kiss, then placed her head against his chest. Finally, she whispered, "It's late. We'd better get back."

"Yes," Aaron agreed, taking her hand and walking back to camp.

Neither Peggy nor Aaron noticed Sara's surprised look, or Tanner's wry grin.

Aaron escorted Peggy to her tent.

"Good night, Aaron," Peggy murmured. "You get some rest, now."

"I will, Peggy." He smiled and turned to walk back to the campfire.

Aaron nodded thoughtfully to himself as he sat down next to Rufus. "Yes," he said, glancing at the fire. "Everything's going to be just fine. Sorry I got so fired up."

Sara frowned. "Don't know what there was to get so sore about!"

Aaron ignored the barb. "Guess I'd better get a few hours sleep, or I won't be worth beans tomorrow."

"Right! I'll take the rest of the night," Rufus said.

"I could do it," Sara offered.

"You're needed tomorrow," Aaron said.

"I suppose so." Sara rubbed her eyes. "But call if you need me, Rufus." She turned to her brother. "You all right?"

"I'm fine," he answered pleasantly. "I've one of Rufus' rifles."

"Well, all right, then," Sara said, wondering about Aaron's turn of mood. She sighed. Her brother was certainly changeable these days. She hesitated. "Please call if you need me, Rufus."

"Will do, Miss," Rufus smiled cheerfully and waved her on. "Young folk!" He shook his head.

A few hours later, Rufus stood up to stretch his back and then settled down by the fire. The young folks had gone to bed. That was good. It'll be light soon enough. He patted his holster. His .36 and

George would be on duty. "Yep," he said to himself, glancing at Aaron's wagon. He chuckled. "Youth. It's a fine thing---if'n ya don't stay at it too long." It was then that another, sharper, pain seized him.

CHAPTER NINE

The next morning, they found Rufus Tanner lying on the ground, eyes closed and barely breathing. George sat beside him and growled at the youngsters as they came near. When he saw Tarney with them, he allowed them closer.

"Good boy. It's all right, George," Aaron reassured, squatting down to feel for Rufus's pulse. "He's still alive."

"Thank goodness." Sara said, kneeling for a closer look.

"Oh! What are we going to do?" Peggy cried.

"I'm not sure, yet, Peggy." Sara sat on the ground and gently lifted Rufus's head onto her lap. "I wonder how long he's been lying here. He's so cold. We have to get him off the ground." She tried blowing warmth on his limp hands and brushed the thin strands of hair off his forehead. "He feels clammy." Sara's worried glance at Aaron spoke what she didn't want to say.

"But he's alive!" Aaron said, determinedly. "We'll get him to Leavenworth--find a doctor. He'll be all right!"

"We've no time to lose!" Sara glanced up at Peggy. "Get some water and bring as many blankets as you can."

Aaron and Peggy sprang into action.

Aaron shouted as he ran, "I'll find something to help us get him up into the wagon."

In a few minutes, Peggy returned with blankets, clean rags and a basin of water. Sara quickly moistened a strip of muslin and put it against Rufus' mouth. There was no reaction.

George eyed Sara.

"It's all right, George," Sara said, "We have to keep him hydrated. And you, too." Sara put the bowl of water on the ground next to the dog.

George sniffed the bowl and took a drink, then moved over to give Tarney a share.

Sara looked worried. "How will we get Rufus up and inside the wagon?"

"I've an idea." Aaron said. We'll make a tarp of canvas from the tent, fasten ropes on each side and make a pulley."

A half hour later, they were carefully lifting Rufus onto the tarp and dragging him to the wagon. Though he was not a large man, in his present condition, he was dead weight and could easily fall off the tarp. They decided to practice first with the flour barrel. When that succeeded, they were ready to hoist him up. Slowly, ever so slowly, they eased him up against the side of the wagon.

George paced the ground, watching every pull of the rope.

Ten minutes later, they'd managed to get Rufus up and into the wagon.

Aaron covered him with two blankets and set three pillows under his head, as Sara instructed. "We'll have to wait and see how he does." Aaron frowned. Rufus had not even opened his eyes. "I think his color is better, though," he added, hopefully.

They'd done all they could for now, Sara knew. She could only hope the rough rocking and uneven trail would not be too hard on the old man.

Peggy knelt beside Rufus, laying her hand on his forehead and closed her eyes. "Please, Lord, let Rufus get better, soon." She glanced up at Sara and Aaron. They nodded in agreement. Peggy began to sing the familiar old hymn, The Old Rugged Cross. Aaron joined in.

"How about Jeannie with the Light Brown Hair," Sara suggested.

For the next half hour, Peggy sang for Rufus.

George seemed to understand that they were trying to help, and quickly plopped down beside his master.

The next task was to dismantle camp, and within an hour they had done so and were hitched and ready to leave. A hurried breakfast of canned peaches and hardtack sufficed. Next, they checked over the map, noting the quickest route to Leavenworth.

"Looks like the main trail cuts off here," Aaron pointed down at the weather-stained map. "Could reach the cutoff about midday---save three hours, but that'll depend." He glanced at the Tanner wagon. "We'll have to slow down for Rufus."

"I know," Sara agreed. "And we'll need to stop every hour to give him water." Sara quickly tucked her red hair under her battered, old straw hat and glanced at Peggy. "Here, Peggy, take this cloth one." She handed her a large, floppy green hat. It's going to be burning hot."

"I don't see any water hole marked," Aaron shook his head. "Let's not fuss about that now. We have enough for the animals and ourselves till nightfall. By then we should connect to the river."

"Right!" Sara nodded. "And since you'll be driving Rufus's rig, be sure to take these rags, keep them damp. Put them on his head once in a while, and try to get some water or moisture into his mouth as often as possible."

Aaron grabbed the rags. "Anything else?" He glanced at his sister. She had dark circles under her eyes. "Think you're fit enough to handle the wagon on your own?"

"Of course!" she insisted. "Besides, Peggy can help!"

"Right! Well, let's go! Come on, Tarney. George will want you close by."

By eight, they were ready to begin their second day of the journey. Aaron was about to climb up into the driver's seat when he glanced back at Peggy. "Peggy thinks we should say prayers for Rufus. Maybe, it'll help. I think it's a good idea. Don't you Sara?"

Sara frowned. "We should get going. Every minute counts." She noticed her brother's disappointment. "Go ahead if you want to. I have to go put this oil on my face." she said turning to go into the wagon.

Peggy and Aaron stood alongside the wagon, waiting for Sara. Peggy smiled as Sara returned and took her place in the driver's seat. "We waited for you," Peggy said. "Remember, Jesus' words. "Where two or more are gathered, there am I. We waited for the 'more.'"

Sara cleared her throat. "Fine, you go ahead." Sara wouldn't remind her brother and Peggy that prayers had done nothing for their parents. She sighed, but she bowed her head, anyway. It was awkward. She felt like a hypocrite. But she knew her lack of faith would only worry them. And it wasn't something she wanted to discuss or think about just now. She'd sort it out later.

By early afternoon, they were following the cutoff trail.

"Heat's sure pouring down," Peggy was trying to tuck her damp, blond hair under the floppy bonnet. "I think Rufus looked better last time we stopped, his color, I mean."

"I thought so, too. He's a 'tough old bird,' Sara smiled. "That orneriness could save him, according to Aaron." Sara sat holding the reins. "This old bench is hard. I can hardly wait to be on a stagecoach. I hear it has upholstered seats, and window flaps to protect from the dust." She glanced at Peggy. "You look a little pink. There's my jar of almond oil next to you just inside the wagon.

Better rub that on."

"Thanks," Peggy said, reaching behind her. She took the slender bottle and poured some in her hand, then rubbed it over her face and arms.

Peggy's face still showed bruises, but the cut over her eye looked better. Luckily, it only needed two little stitches, and Sara thought it probably wouldn't leave a scar.

"You're healing nicely, Peggy!" Sara smiled.

"I know--thanks to you and Aaron. You two have been awfully good to me--and Rufus, too." Peggy sighed, "Poor man."

Sara nodded. "But he somehow had strength to avoid the cholera, didn't he?"

"Yes, and maybe all our prayers helped." Peggy said, glancing at the prairie.

Now that they had traveled a good part of the day and Rufus was showing improvement, Sara realized that she was actually feeling hopeful. It had been awhile. It seemed so many things on the wagon train had pulled her down; getting to San Francisco had seemed more a dream. Now, it seemed more real. She patted her skirt. It was still there---under her petticoat---the little cloth pouch with all the important papers---proof they owned the Robbins Hardware store, the boat The Promise, and Rebel, Aaron's horse. The court could not deny their claim. And even though the papers added to the heat of her dress, the little pouch provided Sara with a much needed sense of hope and purpose. She would guard these with her life.

As Danny and Reeves plodded forward, Sara watched the wind brush patterns across the tall grass. Golden shapes fanned back and forth in waves of mesmerizing movement all across the prairie, as far as the eye could see. She listened to the rhythmic clip-clop of the horses, finding comfort in the sure steady movement. It reminded Sara that they were moving toward their destiny. It was unfolding even now, like the patterns formed by wind. No matter how random, it seemed there was beauty and harmony, as though by a grand design. Was there a design, a reason for everything? Oh, how she wished she could believe again as she once did as a child. It would be a comfort as it was for Peggy. Peggy's faith had not abandoned her. Why was that? Sara pressed her lips together and took a breath. No, she wouldn't think of that now. She'd just stay with her feeling---the wonder of nature. That was enough for now.

She turned to face Peggy. "I'm awful glad you're with us. Thank you for being my friend."

"Well, of course!" Peggy smiled. "Just think of all the fun we'll have in San Francisco!"

CHAPTER TEN

A few hours later, Peggy took over the reins from Sara. They'd traveled silently for a few miles and finally, Peggy glanced at Sara and smiled. "You've been the closest thing to a sister, for me." Peggy's eyes moistened, and she paused for a moment.

"I'm glad you feel that way, Peggy. I do too. What is it, Peggy? You look like you need to ask me something."

"Can I ask you something very personal?"

"Of course! You're part of the family now--sisters, remember!"

"Do you love Mark?"

The question caught Sara off guard and she laughed. "Well, goodness, I…I" She paused to consider. "I used to think that I did."

Peggy smiled and nodded. "He's sure sweet on you."

"I guess," Sara answered, but her throat suddenly went dry. She poured some water into a tin cup and took a swallow. Peggy had asked a sobering question. "I think I'm a disappointment to Mark." Sara frowned as she thought about it. "Mark doesn't really understand how much I want to work in my family's business. He thinks wives should stay home, take care of a family. But you see, before we left, I spent a year learning about our family business. I worked after school in a hardware store. I learned about keeping the books and planning and ordering. The owner was a friend of my father's and he let me do a lot of things. I loved working. I always had ideas, and Mr. Walker was very kind and listened. Of course, people frowned on me working there. 'It's a man's place,' they said. I think Mark thought I'd give it up once I was in San Francisco. But I'm going to be needed at our family store in San Francisco, especially now that Uncle Jacob is ill. First, of course, we have to prove our case—-that all debts have been paid and prove to the court that Mr. Locke is a lying thief who is just trying to take everything our family worked so hard for." Sara took a deep breath. "Now that I'm responsible for Aaron, as well as my Uncle and cousin, I'll need to spend all my time making a go of the hardware store. I'm going to be very busy." She paused a moment, readjusted her straw hat.

"Do you think you'll marry Mark someday?"

"I don't know. But I asked Mark to wait a few years, until

Aaron was on his own, or everything with our inheritance was settled. It could take time." She frowned and bit down on her lip. "Now I'm not sure I want to marry, anyone." The idea seemed newly formed, and forced Sara to glance out at the prairie.

Peggy was all sympathy. "You have a lot on your shoulders now. I'm sure Mark will wait for you."

A burr of conscience picked at Sara. "I should've been more honest with Mark, voiced my doubts---said what I really wanted. I…I didn't want to hurt him, especially now. Mark doesn't believe women should work outside the home. Most people think like Mark. Folks on the wagon train thought it unnatural for women to want to work outside the home. Mrs. Barker said I'd never marry a proper man, if I stepped out of place." Sara mimicked the prudish look. "'It's downright unseemly for a Christian woman to have such selfish notions.'"

Sara took a deep breath, pulling the richness of the air inside of her. Well, maybe she did have selfish dreams. But dreams were important. At times, it was all that had kept her going.

"Are you all right, Sara?"

"I'm fine!" Sara laughed. "Spinning dreams is all. Probably just a silly goose."

"Sara Robbins, you're not a silly goose. You're just about the cleverest girl I know. And dreams aren't silly."

"Some folks think I want too much," Sara said, thoughtfully.

Peggy shook her head. "My momma used to say that God puts the 'wants' in us before we're born. Then the angels spin the dreams."

"Sounds nice." Sara smiled, but countered, "People tend to want a lot of things, and some things that aren't good for them. How do we know what's right and good?"

"Momma used to say that 'It takes a lot of praying and that the heart has to be sweet and open, humble to God. Then the right answer will come.' Sometimes Momma and I used to open the Bible and read passages, listening for a sense that God was speaking to us. The words would jump into our hearts." Peggy put her arms around herself. "It's the work of the Holy Spirit working through us. I sure hated to leave Momma's Bible behind on the wagon."

Sara felt a twinge of guilt. It'd been a long time since she'd read the Word. "Aaron and I have the family Bible." She pointed to a small lidded box. "You're welcome to use it any time."

"Oh, thank you, Sara. Thank you so much!" Peggy beamed. "You'll see. We can pray together and receive messages."

"Yes," Sara nodded, not wanting to spoil Peggy's excitement. If only it were that easy, Sara thought. "But why is it, Peggy, so hard for even prayerful, righteous folks to know what's right or wrong? And why is it folks can't see that slavery is wrong? And why can't others have mercy on women when they're treated so poorly by their husbands or stepfathers? Why do they blame the women?"

Peggy shook her head sadly. "I don't know."

Sara was growing more incensed. "And what was so bad about working outside the home to put food on the table, or even to exercise their natural abilities. Why in the world would some folks be dead set against others wanting nothing more than to make a better life for others? It doesn't make any sense to me."

"Me either," Peggy agreed. "Do you suppose it can ever be different?"

"Of course," Sara insisted, "My Father said that 'ideas are just ideas. They can change. And some ideas are better than others. I know it will change when women get the vote." Sara straightened her back. "Women will change things. And when I get to San Francisco, I'm going to be a suffragette, just like my Mother. I'll work for the vote!"

Peggy looked worried. "I don't know. Women are so different from men--think differently about life and right and wrong."

"Precisely! That's my point. We would vote for things that help all kinds of people---things that men don't find so urgent. Maybe even change the law so that awful stepfathers or bad parents couldn't hurt their children."

Peggy turned to glance out at the prairie. "Like Colwell," she murmured.

"Exactly! By the way, how did you happen to have Colwell as a step-father?"

Peggy took a breath. "When Pa died two years ago, we moved to town to be with Aunt Bertha." Her voice softened. "Aunt Bertha caught pneumonia and died last year. Then Momma went to work at a dry goods store." Peggy frowned. "One day Donald Colwell walks in and offers to take us to California. Momma always dreamed of seeing San Francisco--wanted to be where it was warm. So she upped and married Donald---to be respectable, you know. Then, in a few weeks we set out as part of the wagon train, where I met you."

Peggy clasped her arms about herself and glanced longingly at the prairie. "I miss her so much."

"I know!" Sara said, feeling the same ache in her heart. "But I'm so glad you're going to San Francisco with us. Your Momma would be happy and proud about that!"

"Yes!" Peggy brightened. "And when we get there, I'm goin' get a job, first thing. Help you and Aaron."

"That's very sweet and noble of you, Peggy! What do you think you'll do?"

"Go on the stage. Be a singer!"

"On the stage? You mean in a theatre?"

"Yes!"

"Really?" Sara suspected Peggy didn't know that most folks thought women who performed on stage were "fallen women." Of course, people thought all kinds of things. Anyway, it was Peggy's dream. That was good enough. "That sounds very nice." Sara smiled encouragingly.

"I'll sing and dance and make people happy—-help take their mind off things." Peggy's eyes shown with purpose, but then she frowned. "I ain't had proper training."

"I heard some people are just natural born to it."

"I used to sing in church with Aunt Bertha. And most times, folks made me sing all by myself."

"I think that's wonderful, Peggy. Sounds like you're one of those naturals. You should be very proud."

Peggy drew her lips in a determined manner. "I'm goin' to go on the stage! Ain't nobody goin' to stop me. Not even Donald Colwell!"

"That's the spirit!" Sara grinned. "I know Rufus appreciated your singing. You have a lovely voice. Hope you'll sing some more. I never heard you at the camp-meets."

"Donald wouldn't let me!" She frowned briefly and then added, "I'm not shy when I sing. Ain't that something?"

"I guess that means you're a natural!"

"If you say so," Peggy teased.

"I do, and don't you forget it!" Sara grinned.

CHAPTER ELEVEN

Rufus's condition continued to improve. By early afternoon, he was sitting up and complaining about "too much fussing." Sara decided to make camp early, and was relieved to see the trail turn toward the river. The winding waterway snaked slowly across the land just east of them.

When at last they arrived at the river, they quickly found a campsite. Others had camped there and left a good circle of stones around a fire-pit.

Aaron and Peggy unhitched the animals, led them down to drink, and by the time they returned, Sara had ropes around some trees for a make-shift corral. The girls collected fallen branches for firewood and soon the tent was pitched and a campfire ready. Sara fixed boiled beef jerky, biscuits, canned pears and black tea.

Rufus stayed awake long enough to take a few bites of canned pears. Sara had tried to get him to eat more. "Quit yer fussin'. I don't need no midwife to carry me out of this world!" He glared at Sara, but Rufus' complaining was short-lived. He soon turned over and went to sleep.

"It's better to let him have a peaceful night's rest," Sara said. "We can make up the time tomorrow and be in Leavenworth by tomorrow afternoon, if all goes well."

Aaron and Peggy agreed.

"Besides," Sara reminded them, "we need to wash clothes before coming into town, or they'll smell us a mile away."

After supper, Peggy and Sara went down to the river to bathe and wash clothes. They were careful to stay close to the bank to avoid any quicksand. Then they set the few pieces of laundry out to dry and by the time their chores were finished, the sun lay against the horizon. It was bedtime.

Aaron insisted on first watch. "I'll call when I need you," he assured his sister. "I'll keep Tarney and George can stay with Rufus.

"All right. Goodnight," Sara muttered and trudged off for the tent where she found Peggy already asleep.

Before stretching out, Sara reached into her satchel and pulled out the Derringer that had once belonged to her mother. Placing the small pearl-handled gun under her robe, she wondered what her mother would say. Most likely, she'd say to be very careful. Though it was a small caliber; it could be lethal at close range. Sara worried about being able to use it properly because of her sore hands. It was going to be hard to hold the gun steady. The month-long quarantine had made her hands soft. And holding the reins for just one day made them sore and swollen. She'd have to remember to rub almond oil into them. But hopefully, she wouldn't have to use the gun. Fortunately, Aaron had Rufus's revolver.

Later that night, Sara felt someone shaking her. "Wake up!" Aaron whispered. "Hurry. I need you."

"What is it?" Sara bolted up in alarm.

"Riders! Could be Indians! Hurry!" he whispered. "Better get dressed and stay calm, Sara. Remember, no candlelight till we know who it is.

Tarney was already jumping up and down, waiting for Aaron's command. "Come on, girl, only be quiet!" He grabbed her rope collar and leash.

Sara quickly pulled a dress over her head, and took the Derringer from under her robe, placed it in her skirt pocket, and rushed outside.

"Sounds like more than two," Sara whispered, anxiously, wondering how many more there might be.

They stood together under the dark canopy of trees and waited as the sound of horses drew near.

Tarney began barking and pacing excitedly in front of Aaron. "Stay!" Aaron ordered, grabbing hold of her rope collar. "Hush!"

A groggy Peggy stuck her head out of the tent. "What's happening?"

"Stay there," Aaron commanded. "Riders coming."

Alarmed, Peggy crouched back inside the tent.

"They're getting closer," Sara whispered, straining to see into the dark woods.

A pale moon edged the cottonwood trees in silver, and finally revealed the misty silhouettes of three riders, heading straight towards them.

Why don't they call out? Sara wondered, clutching the side of her skirt.

"They must see us," Aaron whispered to his sister standing beside him. Deepening his voice to sound older, he hollered. "Who goes there?"

"White men, son. White men! No need ta fear!" The man's voice was deep and flat.

Neither Sara nor Aaron was eased by the sound of it. They stood anxiously waiting, guns ready. Rufus's Colt shook in Aaron's hand. The metal felt cold and lifeless. He wondered if he'd be able to keep an aim and hold Tarney, as well.

The three riders stopped in front of the wagons, glanced around camp and prepared to dismount from Indian ponies. A sense of foul purpose emanated from them.

"Better ride on!" Aaron warned, taking a firmer stance and aiming his revolver. The men's faces were hidden under wide-brimmed hats, and their weapons were shielded beneath long heavy coats.

Tarney let out a warning growl and tugged against Aaron's hold on her collar. "Hold still, Tarney!" Aaron demanded, feeling the gun wobble in his hand.

"Well, lookee here, brother Clyde." The shorter of the three men rode closer. "We found ourselves a couple of partridges nesting in the trees!" His voice was guttural and insinuating. He stared at Sara, and then turned to a younger man. "We love partridges, don't we, brother Miles?"

Miles raised his chin and howled like a coyote.

"Miles never had him a partridge, did ya Miles? He's the baby of the family, ya see. Ain't that right?"

"Lance! Leave be," Clyde ordered. Apparently, the leader, he was a heavy-set man and sat astride his horse like a general, and cautiously looked about. "You young'ns alone?" He feigned a casual tone.

"No!" Aaron's voice spiked and he quickly asserted. "My pa's here...and our Uncle, too! They're down at the river. Be back in a minute. So you better get out of here right now!"

"Ain't very hospitable, now are ya?" Clyde sneered. "I ought ta speak to yer pa...have him teach ya some manners."

Suddenly, Sara remembered Hanson's warning, and a column of dread passed along her spine. These men might be marauders, heartless killers who attack lone wagons. Dear, God. What are we going to do? They didn't believe Aaron. The awful fear seemed to pin Sara's feet to the ground, lifeless as a bug under glass. But in a moment, her fear sharpened into rage, and her voice shot out the command. "You and your men stay right where you are. We have our guns on you, and we aren't afraid to shoot!" Sara felt the cold metal of the gun in her hand. All her senses were pointed with it. "You men leave, now!"

"Well," Lance sneered, dismounting and stepping forward. "jist look at that, will ya, Miles?" He turned to the younger man. "Ya see that Miles, she's a brave little partridge, trying to protect her baby brother, and with a big bad, old Derringer, too."

"I like her! I like her!" Miles shouted in glee, revealing a mouth full of half-missing teeth in his child-like face. "Can we bring her home?" he asked excitedly, as though Sara were a puppy dog.

Clyde didn't answer, but leaned forward for a closer look at Sara. As he did, the moon shone on his face, revealing the dark ruthlessness there.

"You leave us alone!" Sara insisted, pointing the small gun. She felt her stomach turn at the sight of him.

"I think ya got it all wrong, Miss. Me and my brothers, we're the Carey brothers. That there," he pointed, "be Lance, and here's my younger brother, Miles." Sara watched the two men nod. "We be want'n ta protect ya. We seen Injuns earlier, right about here!" He dismounted.

"Don't come any closer!" Aaron shouted," reaiming his gun.

Clyde ignored him, but eyed Tarney. "Nice little mutt, ya got there," he offered coolly.

Tarney was snarling and growling, ready to plunge.

"Ain't very hospitable, and she don't fix ta mind ya much." Clyde was judging the threat. Then he nodded a silent direction at the other men.

"What are you doing?" Sara was alarmed to see the other brothers quickly dismount and head for the two wagons. "Tell them to stop!" she demanded and pointed her gun at Clyde's head.

"No need to get riled, miss," Clyde said, "they're jist making sure weren't no Injuns up there."

Lance called out from Sara's wagon, "No one here!"

"Leave him alone!" Aaron shouted, angrily. "He's sick!"

"Come on back, boys!" Clyde ordered. He turned to Aaron. "Ya see, son, we mean ya no harm."

Aaron knew the man was angling for time and checking for weakness. "You men, drop your guns, or I'll shoot." Aaron took aim at Clyde."

"Why sure, young man." Clyde said, smoothly. "As you kin see," he smiled, dropping a gun from his belt. "Okay, boys. Let's show'm. We an't here ta harm."

Sara began sweating and her hand felt wet and unsteady as she held the Derringer. She watched the three men take guns from their belt holsters and dropped them on the ground. The men were too confident. What were they planning? She heard Aaron raise his voice, "Stand aside," he ordered.

"Come on out, Peggy. Get their guns!"

CHAPTER TWELVE

Sara watched the men's startled looks as Peggy hesitantly walked out of the tent. Peggy clutched a blanket about her nightgown and stopped a few feet in front of the tent.

"It's all right, Peggy. Just do what Aaron says." Sara nodded encouragingly. She could only hope Peggy would keep her wits about her. Everything depended on that, now. But Sara's throat went dry as one of the men took a step toward Peggy.

"Well, lookee here!" Lance grinned. "Sure is a purdy sight," he leered as Peggy came near. He doffed his large, black hat, revealing scraggly brown hair. "Kin I help ya, Miss?" he offered smugly as Peggy bent to pick up his gun.

Sara held her breath as Peggy hesitated in front of the men.

"Get his gun!" Aaron ordered.

"I'll give ya, mine, if you like," Miles offered eagerly. His plump, round face beamed.

"Shut up!" Clyde snapped.

"Scrappy little critter ya got there, boy!" Lance glared hatefully at Tarney.

"Hurry, Peggy! Aaron noticed Peggy falter as she bent down for Lance's gun.

Lance's eyes narrowed at Peggy as she picked up his gun. The man shifted his weight suggestively. "You're lettin' a girl do your dirty work, boy. Why don't you come get this yourself? Or aren't ya man enough?" He made an obscene gesture.

Peggy had Lance's gun and tossed it towards Aaron and then moved cautiously toward Clyde.

Clyde, a barrel-chested man with a square face, kept his attention on Peggy. The mean smirk across his mouth never changed, as he waited.

Peggy came nearer to Clyde's boots. And as she bent to pick up his gun, he struck, quick as a rattlesnake, and snatched her up, pulling her roughly against him.

Peggy screamed and struggled against his powerful grip.

"Let her go!" Sara shouted, pointing her gun at him.

"Ya got her, Clyde!" Miles laughed and danced a jig.

"Hurt her and so help me, I'll"... Aaron threatened, but words fell mute as he helplessly watched Clyde pull Peggy in front of him as a shield. If he tried to shoot now, he'd hit Peggy. Fear reamed through his body like a spear.

With his left hand Clyde quickly pulled a colt .32 from his belt and pressed it against Peggy's temple.

Peggy went limp.

"Drop yer gun, boy! Drop it, Miss!"

Aaron and Sara hesitated.

"Better do what Clyde says," Lance warned.

Reluctantly, Aaron put down his weapon, but Sara shakily held hers. She knew if she tried to shoot Clyde, he'd probably shoot Aaron, and she couldn't risk that. Slowly, she bent down and put the Derringer on the ground.

"Now that's more hospitable! Ain't it Clyde?" Lance said, enjoying the theme.

Suddenly, Tarney was barking furiously and tugging on the rope. She saw George moving stealthily around in back of Clyde. And as George lunged at the man's leg, Clyde moved automatically and without letting go of Peggy, kicked George.

George gave a yelp, but regained his balance and was about to leap at Clyde.

"Shoot it!" Lance encouraged.

"No, Clyde," Miles protested. "Don't kill'em. Let me have `em!"

"Shut up!" Clyde snarled, taking aim and firing at George. The bullets dug into the earth, just missing George.

George took off running for Rufus's wagon and ran under it, trying to hide behind the back wheel.

Peggy fainted and sagged heavily in Clyde's arm.

Clyde let her fall to the ground. "Fool girl!"

"Monsters!" Sara shouted.

"You two better shut up, or I'll kill the other mutt."

"I hate mutts," Lance said. "Let me kill it. Prove I kin shoot straight." He grinned.

Before Clyde could answer, Tarney broke loose from Aaron's hold, lunged forward, going for Lance. Even as Aaron shouted, "Stop!" Tarney was jumping up and trying to sink her teeth above Lance's boot. Lance took his fist and punched Tarney down, then kicked her. Tarney landed with a thud on the ground, a few feet from Aaron.

"Tarney! Oh, Tarney," Aaron cried, dropping to his knees. "You killed my dog!" He bent to pick her up.

"Leave it be!" Clyde ordered. "She ain't dead yet!"

Ignoring Clyde's order, Aaron sat on the ground and cradled Tarney in his arms. "I'm here. I'm here, Tarney," he cried, rocking back and forth. "Don't die, please, don't die!"

"Aaron!" Sara beseeched, "Please, Aaron, put Tarney down!" Terrified, Sara watched Lance take aim at Tarney and Aaron. "Aaron! Noooooo!" she cried.

Suddenly, a shot exploded.

A startled look creased Clyde's face.

Lance spun around to see where the shot had come from.

"Out there!" Miles shouted, gleefully, pointing to the woods, where a faint puff of smoke lingered.

"Clyde?" The two men turned to see their brother's face frozen in painful surprise, clutch his chest, and fall face down on the ground.

"Clyde!" The brothers rushed over, dropped to their knees and turned Clyde over. Blood bubbled up from the hole in Clyde's chest. Lance retched and put his hand over his mouth.

"Is he bad?" Miles whined. "What'll we do? What'll Pa say?" Miles knelt beside his brother's body, clutching at his coat.

Sara dashed to grab Clyde's gun, but Lance moved faster and kicked it out of her reach.

"You'll pay for this!" Lance snarled. "You'll all pay for this!" He looked at Sara and Aaron and then out at the woods, not sure which threat to handle.

Peggy, awakening from her faint, looked over to see Clyde's body just a few feet away; she burst out crying, and covered her face. "Oh, no!"

"Stop crying!" Lance demanded. He kept thrusting his gun at Peggy and then at the woods.

Just then a terrifying shout, "Keewaa Keewaka!" came from the nearby thicket.

Sara and Aaron glanced at the woods.

Lance spun around. "What the…?"

Again the cry came, even closer.

Injuns!" Lance shouted to Miles. "Let's get out'a here!" He started for the ponies.

Miles balked, "We got ta take Clyde," he pleaded, trying to raise his brother.

"Leave'em, Lance ordered. "He's dead!"

"No!" Miles cried, "Pa will fix'em!"

"I'm boss now. Git here or I'll whip yer hide!" Lance commanded.

With tears flowing down his face, Miles did as ordered and rushed to his pony and jumped on.

Lance quickly mounted, jabbed his horse, and shouted a retreating threat. "You haven't seen the last of us!" He turned and with deadly vengeance, aimed a parting shot into the thicket.

There was a cry of pain.

"Ya got one!" Miles cheered as they rode away with their threats still ringing through the darkness.

Sara and Aaron stood stunned, numbly looking into the trees. It was several moments before they realized the men had truly gone.

Aaron peered uneasily into the cottonwoods. "Did you see where the shot came from?"

No," Sara answered. She bent over, looking at Tarney. "She's still alive!"

"Get her inside the tent, Sara." Aaron ordered, glancing about. "And stay there with Peggy. I'm going to check the woods."

"No, Aaron! Wait!"

But Aaron had already moved into the dark underbrush and out of sight. "Oh, please be careful, Sara silently pleaded, trying to see into the woods. Moments later, Sara realized there had only been one shot. Did that mean there was only one person out there? Sara wrapped her arms around herself, realizing how chilled she felt. "Peggy?" she whispered, turning to see her friend standing over the body of Clyde. Peggy looked stunned, unable to move. She started shaking.

"Peggy, we need to get you inside the tent." Sara sensed that one more shock would undo Peggy completely.

Peggy murmured to herself, "There's nothing we can do, nothing we can do."

"Peggy, please, I need your help." Sara knew that she had to get Tarney and Peggy inside the tent where they would be more protected. "We can use your blanket to lift her," Sara said, pointing on the ground where it had fallen from Peggy.

"All right," Peggy said flatly, bending down and helping Sara lift Tarney on to the blanket. They carried Tarney to the tent and eased her down on Aaron's straw mattress.

Sara knelt gently stoking the little dog's head. "Please don't die, sweetheart." Sara gulped back a knot of tears in her throat. "Don't know what we'd do without you." She shook her head and glanced worriedly at Peggy. "I guess it's best to let her rest for now. I'll see if anything's broken later." Sara stood up, took a deep breath and squinted into the woods. Everything seemed quiet--too quiet. And yet there had only been one gunshot. If there were more Indians, Sara thought, they would have attacked by now. "Peggy, you stay here and keep an eye out for Aaron. I want to check on Tanner."

Sara stood outside the tent, paused a moment and listened to Aaron trudge about in the underbrush. She was on her way to Rufus' wagon when she heard Aaron call.

CHAPTER THIRTEEN

"I've found him. I found him! It's an Indian...a young buck. Better come give me a hand. He's wounded!"

White Hawk lay on the ground, his eyes closed. A trickle of blood oozed down his upper right arm and darkened the right side of his shirt.

"Looks like the shot grazed him," Aaron said, squatting down next to him. "He's out cold--must have fallen backwards and hit his head. And look there!" Aaron pointed to a revolver half-hidden under a tree root, barely a foot away. Aaron picked up the gun and held it up to catch more moonlight. "It's my gun!" Aaron exclaimed. "Dad's gun, remember?" He looked at Sara, amazed. "He's the one who stole it!"

"Rather ironic, isn't it?" Sara said, shaking her head and kneeling for a closer look.

White Hawk moaned.

Peggy came forward. "Why he's nothing but a boy!" Peggy gasped, staring down at him.

"He's still losing blood," Sara said. "Looks like a surface wound, but I can't be sure. We'd better get him inside the tent."

Aaron scowled. "That's not a good idea."

"We can't leave him lying on the ground, bleeding to death. Come on," Sara insisted. "We can do it together."

"Oh, all right!" Aaron reluctantly bent to pick up the Indian's upper body as Sara and Peggy each lifted a leg.

They carried White Hawk to the entrance of the tent, and laid him down.

"Wait a minute," Aaron directed. "I want to check on Tarney first. There may a problem putting the Indian near her."

As Aaron entered the tent, he was surprised to see George as well. Apparently, he'd snuck in and wanted to be with Tarney. Both dogs raised their heads and wagged their tails. "Well, look at you--seems you're both feeling better." Aaron bent down and gently patted Tarney. "Sara," Aaron called excitedly, "Tarney and George are better!"

Tarney got to her feet, but limped forward on her left leg.

George tried to get up, but it was clear he was in pain. "That's all right. You two just stay quiet and rest!" Aaron whispered, turning to leave the tent.

"We can't put the Indian in the tent, Sara," Aaron frowned. "Too risky. Might scare the dogs. Besides, no telling what the Indian might do when he wakes up. We'll have to put him in the wagon. It'll be better to keep an eye on him, anyway."

The three managed to hoist White Hawk up and inside the wagon. Aaron lit the lantern and gave it to Peggy. "Here, hold this. I'll stand guard."

Sara quickly loosened the blood-splattered shirt. "Raise him up, Aaron, so I can remove his shirt."

"I'm surprised he doesn't wake up," Peggy said, worriedly.

"I'd be here to protect you, if he did!" Aaron assrted.

Sara winced, as she saw where the bullet had grazed his arm above the elbow. "It's not too deep. He'll be fine if it doesn't get infected. I'm more worried about his head. He must have hit it pretty hard."

"I wonder how old he is." Peggy bent for a closer look.

"Hard to say. I'd guess near my age." Aaron grimaced.

Sara noticed Aaron pale at the sight of blood. "Aaron, Peggy can help me. Why don't you see to Rufus? I'm worried about him."

Aaron shook his head. "I don't think I should leave you with the Indian. He might wake up and attack you."

"Aaron! I hardly think he's in any condition to do something to us. I'll call you if we need help."

"Well," Aaron said, "you better keep your Derringer handy. Holler if you need me!"

Peggy faced Aaron. "Are you feeling all right? You look kind of queasy."

"I'm fine!" he snapped and turned to leave.

He paused at the opening of the wagon and looked out at the darkness. Now and then the moon shed some light across the trees. But he couldn't see very much.

"Just be careful, Peggy!" he warned, springing down from the wagon.

Aaron headed for Rufus's wagon, and carefully skirted the body of Clyde, who lay sprawled on the ground near the fire-pit. Aaron startled as a flash of moon-light shown on the man's face. Had the man moved? But no, he's dead, Aaron told himself. But we'll have to dig the grave soon as possible, and it's going to take several hours, judging by the ground. He sighed and rubbed his burning eyes.

"Peggy, I'm going to close the wound, probably no more than three or four stitches, but I'll need your help." Sara knelt close to the Indian, gently taking his arm in her lap.

"You'll want more light, too" Peggy turned up the lantern wick, then set the lantern on a barrel next to Sara.

"That's better." Sara nodded. "We'd better hurry." She didn't want to mention it, but any light could put them all in danger.

"Peggy, reach up there." She pointed. "And bring down that safety-basket. Open the jar of whiskey-spirits and take out several strips of muslin. Bring the needle and thread."

Peggy quickly found the things Sara needed and handed them to her. "Did you want me to keep your Derringer close by?"

"Good idea! I doubt we'll need it. But Aaron will worry. Put it on the barrel next to the lamp."

Sara applied a band of muslin as a tourniquet. Next, she cleaned the wound with a cloth soaked in whiskey and then doused the needle, thread and her fingers. She took a deep breath. "I sure hope I can keep steady and get him stitched up before he wakes."

Sara made small, even stitches in the boy's wound. "Fortunately, it's not very deep," she murmured. But halfway through, she broke out in sweat. She stopped to wipe her forehead with her apron and took a breath.

"You're doing fine, Sara," Peggy encouraged. "It would surely hurt somethin' fierce if he was awake." Peggy frowned, Wonder what would happen if he did."

Finally, Sara sewed the last stitch, then stood and rubbed her eyes.

"I can wrap it, Sara," Peggy offered.

Sara nodded and gave Peggy a clean cloth and a strip of muslin.

After they were finished, Sara stood, but lost her balance and sat on the flour barrel.

"Are you all right?" Peggy asked.

"Yes. I'm fine, just tired. We'll let the boy sleep for now." Sara rose and walked to the front of the wagon. She leaned on the driver's bench, steadying herself and drew in a deep breath.

"You're sure you're OK?" Peggy came close.

"Don't fuss! I'll be fine, Sara answered, more sharply than she meant. "Sorry, guess I'm just tired."

"Sara!" Aaron called from the Rufus's wagon.

"What is it?" The girls asked, quickly climbing down and rushing to Aaron.

"Rufus is awake!"

"That's great news!" Peggy said.

"But he wants to get up and see George."

Sara sighed and stared mutely up at Aaron. "Tell him…tell him he can't. George and Tarney are resting and that George is fine. He can see him in the morning." She was relieved to know that Rufus was better, but thought it best for Rufus not to move about. She didn't want to argue with the old man, but she would insist, if need be.

Aaron relayed the message, stressing that George was resting and didn't need any excitement. Rufus agreed, laid back and promptly closed his eyes.

Climbing wearily back into her wagon, Sara checked on her Indian patient. He appeared to be resting, so she covered him with a blanket, took her gun off the barrel, and put it into her skirt pocket. She shouldn't have left it on the barrel and walked away. She was just too tired. That wouldn't have happened if she'd been more alert. She must remember to keep her wits about her. The boy was sleeping. He looked peaceful. That's good.

After turning off the lantern, she quietly climbed down and stood near the front of the wagon, peered anxiously at the dark trees and dense brush. It seemed so very dark, but soon, her eyes adjusted.

Here and there, branches trembled nervously and limbs reached like arms--underbrush seemed to creep toward her. "Though Bernam Wood be come to Dunsinae," she thought, shivering and remembering the tragedy of Macbeth.

Clasping her arms about her, she quieted her breathing so as to listen carefully. Now and then the hoot of an owl marked the stillness, and nearby, the horses offered their gentle, uneventful, breathing sounds. All else appeared quiet, but Sara remained apprehensive.

I've got to stop this! She told herself. She was frightened, no use denying that. Even the gun in her skirt was little assurance. Were there Indians about? How would she know if they were watching? Would the Carey brothers come back? She shook her head, trying to dispel the fears. Just a few months ago, she would have said prayers

67

to calm herself. Right now, she couldn't. And she missed Tarney being close, always having her good senses to warn them. Poor little Tarney. "You just have to be all right," she whispered to herself.

Sara patted the cloth pouch under her nightshirt as she walked toward the campfire. Maybe she should put the papers in her satchel, but it was such a comfort having them close. She watched Aaron put another log on the fire and then sit beside the fire pit next to Peggy. Sara sighed. I sure hope that's the right thing to do, she thought, as sparks from the fire lifted into the darkness. Anyone within miles could see. Sara shook her head, walked closer, sidestepping the dark shape of Clyde, lying a few feet from the fire. "Keep a water bucket handy in case you hear any horses."

"I know what to do!" Aaron said, testily, and then quickly added. "Sorry, guess we're all jumpy."

Wearily, Sara sat on a log and glanced back at the dead man. "We'll bury him at first light."

Aaron frowned at Sara. "You look about to fall over. Go on-- rest. I'll take first watch."

"No, I'll be fine." Sara bent forward, putting her elbows on her knees, and trying to hold her head up.

Peggy rubbed her eyes, took a deep breath and stood. "Rest, Sara!" she insisted. I'm not all that tired. I'll stand guard."

Sara nodded. "Thanks, Peggy. I'll just take a short nap. Be sure to wake me if Rufus needs anything, or if the Indian wakes up." She headed for the tent. "Peggy, remember to stay close to Aaron!" Once back in the tent, she sprawled out next to Tarney and George, and before long, fell sound asleep.

CHAPTER FOURTEEN

Sara slept through the night and awoke to feel Tarney tugging at the sleeve of her nightshirt. "Leave be!" she protested, turning away and burying her face in the straw mattress.

Finally opening her eyes, she sat up and glanced about. The light filtering through the tent suggested it was past dawn. "Aaron was supposed to wake me," she grumbled, tossing aside the comforter and getting up.

She untied the cloth sack from around her waist, gave it an affectionate pat for good luck and placed it carefully into her satchel. She could already tell it was going to be one of those dreadfully hot days, and she didn't need the extra cloth against her skin. The pouch with her important papers would be just as safe in her satchel. Now she needed to hurry and dress.

Pouring a pitcher of water into a bowl, she hurriedly sponged off, dried and put on her undergarments. Her plain blue blouse and brown skirt were the only clean garments at the moment. She quickly pulled on her boots, and brushed her hair, then tied it back with a crumpled strip of muslin. She briefly stretched the kinks from her back, and grumbled "Aaron shouldn't have let me sleep so long. There's way too much to do!" The first thing she'd best do was to see about the Indian, then tend to Rufus and the dogs. After that they'd dig a grave and bury Clyde.

She heard a gentle scratching and looked about. Tarney and George were waiting by the tent's door flap. She walked to the front flap and opened it. "Look at you! It's amazing! Up and about as if nothing happened." She could hardly believe it. She bent and gave Tarney a gentle hug. "You too, George. I'm so happy you're feeling better!" She noticed Tarney lift her right front paw. "Let me see that," Sara said, carefully inspecting it. "I don't think it's broken. We'll just make sure you take it easy."

She was surprised to see Rufus sitting by the fire-pit talking to Aaron and Peggy. He sat propped against a log, with a blanket across his legs. And though his face was pale, he seemed alert. "Rufus shouldn't you be—"

"Well, sleepy-head," Rufus interrupted, grinning. "The day's half gone. You gonna' lay around an' let us do all the work?" He chuckled as he greeted George with a pat on the head.

"Aaron, you should have woken me, earlier," Sara snapped, frowning at Aaron. She avoided looking at Rufus Tanner.

"You needed your sleep," Aaron replied, pleasantly. "Peggy's been a big help. She helped me dig the grave and bury Clyde, even guarded everything, so I got a few hours sleep, as well." He smiled at Peggy. "We both curried Danny and Reeves." He turned back to Sara. "Used the last of the oats, though."

Sara glanced at Peggy and then Aaron. "So, just the two of you buried Clyde?"

Peggy answered, "Yes, and we took care of the Indian, too."

"That's wonderful!" Sara said, surprised. "How is he?"

"He's awake," Peggy offered, "but he has a terrible headache, I think. You can tell when he tries to sit up. Poor kid." Peggy said.

Aaron shook his head. "He sure don't know how to behave. I offered him my shirt, but he just threw it back at me," Aaron said angrily. "Of course, when Peggy took it to him and offered to help put it on, he was all willing and grateful." Aaron rolled his eyes.

"Aaron," Peggy said gently, "you mustn't take it personal. He knows me better, is all. I'd already given him water and some bread." Peggy glanced at Sara. "He slept through the night, mostly. He woke up once. I lit a candle and gave him some water." She turned to Aaron. "He looked at me like I was a ghost, at first. But when I gave him a sip of water, he took it and laid back. Ain't been no bother!"

"Thank you, Peggy," Sara said, "for all your help. I really appreciate it. You probably need to re—"

Aaron interrupted. "He could've been more grateful seeing as how I found his pony and tethered him with ours."

"Oh, Aaron you're so clever." Peggy beamed at him. "Aaron took the Indian's shirt to coax the pony to come. He was able to get a rope about his neck and everything!"

"Yep!" Rufus added. "He's a mighty clever young man, missy, and don't ya forget it!"

"Yes, I know!" Sara retorted. She was not in the mood to be lectured at about her brother. Turning to face Rufus, she said in a measured and rather formal tone, "Aaron has proved himself many times in these last months. Everyone knows how brave and capable he is! In fact he's one of the most capable people I know!"

"Well, we agree on that!" Rufus grinned, enjoying putting the spur to Sara.

Aaron raised his eyebrows and smiled. "Well, thank you, Sara. And, of course, Rufus has been a big help, too," he added grinning at his friend. "Wait 'til you hear his news! Rufus is going with us to Ft. Leavenworth."

"I know that!" Sara said, impatiently.

"No, I mean he's going to stay there for awhile."

"You don't plan to take the Overland Stage with us?"

"Nope," Rufus replied. "Ain't fit for it yet. My old friend, Mat Skoocome lives a few miles outside of Leavenworth. He raises mules. Says it's a good business, too. We go back a ways. Worked a claim together in California—'49, it were. Likely I'll jest settle in an' stay awhile, 'til I'm stronger."

Peggy nodded, "You see, he doesn't want to be a burden to his granddaughter in San Francisco. Says he'll come when he's better and he'll see us there, too!"

"Yep, that's the plan!" Rufus smiled, approvingly.

"Is there anything we can do for you?" Peggy asked.

Rufus turned to Peggy. "Well, young lady, as a matter of fact, there is. I had in mind to ask Aaron, but—".

Sara interrupted, "I'm sure we'd all be happy to help!"

"Well, then," he began, "I have an old, carved, wooden box in my wagon, jest under the driver's seat. There's an envelope with some money and papers and what not in it. Not much ta value, I guess, but there's a tin-type of Fredrick, my son, and his wife, Maria, just after they married. Both are dead, but my granddaughter might be grateful for the likeness. There's a note to Max Kruger, my solicitor in San Francisco. I believe my granddaughter, Elizabeth Tanner, is in San Francisco. Last I heard. Anyway, her address is on a piece of parchment inside the box. I'd be mighty grateful if you can give the box to Elizabeth or ta my solicitor. He'll know where ta find her. I pay'm ta keep track. So if you have trouble, jest see him."

"We'll do that," Aaron said. "Don't you worry about anything!"

"While I think on it," Rufus said, "I'd like you to sell m' wagon and team in Leavenworth. I won't be needin' them."

"Of course, we'd be happy to help!" Aaron offered.

Rufus nodded. You'd do me a favor if you'd allow the money to help Peggy."

"Oh, Mr. Tanner, I couldn't!" Peggy exclaimed.

"It's not much...an' I won't need more than I have for my trip. You all have been kind, takin' care of me. It'd make me rest easier to know you have a little extra."

"But, Mr. Tanner," Peggy protested, you never know, you might need it in Leavenworth or San Francisco."

Rufus grinned and pointed a scolding finger. "Mind what I said. I don't want to get riled up. Ain't good for me to argue."

Finally, they agreed to do as Rufus asked. After having a breakfast of bread and jam, they were ready to hitch up the teams and head out for the last day of their journey to Leavenworth.

They agreed that the Indian should stay hidden inside the wagon, so as not to bring questions from passersby. And before leaving camp, Aaron drew a charcoal sign on the canvas of Rufus's wagon. It read "For Sale" in big bold letters across both sides.

By midday, they were on the main trail and meeting all kinds of traffic coming and going from Leavenworth. They were soon caught in the flow of many wagons, prairie schooners, carts and riders passing along the several trails fanning out from town.

Peggy wondered if her stepfather was anywhere about. Would she be able to spot him in time? If anything bad happened to her friends, it would be her fault. The terrible thought made her stomach churn.

"Don't worry, Peggy. If Donald tries to slip in with the traffic, I'll see him," Sara said. She knew that Aaron and Rufus, in the other wagon, would be watching as well. "But you'd better stay out of sight." Sara smiled. "Besides, you're the only one that seems to soothe the Indian. He seems better when you're around."

Sara knew that Aaron didn't like the idea of Peggy spending so much time with the Indian. But there wasn't much he could do about that---they both needed to be out of sight.

Before entering town, a family of five, the Stoddards, stopped to inquire about Rufus's rig. They said it was just what they needed for their older son and new daughter-in-law. The eighteen-year-old newlyweds wanted their own wagon for the trip to Oregon. The young man paid Rufus a fair price, which included a fine looking chestnut horse.

"It'll suit jest fine!" Rufus said, grinning. "And it'll help the youngsters git a start n' have a little privacy." He winked at Aaron. "Riding in style to my friend's ranch is exactly what I wanted."

By early afternoon, they were three miles outside of

Leavenworth, near the army fort and decided to stop by the side of the Kansas River. This would allow the horses a break and an opportunity for everyone to wash up. They would take time for a proper goodbye to Rufus and enjoy a final visit.

"I reckon it'd be smart to stay a bit standoffish around folks," Rufus counseled. "Don't fancy questions about the Indian pony."

But questions or interest couldn't be avoided. So many families were camped along the river nearby and there seemed to be an eagerness to share information. Men met in small groups. Children and dogs ran along the grassy slope of the riverbank, and women hauled water or washed clothes. There was an excitement about the place—-like a huge family picnic. A hardy-looking family with eight children seemed determined to be friendly. While they spoke with thick German accents, their intentions were clear. Mr. Foreman, a rather large man with a bald head walked forward grinning and playing a small accordion, with his petite, redheaded wife, Gina, at his side. She offered pieces of smoked sausage and spicy sauerkraut from a china platter. "Dat iz da best sausage ever!"

All agreed. It was a special treat, especially since there'd been little good food in the last few weeks. Finally, the Foremans went on their way, leaving an unexpected void for Sara.

She was overcome with a certain melancholy. It seemed odd, since the Foremans were only strangers. But as she thought about it, she realized they were a reminder of how many friends they'd left behind. And now, Rufus Tanner. Sara found herself close to tears. She hadn't expected that. In spite of the fact that Rufus often provoked her, she had formed a real affection for the crusty old man. She'd tried to convince him to see a doctor. But she doubted he would. He'd smiled that half-ways grin and nodded, 'We'll see how it goes.' Yes, she'd miss Rufus, but Aaron was sure to miss him more. She wondered if they'd ever see Rufus again.

Finally, it was time for their friend to leave. Peggy suggested they form a circle and pray. Sara felt a little awkward, but she joined the others. They said their last farewells, sadly watching Rufus ride away, the familiar scowl on his face. Aaron waved until his friend was out of sight, and then slowly resettled his hat on his head. "I'll miss him," he said flatly.

Sara suspected Rufus was having just as much trouble saying goodbye. Heaving a big sigh, she took the reins from Aaron. Ever mindful of how much they had to do, she turned to her brother, who sat dejectedly on the driver's bench next to her. "We'd better hurry. I want the doctor to see the Indian, then we have to get our tickets for the stagecoach, plus we still have to arrange to sell Danny and Reeves. And we'll need time to arrange for shipping our goods. By then, we could consider a fine dinner at the Planter's Hotel." She was hoping to get a smile out of Aaron.

"I am kind of famished." Aaron agreed. "That sausage kicked up an appetite. Aren't you hungry, Peggy?" he turned to call inside the canopy.

"Yes, and I expect our patient is, as well!"

"Well, then," Aaron snapped, "Let's not sit about jawing!"

"Aaron Robbins," Sara smiled. "You sounded just like Rufus Tanner!"

Aaron scowled, and then grinned.

CHAPTER FIFTEEN

By late afternoon, they'd arrived in the fort town of Leavenworth, a jumping off place for the Oregon Trail, and a stop for the Overland Stagecoach.

"It's so crowded." Sara frowned, pulling the reins tighter. "So many people and wagons." She thought it would be difficult to catch sight of Donald Colwell if he wanted to stay out of sight. But would he have had time? Would the wagon master have detained him. She knew she'd better not let her mind dwell on that, now. She had her hands full trying to keep the team in check.

Sara juggled into position between two large wagons. Suddenly, the one on her right careened frighteningly close. "Rats!" she swore, pulling the reins hard, barely avoiding a crushing blow.

"It's far more crowded than when we came through last month." Aaron scowled. "Better let me take the reins."

Relieved, Sara handed her brother the reins, and rubbed her sore hands together. She removed her straw hat and wiped her forehead on her sleeve. It was hot and it might take an hour getting anywhere in this mess. Many large wagons lumbered about like bilious elephants. There were small horse carts and riders, as well, and more folks walking--all jamming the road and aiming for a place to move ahead. It's a wonder people don't get killed, Sara thought. She shook her head and pulled Tarney closer. The little dog started barking at all the excitement, but was finally anchored between her and Aaron on the seat. Sara worried that Tarney might jump down and look for George. Poor little thing is going to miss her friend. They all would. Sara shook her head.

"You're doing good, Aaron!" Sara said, taking a deep breath and sitting back. She pushed her shoulders up and down and stretched her arms over her head. "That's better," she said aloud. "I need to stretch my legs. Maybe later we can go for a stroll and look at all the interesting little shops. I didn't get to see anything last time we went through Leavenworth," she said, noticing several ladies' dress shops.

A variety of small stores lined the boardwalk on each side of the street and many shoppers were rushing in and out, apparently stocking up for the journey.

"Peggy." Sara turned to face the back of the wagon. "Once our business is settled and we've seen to the Indian, we'll go shopping. You need a new dress. That old one of mine is too big for you."

"I've never had a store-bought dress before."

"You will," Aaron concluded, "and the prettiest one we can find!"

"Has the Indian said anything, yet?" Sara asked.

"No," Peggy replied. "But I think he understands what we're saying. He was real jumpy and kept trying to get up. I finally figured he was worried about his horse, so I opened the back flap and showed him we had it tied in back. He nodded and lay back down. He's been fine ever since. His wound looks a little festery, though."

"You're doin' just fine by him, Peggy," Aaron said, turning to smile at her.

"I like taking care of him." Peggy answered cheerfully.

Aaron's smile faded. "Well, just keep an eye on him. I wouldn't turn your back--can't trust him. Remember, he stole my father's gun. He might try something else, too!"

Peggy frowned and looked disappointed. "He seems nice."

"I think he's harmless," Sara said. "And he did save us!"

"Sure he saved my life," Aaron interjected, "but what was he doing there? Maybe he intended to kill us. Did you think of that?"

"Don't be silly, Aaron. I'm sure he was after an animal or else he could've killed you when he stole the gun."

"Well, that's true," Aaron grudgingly admitted.

"Look down there!" Sara pointed to a small, gray building with a worn sign at the end of the street--Sheriff and Jail. Maybe while we're so close, I should take the time now to report the attack and the death of that man, Clyde. They can probably direct us to the nearest doctor's office, as well."

"Probably save some time, Aaron nodded. "And," he grinned, "maybe find out if there's a reward."

They arrived at the end of the street and pulled the wagon up just beyond the sheriff station.

"I'll stay and guard the Indian," Aaron announced. "Hope it doesn't take too long. I'm famished and so are Peggy and Tarney."

"I'll hurry," Sara answered, getting down from the wagon.

This shouldn't take more than a minute, she assured herself. Besides, it was her civic duty.

Sara walked determinedly to the Sheriff's office and paused a moment to notice its unusual door. The door had been overlaid with copper, so that it appeared green and old. Its surface, riddled with buckshot, hurt her knuckles as she knocked. Not very welcoming.

A man's voice bellowed, "Enter!"

Sara turned the iron latch, and entered a dark and hazy room. It was darker than she expected and smelled of sausage and stale tobacco. A man sat in a wooden chair, his back to the door. He didn't move and it seemed to take forever for him to acknowledge her.

"Shut the door!" he muttered. "What do ya want?" His voice was flat and nasal. He spoke without turning around.

"I'd like to speak to the sheriff," Sara replied, polite as possible, unaccustomed to such rude behavior.

Sara quickly glanced about. It was a small, poorly lit room, containing two cells and one desk. A meager shaft of sunlight poked through a greasy barred window at the front. The place gave Sara a creepy feeling, and if not for the task at hand, she would have walked out.

"I said I need to speak to the sheriff," she asserted again. "I'm in a bit of a hurry," she added, her tone hinting displeasure.

"Sheriff's out, Ma'am," he said, turning slowly to face her. "I'm the deputy." He leaned forward on a stack of messy papers, picked up a tin cup and sipped at it. His long thin face and deep-set eyes glared at Sara.

The man's glare and manner were unsettling. But perhaps he had cause for it, Sara thought. He didn't look well. She guessed his age to be in the twenties, but he could be older. Pockmarks scared his weathered face, his dirty brown shirt looked two sizes too large. There was something wretched and sad about him, as though he'd stayed too long in this place and had become as old and faded as the walls.

"Sheriff won't be back for several hours," he stated, quickly averted his eyes, and then casually tapped a pencil on the desk in front of him.

"I need to know where to find the doctor's office."

He pointed, without interest. "End of this street."

Sara sighed. She wanted to be gone, but knew it was her duty to inform the authorities of what happened. Maybe she could help them catch those terrible men. "I need to tell the sheriff about three men who attacked our camp, threatened us. They tried to kill us and one of them was shot. We had to bury him and—"

"Well," the young man turned to face her. "My Pa's gone, so I guess you'll have ta tell me. I'm his deputy."

"I see," Sara hurried to explain. "Well, these three men rode into our camp. One of the men, I think his name was Clyde, was shot by an Indian hiding in the bushes. I don't know why the Indian was there—"

The deputy narrowed his eyes and gave Sara a piercing look. He was interested.

"You see, the man was about to shoot my brother when the Indian fired and killed him. I…guess the Indian saved---"

"Hold on! You say an Injin' shot a white man?"

"Well, yes… but you see, he was injured as well. Shot by Clyde." She saw the scowl of doubt and hurriedly continued. "I believe the Indian saved our lives. Now we need to help him."

The deputy's gray eyes narrowed. "So this "redskin" shot the white man?"

"Yes, but--" Sara saw the hostile look and did not like the implication. "The Indian saved our lives, and he's but a boy and injured." She stopped short again, seeing his interest spark. It was clearly not a wholesome interest.

"Do you know his full name?"

"The Indian?"

"No, the white man!" he snapped.

"I think they said Carey brothers. But the one shot was called Clyde. And the others," she thought for a moment, "The others were called Miles and Lance, I think."

"I see," he said, eyeing his pencil carefully, pausing and thinking how to proceed. "Sound's like you tangled with the Carey Clan, all right--old man Lumis's sons." He smiled, revealing decayed teeth. "That Injun. You say he's injured? Think he might still be in the area? Was he alone?"

"I…I…" Fear edged down Sara's spine. The deputy was more interested in the Indian boy than the criminals. For a moment she couldn't think.

"I asked ya a question!" The deputy's voice demanded.

Caught off guard, Sara answered too quickly, showing her anxiety. "No!"

The deputy examined her critically.

Trying to muster authority, Sara said, "He's--he's gone from there. Why do you need to know?"

"Cause I'd track him down and hang him!"

"You mean you'd hang him even though he saved our lives? It was self-defense, if anything!"

"Can't let the varmints git away with it." He rose from the chair. "You'd tell me the truth now, wouldn't ya? Or jest maybe you're an 'accessory'?" He seemed intrigued by the idea.

A little pain lashed across Sara's forehead. Oh, no! She had to get out of there as fast as possible! "Well," she said, edging closer to the door, and trying to sound business-like, "I just wanted to report that information to the sheriff. As she approached the door, her knees began to shake.

"Hold on there, Miss! I ain't finished with ya!"

CHAPTER SIXTEEN

Sara froze. Heart racing, she turned to face the deputy. "What do you want?"

The deputy's eyes narrowed as he edged closer, backing her against the door. "What I want and what I get, now that's two different things."

"I must be going!" Sara insisted, fumbling for the door handle at her back.

The deputy leaned closer, his foul breath hovering between them. "I gotta show you something."

"What?" Sara snapped, suddenly angry and stiff with indignation. "I don't have time for this kind of—-"

"Yeah, ya do!" He glared. "It's yer duty, m'am, or maybe I'll keep ya, til my dad gets back?"

Sara flinched, but didn't move. "Please hurry," she said, trying to sound firm. The deputy ambled back to the desk and looked through a stack of posters. "Yep," he nodded, pleased with himself. "Got it right here." He brought the poster to Sara and held it close. "Is this the man was shot?"

"Yes," Sara answered in surprise, "that's the man who tried to kill us."

"He's a mean one," the deputy smiled in satisfaction. "His kin, old man Lumis, will be wantin' ta know all about it. Where'd you say it happened?"

Sara felt compelled to answer, "About two days back along the trail. We were camped there, by the river."

"You goin' ta be around town?" he asked, slowly.

"No," Sara said quickly. "Why do you ask?"

"He's part of the Carey Clan—-meanest bunch of men around. I know 'em pretty well. Lumis might take it better if I tell him, or better still, if I have the varmint that killed his kin."

"Well, we won't be around," Sara said, emphatically.

"Might have cause ta detain ya," he smiled. "'spect his kinfolks will want ta know where Clyde's buried."

"I'm leaving today."

"Well," he said, making light of it, "guess I can't blame ya." He walked back to the door and blocked the opening with his arm as Sara was about to open it. "I'd hate ta have ta explain anything to ol'Lumis Carey. You goin' on the stagecoach or caravan?"

"Stagecoach!" she answered, and immediately regretted it. "I have to be leaving now," Sara insisted, pushing aside his arm. She felt her face flush. "Just inform your father, the sheriff," she ordered and marched out.

"Oh, I will ma'am, I surely will." The deputy slouched in the doorway and watched Sara hurry to her wagon. He'd remember that wagon, he thought. No question 'bout that. Oh, yes, he'd remember that wagon and 'specially that uppity young lady with the red hair. She'd need to be brought down a peg or two! No question 'bout that. And he was jest the man to do it!

"Come on! Let's get going!" Sara called, running to the wagon. She quickly climbed up beside her brother. "Hurry! We've got to get away from here!"

"What's wrong?"

"I'll tell you later. Just go!" she urged, glancing back toward the Sheriff's Office where the deputy remained in the doorway, eyeing them.

Aaron clicked the reins and Danny and Reeves surged forward, up the street. The traffic had thinned some, and they easily made a right turn off the main thoroughfare and soon spotted a large shingle with black and white letters announcing "Doctor Lewis – Surgery, Bones Set, Etc."

"There it is!" Sara cried with relief.

"Let's hope he's in."

"What happened with the sheriff?"

"He wasn't there, but his son, the deputy, was and he knows about the man who was shot—-showed me a wanted poster. It's the Carey gang and they're wanted for murder and robbery." Sara hesitated a moment, debating whether to tell Aaron. "But he was more interested in the Indian—-said they'd hang him, if they caught him."

"Why?"

Sara lowered her voice. "It's obvious! He hates Indians. We can't let him know the Indian's with us. The deputy mumbled something about being accessories and detaining us." Sara pinched the bridge of her nose, aware of the tension building there.

"What the blazes have we gotten ourselves in for?" Aaron

scowled.

"If the sheriff's anything like his son, we could be in trouble. We'd better hurry and get his wound looked after and then find him a place to stay. I don't think he's ready to go on the stagecoach."

"That's going to delay us!" Aaron protested.

"Not so loud," Sara frowned. "I don't want Peggy to hear."

Aaron glanced to the back of the wagon where Peggy appeared to be sleeping. She was leaning against a small barrel, her head back. The Indian was a short distance away, lying on the mattress. "She should be sleeping on the mattress, not him! Besides, she's been up half the night, looking after him." Aaron shook his head. "He's more darn trouble than a barrel of rats!"

"We're here." Sara announced, relieved, as they pulled up to the doctor's office. "I'm sure it won't take long." She gave her brother a confident smile as he drew Danny and Reeves to a halt, then climbed down and marched up to the entrance. The sign in the window read, "Open, Walk In."

Upon entering, a little bell tinkled, announcing her arrival. She walked in and stood waiting a moment. But when no one came, she called, "Hello!"

The outer office was empty of patients, but it appeared to be a pleasant room, furnished like a family parlor. She supposed the Doctor lived there, as well, for a lingering aroma of corn-beef and cabbage was masked by the stronger smell of oil of cloves, which was pungent but not unpleasant.

Before long a middle-aged man with a small, pointed beard came through the door. "I'm Doctor Lewis," his round face smiled. He wiped a stubby hand across his yellow, satin vest. "How can I help you Miss--ah?"

"Miss Robbins," Sara clarified and continued with a sense of urgency. "I'm so glad you're in, Doctor Lewis," I have a patient for you out in the wagon."

"And what seems to be the trouble, my dear?"

"I'm concerned about a wound. There's a young man--"

"Won't you sit down?" he advised kindly. "You look a might peaked yourself. Please sit there." He pointed to a gold, brocade loveseat and came to stand near her.

"Thank you, doctor, but I'm fine," Sara resisted. "I don't mean to be rude doctor, but we are in a bit of a hurry."

The doctor apparently wasn't accustomed to having his

directives denied. "But, you must take time. People hurry so much nowadays. Too many of the good things, the genteel things in life, get put asunder. Don't you agree?"

Sara cleared her throat. "Yes...uh, I need you to take a look at the wound. I did all I could, cleaned it out, but it started to fester yesterday. I didn't want to tell the others, but I'm very concerned about the young man."

"Others?"

"My brother and a friend. We're on our way west."

"I see," he responded knowingly. "Well then, why don't you bring him in?"

"Oh, thank you Doctor Lewis," Sara said, rushing for the door. "I'll be right back."

Outside, Sara told Aaron the good news. "The Doctor will see him now."

"How much is he going to charge?"

"Good heavens!" Sara frowned. "I never thought to ask."

"Didn't ask?" Aaron blurted. "But suppose it's more than we can afford? We have to buy the tickets and there's Peggy's fare and--"

"She has some of Rufus' money. He gave her the wagon, remember?"

"But—"

"Aaron! We have to do the most important thing, and that's to take care of a wounded boy."

Aaron looked about to argue.

"Suppose it was you hurt--"

"All right, all right! Just don't nag!"

Sara sighed and shook her head.

Aaron soon helped a reluctant White Hawk down from the wagon. He turned to Sara and Peggy. "I'll take care of this. You two stay here, in case the deputy comes along."

The girls agreed to remain in the wagon, but to Aaron's annoyance, the Indian refused his help into the office. White Hawk painfully struggled up the walk and with great effort, straightened himself. Suddenly, he balked at entering, and turning back, motioned for Peggy.

"Come on!" Aaron insisted, crossly. "Let's not waste any more time."

White Hawk stubbornly refused to budge until Peggy finally climbed down from the wagon and joined them, but as soon as they entered the office and saw Doctor Lewis' reaction, they knew they had a problem.

"Well! No...no one told me," the doctor sputtered. "I had no idea! The young lady said nothing about an Indian!"

White Hawk stiffened. Clenching his fists, he stood straight as a tree and glared at the shocked doctor.

"What's wrong?" Peggy asked, turning to Aaron.

"I'm sorry, but I must refuse to treat your...friend." The doctor looked from Peggy to Aaron, barely glancing at White Hawk. "I'm so sorry, but I can't help you. It's against policy to treat a savage. I'm sure you can understand."

"Understand?" Aaron exploded, "Why you sniveling old hypocrite! What kind of a doctor are you?"

"I must ask you to leave," Doctor Lewis said tightly.

"This is terrible," Peggy cried, wringing her hand. "I thought he would help."

"He doesn't know the meaning of the word," Aaron spat out, and turned to White Hawk, "Come on. Let's get out of here."

"Oh, please, doctor," Peggy begged. "Please help our friend. He's injured...he saved our lives."

"No!" White Hawk suddenly spoke up, face rigid with anger.

All three gaped at White Hawk in amazement.

Aaron regarded the Indian boy thoughtfully. "Why didn't you say something before?"

White Hawk ignored Aaron's question, walked to the door, then turned back to glare at the doctor. Hatred flashed in his eyes. "You medicine man---no good."

Startled, the doctor put a few feet's distance between them. "Well!" he exclaimed, "You'd all best leave before I have to get the sheriff." White Hawk's glare forced the doctor to back up a few more feet. He appealed to Peggy. "I think you'd better get your friends to leave."

"Leave," White Hawk said, continuing his threatening look.

Aaron piped up, "Come on," he ordered, opening the door.

"Oh, this is awful," Peggy said, trying to give White Hawk a hand through the door. But he suddenly staggered, and was about to fall. "Here take my arm," she offered.

"Hurry up!" Aaron called impatiently to Peggy. "Let's get out of here."

Sara saw them coming and knew that something was wrong.

Aaron looked angry as a hornet, and Peggy, pale and grim.

"What happened," Sara asked, as she helped get White Hawk into the wagon.

"It was terrible, the doctor refused to help us--"

"He hates Indians," Aaron cut in. "Let's get out of here." Aaron quickly seated himself in the driver's seat and called, "Gee up!"

As they pulled out into the street, a wagon passed by, nearly tipping into them.

"Watch where you're going!" Aaron shouted angrily, but the driver merely waved him on good naturedly.

"The doctor actually refused to treat him?" Sara could hardly believe it.

"Yes," Peggy answered from the back of the wagon where she was helping White Hawk onto the mattress. She smiled down at him. "He can talk. What's your name?"

"You do have a name, don't you?" Aaron piped up from the front.

"Yes!" White Hawk replied stiffly, trying to prop himself up on one arm.

"Well, what is it?" Aaron demanded.

"White Hawk!" his voice challenged.

"That's such a pretty name," Peggy offered, trying to forestall conflict. "His name is White Hawk," she repeated.

"I heard," Aaron answered, less than enthusiastically. He sighed and turned to Sara. "Now what are we going to do?"

"We should try to have his wound tended as soon as possible, and--"

"Look over there!" Aaron pointed to a sign, which announced, Blacksmith. And there, next to it, was a second sign saying Animals Doctored. "I want to have Tarney looked at. I don't think anything's broken, but she seems a bit sluggish." Aaron glanced down at Tarney who had curled up on the seat between them, and barely moved. "She's most likely just sore. Maybe, he'll take a look at her." He glanced hopefully at Sara, "It won't take long."

Sara agreed." That's a good idea." She stroked Tarney's head. "You'll feel better, soon, little one. We want you in good shape because we've a big journey ahead of us." Tarney raised her head listlessly as Sara touched her nose. "She's kind of warm--and probably thirsty, too. Aren't you, sweetheart?"

"Aaron!" Peggy called from the back of the wagon. "I've heard that sometimes animal doctors help treat people, as well. Maybe he'd help White Hawk."

Aaron frowned, but nodded. "Probably a good idea, Peggy." He didn't want her to think him unfeeling. "White Hawk's likely hungry, too." Aaron added, and then his conscience demanded. "We're all famished."

Sara was pleased by Aaron's concern. "Thanks, Aaron. We'll stop and get something to eat soon." She was hungry, as well, and feared that if they didn't get food soon, tempers would flare, especially her own, but first things first. Hopefully, the animal doctor would help.

CHAPTER SEVENTEEN

The blacksmith's shop was an open stall in a barn-like building at the end of the street. They heard the clanging of metal pounding upon metal and smelled hot iron. The Animal Doctor sign hung directly under the Blacksmith sign. And as they pulled up below the two signs, Aaron called out to the blacksmith, "Is the animal doc here?"

The blacksmith set down his heavy tongs and sauntered towards them. "What can I do for you?" he asked in a booming voice. The voice matched the man, for he was tall and muscular with bright, coppery-colored hair and a ruddy complexion. Wiping his forehead with his dirty sleeve, he beamed at the young people. "What can we do for ya?" he repeated.

Before they could answer, the man's attention went to Danny and Reeves, and he ambled over for a closer look. "Man, they're beauts! I dinna see anything like them since I was a wee'un in the old country. Where from?" He addressed the question to Aaron.

"Originally from Boston. But we lived in Omaha, Nebraska Territory the last three years, so they've grown up there, too. They're Morgans."

"Aye, fine, they are!" He said with a slight brogue, examining their rich, chocolate-brown coats. "Deep-chested, and the shoulders and forelegs well-placed. They'll have a longer stride and strength, and get across the country's most fearsome obstacles, but it'd be a shame to take them." The blacksmith moved around examining the horses. "Great strength in the hind quarter. You're a lucky lad to have them. But you should na take them into the bad grass area. Their stomachs weren't made for it."

"Nobody warned us."

"Well, I'm saying. Oxen can handle different grasses and shrubs, but not them fine looking horses. They do na have the stomach for it. It'd be a pity to take them. There'd be no escaping the worst."

"Sir," Sara interrupted, needing to get on with their business. "We're looking for the animal doctor. We've a sick--"

"They're not sick?" The very thought seemed to upset the

blacksmith.

"No--it's our dog, Tarney," Aaron quickly answered.

"Aye," he said, not taking his eyes from the Morgans. He stood alongside Danny and stroked the horse's head.

"What do ya call them fine animals?"

"Danny and Reeves, sir." Aaron offered, appreciating the man's interest.

"You've come ta the right place, but the doctor's out."

The blacksmith noticed the disappointed looks and quickly added. "He'll be along soon now. You'd be welcome to come in and wait in the shade of the barn." He pointed to the back of the building and paused for a moment. "Are ya a mind to be selling these two fine animals?" He addressed the question to Aaron as he jumped down from the wagon.

It was Sara who answered. "We might." She tried to sound very business-like. "We can discuss the matter if you wish---Mr.?"

"Tommy McGinnis, at your service!" he beamed. "I'll be happy to discuss the situation with your father, Miss."

Sara hinted at humor. "You'll want to speak to me, sir, as I'm in charge of the transaction."

Mr. McGinnis raised bushy, red brows and looked to Aaron.

"My sister takes care of the finances," Aaron said with a slight frown and a note of apology.

"I'm Sara Robbins, and this is my brother, Aaron." She turned her head to include Peggy who stood in the opening of the wagon, "and this is our friend Peggy O'--." Sara stopped short of mentioning Peggy's last name. It occurred to her that Donald Colwell might still come looking for Peggy and the less she was seen and known about, the better.

Peggy, however, gave an enthusiastic smile and added, "We've another in our party--Mr. White Hawk, but he's resting," she pointed to the back of the wagon. Her smile faded, however, as she caught Aaron's frown.

Tommy McGinnis bowed slightly, "Nice ta meet you all. My friends call me Mac." He stepped forward to shake Aaron's hand. "Come on in ta the shop," he said, "I'll brew a spot of tea for ya." He grinned at the girls. "Though it's a wee bit warm for it." He pointed to a place inside the barn. "You can unhitch yer team, if you've a mind. It'll be cooler for them and I've got some hay and oats. I'd be glad for the company, as well."

Sara glanced at Aaron. She wasn't sure what to do. But if they had to wait for the doctor, it seemed like a pleasant offer. Besides, she needed to stretch her legs and a little shade sounded appealing.

"Water trough's handy, on the right, as you enter." Mac encouraged.

"That's mighty kind of you, sir." Aaron said.

"See you have a pony, there." Mac was studying the little horse.

"Belongs to a...a friend of ours," Aaron volunteered.

Mr. McGinnis shook his head, thoughtfully. "She's in need of some good graining. Been rode hard. Pretty little thing--what are ya asking for her?"

Aaron quickly answered, "She's not for sale."

"What might ya be asking for the others?"

"One hundred and twenty, each," Sara announced firmly.

"Well, that's a might steep for me." He wiped his chin with the back of his hand. "Would ya take less, maybe eighty a piece?"

"Afraid not." Sara stated, pleasantly.

"Sure are a fine pair. Would ya take ninety?"

"They're very special, sir. I'd like to help, but we have to get our price," Sara said with authority and added, "Besides, we have the possibility of another offer." She sounded very sure of herself.

Aaron glanced at Sara as if she lost her mind, and was about to contradict her when she spoke again.

"I'll tell you what, Mr. McGinnis, we need to see the animal doctor about our dog, Tarney, and make arrangements for our goods to be sent on and talk to the man about our horses. Perhaps we could discuss a possible transaction later. Maybe," she added, "you might consider one hundred and ten?"

"Well," he said, shaking his head and weighing the offer. "I'd sure like to have them. I'll be thinking on it."

"Good!" Sara said brightly. "How long do you think the doctor will be?"

"Doc Surtees is out ta the Donaldson's place. Gone most of the morning. Should be back soon. You best take your dog back there where it's cooler." He pointed to a stall.

"There's a jug of water. Help yourself."

"Thanks, Mr. McGinnis. We're happy to pay for the feed."

"No need, son. You just rest now, and take some grain ta the bonnie horses." Mac nodded pleasantly, "You and your friend are welcome to whatever ya need." He turned toward his shop. "I'd be obliged if you'd keep me in mind for the horses."

"We will!" Sara smiled. "And thank you."

"Thanks again," Aaron added as he watched the tall, burly man walk away. Then he took Tarney and carried her to the back of the barn and gently laid her down in a stall on some cool hay. The hay smelt clean and fresh, and offered a good place to stretch, and hopefully, stay out of sight.

CHAPTER EIGHTEEN

Doctor Surtees finally drove up in his little lorry. The blacksmith rushed to assist him down off the rig, whispered a few words, and pointed to the middle of the barn.

The doctor, a tall, elderly man with a decided limp, came toward them. He extended his hand. "Sorry you had to wait for me." Deep-set, blue eyes crinkled with humor. "You must be Aaron," he said, shaking the boy's hand. "My name's Frank Surtees. How do you do, Miss Robbins?" He smiled at Sara and turned to the problem at hand. "Is this the little dog?"

The doctor shuffled over to Tarney, knelt, and spoke softly. "I hear you're not feeling so good. But we'll have you fixed up in no time." He motioned to Aaron, "Why don't you bring her over to my table there." Doctor Surtees stood up and shuffled to a small metal-topped surgical table as Aaron brought Tarney to him. "How did this happen?" he asked Aaron.

"She attacked a man who was threatening us, and he kicked her."

"Brave little girl, aren't ya?" the doctor said, his hand gently probing along Tarney's stomach. "Seems some folks are born naturally cruel," he sighed, continuing his examination.

"The man who kicked her is part of the Carey gang we're told." Aaron watched the doctor, intently.

"I've heard about them. They say they're from around here, though I've never run across them myself. I hear they're a mean bunch." He moved his hand expertly along Tarney's side. She lay quietly, not making a sound, her big brown eyes watching every move.

Next, Doctor Surtees looked at her teeth, felt along her head and inspected her ears. He took his time. "You're doing just fine," He encouraged and turned to Aaron. "She sure is good-natured."

"Yes, sir. She's part of the family," Aaron said, his voice full of emotion. He cleared his throat, "We're on our way to San Francisco. Do you think she'll be well enough to travel on the stagecoach?"

"Stagecoach, eh? That can be mighty rough. You might want to keep a pillow handy for her, and set her in a little box so she won't get tossed about too much. She's bound to be sore awhile, but there's no evidence of rupture or broken bones."

"I didn't think so, either," Sara said, relieved

Aaron proudly asserted, "My sister's good with medical things."

"That's certainly wonderful." Doctor Surtees nodded in appreciation. "I expect you can manage just fine, then." He beamed at Sara. "Just make sure she doesn't run about too much. Her front, right leg is likely sprained. She'll favor that. Might give her a worming in a week or so, when she's better." Doctor Surtees shook his head." They're apt to pick up all kinds of things along the trail. But for now, I'd say she was fine!"

"You mean she's really all right?" Aaron asked, half believing.

The doctor smiled warmly at Aaron. "I'd say so."

"Hallelujah!" Aaron exclaimed, jumping for joy. "That's wonderful! Hey, Peggy," he called at the wagon, "Did you hear--Tarney's going to be fine!"

"Oh, thank you so much, Doctor," Sara said. "Is there anything special we need to do for her?"

"Just keep her comfortable, and give her good scraps. Need to build up her blood," he said, moving over to a small, white metal cabinet a few feet to his left. "I'll give you some medicine. Give this to her, next week, for three days. Should cure what ails her."

Just then there was a loud shriek from the front of the barn.

"Aaron, come quick!" Peggy yelled, running toward Aaron and Sara. "It's White Hawk. He's trying to run away!"

They rushed to the front entrance of the barn where they saw White Hawk at the back of the wagon, trying to untie his pony.

"White Hawk! Stop it!" they shouted, running up to him. But White Hawk ignored them as he struggled to untie his horse. He couldn't get the knot undone , and grew more and more agitated. He staggered a little and grabbed at his arm.

"Please, White Hawk," Peggy cried, rushing up to him and attempting to get the rope. White Hawk resisted, pushing her away.

"Take your hands off her!" Aaron shouted, racing up to White Hawk and shoving him. White Hawk stumbled momentarily, but regained his balance quickly. Suddenly he crouched and glared at Aaron, daring a fight.

Just then, Sara ran forward and moved in between the two. "Stop it! Can't you see you're drawing attention!?" She pointed to the entrance of the barn where four people stood staring at them. An older woman cried in dismay, "There's a kid and an Injun fighting!"

"Can't you two get along for a second?" Sara whispered, trying to draw Aaron aside. "What would happen if you attracted a crowd?"

Aaron wouldn't budge and continued to glare back at White Hawk, eager to fight. "He'd better not go pushing Peggy!" Aaron rolled up his shirtsleeves.

Peggy rushed to explain. "It's my fault. He didn't mean anything!" She pulled at Aaron's sleeve. "Please don't fight!"

"All right," Aaron snapped. "We'll see about it later! Get back inside the wagon," Aaron commanded, looking at White Hawk.

But the tone of his voice only increased White Hawk's anger. The Indian stood his ground. Now it was a stubborn battle of wills as the two stood glaring at each other, each refusing to move first.

"Please don't make trouble," Peggy pleaded. "Can't you see he's sick? He needs our help."

Aaron scowled at Peggy's words.

Suddenly, White Hawk whirled about, ignoring everyone, and began tugging at the rope again. But WalksThrough kept moving, tightening the knot and anchoring himself to the wagon. Sweat poured down White Hawk's face. Suddenly, his knees buckled and he fell to the ground and stayed there pounded his fists in the dust.

"Oh, no!" cried Peggy, rushing up to help.

"Now look what you've done, Aaron!" Sara said. "Can't you see he'd not well?"

"Oh, White Hawk!" Peggy exclaimed. "You're bleeding again!"

"It's his own fault! He's stubborn and ignorant as a savage!" Aaron said. But when he saw the crowd gathering, he regretted his outburst. "Better get him inside."

Six people had gathered around the doorway, and when they saw White Hawk fall and blood coming from a wound, they murmured amongst themselves. "That boy's nearly killed the Indian."

Just then, Doctor Surtees came walking toward them. "Seems we have a sick young man here." He smiled good naturedly to the people. "I'll be taking care of things. No need to worry. You can go about your business," he said to the onlookers, and stepping close, leaned over to talk to White Hawk. "I'd like to have a gander at that wound, son. It looks to me like it needs a bit of antiseptic."

White Hawk remained rigid and would not look at the doctor. His eyes continued to challenge Aaron, who had assumed an air of the 'injured party.' Doctor Surtees squatted low and whispered into White Hawk's ear. "I know you want to leave. I think I can help."

White Hawk gave the doctor a skeptical look.

"I said I can help you leave. You understand?"

Sara, who had been standing near, heard the doctor's offer to help, and she knew it was as much an offer to help White Hawk save face as well. "Please let him help us. We don't want a crowd," she appealed in a low whisper.

Aaron stood back, watching the on-lookers crowd closer, and he heard a comment about "White folks have no business meddling with Indians." It made him uneasy and embarrassed, and from the looks on people's faces, he could tell there was no sympathy for the Indian. Suddenly it made Aaron angry. People were disgusting, he thought. He decided to do something. He marched up to White Hawk and whispered, "That crowd could be a problem for us. Why don't we set this aside for now? Let the doctor help. That way you can leave sooner. That's all I want, same as you." It was as much of a peace offering as possible in public.

White Hawk seemed to understand. He nodded grimly at Aaron and started to get up, but his balance was off and he staggered. Just then, Mr. McGinnis, who had been busy in another part of the barn, came forward, quickly offering a hand.

"I've got a hold of ya. There," he said, lifting the boy to his feet. "Come this way." Mac led White Hawk to the back of the barn, and helped him sit on a wood barrel. "Doc will have ya fixed good as new." As Doctor Surtees came toward White Hawk, Mac hurried to shoo away the onlookers.

Doctor Surtees made a careful inspection. "Seems someone already stitched it up for ya. I'll just clean it out. It's going to hurt some," he explained, as he removed his surgical instruments from a cabinet. "You're lucky the bullet didn't lodge. Tore up the flesh, but there are no bones shattered. Yes, you were one lucky young man."

Doctor Surtees returned and began cleaning around the wound. He was gentle and worked as quickly as possible. It was obviously painful, but White Hawk held still, keeping a stoic look on his face. He appeared peaceful, as though his mind were somewhere else.

Aaron wondered how he could take such pain and not cry out. He respected the Indian for that. It was hard to watch, but he forced himself. Somehow, it seemed only right. And though he felt like gagging, he stayed watching, fascinated by the way White Hawk withstood the pain.

"We're almost through now," Doctor Surtees assured, cutting away the last of the raw puffy flesh. "You are very brave. I wish I had some Laudanum for you, but it's all gone. Hold on...I just about have it..." The doctor was sweating. "Wipe my face, will you?" he asked Aaron.

Aaron picked up the towel and did as the doctor instructed. Finally, Doctor Surtees finished cleaning the wound and began applying medicine on a dressing. "This must stay on today. I'll give you another poultice for the next few days. But you must be careful and not use your arm at all."

"No use?!" White Hawk blurted, suddenly stricken. He looked shocked, and then turning abruptly, ran for the front of the barn, intending to leave.

"Wait! White Hawk wait!" implored Peggy, calling and running after him.

"Your arm is fine!" Doctor Surtees called, trying to stop him. White Hawk had misunderstood. "Come back! We're not through yet. You have to pay me!"

Doctor Surtees's words stopped White Hawk instantly and he spun around to glare back at the doctor who stood about fifteen feet away.

"How much?" demanded White Hawk in a cold, clear voice.

Doctor Surtees shook his head and sighed. What a proud young man he is, thought the doctor. His instincts had been right. "White Hawk," the doctor explained, "your arm will be fine in a few days, but I need to talk to you, in private." He motioned to a corner stall away from the others. White Hawk reluctantly followed. "You'll need to rest for a few days. I know the others want to leave. They'll worry about you, and I'm worried about them."

White Hawk frowned, not understanding, but Doctor Surtees cleared his throat and continued. "I want you to do me a big favor. Go with them for a few days, keep an eye out for them. I think that would be best for all of you. Will you do that for me...as payment...as what you owe me?"

White Hawk was still trying to figure out what was in the man's mind, and it was not what he said, but what was under his words that escaped understanding.

"Will you pay what I ask?"

White Hawk stared at the old man, saying nothing for a long

while, and then slowly nodded his ascent.

"Good!" The doctor nodded. "Well then, that's taken care of." He smiled, turned from White Hawk, and walked back to stand beside the Robbins children. They stood mouths open as White Hawk calmly walked over to the wagon, climbed in and took his place. Peggy eagerly joined him.

Sara hadn't quite understood what had happened, but she was grateful for the change in attitude. However, there was still the matter of what to do with White Hawk. She turned to Doctor Surtees.

"My brother and I have a problem. You see, we're catching the stagecoach this afternoon, and we need to find a place for White Hawk...someone to care for him till his wounds heal. Do you know anyone in town who could help?"

Doctor Surtees shook his head and looked down.

CHAPTER NINETEEN

"Aaron and I will contribute to his board for a few days. You see, he saved our lives and we--"

"I'm afraid I can't be of any help, my dear, though I would if I could. My wife, unfortunately, is deathly afraid of Indians, and she's an invalid." He sighed. "I couldn't ask her to take the boy in. And as for anyone else..." his voice faded.

Sara looked at Aaron. He was scowling.

"My best advice is that you take the boy with you for three days on the stagecoach. He'll be much safer than he would be in the town. Believe me."

"I see," Sara said, disappointed. But not wanting to make the doctor feel more burdened, she nodded. "Thank you so much for your kindness. We'll take care of the problem, don't you worry. What do we owe you, sir?"

"Nothing," he said, grinning.

"Nothing?" Aaron and Sara looked at each other, thinking they'd not heard him right.

"It's been taken care of," said the doctor, picking up his jacket, preparing to leave. "I have another appointment. You'll have to excuse me."

The two young people stood there dumbfounded, but as the doctor started walking away they recovered. "We can't thank you enough, Doctor."

"White Hawk is the one to thank," he said, waving as he left them. Sara and Aaron waved goodbye and headed to the front of the barn. "I wonder what White Hawk paid him? I didn't see him give him anything," Aaron stated.

As the doctor got into his carriage, they waved farewell again, to Mac as well.

"We'll be back later, after we've done our errands," Sara shouted as they took off in the wagon.

"Now what?" Aaron frowned.

Sara shook her head, "I'm so tired, I can't think."

"You need some food. That'll help."

"We've too much to do! We have to get tickets, sell the wagon, and the horses, have our goods taken care of, get cleaned up. It just seems too much. I can't do it all," she admitted.

"Sara, you stay in the wagon with Peggy and keep an eye on White Hawk. I'll go see about the tickets. That's what's worrying you most. I'll explain we'll be paying for them after we sell the wagon."

Sara sighed. "But that'll make two trips. We don't have that much time."

"But, it'll be better to have the tickets reserved. I've heard of people doing that."

Sara put her hands over her eyes and shook her head. "I can't make any decisions right now...I'm too--"

"Aaron, Sara!" Peggy called excitedly, coming up front. "Guess what? White Hawk says he's going with us on the stagecoach for three days."

"What?" exclaimed Aaron.

"He wants to come with us. Said he'd be closer to where he wants to go."

Bristling, Aaron turned to Sara. "No! He can't come!"

Sara ignored Aaron's outburst. "Did he say he <u>wanted</u> to come?"

"Yes," replied Peggy and then bit down on her lip. "I guess it was my fault. I kept saying he'd be better off with us than staying in this town. He agreed."

"You had no right, Peggy!" Aaron's temper flared.

"I'm sorry. I didn't mean any harm."

"It wasn't your decision!"

"Stop it, Aaron!" Sara lashed out. "Peggy was saying what she thought was kind and right." She turned to Peggy. "You didn't do anything wrong. Aaron's just hungry and upset."

"I'm so sorry if I've caused problems," Peggy apologized, tears forming.

White Hawk suddenly appeared in the opening. He'd heard the conversation. "I go!" he said looking at Sara and ignoring Aaron. "I go on stage. Same you go." His tone was full of resolve.

"And how are you going to pay for it?" taunted Aaron.

"Wait just a minute!" Sara insisted. "Let's think. White Hawk, you don't have any money or clothes do you?"

"No!" he responded emphatically, standing taller, apparently proud of the fact.

Peggy tried to explain, "You'll need money for a ticket and some clothes."

"Wait a minute, Peggy, White Hawk. I need to talk to Aaron about something. Come on Aaron. I have an idea and I need to stretch my legs. Let's go over by the saloon for a minute."

It took some convincing, but Sara finally got Aaron to agree to discuss the matter. "Of course, we owe him our life. And Doctor Surtees said White Hawk took care of Tarney's expenses, as well. And besides our obligation to him, I feel sorry for him."

"Sorry?"

"He's not feeling well, and we're the only ones he has right now."

Aaron planted his hands on his hips and thought about it. "Where will we get the extra money?"

"We have to see how much it'll cost for the smaller journey of three days. It can't be much."

"And what about clothes?" Aaron sounded dubious. Suddenly he understood. "You mean I'm supposed to give him mine?"

"That would be good of you, Aaron."

"I guess I have no choice!"

"No choice?" Sara's impatience erupted. "Why you little hypocrite! Nobody's forcing you to do a thing. Grow up!" she snapped, and pivoting sharply, she stalked off.

A couple of men standing nearby began to laugh aloud. Apparently, they'd overheard. Aaron turned beet red. Then he put on a determined face and marched back to the wagon. Sara was right. They had a job to do. "You're right, Sara."

Sara nodded. "And I agree to sell Father's watch if need be. How about you?"

Aaron glanced down. "All right," he answered tightly.

"Good. Now, let's go buy the tickets."

As they approached the main thoroughfare, they saw a number of people running up the street and gathering in front of the Planter's Hotel.

"I wonder what all the excitement's about?" Aaron said, straining to see.

"It's a big, red Concord stagecoach!" Sara exclaimed. I wonder if that's the one we'll be taking."

"I sure hope so," Aaron said. "I've never seen anything like it."

"Me either," Peggy added. "It's so shiny and new, like from a fairytale." The coach appeared to be the most elegant thing, with its large, red body and bright, yellow wheels. A driver sat up front, stiff and tall, and as regal as a king in his bright, red shirt. He was encouraging everyone to come and see his magnificent coach.

"Think I'll go and take a look," Aaron announced.

"We'd better get the tickets right away," Sara said, eyeing the coach. "It looks ready to depart." The stagecoach was stopped in front of the Pike's Peak Express Office - Stagecoach Tickets sign.

"I'll do it," Aaron said, hoping to get a better view.

"No, you wait there," Sara said, pointing to a place on the street newly vacated by a large wagon. "We won't be able to get our wagon any closer with that crowd, and I'll be fast." Sara stepped down from the wagon before he could open his mouth.

Aaron watched Sara rush up the street and disappear in to the Hotel's ticket office. "She'd better hurry," he grummbled, watching the crowd gathering around the red coach.

Before long, a young man walked up to Aaron's wagon. It was the deputy.

"Is that your pony back there?"

"Belongs to a friend of mine," Aaron answered, not paying much attention to the man.

"You say it belongs to a <u>friend</u> of yours?" the deputy asked, dubiously. He was eyeing the length of the wagon now.

"That's what I said, mister," Aaron retorted.

"This your wagon?" the deputy inquired accusingly.

Aaron responded to the tone. "I don't see how that concerns you." He watched as the deputy bent to look beneath the wagon. "I don't know who you are, but I don't like people snooping around," Aaron flared.

"Ya don't, huh?" The deputy sneered. "Well, ain't that a shame? 'Cause I'm the deputy and I got a right!" He continued walking around toward the back. "Think I'll jist have me a look around inside."

"Hey! You hold on there!" Aaron shouted, scrambling off the wagon. Tarney began barking and following after Aaron. "What do you think you're doing there?" he said, as the deputy began opening the back flap.

CHAPTER TWENTY

Sara rushed in to the Hotel and located the ticket office, which was off to one side, in a separate room. Upon entering the waiting room through a glass door, she noticed that the ticket office was nearly empty, except for four men sitting about on narrow wood benches. One man was asleep with a newspaper covering his face and snoring loudly. Another, very old man with a long, white beard, sat closest to the ticket counter. He glanced curiously at Sara as she moved up to the counter, and then offered a wide-faced toothless grin.

Sara returned a tentative nod and directed her attention to the ticket agent behind the long wooden counter. He was too busy to notice her and kept mumbling in irritation.

"Sir?" Sara tried catching the clerk's eye, but he didn't look up. His name was printed on a small wooden sign resting on the counter: Josiah Wertle, Clerk.

"Mr. Wertle?" Sara inquired, raising her voice.

The clerk looked up in surprise. "Oh, I'm sorry. I didn't hear you, Miss." He nervously cleared his throat. "Can I help you?" He looked about confused, as if expecting someone else. The man's thin neck and beaky hat made Sara think of a chicken.

"Yes. I'd like to buy four tickets for San Francisco. However, one is only for part ways--probably three days worth." As she gave the order, her gaze was drawn to a large map that covered half the wall behind Mr. Wertle. The map depicted the various routes to California and places in the west. Sara was amazed to see the distance they had already traveled. And in thirty-five days or so they'd arrive at their final destination. Sara noticed a red dot where San Francisco was marked on the West Coast. A sudden surge of excitement ran up her spine, and she couldn't take her eyes off the mark.

The ticket man cleared his throat again. "I see. And when did you wish them?"

"Today. This afternoon. Soon as possible."

"Oh, dear me," he exclaimed in a rather high-pitched voice. "That's not possible. That's certainly not possible."

"But...but, I have to leave today!"

"Dear me," he fussed, "the last coach left hours ago."

"But it can't have!" Sara protested. "What about that bright, red coach out front?"

"Oh, gracious, no. That's a private coach. Belongs to Cass Bartlett and his partner, Bill Russell. It's...it's very private. The regular coach leaves at eight a.m. tomorrow, and I must warn you, there are only four places left."

"Oh, no. This is terrible. We've counted on leaving today."

"Sorry, Miss, I'm afraid there's nothing I can do." Mr. Wertle tapped his visor, "We're hoping to put more coaches on, but we have only one a day right now. If you wish to leave tomorrow, you'd best get your places today. It's the best I can do."

"Well," Sara sighed, trying to rally and make the best of it. "We'll take the four for tomorrow, then."

"Fine," Mr. Wertle nodded. He pulled the tickets from a box and began figuring the cost. "That'll be six hundred and fifteen dollars." When he saw Sara's look of dismay, he hurriedly explained, "That's one hundred and seventy-five each to San Francisco and one at ninety dollars for part ways."

Sara took a deep breath. "All right. I can give you three hundred now and the rest in the morning." She sounded confident.

"Oh, dear me, that's not possible--not how we do business."

"What do you mean?" Sara's heart began pounding.

"Well, we only allow that kind of reservation for..." He cleared his throat uneasily, "for established customers, ones who usually stay at the Hotel."

Sara put on her managing voice, "Then you may consider me the same."

"Are you staying at the Hotel?"

"How much is it for the night?"

"It's three dollars for the room," he announced, looking at her thoughtfully, "and two dollars extra for each "guest."

"The room charge includes one guest, I assume," Sara quickly counted out nine dollars and placed them on the counter.

"Do you have luggage?"

"No, Sara smiled eagerly. "Only my satchel."

"Oh dear!" Mr. Wertel looked away. He'd been warned about such women. Though her appearance suggested otherwise, his better judgment demanded care. The fact that she had no luggage was the most telling piece of evidence, however. He knew what he must do. "I'm sorry. I don't believe we have any accommodations to your liking."

"Nonsense! May I see the room?" Sara insisted. "I'm very tired and cross, and I have no intentions---"

Henry interrupted. "I'm afraid there is nothing I can offer at this time."

"What utter nonsense! I've just made a deposit and expect to have my room immediately." Sara face was turning red.

"Sorry, there's nothing I can do!" And with a final flourish of his hand, waved her away as though she were a moth.

Just then, a dark-haired and very handsome young man walked slowly up to the counter where Sara stood. He bowed and smiled at her with mischievous humor. "May I help you, Miss?"

"I don't think so," Sara answered heatedly. "This man has merely made a mistake. I gave him money to pay for a room."

"Most likely a misunderstanding," the young man offered a smile. He turned to Hotel clerk, "Henry, I'd deem it a personal favor if you'd accommodate this young lady. I'm sure you can find her a room." He nonchalantly withdrew a five dollar gold piece from his vest pocket and set it on the counter.

"No, please!" Sara protested. "I have a reservation!"

Sara's protest was politely ignored as Henry turned and picked up the coin and took a key from the back peg. "Here," he said peevishly, tossing the key on the counter. "It's room 12, just down the hall from Mr. Bartlett's. Apparently, Mr. Bartlett is vouching for you." Henry's suspicions about the young women were amplified by this turn of events; however, he reasoned that a gentleman had certain "privileges." Turning abruptly, he went about his business at the end of the counter.

"That is the rudest, most insufferable man!" Sara exploded in fury as she picked up her satchel and headed for the stairway. The faster she could get away from him, the better.

"Could I help you with that, Miss?" The young man rushed to keep up with Sara.

"No, thank you!" she replied sharply. She was still very angry and did not like being retrieved by a stranger. She paused for a moment. "Thank you for your help, Mr.?.."

"Cass Bartlett at your service, Miss...?"

"I'm Sara Robbins. Again, thank you. Now if you'll excuse me," she said, struggling with her satchel.

"Perhaps, I could help with that." Cass smiled.

"No... no... I can manage," she said, suddenly glancing up into the bluest, most penetrating eyes she had ever seen. His gaze seemed to hold her captive, and a jolt of heat raced through her. "Goodness!" Sara exclaimed, shocked at her reaction. She felt dizzy, off balance. "I...I...can manage." she stumbled over words, feeling her face grow warm. It seemed to take forever before he doffed his hat and turned from her. Sara watched the imposing young man as he moved through the lobby. She guessed he was about twenty-three or so. He appeared to be well dressed in the Eastern style with a beige, linen suit and brown, silk vest, worn fitted. His shoulders were broad and his hips slender. Sara noticed him walking toward a hallway next to the ticket counter, but he turned suddenly as though he sensed her watching him. He smiled and doffed his hat once again.

"Well!" Sara exclaimed, turning away indignantly. "Well!" she said again, her temper rising. He's probably some conceited rich young man from the East who thinks they can buy acquaintances. "Humph!" she stated aloud, only to realize that people were staring at her. Suddenly self-conscious and too unsettled to walk through the lobby and up the stairwell for all to see, she turned and valise in hand, marched toward the street. Once outside, Sara took a deep breath. Cass Bartlett had left her feeling shaken. Of course, she told herself, it was just that unpleasantness with the clerk. Besides, she reassured herself, it's not important. Right now she had to find Aaron. But as she came out of the hotel, she realized Aaron and the wagon were nowhere to be seen.

CHAPTER TWENTY-ONE

Oh, dear, where is he?" Sara glanced anxiously about. Aaron certainly wouldn't leave without telling her. Maybe something terrible happened. A small pulse of pain flashed across her forehead. No, she must stay calm, she told herself and took several deep breaths. Once again, she glanced up and down the crowded street. Near the end of the street, she caught sight of Peggy waving and running toward her.

"Here I am, Sara," Peggy rushed, out of breath.

"Thank goodness! I didn't see the schooner."

"Wait till you hear what happened!" Peggy said, trying to catch her breath. She grabbed Sara's arm and rushed her forward. "Come on! We can't talk here."

"Where's Aaron and the wagon? What's happened?"

"You remember that deputy?"

"Yes, of course."

"Well, he came snooping around the wagon, and he and Aaron about got into a fight. The deputy kept asking questions, said he was go'n to look inside the wagon. He wanted to know if we'd seen an Injin. He even asked about you. Was there a red-headed gal in our party? You should've seen Aaron. Of Course Aaron didn't know it was the deputy. I figured it might be, so I set to work. But oh, Aaron was so brave--told the deputy to mind his business."

"Well, what happened?" Sara asked, fearing the worst. "See, I knew the deputy would poke his head in the wagon no matter what Aaron said, so I hurried and got White Hawk all dressed up in Aaron's jacket and put his long, black hair up under Aaron's hat, turned him sideways, and I sat shadow-like next to him. And when the deputy looked inside, there was White Hawk, sitting straight as a stick and looking every inch a gentleman."

"Well, then what happened?"

"The deputy just grunted, pushed back the flap and took off. He looked real cross, but there wasn't anything he could do."

"I hope that settles it!" Sara said. The deputy could cause them a lot of trouble, she knew, but resisted mentioning it.

"Aaron told me to tell you that you can't be seen with us until he's sure the deputy's not around. He took the wagon over to the storage depot to get started with the packing. You're to meet him there, but be real careful."

The girls continued walking down the street toward the storage depot. Sara stopped abruptly. "Peggy, there's nothing for you to do at the storage depot, so why don't you take the key and go back to the hotel. That way you can start washing up." She looked down at Peggy's worn, brown leather shoes. "Maybe there'll be time to buy you some shoes and a dress."

"That would be wonderful!" Peggy agreed, then shyly balked. "I don't want to go to the hotel by myself. I ain't never been in one. I won't know what to say or do."

"All you have to do is walk inside and head for the stairs. Our room is on the second floor--number 12, and there's a bath at the end of the hall."

"What'll I say if anybody asks me what I'm doing there?"

"Just smile and say you're with the Robbins family."

Peggy looked doubtful.

"Just remember, you're part of the family now. And I'll be along soon."

Sara watched to make sure Peggy got into the hotel, then turned and hurried to the storage depot to meet Aaron.

"We're almost through," Aaron announced proudly as he saw his sister enter. "We've got most everything on the list weighed. Of course we didn't have a whole lot." Aaron continued checking things off as two men removed them from the wagon. "Didn't see that deputy, did you? He sure is after the Indian." He glanced at White Hawk who stood sullenly a few feet away.

"No, thank goodness. Peggy told me about what you did." Sara was momentarily distracted as the two men began lifting a small barrel of household items that she had packed over three months ago. "Please be careful. My mother's special teacups are in there."

The men nodded matter-of-factly, and continued rolling the barrel into a dark corner. Sara wondered if anything would arrive in one piece, or in fact, if anything would arrive at all.

Their things would be shipped on large wagons, then unloaded onto smaller ones to cross the mountains. Anything could happen and she felt so very helpless. But as she stood watching, she reminded herself that the most important thing was that she and Aaron and their friends were safe. She was not about to let "things" control her life. Sara nodded assurance at Aaron. "It looks like everything's going well. You're doing a good job."

Aaron smiled. "I asked about the horses," he explained. "They offered the same as Mac, and I think we should let Mac have them." He looked hopefully at Sara.

"Good idea, Aaron."

"Sara, why don't you finish this, and White Hawk and I will take the horses over to Mac's. It'll save time. We can meet you back at the hotel. Better take Tarney with you," he said, "and give her a bath." Aaron turned to White Hawk. "Maybe Mac can care for your pony overnight--keep him out of sight."

White Hawk stubbornly shook his head. "No! Stay with WalksThrough."

"White Hawk--" Aaron began to argue.

Sara interrupted, trying to forestall another scene.

"White Hawk, I need to tell you something," she said, motioning the him off to the side where they couldn't be overhead. "Peggy is waiting for you at the hotel, and she'll worry if you don't come with us." Sara paused for a moment to let the idea settle. "Do you understand?"

White Hawk didn't look happy, but nodded. "I go."

Sara was relieved. She did not like the idea of any of them being separated, especially with that suspicious deputy lurking about. Plus, underlying everything was the fear that Donald Colwell might show up. The hotel, she thought was the safest place. They'd be out of sight until they caught the stagecoach in the morning.

"Right now, I can't think of how to get White Hawk into the hotel and inside without being seen?" Sara frowned.

"Don't worry, Sara. I have an idea. We have to hurry now. Just finish this, and I'll see you at the hotel--room twelve, right? My sister will pay you," Aaron added a nod to the manager as he left with White Hawk and the horses.

When the freight men were finished, the manager walked over and presented the bill of lading to Sara.

"I think you'll find everything's in order, Miss Robbins. And we have your destination address." He pointed at the paper. "Is this correct?"

"Yes, thank you," Sara replied, suddenly feeling more hopeful. "I understand that the goods will arrive in three to four months.

"Yep, unless we run into some bad weather, or such. Never can tell--can't guarantee." His face flushed, but he smiled assurance.

"We're dependable as any."

"I appreciate that," Sara said, and began withdrawing money from her satchel. "Here's three-quarter payment now," she offered the bank notes and silver dollars. "You'll have the rest on delivery."

The manager frowned. "That's not what we usually do, Ma'am." He looked at the four boxes and two small barrels, then shifted his ample weight.

"Well," Sara began, "sounding very business-like, that's how it's done in the East, and it's only fair. You have our down payment and my goods if I forfeit." Sara stood firm and looked the man straight in the eye. "The goods are worth more!"

"All right, all right," the manager sighed, taking the money.

"Thank you," she said, primly, bending to pick up Tarney and her satchel. It was awkward trying to juggle both. She was about to step forward when she noticed with alarm that the deputy was walking into the front of the freight building. He was followed by another, older man.

Fortunately, it was rather dark inside, and she didn't think the deputy had seen her. She bent her head against Tarney and whispered. "Mustn't wiggle or make a sound." Sara backed away and headed for a narrow side door near the rear of the building. She stopped suddenly and stood behind some barrels to watch as the deputy walked up to the manager.

"Afternoon, Sheriff, Deputy." He nodded, without looking directly at them.

"Who owns that?" The deputy pointed to Sara's wagon.

"The manager replied, "Belongs to the Robbins."

"Robbins', eh? Did they have an Injin pony?"

"Well, I guess, maybe."

"That's them, Dad! I knew it!" the deputy exclaimed.

The manager looked puzzled and pointed to the back.

"Seems they did have a pony. But you can ask that girl back there." He pointed to where Sara had been. "Well," he said, "she must'a gone out the back."

"Trying to sneak out, most likely, Dad."

The sheriff scowled. "We'll get her, Son," he said, hurrying for the rear door.

"What'd I tell ya, Dad, that gal's the one!"

"We'll pick 'em up, Son. You were right! Ya did good, for once in your life."

CHAPTER TWENTY-TWO

Sara managed to sneak out of the Freight and Storage Depot and back to the Planter Hotel without being seen by the sheriff and his deputy son. Now her main concern was getting Tarney up to their room without being stopped by the hotel clerk, Henry. The hotel rules didn't allow dogs, and Sara felt sure Henry would hold to that..

Entering the lobby, she glanced at the clerk's counter. Fortunately, Henry's back was turned. He appeared to be checking messages in the little boxes that lined the wall in back of the counter.

Quickly walking through the main lobby across the green and yellow floral-patterned carpet, Sara headed straight for the staircase. She dared not look back nor glance at the people seated in the lobby, though she knew some were watching her.

Two women voiced surprise at seeing her march in with a dog. Tarney's wiggling, made it more difficult to carry the satchel. "We'll be there soon. Just be still another few minutes," Sara whispered. Her arms grew heavier by the second as she climbed up wide stairs to the landing. Finally, she reached the landing and set Tarney down.

The hallway was deserted. "That's a relief," she muttered, starting down the hall to find her room.

Suddenly a door opened, and a young man walked out of his room. "Good afternoon, Miss Robbins." Cass Bartlett smiled at seeing Sara. "I hope you found your room suitable?"

"I'm sure...it's fine..." Sara replied, flustered. "I haven't seen it as yet," she added regretting her need to explain.

"Well, if it isn't, you just tell me and I'll take care of it for you."

"I'm sure that won't be necessary," Sara answered politely, but avoided looking at him. His presence was unsettling, and she wished he'd move away, but instead, he seemed to draw closer. Then he bent to pet Tarney.

"Sure is a cute little pup."

"She's full grown," Sara corrected.

"Ah, yes. Well, she's very pretty." His face clouded with concern. "She appears to have a sore paw. Did you know that?"

"Yes, of course." Sara struggled to pick up the suitcase again.

"Here," Cass said, rushing to help. "Let me get that." And

before Sara could protest, he took the case from her. "Room twelve, isn't it, Miss Robbins?"

Sara was too tired to protest. "Yes," she said, following him down the hall to the door of room twelve. Once there, Sara stopped abruptly and turned to face him, indicating that she had no intention of having him carry the suitcase over the threshold. "I can manage myself," she said bluntly.

"Oh, yes...of course," he hesitated, not quite understanding.

"I have someone to help. Thank you."

"I understand." Cass looked disappointed. He concluded that Sara's discreet wording was a signal that there was a gentleman on the other side of the door. He set the suitcase down, bowed and stepped back.

"Thank you," Sara said, and waited for him to leave before knocking on the door.

When Cass finally turned and disappeared down the stairs, Sara glanced up and down the hallway, than knocked on her door.

"I was gettin' worried," Peggy whispered, opening the door. "So glad it's you."

Sara rushed in, set Tarney and her satchel on the carpet and plopped down on the bed. "I'm so tired I can hardly talk, but everything's taken care of. Aaron and White Hawk will be here soon."

"Can I get you something? Would you like tea? I could go downstairs..."

"No, thanks, Peggy. I just want to close my eyes for a few minutes."

"I'll hang the clothes and put things away," Peggy said, needing to be helpful.

"Suit yourself," Sara murmured. "I'll take my bath later...call me...in a few minutes."

Tarney jumped up on the bed beside Sara, gave a sheepish glance at Peggy, and when she wasn't told to get off, she settled down next to Sara. Before long, both were sound asleep.

Peggy put away the clothes and straightened Sara's traveling dress. She was in her own dreamy mood and didn't realize the passage of time.

More than a half-hour went by before Sara awoke. She sat up with a start. "Where's Aaron?" she asked, confused. "I thought I heard his voice."

"He hasn't come yet," Peggy answered.

Sara sat shaking fragments of sleep from her mind. "I guess he'll be along any minute now. I'd better get my bath.

Everyone will want to wash up and eat." She rubbed her eyes, trying to wake up. "Since you've already washed, you could go and get your new shoes. The stores will be closing soon. There's five dollars of Rufus' money in my satchel."

"Oh, no. I don't think I should spend it now. You might need it later."

"Fiddlesticks. That's what he gave it to you for, isn't it--for things you need."

Peggy wrinkled her forehead.

"For heaven's sake, Peggy, take it and be done about it. You'll need shoes for the trip, and I don't want to worry about you!"

Peggy finally relented and took the five dollars. "I'll be quick as I can," she called from the doorway.

Sara shook her head in frustration as Peggy left. Why did Peggy's humility bring out the worst in her? Her own sense of guilt for being cross with Peggy was irritating as well. But she was too tired to sort it out now.

Sara gathered up her clothes, a couple of towels, a bar of soap, and quietly opened the door. Fortunately, there was no one in the hallway. She whispered to Tarney, "Come along girl. You're going to get a bath, too."

Tarney eagerly followed, and as they entered, Sara was pleasantly surprised to see the bathroom was a commodious and elegant room with a brass tub that had hot and cold water faucets. It was the first real bathtub she'd seen in months and discovered that it even had warm water. Oh, how she wished she could just stay and luxuriate in it, but there wasn't time. Aaron and White Hawk would be back soon and wanting to clean up as well. When Sara finished, Tarney wiggled in anticipation as Sara picked her up and set her in the half-full tub. The water was still warm, and Tarney settled in, allowing herself to be bathed.

Meanwhile, Peggy walked down the main street, looking in the shop windows until she saw a dress shop with a wonderful green, satin dress in the window. She wanted a closer look and stood awkwardly in the doorway, not sure if she was allowed to enter just to "see something," but she decided she had to see the dress. There were only four people in the shop: a young couple and two women besides a middle-aged clerk.

As Peggy entered, the sales clerk took the green satin dress out of the window and held it up in front of a young woman with long, reddish brown hair who glanced for approval at the young man standing at her side.

"Suits her, Mr. Bartlett, doesn't it?" the clerk said.

Cass doffed his hat. "I'm not much of a judge..." he groped for the right words.

"Well? Do you think it suits me, Cass?" the young woman asked, twirling around in a flirtatious manner.

"It's a little..."

"A little risque?" she grinned, mischievously.

"You could say that, Lucille," Cass chuckled.

"I'm going to wear it on my honeymoon. Do ya think Russ will like it?"

"I expect he'll like you in or out of anything," Cass returned, suggestively.

Lucille smiled and continued preening and sashaying about in front of Cass. It seemed they were both delighted at the shocked expression of the clerk.

Peggy stood in rapt attention watching the young couple. Besides being the handsomest pair, they looked so happy, and the dress was the most beautiful she'd ever seen. Suddenly, a rather indignant clerk turned and walked toward her. She was an imposing woman, tall with sharp features and an officious manner. She eyed Peggy critically, noticing the too long and too worn out dress. "May I help you, Miss?"

"Yes," Peggy answered quickly, feeling her face flush. The attractive couple were watching her, she thought with alarm. "I'm interested in a dress...like that there." She pointed to the green satin dress. But it was as if the clerk had not heard her correctly, for she walked briskly toward an armoire in another part of the shop, and motioned for Peggy to follow.

"Over here, Miss. What size?" she asked curtly.

"I'm not sure," Peggy hesitated. "I've always made my own from an old pattern...I..." words failed as the women eyed her impatiently.

"Ladies' small," the woman frowned, and selected a plain blue, cotton print dress. However, she was distracted by a nod from the young couple as they appeared ready to buy.

"One moment," she said, dismissing herself, and rushing to the counter. As the clerk attended the couple, Peggy noticed the young man more closely. He was very handsome, tall and well-built, with wonderful dark, brown, curly hair and blue eyes. She thought he was just about the best-looking man she'd ever seen. She watched as he handed the clerk ten dollars.

Ten dollars! Peggy gulped, amazed. She only had five dollars. She'd never been able to afford such a dress. But, she reminded herself, she was going to work hard and some day she would have a green, satin dress.

"Thank you, Mr. Bartlett." The clerk smiled and began wrapping the dress in brown paper, then tied it with string. Nodding at the young woman, the clerk handed the package to Cass.

"Thank you, Mrs. Lawson," Cass said, bowing very formally at the clerk. Then with a wide grin he took Lucille's arm.

Peggy watched as Cass and Lucille happily walked out of the store. A perfect couple she thought. Peggy wondered if she'd ever have a sweetheart of her own, especially one so handsome and generous.

The clerk finally returned to help Peggy. "Have you decided?" she asked.

"I..I...haven't decided," Peggy answered hesitantly.

"I'll be up front if you need me," the clerk said stiffly, then turned and walked away.

Peggy felt that somehow she was a disappointment to the clerk, and for a moment she felt the familiar dread of having done something wrong again. But suddenly, she was angry. How dare she! She didn't like being treated as someone to be gotten rid of as quickly as possible. She raised her voice. "I haven't found what I like!"

Peggy's anger drew a shrug from the clerk.

Still, it felt good to have spoken up. Peggy held her head firm and walked to the door of the shop. She'd not do business with such a rude clerk.

Unfortunately, coming into the store and directly in front of her was the deputy. He glanced briefly in Peggy's direction, but apparently didn't remember seeing her before in the wagon.

Walking deliberately up to the clerk, the deputy asked, "Mrs. Lawson, did ya see a young woman in here with long, red-brown hair? I thought I saw her leave, jist a minute ago."

"Yes, there was such a woman in here," she said.

"Was her last name Robbins?"

"I wouldn't know," she said, raising her eyebrows.

Peggy nearly gasped aloud at hearing Sara's name. She had to get out of there as quickly as possible, and without drawing attention. She moved a few feet closer to the doorway. Peggy felt the deputy's eyes watching as she exited the shop, and she didn't dare look back until she'd gone down the street a ways.

Back at the shop, the deputy's recognition was slow. It took him a few minutes to connect Peggy with the red-headed girl he was seeking.

"Mrs. Lawson, do ya know where I can find that girl?"

"Mercy no!" she answered, and then remembered. "She's with Mr. Bartlett, and he stays at the Planter's."

"I see," the deputy said, smiling. "Obliged to ya," he mumbled, and turned away, quickly leaving the shop. He walked confidently down the boardwalk, smiling and tipping his hat at folks. One day, they'd give him the respect he deserved. Yes, he told himself, it was near as an egg under a bird.

CHAPTER TWENTY-THREE

Downstairs, the deputy leaned across the reservation counter questioning Henry. "You say that red-headed gal is a friend of Mr. Bartlett's?"

"You'd best ask Mr. Bartlett," Henry answered quickly. And while he had no use for the deputy, he wished to conclude such onerous business and pointed to a table in the dining room. "You can find Mr. Bartlett over there. The one in the dark, blue, dinner jacket."

Without a word, the deputy turned and headed into the dining room and strolled up to Cass' table. Cass, who was alone, looked up at the stranger.

"You Cass Bartlett?"

"Yes." Cass saw the metal star on the shirt of the pocked-face young man. "You the sheriff?"

"Deputy."

"What can I do for you?"

"You know a gal named Robbins?"

"Well, that depends." Cass smiled at the thought of Sara. "What about her?"

The deputy took that as an invitation to sit down on the opposite chair. He dug his fingers into the pattern of the white damask table cloth. "Seems this gal has a reputation. You know. One of <u>those</u> kind."

"That so?" Cass answered, taking an instant dislike to the man. He watched the deputy avoid his eyes and shift his gaze to take in the room.

"You're sure about her?"

The deputy grinned knowingly. "Yep."

"And how does that concern me...or you?"

"Well, I want to ask her a few questions about a murder." The deputy scowled at the nonchalant young man. Mr. Bartlett seemed too rooster-sure of himself. The deputy raised his voice, leaned forward and pushed. "She's connected with the murder of Clyde Carey by an Injian."

"That so?" Cass said with casual disinterest. "I can't be of any help to you, deputy. I hardly know the girl. Besides, I think she's gone." He slowly sipped the last of his cordial.

"Not likely gone, Mr. Bartlett. She's expecting to take the stagecoach tomorrow. I want to question her 'afore."

"If I see her, I'll tell her you're looking for her."

"Make sure you do, Mr. Bartlett," he warned. "It wouldn't be good for you to get involved in this." Without another word he rose from the table and walked away.

Cass watched him leave. He knew the reputation of the sheriff and his son. He'd heard they were mean as badgers and likely in cahoots with the Carey gang. He wasn't surprised.

Cass stayed in the dining room, purposefully finishing his coffee and wondering how he could help Miss Robbins. The best thing for him to do was to talk with her as soon as possible. And suspecting the deputy might follow, Cass went upstairs to his room and waited. After half-an-hour, he cautiously left and walked down the hall and knocked on the door of room twelve. No one answered, so he tried again, keeping his voice low.

"Miss Robbins? It's me, Cass Bartlett."

Sara recognized his voice and slowly opened the door a ways. "Yes?" she questioned, uneasily.

"May I see you for a minute? I just had a visit with the deputy, and I thought you might like to know about it."

"Yes. Yes, I would. Just a moment," Sara said, alarmed and quickly stepped out of the room. She closed the door behind her and glanced anxiously down the hall. "What did he say?"

"Perhaps we should discuss this more privately. I'm at your disposal, Miss Robbins." Cass saw the worried frown.

"Would you care to join me in my room? It's just down the hall?"

"Yes, that would be better," Sara answered hurriedly, too concerned to think of the impropriety.

"My room is number 16."

"I'll be right there!" she said, quickly turning to re-enter her room.

Cass waited a moment, but when Sara did not immediately follow, he assumed she was waiting for a chaperon, or perhaps a more propitious time. He started down the hall, but he'd barely gotten to his room when he heard Sara's door open and saw her rushing toward him. She was alone. He quickly gestured for Sara to enter, and then with a final glance in the hall, closed the door.

Wasting no time, Sara marched a few feet into the room and abruptly asked, "What did the deputy say?"

"Says he wants to talk to you about the murder of Clyde Carey. Thinks you and some Indian are involved." He watched her expression grow from alarm to anger.

Sara began pacing around the room, hugging her elbows. "How dare he! I'm the one who told him about it. White Hawk saved our lives against a common criminal. I won't have him calling it murder! Why the very idea!" she fumed.

"And he knows you plan to be on the stage tomorrow."

"Oh, Blast!" Sara cried. "This is terrible. What ever are we going to do? There has to be a way!" She continued stalking about the room, shaking her head. Suddenly, dejected, she crumbled on to the small, red velvet loveseat. "How in blazes are we going to get on the stage without him seeing?" She hunched forward, elbows on her knees.

"I'm sorry, Miss Robbins, you seem to have quite a dilemma. Is there anything I can do?"

"No, I'm sure we'll think of something...it's just my head feels like cotton...at the moment."

"Have you had anything to eat?"

"No, we haven't," Sara answered, shaking her head, and suddenly thinking of Peggy and Tarney. They'd be equally famished.

"That's an easy problem to solve," he said, walking across the room to pull upon a long, gold cord that hung against the damask covered wall.

Sara looked puzzled, "I was told the dining room was closed."

"Don't worry about that," Cass smiled, happy to be able to do something to help. "I'll have Y Lui fix it. What would you like--ham or chicken?"

"Anything! Oh, but we wouldn't want to be a bother."

"You aren't, I assure you, Miss Robbins." Cass walked back to sit down on the arm of the love seat next to Sara.

"Did the deputy say anything more? Did he mention the Careys?" Sara's face grew stern.

"Yes, why?"

"It's just that the men who came into camp were mean, known criminals--said they'd try to hunt us down." She held her hand against her forehead. "We have enough trouble as it is."

117

"I see," said Cass studying her with concern. He noticed the green eyes brim with moisture, and the sight of her trying so hard not to cry gave him an odd feeling. Whoever was supposed to offer her protection was nowhere to be seen. He'd give the rogue a piece of his mind, he would.

A knock on the door sent Sara scurrying behind the love seat.

"Don't be frightened, Miss Robbins. It's probably Y Lui," he smiled, walking confidently to the door.

The knock on the door, did in fact, turn out to be Mr. Lui, the Chinese cook, a short man, with a thick, black braid down his back. His broad smile radiated good humor as he stood at the door nodding and bowing.

"Y Luis, my friend would like something from the kitchen. Is that possible?"

"Yes, yes. You askee me, yes," he beamed.

Cass turned to Sara. "Would you like a chicken sandwich or perhaps ham, Miss Robbins?"

"That would be wonderful!" Sara exclaimed, and forgetting any fear, rushed to the door. "Can I order two?"

"Su', Missy. Yo' askee, two o'so good." Lui responded, nodding to Cass. "Two bery good," he chuckled, grinning at Cass and then turning, scampered away down the hall.

"You must be hungry," Cass said, glancing quickly down the hall before closing the door.

Oh, I am, and I'm sure my friend is too."

"I see," Cass said, turning back into the room. Her comment confirmed his opinion that Sara was with a man and was thinking of him. Cass cleared his throat and sat back down on the love seat. He wanted to know more, but decided to wait and let her explain, in her own time.

The anticipation of food revived Sara a little, and she took a chair opposite Cass and began looking about. "Your room looks different from ours." Sara noticed heavy, red satin drapes, which covered three long windows. Two gilded chairs were placed on either side of a marbled fireplace and above that hung a huge, ornately carved, gold mirror. It was very beautiful she thought. Sara had only seen such opulence in books. "Louis the Sixteenth?" she asked.

"Why yes," Cass answered, pleased. He glanced about the room, as well. "This is the owner's suite." He was glad to see Sara's interest and change of mood. "Russell Hammond's a friend of mine and business associate. He insists I stay when passing through. It is a pleasant room, I suppose, though a bit formal for my taste. It reminds me of my Father's house, he said, ruefully and pulling his gaze back to Sara. His voice was warm and kind. "Perhaps at another time you'll allow me to arrange these quarters for you?"

"Good heavens, no!" Sara objected, and then caught herself. "I'm sorry," she apologized. "I didn't mean to sound so rude--so ungrateful. You've been most kind, Mr. Bartlett. It's just that I hope never to see this town again. You see, we've had delays and we're trying to get to San Francisco as soon as possible. We'll be staying there."

"I see," he said, hoping for more information. He paused a moment, then finally asked, "Do you have family there?"

Sara cleared her throat. She hoped he couldn't hear her stomach rumbling. "My Uncle Jacob...Jacob Robbins, and his daughter, Clara. She's only ten." She noticed his thick dark brows rise. "Do you know my Uncle?" she asked hopefully.

"The name sounds familiar, but I can't say," he smiled, revealing perfect strong, white teeth. "It's been a while since I was home."

"You've lived there?" Sara leaned forward.

"I grew up there." He put his hand through his thick nearly black hair and cleared his throat, "I left to go east--to college. After that, I traveled for six months." He rose from the love seat, walked to the window and glanced briefly about. He pulled his hand across the back of his neck. "Things change faster in San Francisco than most places, so, you see, I've lost touch; don't exactly know what's happening there."

"But how interesting for you, traveling, I mean." Sara felt a need to cheer him. She thought there was something wistful, almost sad, about the way he mentioned his home and being gone. She watched as he began pacing the room. Her original impression of Mr. Bartlett being a spoiled, rich young man was becoming somewhat modified. Certainly, he hadn't shown anything but kindness and concern for her, and that appeared quite genuine.

Such consideration was the mark of a gentleman, a person of character. Still, she quickly cautioned, she shouldn't rush to conclusions. After all, her experience with men was rather limited, and she'd been warned by several women on the wagon train to be "on guard" for handsome young men who <u>appeared</u> to be "good and seemingly kind." She suddenly remembered her father's warning, "There are unscrupulous men who would seek advantage over you, daughter. A man must prove his character, and that takes time. Do not rush your better judgment." Prudent, she must be, she reminded herself, and decided the best thing would be to thank him and leave.

"I really must be going," Sara said, somewhat reluctantly. "I appreciate your concern."

CHAPTER TWENTY-FOUR

Cass smiled, warmly. "I'm sure the food will be here momentarily, and we haven't solved your problem."

"I do appreciate your help, Mr. Bartlett, but---"

"Please call me Cass. I'd like to be of assistance. Perhaps there is something I can do. You see, I too, am leaving for San Francisco tomorrow. And I have at my disposal a large and rather comfortable coach. Perhaps you've seen it--the new red and gold one down the street."

"Oh, yes! It's beautiful!"

"And quite comfortable." Cass was thinking that Sara's presence would add some credibility to his story of scouting way stations for a new coach line. And he felt he could easily convince her that it would be simpler for him to deal with the deputy problem.

"Miss Robbins, have you considered the hardships of the Overland Stagecoach?"

"I'm not sure I understand."

"The regular stagecoach is uncomfortable and dangerous--all that jostling about. Why, I've known men to have bitten through their lips after falling asleep."

"So I've heard." Sara frowned and then smiled. "I believe my experience on the wagon train has prepared me quite well for any hardship." Sara suddenly felt the urge to defend herself. "I'm no fragile flower, Mr. Bartlett, nor do I aspire to be." It irritated Sara that he was obviously used to a more self-indulgent woman, the type that Sara couldn't abide. "I'm actually looking forward to this part of the journey," she added with a note of pride. "It's a challenge!"

Cass nodded respectfully. "Yes, I can see you are a woman of character. And that is why you would make a fine traveling companion--you and your companion, of course," he smiled.

Sara was about to explain about his misunderstanding of the "companion" when there was a knock at the door. She froze as Cass went to answer.

It was Mr. Lui with a large tray which he carried into the room and set down on a little table in front of Sara. He waited a moment, apparently expecting her to look over the contents under the silver cover. "You 'ikee?" he asked, smiling.

Sara did not move.

"Thank you very much, Y. I appreciate the extra trouble." Cass nodded, approvingly.

"No troub'e. I see lady 'ikee!" He grinned at Sara. "You say anytime--day--night," he added, winking at Cass as he backed away and withdrew through the door.

Sara stared at the tray of food in front of her. Besides the two sandwiches, there were rolls and small sausages, as well as four hard-boiled eggs stuffed with something that smelled wonderfully of ginger. It was more of a feast than Sara had seen in awhile. Everyone would enjoy this, she thought, hoping Cass would let her take some back to share with the others.

"How about a toast to our possible joint effort? I hope you and your friend will take pity on a lone sojourner. At least, think about it. You can let me know tomorrow morning early, after you've consulted with your friend."

Sara frowned. "But I've already paid for the tickets!"

"I can arrange to have that returned."

Sara felt her face flush as he bent closer. "That's certainly very generous of you Mr. Bart—"

"Cass, please. You'd do me a favor!" Cass went over to a large, black-lacquered, Oriental cabinet and opened it. He withdrew two small crystal glasses. "This very special occasion deserves the best. And this is the finest imported liquor from Holland. I think you'll like it.

Sara smiled and took the delicate glass with the brown liquid. "Mmmmm. It smells like chocolate," she said, savoring the aroma.

"Precisely." Cass beamed. "To our adventure, our challenge!" He lifted the glass and in one gulp, finished it.

Sara lifted her glass in the same spirit and drank the whole thing in a swallow. But suddenly the hot liquid burned her throat. "This is alcohol!" she sputtered, shocked.

"Yes, and the best there is!" Cass laughed. "Perhaps you'd better not try to gulp it. Is this your first taste?"

"Of course! What do you think?" Sara stood.

"I think you are a charming and intriguing young woman!"

"And you, Mr. Bartlett, are a rogue and a scoundrel! I've heard all about your kind. Men that--men who…who try to take advantage--ply helpless young women with drink and then--then—"

"Then what?" Cass asked, amused to see her struggle between control and rising temper. She looked about to explode, and at the same time, utterly charming. Cass couldn't help laughing. But when he saw how close to tears Sara was, he rushed to apologize, "I didn't mean to offend—"

But before Cass could stop her, Sara starched herself together, doubled her indignation and marched for the door, not however, without grabbing a fistful of eggs in one hand and the precious sandwiches in the other. She was, after all, a lady, albeit a practical one.

Sara stormed back to her room, ready to explode with indignation. She could hardly wait to tell Aaron.

"What happened?" Peggy whispered, gingerly opening the door to let Sara in.

Sara sputtered, "That man--that rogue!"

Peggy gave Sara a hush sign, and pointed to where Aaron lay sprawled on the floor.

"What? Oh!" Sara said, stopping abruptly. Aaron was sound asleep on the floor, while White Hawk lay on the bed. "Oh, Phooey!" Sara flounced down on a chair.

"Sara, what happened?" Peggy had never seen Sara so upset.

After a few deep breaths, Sara gained sufficient control to whisper the "event" to Peggy.

Peggy was all sympathy when she heard what happened, and even volunteered to forgo the sandwich as a stand of honor, as though the food was tainted by immoral association. Such a sacrifice was not deemed necessary. Both girls ate heartily and shared with Tarney.

It had been a long, tiring day and sleep was most welcomed.

Sara and Peggy agreed not to tell Aaron about the "near catastrophe" with Mr. Bartlett. "Heaven knows what Aaron might do. And certainly, under no circumstances will we open the door to Mr. Bartlett, even if he crawls on his hands and knees and begs forgiveness!"

They would put this day behind them.

Peggy knelt beside the bed, ready to say her prayers, and coaxed a reluctant Sara into kneeling next to her.

Though Sara felt a twinge of guilt for her lack of faith, she didn't want to disappoint Peggy. She hoped that God, if He was there, would not judge her hypocrisy too harshly, and ventured a sleepy thought that perhaps God understood her state of mind.

The next morning, Sara was first in line at the ticket counter. "I certainly didn't expect anything like this," she exclaimed, not caring who heard her raised voice. "That's totally unreasonable!"

"As I said, those are the rules!" Josiah Wertle's eyebrows darted up and down under his green-beaked cap. "Now, if you'll move out of the way Miss Robbins, I have work to do. No…please do not come around the counter. No! no, Miss, this is very irreg--"

"Rules? What rules?" Sara interrupted and persisted in following Mr. Wertle behind the ticket counter.

"I'm truly sorry, Miss, I don't make'm. That's just the policy." He tried to avoid her, but she followed closely into the baggage area. Her voice carried into the office as well. It was impossible to ignore her.

Sara's voice rose in indignation "I've never heard of such an outrage! We paid our money and everything!"

"I understand, Miss. You'll get your money back. But that's all I can do." He tossed his hands up in helplessness.

"Nonsense!" she insisted, pursuing him as he lifted baggage onto a cart.

Mr. Wertle's long face reddened by the minute and he kept plucking at his cap and pulling it over his forehead. People in the waiting room were watching and the picture of an angry and desperate young woman questioning management policy was almost more than Mr. Wertle could bear. Nothing he said seemed to deter her. Now he didn't know what else to do or say; he'd just have to call the sheriff.

Sara tried pleading. "If it's a question of more funds to pay for our dog, we can manage!"

I've tried to make it clear. It isn't <u>just</u> the dog." He glanced furtively at the Indian boy sitting next to Aaron on a bench in the waiting room.

Aaron caught the look and scowled back. He was about to jump up, for he felt like punching the self-righteous worm of a man. However, a stern look from Sara and a wave of her arm reminded him that he'd promised to stay calm. He knew that their only hope was to get Mr. Wertle's "pity on a helpless woman." Apparently, that ploy hadn't as yet worked. Sara didn't appear all that "helpless." He watched his sister keep pace with Mr. Wertle.

Unfortunately, they were all too preoccupied to notice the

unshaven man entering the ticket office. But as soon as he spoke, a chill of recognition engulfed them. Sara whirled around in alarm to see Peggy's stepfather, Donald Colwell, stagger up to Peggy, grab her arm, and roughly pull her up. Peggy shrieked in pain.

"I knew I'd find ya, girl." His huge body and voice seemed to fill the room with foulness. "I warned ya not to run off." His voice was slurred. "I told ya what I'd do!" He turned around suddenly to face the room but momentarily staggered. "This sshere's my daughter—-trying to run out on her Pa!" He pointed to White Hawk and Aaron. "I knew I'd find her with this riffraff!"

CHAPTER TWENTY-FIVE

Colwell had surprised them so completely that it took a moment or two before anyone realized what was happening. Colwell had Peggy by the arm and began pushing her toward the door. She struggled, trying to pull away, "Let me go! Let me go!"

"This will teach ya to disobey!" Donald said, cruelly twisting her arm and shoving her closer to the door.

Tarney growled a warning then suddenly sprang forward and grabbed Colwell's pant leg. But a powerful kick shook Tarney loose and sent her yelping and sprawling through the door. A split second later, Aaron and White Hawk rushed at Colwell, shoving him roughly through the door and on to the boardwalk.

Momentarily off balance, Colwell spun Peggy around on the boardwalk where she fell roughly against a post, knocking into several people. She managed to cling to the post as Aaron and White Hawk gave another hard push to Colwell, forcing him to let go of Peggy and then propelling him in to the street like a giant top, spinning out of control.

"Peggy! Sara cried, rushing to help. Sara put her arm protectively about her and they stood on the boardwalk, watching in alarm as Aaron and White Hawk pursued Colwell. At first, Colwell fell on his knees in the dusty street. And though somewhat drunk, he quickly regained footing and with a murderous glare, got up and wheeled around to face the boys. "Think ya kin best me, do ya!" he bellowed.

Before Colwell could rush forward, White Hawk came up to within three feet, and calm as a rattlesnake, plunged his right arm straight out. It got Colwell's attention. As Colwell lumbered forward, White Hawk struck, surprising Colwell with a doubled-legged jump kick to the stomach.

Colwell reeled back, grabbed his stomach, and fell to his knees. A swirl of dust kicked in his face and he coughed and shook his head. He was winded and stunned. The blow had caught him off guard, but that wasn't the worst of it, for he heard jeering comments from the small crowd that had gathered. More people came running to watch the fight "between 'a grow'd man' and a youth."

Several people taunted Colwell to "Get up and fight like a man!" Someone else shouted, "Kill the Injin." A woman hollered, "Get the sheriff!" As the circle of on-lookers grew, people shoved and pushed to get a better view.

Two burly men stepped forward and formed a wall against Aaron, deliberately holding him back. The taller man said, "Let's see what the Injin can do first, son."

White Hawk was now alone with Colwell who was still down, and snorting like a bull. White Hawk stood legs apart, waiting, hoping the man would stay down. His arm ached and his head began to pound. Could he do this? Even at his best, he'd be no match for such a large man. But I am younger and faster.

He watched Colwell carefully, judging the man's balance. He saw Colwell's weakness as he leaned forward on his right knuckle before standing. Once on his feet, the man's eyes squinted against the sun. He began circling. White Hawk moved to keep the man's head turned to the sun. He heard the crowd begin to shout and call. Several women gasped as they realized the fight was continuing.

"Stop it! He's just a boy," yelled a dark-haired older woman. Others countered, "Get the Indian!"

The taunts meant nothing to White Hawk. He shut his mind to everything but the man he faced. He crouched, waiting for Colwell to throw the first blow. Colwell swung a powerful roundhouse that White Hawk dodged. Over and over White Hawk forced Colwell to swing at him. White Hawk darted away, increasing the size of the circle, forcing Colwell to pursue. Colwell's fists pummeled air, missing White Hawk over and over, but it wasn't long before White Hawk tired. Beads of sweat appeared across his brow. His throat felt dry and coarse, and he knew his strength was leaving. He wondered where Aaron was, and then caught sight of him in the front line of the crowd. White Hawk wondered what he would do. Would the white boy come to his aid?

Suddenly there was a gasp from the crowd as Colwell pulled a Bowie knife from his belt and sliced the air.

"I'm not playing any more, Injin! I'm go'n to kill ya." Colwell seemed to gain a burst of energy and rushed forward, knife in hand.

White Hawk backed away, and barely sidestepped a lunge from Colwell. The knife missed him by an inch. Next time youthful agility might not save him.

Just then, Aaron broke free and pushed through the wall of

spectators. He rushed into the circle and moved up toward Colwell's back. Tarney stayed beside Aaron, barking and making a distraction. But Colwell was not easily side-tracked. He had the advantage and raised his knife and moved quickly to strike White Hawk. Aaron moved in back of Colwell and gave a shattering yell close to Colwell's ear.

Startled, Colwell spun around to jab the knife at Aaron, barely missing his shoulder. Aaron jumped to the side. And then, in a flash, White Hawk sprung at Colwell, hurling his whole body at him. One foot hit Colwell's chin, and whipped his head to the side. He grunted in pain, spilled backwards and crumpled to the ground. The knife fell in the dust beside him. Colwell lay on his back with a trickle of blood oozing from his mouth.

Aaron rushed to get the knife and held it pointed at Colwell's throat.

White Hawk stood glaring defiantly at Colwell, victory in his wide stance. Then he spat out his disgust and shook the dust from his leather leggings.

The crowd suddenly began to cheer. The fight was over. The boys had won. Colwell lay on the ground, dazed and gasping for breath. He uttered curses between gulps of air, and glared at the jeering crowd, not quite understanding that the fight was done and he'd lost.

Sara and Peggy rushed forward, trying to push through the crowd. "Let us through!" Sara cried. "That's my brother!"

Unexpectedly, the crowd parted.

"There they are!" cried the deputy, as he and the sheriff shoved their way into the heart of the circle. "I knew it was jist a question of time!" The pocked-faced young man grinned in a show of superiority. He acknowledged the crowd with a sweep of his hand. "These young'n are wanted in refe'n to a murder. No need for good folk to alarm. We'll take care of 'em." And with that, he herded them ahead into a tight little circle near Colwell. "Better hold that yapping dog of yers or I'll shoot'm dead now."

"Take your hands off me! Sara protested stormily as the Deputy grabbed her arm and shoved her forward.

"Take your hands off my sister!" Aaron raised the knife he still carried.

"Resisting arrest are ya? Yer in enough trouble as it is, protectin' a murderin' Injin!" He pushed Aaron.

Sheriff Tuffs drew his gun. "Hand over the knife, boy!"

As Aaron reluctantly handed it over, the sheriff bellowed a question to Colwell, "What's this about?"

Colwell, who had managed to stagger to his feet, stood brushing himself off. He nodded as he swaggered confidently over to Sheriff Tuffs. "Sure glad ya came along. That Injin was 'bout to kill me. Damn near got my kid, too." He indicated Peggy. "My daughter thar, she run off. Now I s'pect it was the Injin got a notion to take her off"

"He's lying, sheriff!" Peggy protested, struggling to wrest herself from the deputy's grip.

"He yer Pa?" Sheriff Tuffs eyed Colwell and then Peggy.

"No! He's my step-father!" She saw Colwell's mean look, and knew that he wouldn't hesitate to hit her.

"Listen sheriff," Colwell tried to sound reasonable. "I'm her legal kin. I married her ma proper-like. So she's mine!"

"Sheriff," Sara interjected, "this man is her stepfather, but he beat her so hard she ran away to save herself and--"

"She's lying!" Colwell bellowed. "They run away from a wagon train! She's trying to save herself."

The onlookers watched and speculated as to who was right. But finally, seeing the fight was over, thought the domestic quarrel less interesting and left the scene. The crowd began to thin out as the sheriff announced, "I'm taking ya all to jail. We'll see what this is about. Come along," he ordered, leading the youngsters and Colwell at gunpoint down the street toward the jail. The deputy brought up the rear, grinning.

Tarney ran alongside Aaron as the procession moved along the street. Folks stopped and stared, and some made rude made comments about how "Injin can't be trusted."

Sara kept her eyes straight ahead, looking back only once. Her heart sank as she saw the Overland Stage Coach pull away from in front of the Planter's Hotel. There will be another one tomorrow, she told herself.

At the jail, Sara was relieved to see that they were separated into two cells, a separate one for Colwell. But it was unsettling as he stood glaring and cursing them through the bars. Sheriff Tuffs warned him a number of times to quiet down and told the youngsters they would be detained "indefinitely" if they caused trouble.

Sara protested, but she only succeeded in irritating the sheriff, changing nothing but his temper for the worse.

The sheriff sat at his desk, staring down at a cold cup of coffee. "Ya got us stuck in a barrel," he said, frowning at his deputy son, Ronny.

"No Pa," Ronny shifted his weight uneasily. "Ya see, I knew we'd catch'm, so I already sent word to old man Carey that we had his son's killer. Told 'em we was keeping him here, accessories, an' all. They'll be thanking us. It'll be jist a day or two till the whole town knows what we done. We got us a killer!" He grinned with pride at his father.

CHAPTER TWENTY-SIX

Sheriff Tuffs' eyes narrowed. "What'll we do if ol' man Carey decides ta get mean? Hangin' an injun's one thing, but we got kids here. And this Colwell--." He glared at his son. "Ya sure got us in a fix!"

"No, Pa, it'll be fine. I swear." Ronny gave his father a nervous smile, and then stalked angrily over to the cells. "Ya all stand back against that wall, ya hear!" He saw Colwell ignore him, and it put a spur to him. He stood with his fists flexing around the iron bars and glaring at the big man. He had an uneasy sense that maybe Colwell could rip the bars out with his bare hands. No one was strong enough to do that, he told himself, and gave his gun holster a reassuring pat. Colwell best remember who was boss.

Sheriff Tuffs worked a finger around the edge of his thin lips, his voice barely audible. "Maybe we ought ta let the kids go. Give Colwell jurisdiction over them. That way we ain't responsible."

An alert Colwell responded. "Ya have an idea there, sheriff. You can keep the Injun. I'll take care of the others. I gotta protect my kin--ya understand." He glanced favorably in Ronny's direction. "You'd do the same fer your boy!"

"Sheriff!" Sara called in alarm. "There are a few things you don't know as yet. Can I talk to you privately?"

Sheriff Tuffs reluctantly got up and strolled over to Sara's cell.

"Look sheriff," she said, waving him closer, "I want you to see Peggy's arm." She pulled up Peggy's sleeve, revealing a large bruise.

Unmoved, the sheriff just stared.

"Don't you understand? That man there," she pointed to Colwell," tried to kill her. If you let him out or let him near us, he will do something terrible. You've got to believe me. Wait! Show him, Peggy. Show him the rest."

Peggy resisted. "I...I can't."

"It's the only way," Sara pleaded.

Mortified, Peggy slowly lifted her skirt, revealing dark, ugly bruises down her thighs. Only Sara had seen the bruises and now the startled looks from Aaron and White Hawk made Peggy feel even more embarrassed.

"He do that to ya?" Sheriff Tuffs scowled.

"Yes, Sir," Peggy muttered, keeping her head down. "She's lyin'!" Colwell yelled.

A murderous glare from White Hawk drew Colwell's attention. "That Injun's a killer for sure. Ya ought a keep him away from my daughter. Jist look at him, Sheriff. How'd ja know he didn't do those marks?"

Peggy exclaimed, "I wouldn't lie about a thing like that. He…he," she pointed at Colwell, "tried to kill me. Ask anyone on the wagon train. They heard him threaten me. We left the train and got attacked. Those Carey men would have killed us, too. Then White Hawk came to our rescue. He got shot." Peggy hid her face and turned away!

"I see," the sheriff said, not entirely getting the picture, but it was enough.

Aaron saw the hesitation. "They wounded White Hawk. See for yourself."

The sheriff abruptly moved away. "I don't need look at no Injin." He ambled back and sat down at his desk. Turning his back on the cells, he began shuffling papers in front of him.

Sara could see that the sheriff didn't quite know what to do, and she suspected, as well, that he had a long-buried speck of decency. After all, he'd let them keep Tarney in the cell, and even gave her a dish of water. Just maybe, Sara thought, there was something she could do.

Quickly, she came up with the idea that she hoped would get her back to the Planter Hotel. Once there, she'd try to get help from Cass Bartlett. Hopefully, he hadn't left, and was willing to talk to her. It was a chance she'd have to take.

"Sheriff, I understand we may be detained for questioning. However, there are a few "feminine things" that Peggy and I need. I'm sure you understand." She tried her most modest look. "I should run back to the hotel and get them. I'll come right back. After all, my brother's here...I give you my word."

The sheriff looked away a minute, deliberating. He set his fingers against his mouth and worked them as he discarded ideas. Finally, he settled on one. Maybe the young woman's leavin' would give him time ta figure out how ta stop "all hell" from breaking loose. "I'll let ya go, but my deputy here," he nodded at Ronny, "will take ya and bring ya back."

He turned to his son as they left. "Be quick about it!" He spat sourness into a spittoon next to his desk.

"I'll be quick, you'll see!" Sara said, as she rushed out the door, followed closely by the deputy. She ran as fast as she could along the boardwalk, not caring what people thought as she darted and dashed between them. Two whole blocks seemed like miles. But she didn't stop until she rushed in to the lobby of the Hotel. The deputy was right behind and nearly careened into her back as she stopped abruptly to glance about. She'd prayed that Cass would be there. But he wasn't in sight.

The deputy shoved her forward. "Hurry it up!"

As Sara passed the reservation desk, she noticed a corner of her carpetbag satchel sitting on the floor behind the desk. Thank goodness she'd transferred her important papers back around her waist. But everything she'd need for the trip was in that satchel. Now, she had to get help. She saw Henry Wertle look up in surprise and then shock as he saw her being prodded by the deputy.

Henry Wertle paled, then stammered, "It's check out time, Miss Robbins."

Sara raised her chin. "I believe I have fifteen minutes or so," she announced, haughtily. "Just leave the baggage there, Henry," she added in a tight, calm manner. I've left something in my room. I'll be right back." Sara held her head high and didn't look around her for she knew people were gaping. At the stairwell, she turned to the deputy. "I need a moment of privacy for some "personal" things. I'd expect you as a gentleman to wait for me in the lobby."

The deputy hesitated. He knew folks were watching and listening and wouldn't take kindly to him depriving a lady of her "personals." Reluctantly, he gave in and warned. "I'll be up after ya in five minutes." Then he turned to his audience: two men and an older woman sitting near the stairway. "She's a suspect in the Carey murder." He nodded smugly.

Sara quickly climbed the stairs then turned and glanced back. The deputy was standing below, his elbow on the banister and watching her steady as a lizard. As she landed upstairs, she turned, looked down, and gave the deputy a reassuring little smile and then went straight to room sixteen, praying that Cass would be there. He was her only hope now. Her heart was pounding as she knocked on the door, and took a deep breath when she saw it open. Much to her surprise, a redheaded young woman greeted her.

"Oh! I thought this was Mr. Bartlett's room."

"It is," the young woman smiled at Sara. "You must be Miss Robbins?"

"Yes," Sara answered surprised. "I'm in an awful hurry. Is Mr. Bartlett in? It's quite urgent!"

The girl turned her head, "Miss Robbins wants to see you!"

"Let her in!" Cass answered as he strolled into the sitting room wearing a dark, blue suit and carrying a camel-colored jacket. "I didn't expect to see you," he smiled. "We were just about to leave. Oh, excuse my manners. Let me introduce you. Mrs. Hammond, Lucille, this is Miss Sara Robbins." Cass saw Sara nod and frown. Cass quickly explained, "Mrs. Hammond is the wife of my good friend and business partner, Russell Hammond."

Sara leaned against the door."I...I.." Sara faltered, "I need to sit down," she said, feeling lightheaded.

"Are you ill, Sara?" Cass rushed to take her arm.

"No. No." Sara waved away his concern as he led her to the settee and sat beside her.

"Lucille," Cass asked, "would you please get Sara some water from the decanter. I put it on the side table." He knelt before Sara and looked into her eyes. "Now, tell me. What's wrong?"

Sara's words gushed out. "We're in awful trouble. The sheriff is holding my brother and our friends, Peggy and White Hawk, at the jail. You see, my brother and Peggy--well, the sheriff thinks that White Hawk murdered someone, and he's trying to hold us all, and we were told we couldn't take our dog or White Hawk on the stagecoach and then, Peggy's stepfather came after us, there was a fight and…and…and now we're trying to get away."

"I see," said Cass, standing up. The story was confusing, but obviously Sara was in a real danger. "You say they're at the jail now?"

"Yes, and the deputy is waiting for me downstairs. He'll be up any minute! I don't know what to do." She glanced nervously at the door.

"Stay put. I'll see," Cass said, quickly going to the door and opening it. He looked down the hallway. "No one's there," he reassured, closing the door and coming back to sit beside Sara.

Lucille reentered the sitting room carrying a crystal decanter and goblet. She poured a little water into the glass and gave it to Sara. "Sounds like you've a problem with that pasty-faced deputy." She shook her head. "He's awful full of himself, but I don't think he'd harm you." She glanced at Cass. "Of course he knows better than to mess with me or Russ. If he gives you any trouble, tell him you're friends of Russell Hammond. Thankfully, Russ will be back this afternoon."

"Wait a minute," Cass said, standing between the two women. "I've an idea." He glanced critically at Lucille. "Both of you walk over there," he ordered. "Yes, you're about the same height, have nearly the same color hair. If you two change dresses--"

Lucille suddenly understood and clapped her hands. "You want me to pretend I'm Sara and take the deputy on a wild goose chase. What fun!"

"Yes, now hurry!" He turned to Sara. "You'll wear Lucille's green satin."

"I saw that in a melodrama once." Lucille grinned, getting into the spirit. "It'll serve him right!"

Cass explained to a still confused Sara. "After you change, we'll take the coach and pick up the others at the jail. I think I can handle the sheriff."

As Sara and Lucille hurried to the bedroom to change, Cass paced impatiently in the sitting room, working out the details of his plan. Lucille would wear Sara's dress and distract the deputy long enough for Sara and him to get through the lobby and out to the stagecoach. But timing was critical.

The girls quickly finished their dress exchange. Lucille's long hair was carefully tied in back as Sara's had been.

"Please hurry!" Sara urged. She glanced at the door while Cass explained his plan.

Soon Cass and Lucille left the room, taking up their positions in the hallway. Lucille waited in the hall near the back stairs. Cass sat on the top stair of the main top landing and Sara stood in the room with the door slightly ajar. She felt her heart pounding and wondered if anyone else could hear it. It was hard shoving her fears aside for she kept seeing Donald Colwell's face and wondering what was happening at the jail. What if the deputy discovered their plan? Her anxious thoughts were interrupted. Cass was giving his foot-stamping signal down the hallway. Apparently, the deputy was coming up the stairs.

"Oh, excuse me, deputy," Cass said loudly. "I was just pushing down my boot. I'll move out of your way, in a second here," Cass deliberately jockeyed for space at the top of the stairs.

"Move over!" the deputy growled, annoyed to find his way blocked. As the deputy looked past Cass, he saw his quarry going down the hallway toward the back stairwell. "Stop right there!" he called, pointing. But Cass was still in his way. "Confound it, move over! He shoved Cass aside and bounded after the young woman. "Stop! Stop!" he yelled, as Lucille disappeared down the back stairs. Moments later, the deputy had vanished down the back stairwell. Cass signaled Sara, and she rushed to join him at the top of the stairs.

So far the ruse was working, for Sara and Cass were down the stairs and crossing the lobby with no one stopping them. They hurried past Henry's desk. Without hesitating, Sara bent down and picked up her satchel.

Startled, Henry's mouth dropped open at the sight of Sara in a rather shorter than proper, green, satin dress. It seemed to confirm his worst suspicions--she was a saloon "entertainer." "Well, I say, Miss," he motioned feebly for them to stop, but when they didn't, Henry reluctantly doffed his hat and in confusion watched Cass and Sara leave the hotel.

CHAPTER TWENTY-SEVEN

The shiny, private, red stagecoach with four, large horses was in front of the hotel. Cass quickly took Sara's satchel and gave it to Zek, one of the drivers. Another driver, Orleans Freemont, sat ready, reins in hand.

"Wait! Sara cried. "There's White Hawk's horse." It stood tied to one of the hotel's hitching posts. Sara turned to Cass. "I guess Mac brought it there, thinking we'd be tying it to the earlier stagecoach."

"No problem. We'll take it with us." Cass said, quickly explaining to Zek what they were going to do, and in moments the coach lurched forward, heading down the street, with the pony trotting behind.

Everything had happened so fast that Sara had no time to think about what she was wearing. Once safely seated in the coach, she looked down at the low-cut neckline, and tried to pull the lace up to cover more. She wished she had something to cover herself with.

"That's very--ah--very becoming on you." Cass nodded and smiled. He could see Sara fidget with the lace bodice, apparently uneasy about the dress. He thought she hadn't heard. "That dress looks good on you, the color and--all."

Sara frowned, feeling hot tears brimming. She swallowed hard, took a deep breath and turned away.

"I didn't mean anything disrespectful. Really--."

Sara couldn't speak, but in a few more minutes they were at the jail. As the horses stopped, Cass quickly got out of the coach and turned back to Sara.

"Stay here—out of sight. I'll be right back." And without another word, he turned and walked inside the jail.

As Sara watched, it took all her control to do as Cass ordered. She should be the one to go and get them, she told herself. But she knew she must have patience and trust Cass. Trust him? She hardly knew anything about him. What if he did or said the wrong thing. Sara bit down on her lip. The tension was almost more than she could bear.

The wait in the stagecoach seemed eternal. Even the horses were restless, eager to be going. Sara's hands were little pockets of sweat, and her mind raced with worry. She wondered what had happened to Lucille. She hadn't seen the deputy come back.

Finally, Cass came out of the sheriff's office with her brother and friends in tow. Aaron ran to her and Peggy squealed with delight at seeing Sara. White Hawk could hardly believe his eyes when he saw WalksThrough, and rushed over and placed his head on his pony's neck.

"We have to hurry!" Aaron reminded sharply.

"I ride!" White Hawk scowled.

Cass shook his head and quickly explained that it was better for him to stay inside the stagecoach. "Be less of a problem for everyone. Once out of town, you can ride safely."

White Hawk agreed and everyone climbed into the stagecoach. Tarney was offered a little folded up blanket that made a perfect resting place on the floor of the stagecoach. Soon they were on their way.

Aaron wanted to know how Sara and Cass had escaped and Sara wanted to know what had happened inside the jail.

Cass explained, "The sheriff was worried about the Carey clan putting a 'spur' to the town, and 'all hell' breaking loose. He didn't want an unscheduled hanging, especially of youngsters." Cass grinned, "Sheriff Tuff's fears and a few silver dollars made up the difference."

"What'll happen to your friend, Lucille," Sara asked.

"She'll be fine. I reminded the sheriff that Russell Hammond could create just as much havoc as the Careys if anything happened to his new wife. I saw the look on his face. There won't be any trouble for Lucille."

For Sara, the best news was hearing that Colwell would be detained for several days. They would be gone and on their way before Colwell could be after them again. She glanced at Peggy, who had not stopped smiling. Maybe, just maybe, they'd seen the last of Donald Colwell. Sara took a deep breath, and turned to Cass. "Mr. Bartlett we can never thank you enough," she said. "You saved our lives, in spite of my rather rude behavior."

Aaron eagerly leaned forward to extend his hand. "I doubt there's any way to repay you, sir, but if there is, please tell us," Aaron earnestly shook his benefactor's hand.

Cass smiled. "I explained to your sister that I was going to San

Francisco myself and would enjoy the company. So you see, you've already paid me."

"That's fantastic! Isn't it Peggy?"

Everyone agreed that the day had been saved, especially after Sara explained all that had happened.

Sara finally settled back into the plush, red leather seats of the coach, willing herself to relax. Soon her heart filled with relief as the town faded from view and scenery took on the familiar look of the prairie.

She glanced at Cass and studied his face. A handsome face, she thought, with a strong jaw—-perhaps indicating a stubborn steak? But there was kindness, too. And he had, she knew, gone out of his way for their welfare. Her distressing physical reaction to him, she thought, was understandable, given her "mental state", getting the ticket and all. She clutched the hanky in her hand, shook her head as though scolding herself. Fortunately, all that was behind her. She took a deep breath. She'd hoped to thank him properly, but he appeared lost in thought, and she didn't want to disturb him.

Cass sat opposite Sara staring out the window. He was alert, but relaxed. After explaining what happened with the sheriff, he'd not said much, believing a quiet time to adjust was helpful, so he'd kept his eyes on the passing scene. He hadn't been completely honest about his motives for taking them along. But now was not the time to explain, he thought, feeling a prick of conscience. But to be fair, he would be helping the youngsters, as well. Still, there was that nagging little conscience. He could only hope he'd done the right thing.

He saw Sara watching him. "You wanted to ask me something?"

Sara looked down at her hands a moment, "I--" she spoke softly, her heart full of feeling. "I don't know what we'd have done without you--your help. Thank you so much, Mr. Bartlett."

He looked at her thoughtfully. There was a pause. "You're entirely welcome, Miss Robbins," he said rather formally, then winked, and held her eyes.

Sara was caught off guard. Her stomach turn flip-flops, as a flash of heat raced through her. She touched her face as his eyes held hers. She must be beet red. Oh, dear! This was not at all what she'd hoped for.

They traveled comfortably for several hours until, by late afternoon, the dust and heat of the trail finally caught up with them.

Everyone grew quiet, each making a corner of the coach a place apart.

At times the coach jostled and rolled or rocked forward and back on its leather under-straps. Cass explained that these were the latest improvements in carriage suspension. But once they hit a deep rut and were thrown against each other, like dice in a cup. No one complained, however, for they were happy to be alive and very grateful to be on their way.

Aaron kept reminding himself that in just twenty-eight to thirty-five short days, they'd be in San Francisco, if all went well. And of course it would, he told himself. They'd come through so much. He wondered how his friend Rufus Tanner was and hoped he felt better. He wanted to believe that he'd see him again. He and Peggy had said a prayer for his recovery. He was grateful that Peggy believed, because, at times, it was hard for him. But he didn't want to think about that. He shook his head and glanced across at White Hawk who was sound asleep, all curled up in the corner. Aaron wondered how he could sleep in such a position, comfortable as a cat. He thought about what they'd been through together. He's not really so bad--fights good. But it sure made him bull-crazy mad to see Peggy give the Indian all that attention. Well, he sighed, he'll be gone and out of my hair in a day or two.

Aaron pulled back the red, leather, window curtain and watched the ground move swiftly past. The speed was exciting. The very light of day seemed to race along ahead of them like arms reaching across the land. From time to time, groups of startled antelope darted away--fast they were. Oh, how he'd love to run with them, run and run and never tire. He remembered how he and his father used to race in the fields in back of his home. The memories tore at him. His Father. Oh, God, how he missed him. Dad, he whispered to himself, we're on our way. He swallowed the bitterness in his throat. Don't worry, Dad. I'll make you proud, I promise. I'll take care of Sara and Peggy, too. We'll get back the hardware store and Rebel, too. Don't worry. I promise.

Aaron bit down on his lip and turned to watch Peggy. It bothered him that she woke up every so often to check on White Hawk. And even as the Indian slept, she occasionally wiped his forehead with a handkerchief. Guess I'll just have to put up with it for now. It'd only be for a couple more days.

Once, when Aaron was half asleep, Peggy's tenderness evoked a memory that entered his dream. He remembered being five-years old--in bed with whooping cough. His pony had died two days earlier. He couldn't breathe. He was choking. Then suddenly his mother was there, and he felt her cool hand gently brushing the hair off his forehead.

"Aaron? Aaron! Wake up, honey!" Sara gently touched his shoulder. "There, there--you're having a nightmare!"

"Oh!" he said, startled awake. "Sorry," he looked around. "I fell asleep," he admitted, sheepishly.

"You're lucky!" Cass said, sensing Aaron's embarrassment. Aaron reached for Tarney and placed his hand on her head. "I was worried about her." He said, and then regretted the lie. He closed his eyes again and pretended to sleep. He needed to think about the future, not moan about the past like a child. After all, he'd be captain of a fine boat, very soon, now. He could imagine himself sailing up the Sacramento River. He saw himself standing at the helm of the The Promise. Peggy was there and Rebel. He saw his shiny, sleek, black horse, running like the wind. Oh, he could hardly wait to see Rebel. We'll have a wonderful time, a great future.

They stopped to rest and change the team at a way station during the day, and at noon they picnicked on the prairie, but there was no shade, only glaring sun and choking dust.

Sand swirled through the open windows and covered everything. By late afternoon the passengers were weary and looking forward to food and a safe place to stretch out for the night.

The long, hot day finally drew to a close. They had traveled forty miles, more than twice the miles they would've made on the wagon train.

As the red sun sank under the horizon, the colors of the prairie grass darkened and the sky deepened to indigo.

Finally, they saw their destination. The driver, Orleans, gave a blast of his horn as they came near.

A little, gray, sod house stood against a bare landscape. At the side of the way station was a small corral, and off to the right, on the other side of the barn, there appeared to be a chicken coop and a pig enclosure. It's a regular little farm, Aaron thought.

CHAPTER TWENTY-EIGHT

Jake Randall and his wife, Molly, stood in front, waiting to greet the new arrivals. Jake waved a lantern. Molly, a tall, spare woman with long, thick, grey hair tied back, stood with her arms open and a wide smile across her face.

"Mighty glad to see you safe and sound!" she said, shaking her head. "See any anti-abolitionists?"

"No," Cass answered. "Why?"

"A couple wagons were attacked not far from here."

"Now, Molly," Jake warned, walking up to Cass. "We have guests wanting rest and some good grub."

"Right ya, are, my love." Molly rushed up to Cass. "You're a sight for sore eyes," Molly said, welcoming everyone with large friendly gestures. "Come on in, refresh yer selves."

The drivers, Orleans and Jake, took the coach and horses toward the barn. Cass and the others followed Molly inside.

Sara noticed that the gray, sod home had two front windows with glass panes. White curtains helped to give the room a homey feeling. The room was probably no more than eighteen by twenty feet in all, with nine cots spaced head to head along two walls. The dirt walls had been whitewashed and several lanterns cast a soft warm yellow around the room. Smells of homemade bread and venison stew came from a black, iron stove in a corner of the kitchen area. "It smells wonderful in here," Sara said, looking about and wondering where to put her satchel. She felt a little embarrassed about her dress and held her satchel at the front. Fortunately, Molly didn't seem to regard her saloon costume as anything unusual.

"Jist make yer self ta home," Molly shouted as though someone might not hear. "Supper's near ready. Soon as Jake and the boys get here. Ya can throw down that satchel on any bed." She smiled at Sara and Peggy. "One's good as t'other. There's a fresh pitcher o' water and a basin fer washin' up. You ladies go first. Sure is nice havin' ya---been a while since I had a chat with ladies."

Sara noticed disconcertedly that the beds had very thin mattresses: apparently, they were all expected to sleep in the same room. Sara reminded herself that she was a guest and that this arrangement was probably better than sleeping in a tent outside. A long wood table had been placed on one side of the room and was set with three pitchers of milk and four large loaves of bread.

"Yer lucky, Cass. I had a hunch ya might be bringin' others." Molly tied a clean, white apron around her gray dress as she spoke. "I never know what to expect from you and Russell Hammond. By the by, have ya seen Russ lately?"

"About a week ago," Cass offered. "Russ and I and a couple other men are putting together another coach line to compete with the Overland Stage Line. Business appears ready and waiting. Russ claims our new passenger coach can cut the time. If the Pony Express can do it in twenty-five, we figure, we'll do it in twenty—nine. We'll see. This is a dry run. Russ has ordered another two coaches like the one we're transporting. Said to tell you to get ready, stock up and add a room so you can sleep twelve more passengers twice a week." Cass grinned. "You know Russ, nothing by halves."

Molly sighed. "That many halves can raise a whole batch a trouble. I'd say that young man's eyes too big for his pocket book. Likely a war could change all that. It's come'n to a head. Though," she said, pushing back gray hair from her forehead, "I expect Jake will go along with Russ's plans. That young'n could wrangle an elk out'a his horns."

Cass laughed. "We'll talk later. Right now, I want you to meet some new friends of mine. Molly, this is Peggy O'Neil, Sara Robbins and her brother Aaron and their friend, White Hawk."

"Well, I'll be jiggered!" Molly slapped her thigh. "I near forgot my manners. Glory be, yer' all welcome to my home." Her last remark was directed to White Hawk, who stayed by the door. Molly's generous nature was so obvious and natural that White Hawk did not take offense. He nodded, as if understanding, but turned and walked outside and headed for the barn.

"Time to eat," Molly announced, standing in the doorway and ringing a little bell.

Jake, Zek, and Orleans came bounding through the door. After hurriedly washing in a bucket next to the well outside, everyone gathered around the long table. Molly brought a big bowl of steaming venison stew to the table. It was brimming full of potatoes, carrots and turnips. Molly quickly served everyone a big bowl. "This is for the boy. Jake you take it to the barn and make sure he's fine for the night. Seems he's shy around strangers."

When Jake returned, he reassured everyone that the Indian boy had taken the food and insisted on staying the night in the barn beside his horse. "He's all set. I told him to suit his self. He's bunked 'n settled beside his pony." Jake noticed Peggy's frown. "He'll do fine. Don't worry." He nodded to Cass. "He ain't used to white folks, I expect. Well, now, let's eat," he said sitting down.

Orleans, a tanned, leathery-faced man with a black beard, reached out and was about to grab the bowl when Molly bent over him and whacked his hands with a wooden spoon.

"Ya old mule skinner! Ya know better'n that round here."

Chastised, Orleans acted meek as a child and scratched his beard.

Jake was seated at the head of the table waiting to say grace. Everyone bowed his or her head. "Lord, we thank ya for this day, for good food and for the fine woman who cooked the vittles. Make our conversation amenable to you, Lord. Amen!" He glanced around. "All right ya old mule hogs--let her roll!"

Supper was a noisy affair. The appetite for conversation was as strong as it was for food. The small room seemed to vibrate with the sounds of laughter and men's voices. Good food and warmth from the corner stove offered homey comfort.

When Sara finished a delicious bowl of stew, it was all she could do to keep her eyes open. All conversation seemed to melt past her understanding. There was talk about the drought, about the democrats splitting into four groups, and the possibility of a war between the states. Jake felt strongly, sympathizing with the South. "Buchanan and his cronies are about as helpful as magpies—-talk, talk, talk is all they do. Don't know much about that Lincoln fellow. Douglas is a good talker. But that don't help much these days."

Jake shook his head vehemently. "King Cotton's gettin' a bad deal. They want to sell direct to Europe, and it tain't fair, fer as I kin see, fer the North to tell the South what to do or where to sell."

Zek agreed, pointing his fork, "The boys up North want their cut, tain't right to deny it and blame it on segregation."

Molly joined in, "Now what I hate to see is what South Carolina's done over this slavery thing. She tried to pull away once before and now there's talk she'll do it if Lincoln gets elected. Then other folks might take a notion. It took years ta get us all together, and it weren't easy. Now all the country is fallin' a part. What'd ya think, Cass?"

Cass nodded, "Things appear to be coming to a head, all right. One good thing--there's a wireless coming in--be part of the prairie next year, going from coast to coast. Might help to unify the country. I'm in favor of keeping the country together. I heard talk back East of separating out California. That'd be wrong-headed thinking." Cass looked over at Jake. "Russ hopes the faster mail will pull us together."

"Might at that," agreed Jake. "Which way will San Francisco lean if we come to war?"

"From what I hear," Cass offered, "there are a lot of Southern sympathizers. There's a group that wants California divided, give the South another slave state. They might use war as a pretext. It's hard to tell. I'm eager to know the drift of things, first hand. I'll do whatever I can to preserve the Union. But the slavery issue will have to be solved, sooner or later. England already outlawed it. We should. It's an evil that could destroy us as a country."

"I agree!" Sara interjected. "It's just wrong for a country or anyone to think they can own a human being. It's just wrong!"

Cass smiled at Sara. "Seems you feel pretty strongly about it and have given it some thought."

"Of course, I have," Sara responded heatedly, annoyed that that Cass would assume otherwise. She added. "And I would hope that anyone with a heart or brain would agree. People aren't machines--things for profit. They're not objects!"

"You're right, of course, Sara," Cass returned calmly.

Zek added thoughtfully, "I think yer right in principle, but England didn't have a whole economy tied up in slavery like the South. There's more at stake, here."

"Then," Sara said heatedly, "you have to ask what kind of country or principle is it that holds the purse higher than a human being."

General comments and nodding heads were ready for more debate, but Molly quickly guided the conversation into memories of good times they'd shared in San Francisco. Jake, Molly, and Orleans had known Cass' father in San Francisco when Cass was just a boy. Jake regaled everyone with tales of old Charles, "Chuck" Bartlett, and their days in the Mexican war in 1847. They went on to talk about their mining days in '49, and how little Chuck had been such a hell-raiser. Jake finished with the story of how Chuck senior had saved his life, dragged him half-dead out of the Russian River.

These stories were as familiar to Cass as last season's boots, but he listened politely, as he always did to stories about his father. It was obvious that they cared about him.

"Ol' Chuck never forgot his friends. I owe this job to him and your friendship with Russell Hammond," Jake beamed. "Yep, your Pa must be right proud of you, seeing ya graduate from Harvard an' all. You gonna set up law practice in Frisco, son?"

"I don't know," Cass answered, somewhat thoughtfully.

"I figure it'd make yer ol' man mighty pleased."

"Suppose so," Cass replied without much enthusiasm. In fact, he wondered if it would please his father. He had seen little of the man in the last four years—-hadn't had a serious talk in more. It was unsettling to have these people talk about his father with so much more feeling than he could muster. It bothered Cass, made him realize his own lack. He wondered when that started. Just after his mother died, he supposed--when he'd been hustled off to boarding school. After that he'd only come home on a few holidays. He'd gone east to college and spent the last half year traveling.

The father-son relationship was strained by years of distance—-both physical and emotional. They'd developed polite behavior, but a behavior, he realized that never touched the raw feelings beneath. It had begun soon after his mother died. After that, his relationship with his father felt blunted to the point of uselessness, but Cass knew in his heart something deeper existed. It was that potential that made him uneasy.

CHAPTER TWENTY-NINE

After supper was over, Jake pushed himself back from the table, rubbed his stomach, and snapped his wide red suspenders. This was the signal to begin the evening's entertainment. There would be the traditional card game and story telling for the men.

Molly cleared away the table with Sara and Peggy's help; however, she refused their offer to wash the dishes.

"Mercy, you're guests, and tired ones at that. Don't fret yerselves. I'll do 'em in the mornin.' Water's jist outside the door. Ya go on git into yer nightshirts and on ta bed." It was a kindly meant order and they agreed. Molly had hung a little sheet across a corner of the room to allow for privacy.

While Sara was getting herself ready for bed, Molly fluffed up the straw mattress and pillows.

"Peggy, come here," Sara whispered from behind the sheet. "I want you to have the green satin dress. Come and try it on. Here, take it."

"Oh, it's beautiful," Peggy said, touching the dress. "It's just too beautiful." Peggy wrinkled her nose. "I couldn't."

"Nonsense. I want you to have it. You'd be doing me a favor." Sara was too tired to argue. "Please take it!" Sara came from behind the curtain, a blanket covering her night gown. She pushed the dress at Peggy, turned and took a bed close to the changing area.

"Oh, thank you, Sara." Peggy held the dress close, and then went behind the curtain to put it on. When she came through the curtain to show Sara, all the men stopped playing cards and gawked at her. Orleans whistled, and Zek grinned.

"You look beautiful, Peggy," Aaron said, putting down his cards to stare spellbound. The soft glow of two oil lamps appeared to cast a magical spell about her. Peggy's hair was like spun gold and the green, satin dress shimmered.

Sara rose up on her elbow and watched the faces of the men. It was true. Peggy was transformed. This was a new Peggy, no longer the dowdy, ragamuffin child. Sara smiled as she saw Peggy twirl about, basking in the glow of appreciation. This must be an important moment for Peggy, Sara thought "You look delightful,

Peggy!"

"Sure a sight fer sore eyes!" Jake said. "You'd think we was in 'Frisco at Dolly's."

Peggy continued to show off the dress, doing it the same way she remembered Lucille showing off for Cass. She placed her hand on her hip and bounced a little from side to side.

Cass was quick to catch the similarity. "That dress looks better on you than..." Cass caught himself. "It looks especially nice on you."

Peggy spotted Jake's guitar sitting in the corner. "I had one like that once," she volunteered.

"Can you play?" Molly asked.

"I used to...a little," Peggy responded shyly.

"Well here, give it a try," Jake said, going for the guitar. "We'd sure like a little music from a purdy gal, now wouldn't we?"

"Yes, please," everyone encouraged.

"It's been awhile. My calluses are near gone." She glanced at Aaron for reassurance.

"Go ahead, Peggy! Give it a try," Aaron insisted.

Peggy looked about."Where's White Hawk?"

Aaron frowned. "He's at the barn; wants to stay with his horse."

Peggy appeared disappointed. "Oh, yes, of course," she said, taking the guitar and settling on a bed. She tuned the instrument, turned from view, and began singing-- softly at first, as though telling a story to a child. Her voice was sweet and husky which added a sense of intimacy. And though her strumming was simple, it seemed charming as she sang a familiar song about a young woman whose sweetheart had gone off to sea, never to return. The sad lyrics struck a lonesome chord in the men, and their hard-weathered faces softened with memories of loved ones left behind.

As the evening wore on, Peggy faced her audience. Her voice grew stronger as she filled requests. Molly asked for "Amazing Grace." Jake wanted "Jeannie with The Light Brown Hair."

When she concluded, the men jumped up, stomped their boots and cheered. "More! More!" they demanded.

"Mercy!" Peggy exclaimed, overwhelmed and delighted. "But you all must be awful tired."

"Nonsense!" Molly bellowed. "We kin sleep any time."

Everyone begged Peggy to continue, and she did, drinking in the praise like a thirsty plant. The more she played, the better she felt.

Sharing and being appreciated changed the very boundaries inside her. It seemed a magical night, and she knew that something special was happening to her, and she would never be the same again.

Finally, it was late and Molly gave the signal for them to retire. With reluctance, they rose and ambled to their beds. The men pulled off their boots, promptly found mattresses. Jake and Orleans picked up their rifles and went outside to take first watch. Rumors about raiders in the area had left the men on alert.

Peggy changed out of her "costume" and put on a nightshirt and then silently crept to her bed.

"You were more than wonderful, Peggy," Aaron whispered from the next bed. He raised his head up and smiled at her.

"Thank you, Aaron. Goodnight."

Aaron lay back down, resisting the desire to talk. There was so much he wanted to say to her--to tell her. He could still see her singing. He remembered how their eyes had met, the softness she seemed to set inside of him. The feeling drew deep, filling his heart. On such wonderful thoughts, Aaron finally closed his eyes and went to sleep.

Peggy stayed awake for a long time, listening to the soft mewing sounds and gentle snores around her. It was comforting--part of this special day. She would always remember--the day she was set free. Finally free from her step-father and free to be herself. Oh, how she hoped her mother had been looking down from Heaven. Don't worry momma, Donald Colwell can't hurt me anymore. Thank you, Lord, she whispered and quietly said her prayers, and then curled up like a baby, snug and secure for the first time in months.

At dawn the next day, and only a few miles east of the way station, Lumis Carey gave the signal for his men to halt. Five riders obediently reined their horses to a stop.

They were close enough for now.

The three Carey brothers, their father, Lumis, and one other man who'd recently joined them, wearily dismounted and stood quietly eyeing their intended quarry in the distance.

In the first dim light of day, the way station looked dark and helpless. Lumis smiled knowingly. "Most likely they're still asleep. We'll catch 'em by surprise." He spat on the ground, motioned for his men to gather round. They dismounted and took their places, huddling about the old man.

Lumis took his time and waited silently until everyone settled down and gave their undivided attention. He scanned the faces of the men, and then looked down at the sod, as though measuring something between two elements. His attitude held the air of ritual.

Lumis Carey, leader of the clan, was a short, fat-featured, stubble of a man with a coppery beard and a ritualistic turn of mind. He was born with a game leg and eyes of different color: one green, one brown.

At the moment of his birth a cock crowed, and a passing fortune-teller decreed the babe would be a man of special powers. Lumis accepted the truth of that.

He squatted, and then teetered momentarily on his uneven leg, trying to gain a footing against the rough ground. He finally steadied. "Hand me yer bowie knife, Colwell," he frowned at the tall man on his left. He grabbed the knife and plunged it into the soil, splitting the ground like a carcass.

"This here's the house--over thar's the corral," he said, carving the line deeper. "Colwell," he addressed the stranger without looking at him, "in back of the house thar's a rise in the ground. They can't see or hear ya comin' back thar, and beyond it drops on down into a dry river-bed. You and Miles head on towards the corral that a way." He drew a line with the knife, pointing the distance from the house. "Jist move on back ta here. Get the horses out fast and head up the gully." His beady eyes sought confirmation as he looked into Colwell's face, but Colwell's expression remained impassive. "Ya understand?"

Colwell nodded.

"Me and the boys will meet ya up here," Lumis continued, jabbing the point into the sod. He scowled at Colwell. "Ya understand?"

Colwell offered a perfunctory shrug.

"Thar's a clump o' rocks at the end of the gulch where the old river meets. Wait thar. Ya understand?"

Colwell gave a meager, "Ya."

"All right!" Lumis announced loudly. He spat, clearing unpleasantness from his throat. Colwell's attitude was raising his gall and making things harder for him and his boys. Sensing Lumis' uneasiness, they moved closer. "Maybe six horses in the corral, maybe twelve," Lumis continued. "Depends on if they've brought any spares. We could git lucky!" His eyes squinted up at the sky and lingered for a moment, watching a small cloud change its form. The sky seemed to add territory to his thoughts, and certain signs added confidence. He believed the portents foreshadowed a favorable result. He finally nodded, got to his feet and stretched his legs. He eyed Colwell as he replaced the man's knife in his own sheath.

Colwell merely shrugged, giving no indication of his feelings.

Lumis glanced about. "Yep," he said, "we could git real lucky."

The raid on the way station would be the biggest haul since they'd raided Black Kettle's camp last year. He'd waited two weeks to attack the way station, studying the situation, and now the signs were right and fate was rewarding him, giving a bonus. It would be payment for the loss of his son. Lumis smiled at the thought. It was likely the Injin kid he intended to kill was from Black Kettle's camp, and according to Colwell was traveling with his daughter. Colwell offered three-hundred dollars reward to get the girl, and he could keep any horses they found. Yep, the signs are right and proper. The notion filled him with a heady confidence. There was only one thing bothering him--Colwell! He didn't trust the man, and he could see it was mutual. The man's dark brooding manner lingered about him like a plague, deliberately creating doubt. Even now, he was standing apart, off to the right side. That was not a good omen. It whipped the old man's temper and he snapped, "Dammit! Move the hell over--over thar!"

Colwell glared, mute as stone, but did as told. He smiled insolently.

"I'm warnin' ya, Colwell. Just keep outta my way and stay close to Miles."

"Make sure he does his part." Colwell glared at Miles, who was looking about confused.

Lumus snarled, "Jist follow orders, Colwell--or else! Miles, pay attention here!"

At the sound of his name, Miles' vacant eyes lit up. He beamed at Colwell, round-faced and innocent as an angel, but the smooth face stayed grinning.

Colwell's temper coiled tight, but he saw Lumis' look and eased back. Lumis, he knew, would as soon shoot him in the back as look at him. He reminded himself that he was little better than their prisoner. Back at the jail it had seemed reasonable to join up with the Careys. But once they killed the Indian, took care of the kids, and he had Peggy back, it would be another story. For now, he would bide his time, make plans. He'd think of ways to out-fox the old buzzard and keep the money for himself. The idea smoothed the raw edges of his feelings as he heard Lumis give the order to mount up.

The sky lightened. It was time to move. The men quickly took their places. Colwell rode alongside of Miles, as the men spurred their horses and were off. They would make their strike and be back on their way to Leavenworth in less than an hour.

CHAPTER THIRTY

Sara awoke before dawn, not quite remembering where she was. The room was fairly dark; a bit of gray light came through the two windows on either side of the door. It was early, perhaps no more than five. Somewhere a rooster crowed.

Sara sat up and looked around. Rows of wooden beds held sleeping forms, and only the soft murmuring of men's breathing and gentle snores disturbed the quiet. She looked at Molly and Peggy's cots, expecting to see them still asleep. But Molly wasn't there and Peggy's blanket had been set back, neatly folded and placed at the bottom of the cot. Peggy's probably gone to the outhouse, Sara thought. The idea of using the outhouse spurred her to action. She quickly laced up her boots.

Tarney noticed Sara and jumped down from Aaron's bed and came wagging her tail, then ran for the door.

"Tarney," she whispered. "Just be patient." Sara picked up her satchel and tiptoed over to the table, took a large towel and one of several washbasins, and headed for the door. She hesitated for a moment, looking about. No one stirred. Apparently, she and Tarney hadn't disturbed anyone. They quietly tiptoed out.

Outside, the air felt cool and fresh, and everything appeared still and peaceful--a beautiful gray morning, with just a faint hue of pink at the horizon.

Sara glanced toward the barn. Its gray, weathered wood blended in with the sky and a large, rooster weather-vane, stood at the top of the two-story building. Sara noticed Zek leading a horse into the corral. The fenced in area was divided into two sections--half held six horses, and in the other, four mules were bending over their morning feed.

Before long, a side door of the barn opened and Molly walked out, carrying a milk bucket and a basket. She smiled at Sara and began walking to the house. "Good morning, young lady." She beamed at Sara. "How'd ya sleep?!"

"Very well," Sara replied heartedly, not wanting to disappoint Molly. It wasn't her fault she'd had nightmares.

Molly grinned. "That young friend of yers was so eager to help.

Picked up these eggs." She held up a woven basket. "Said she'd grown up on a farm and missed finding eggs and milking. Did a right handy job of it, too. We'll have fried eggs, bacon, and oats with fresh cream for breakfast. You can thank Peggy."

"I will." Sara nodded. "She's a big help to me, too. Did you see White Hawk?"

"Yep. Grooming his pony." Molly chuckled. "He was mighty happy to see Peggy."

Sara quickly changed the subject. "I thought I'd better wash up before everybody wakes." She held up the towel and pan. "I just helped myself."

"Good girl! The outhouse is around the side and there's a little place smack at the back where ya might take a private wash. Zek and Peggy have finished." She turned to walk inside. "Best hurry," she said, adding, "I'll keep an eye out for the others, so as not to let anyone bother ya."

After drawing a bucket of water from the well, Sara walked to the rear of the house with Tarney close at her heels. "Don't worry, you'll get your drink of water first. Now just stay quiet."

Behind the house, things were as she'd hoped--private and protected. A sod fence about three feet tall offered shelter from wind and view. Sara set the heavy bucket and her satchel to one side, and looked about.

The back of the house had not been white washed, and showed its sod origins. Several feet of sod was built up near the foundation and extended from the back of the house and out a few feet. Strange little mound, Sara thought. Maybe it's a storm cellar. Could it be a grave? No! Heavens! What thoughts. Last night's nightmare was infecting her day. Mustn't allow that! She sighed.

Oh, how she needed this time, this rare moment of privacy and freedom. But she couldn't dawdle. Breakfast would be called soon and she wanted to help.

"Here, my sweet girl," she whispered to Tarney, pouring fresh water in the basin and setting it down.

After Tarney had finished, Sara carefully set out the towel, poured fresh water into the basin and placed the bar of sweet jasmine soap into the water. Next, she spread out her blue cotton dress on the grass, brushing out the wrinkles and then laid out a clean petticoat and fresh chemise. Everything was prepared and waiting. Unbuttoning the top of her nightgown, she let it fall to her waist. The air felt cool and soft on her skin, as she lathered soap across her shoulders and under her arms. The soothing emollient revived her sense of things. Soap and water, such basic provisions, put things in perspective. How fortunate to be here and to be traveling on a fine stagecoach. A little like Cinderella--only without a glass slipper, she said smiling, glancing down at her worn boots. She felt so grateful to Cass for helping them. What a kind young man, he is—-so courteous and respectful. She smiled. Just thinking about him made her feel warm all over.

The dove-gray sky turned pink then gold as the sun moved over the horizon. Mercy! She'd lost track of time. She quickly dried herself, put on her clothes, and stood brushing her hair, quickly braided it and tied the end with a strip of muslin.

She was about to discard the basin of water and wrap her soap in a cloth when she heard movement from the side of the house. She whirled around. "Cass!"

He stood sheepishly grinning."<u>Good</u> morning!" His voiced emphasized the "good," and his grin was suggestive.

"How long have you been standing there?" Sara felt her face flush. "Oh!" she cried. Had he seen her naked?

"I'm sorry. I didn't mean to scare you."

"Well, you did!" Sara's embarrassment gave way to anger. "What do you mean sneaking up like that?"

"Hold on. I wasn't <u>sneaking</u> up."

"Just how long had you been spying on me?"

"Spying?!" Cass retorted sharply.

"Yes, spying!"

"Miss Robbins, I'm not in the habit of spying on little girls."

"Oh! Of all the nerve!" She fumed, and in haughty indignation, bent to pick up the soap. Unfortunately, it oozed out of her hand and fell to the ground, inches from Cass' boots. Undaunted, Sara tried to grab the precious soap but, once again, it slithered away out of reach.

"Here, let me!" Cass volunteered, amused by Sara's fiery determination. Her face had turned scarlet.

"Don't touch it!"

As Cass made an attempt to help, Sara rushed forward, shoving him out of the way. However, in doing so, she knocked over the basin of water, and it spilled all over Cass' legs and boots. This hardly fazed Sara, for she was angry enough to have heaved the basin at him. But it was even worse seeing his reaction.

He laughed. "We'll have to do this more often, Miss Robbins." He shook his pant leg. "Do you suppose we could share a towel as well?"

Cass' insinuating grin and those mischievous blue eyes only angered Sara. Quickly, and without a word, she gathered up the soap and satchel, and indignantly marched towards the side of the house.

"Come here, Tarney!" she demanded crisply.

"Sara wait!" Cass ordered, his tone suddenly changed.

Sara, head high, and determined to ignore him, started walking. It was only a low growl from Tarney that stopped her. She turned then, to see Cass coming after her. He made a motion to silence, his eyes narrowed in a frown. "Quiet!" he whispered.

"What is it?" Sara asked, alarmed.

"Riders. I can't tell how many. Wait. I'll go see. Keep Tarney here and quiet." He motioned her to stay back as he disappeared around the corner.

A chill pulsed down Sara's spine as she picked up Taney and clutched her closer.

Cass slowly edged his way along the side of the house toward the front. He could hear men shouting and horses thundering within feet of him. Cautiously, he peered around the side. He saw three riders circling in front of the station, their weapons drawn, their horses pounding the ground in confusion, raising plumes of dust. Instinctively, Cass reached for his Colt. It was not there. "Damn!" he swore.

Suddenly, the riders opened fire. As the deadly blasts ripped into the way station, Cass heard muffled shouts and cries from within. "God!" Cass swore, pounding his fists helplessly into the wall.

Inside the way station, everyone scrambled for protection. Confused shouts and orders came from all directions as Jake and Orleans raced for their guns. Aaron lunged for the floor, pressing his body flat against the dirt. Bullets whizzed inches over his head and tore into the walls like claws, flinging dirt onto the floor and shattering the windows.

Jake pulled the heavy wood planked table over on its side, attempting to use it as a shield. "Stay down!" he ordered, as Aaron and Orleans inched their way toward the back of the room.

There was a momentary lull in the volleys. "Everyone get over ta the stove," Jake shouted.

But as Orleans crawled toward the stove, a bullet caught him in the leg, and he crumpled up. "I've been hit," he cried.

"Here!" Molly yelled. She tossed a wad of clean cloth to Orleans. "Tie it around yer leg and get over here." Molly was bending down next to the iron stove. She pushed aside a small, oval, rag rug to reveal a wooden square with a handle on it. She lifted the square trap door and motioned to Aaron.

As Aaron came close, she pressed a pistol in his hand. "Follow me down the cellar. Jake and Orleans you follow!"

"Hurry!" Jake demanded roughly. "Molly get ahead ta help Aaron. Go on, Son. Step down. I'll help Orleans."

Aaron quickly climbed down, holding the gun in one hand.

"Move along, son," Jake urged, holding the trap door.

"But Peggy and Sara?"

"Likely safe in the barn!" Jake frowned. "Now get goin, or we'll all be shot."

Aaron followed Molly down five narrow steps. It was a passageway cut into the ground and dark as a grave.

"Keep yer hand on th' one in front of ya," Jake said, "and move along quickly. It taint more than ten feet to go."

Aaron couldn't see a thing and he choked on the musty, sour smell. As his hands brushed against the dirt walls, loose soil crumbled down on his head, and he had a sense that bugs might be crawling up his legs, or spiders falling on his head. He could hear muffled gunshots just a few feet over him. Finally, at the end of the tunnel, he saw shards of light leaking around the edges of a small doorway. Molly was already pushing against the door, but it didn't move.

"Gimme a hand, son," Molly said, straining.

Aaron quickly added his shoulder and pushed. The old wood door burst open and fell to the ground.

Momentarily, light blinded him, but Aaron soon realized he was outside at the back of the house, and then he saw his sister and Tarney.

"Oh, Aaron!" exclaimed Sara, rushing to hug him. She wrapped her arms around him, crying. "I was so worried."

"You all right?" Aaron asked, pulling away.

"Yes, I'm fine," She wiped her eyes with her sleeve, and glanced about. "But Peggy and White Hawk?" She looked to Jake.

"She went ta check on White Hawk before it all broke loose."

Jake scowled.

As Cass came around from the side of the house, Jake asked, "How many?"

"Three in front. Maybe more." Cass walked over to Sara. "You all right?" But there wasn't time for answers as a volley of shots rang through the air.

CHAPTER THIRTY-ONE

"Here's yer gun, Cass." Jake quickly handed him the Colt 45. Turning to Molly, he directed, "Take the young'uns to the barn, down through the gulch." He explained to Cass. "We're too exposed here. There's a safe place inside the barn-—a storm shelter—nobody will find ya. Molly will show ya. Take the riverbed, circle around, out of sight, till ya get to the barn. It's yer best chance. The gulch lies about twenty feet back of us and arcs around to the corral. Molly will tell ya when to make a run for it. Ya got that?"

Everyone nodded.

"Cass, you, Orleans and me will stay here surprise 'em-- have a hunch they think we're still inside. Meet ya soon's it's clear."

Aaron protested, "Let me stay and help!"

"No," Cass frowned. "You protect the girls. Now hurry up!"

"Right!" Aaron nodded, rushing ahead.

Cass watched his friends crouch along the grassy path towards the gulch and then disappear into the riverbed. He could only hope that the tall grass along the top provided cover.

Cass suddenly felt his chest tighten. What has he gotten his friends into. He pounded his hand into his fist. I must've been crazy to bring them along," he said, furious with himself.

"Come on, Cass!" Jake warned, "No time to ruminate." He turned to Orleans. "Can ya walk?"

Orleans nodded a painful yes, and slapped his gun holster. "I kin shoot better'n most kin walk."

They stood at the back of the way station, listening. Jake pointed, "You head over ta the right side, and Cass and I'll take the left. Pull around once and shoot, Cass and I'll surprise 'em from the other side."

Sara and Aaron followed Molly's long strides as she led them up the dry riverbed. Pausing, Molly stopped to look at the ground. "Two riders been through, not long ago." She poked her head up to look about. "I don't see any other horses in the corral, 'cept ours." She kept her voice low. "You two stay close ta the bank, so's ya kin jump up and run when I signal. Ya'll run ta the barn. There's a little shed in the back, and another root cellar under the work bench." She squinted at the corral. "I don't see Zek, but he might be in the barn."

They crept closer—now only a few yards from the corral. They saw the horses running in circles, and bunching up, threatening the pole fence.

Molly turned to Sara and Aaron. "Ya stay close to me. If somethin' happens, head to that little cellar hole Jake mentioned. It's enough for three or more 'an keep yer dog quiet." She eyed Tarney. "Seems she knows enough to be quiet."

Aaron nodded.

"You two wait for my signal." Molly stood up and rushed toward the barn door, gun in hand. But just a few feet from the door was a body lying sprawled across the opening. It was Zek. "Zek!" Molly whispered, quickly bending. She touched his wrist, checked his pulse. "He's alive," she whispered. "Better get him away from here." She stood and glanced about. When she didn't see anyone, she grabbed Zeks' boots, pulled him along the ground until she got him to where he'd be out of sight, then rolled him over. No blood showing. That was good and his pulse was strong. Likely he'd been knocked out. She picked up her gun and motioned for the Sara and Aaron to follow.

They hurried forward. Once inside the barn, Aaron glanced about, hoping to see Peggy or White Hawk "Peggy?" he whispered, looking at the stalls. There were six open stalls on each side and three further down that had walls of sod separating them. Sara couldn't see much because only slivers of light nudged through cracks in the walls and drifted in from the top hayloft at the front. The air was dusty, and dry and made her nose itch. She held her kerchief over her nose.

Tarney, who had stayed close, suddenly dashed forward. And before Aaron or Sara could stop her, she darted for a stall at the back of the barn.

Aaron snapped his fingers twice, and whispered her name. There was no response. Aaron was about to run after her, when Molly pulled him aside. She shook her head, cautioning him to wait and listen.

Sara stood behind Molly. All she could hear was the pounding of her heart.

Finally, Molly moved a few steps, and signaled Aaron and Sara to stay behind her. Holding her gun at the ready, Molly slowly moved up the middle of the barn. A sound caught her attention, and she rushed ahead, gun pointed. "Come out or I'll shoot." She stepped cautiously until she could see into the stall. "Well, Glory be! It's yer friend!" Molly exclaimed." He's got her all tied up."

"Peggy?" Aaron and Sara ran forward.

"Oh, Peggy!" Sara cried, as she saw Peggy cowering in the corner. She was covered in straw and dust, her arms and legs bound with leather straps, a dirty rag strapped across her mouth. She could barely move, but her eyes spoke terror as she shook her head.

Aaron quickly knelt and began untying the leather thongs that bound her wrists and ankles, while Sara worked to untie the strap holding the gag.

"We'll get you free soon," Aaron whispered. But even as he got her hands free, Peggy kept squirming and shaking her head.

Suddenly a giant shadow fell over them. A large man stepped out of the opposite stall, and before anyone knew what was happening, rushed up behind Molly and stuck a gun at her back.

"Colwell!" Sara screamed.

"Drop it!" Colwell hissed, shoving his gun harder in Molly's back. "Drop it!"

Molly let her gun fall.

Colwell shoved it aside with his right boot, and then jerked Molly forward, using her body as a shield. "You too, boy! Drop it!"

Aaron hesitated.

"Now! And keep that mongrel back!"

Tarney inched forward, growling, ready to spring. "Stay!" Aaron demanded.

Tarney's teeth were bared, her eyes fixed on Colwell. "Tarney! No!"

Tarney backed away at Aaron's command, but stood beside him, ready to strike.

"Throw down the gun, or I'll plug yer dog now!"

Aaron threw the gun to the ground.

Colwell glared. "All right. You three move over there." He shoved Molly forward and pointed to the place next to Peggy. "You!" he motioned to Sara. "I've changed my mind about keeping her tied. You," He swaggered a foot closer to Sara, his manner a threat as he held the gun near her face. "Finish untying her. Hurry! I ain't got all day!"

As Sara crouched next to Peggy, her hands shook so hard she had trouble undoing the leather strap. "Hold still," Sara whispered.

Peggy shook with fear, making it harder to untie the leather knot. Sara finally managed to get her feet and hands free. She began to untie the gag when Colwell shoved her aside.

"Back away—-over there--in the corner. All of ya."

Once they were huddled in the back of the stall, he rushed forward a few feet, grabbed Peggy's shoulders and roughly pulled her up. She struggled a little, but Colwell quickly overpowered her, grabbing her wrists with one hand. "Ya all stay nice and quiet now or I'll put a bullet into the first one what moves. He suddenly spun Peggy around, so that she became his shield.

"Miles!" Colwell called, barking the order toward the last stall near the front of the barn. "Get over here!"

Creeping out of the nearby stall, Miles, confused and terrified, shuffled hesitantly into the center aisle and walked a few steps toward Colwell. He didn't glance at the prisoners.

"There's rope and leather over there." Colwell pointed to some leather straps hanging on a nail nearby. "Get 'em and be quick-or I'll--" Colwell cursed under his breath as the slow moving Miles walked meekly over to a tangle of ropes and straps hanging against the wood-slatted barn wall. "Is this what you want?" he asked, hopefully, taking a handful.

Dutifully, Miles brought back several strips of leather and a length of rope. "Did I do it right?" Miles asked eagerly, setting the leather and rope down at Colwell's boots.

"Yeah, yeah," Colwell offered disgusted. Colwell's eyes slanted across Mile's face. His words had prompted a smile. "Now tie 'em." Colwell saw the confusion on Mile's face. "Damn," he swore under his breath as he saw Miles bend and wrap the rope around the three sets of legs. "Since yer so smart, boy, I'm go'n to ask ya to help me more."

Miles grinned eager as a puppy.

"Get that gun over there!" he pointed to the colt Aaron had dropped. "Get it an' bring it here."

Without hesitation, Miles retrieved the gun, carried it proudly and set it down at Colwell's boots.

"Now the other one, Miles."

Miles quickly retrieved Molly's gun which lay closer to the center and then handed it to Colwell.

"Good boy!" Colwell smirked sarcastically. "Now I have two guns. I'll give ya one, if you do something fer me."

Miles shook his head, agreeing.

"Keep yer gun on the three of them and that mutt. Don't let them move from here. I'm taken' my daughter and checkin' the horses. Remember they killed yer brother. Don't let 'em go."

"Don't let 'em go!" Miles repeated, nodding.

"Good, now you keep that gun on them and if anyone tries to leave, ya kill'em!"

Miles repeated, "If they move, I kin shoot em. Jist like when I go huntin'."

"Yep. Jist like." Colwell started backing up with Peggy pushed in front of him. He was close to the main barn door. "Yer pa will be right proud when he comes fer ya."

Miles grinned, eager to do right. He stood, legs wide apart, and held the colt firmly with both hands, all the while pointing into the stall. He frowned at his three prisoners with a determined stare.

Donald Colwell continued backing away, pushing Peggy. He gripped her arm at her back and warned the others. "Now ya all behave real nice for Miles, Miles don't git riled."

As Colwell and Peggy came to the large barn doors, he ordered her to push the door open.

"I can't," Peggy murmured.

CHAPTER THIRTY-TWO

Colwell moved quickly, pulling Peggy into his hip, like a sack of flour, and with his other hand, shoved the door. It made a scraping sound as it opened to bright morning light. He paused, taking time to adjust his eyes. He squinted at the corral, a few feet away. No one in sight. That was good. He'd have Peggy and be gone before----.

Suddenly, from the loft, ten feet above his head, a volume of loose hay came pouring down. "What the?" Colwell said, stepping back. He glared up and aimed his gun. Momentarily, he dropped Peggy. She fell and rolled out of the doorway.

"KEEEWA KEEEEEWAAAAAKA!" came a cry from above, as White Hawk swooped down, arms outstretched and landed hard on Colwell's shoulders, knocking him down.

Colwell grunted, crumpled to his knees and fell chest down against the dirt floor.

White Hawk tumbled off to the side, quickly scrambled to his feet and reached Colwell's gun.

Colwell's sat up, confused. It was as if he were seeing a ghost. "What the?" He glanced at the door where Peggy stood cowering. "Miles," he shouted words like venom, "Kill the Injin!"

Tarney began barking.

"Kill 'em!" Colwell demanded.

The barking confused Miles. He pointed his gun first at Tarney and then at the Indian. "Back up…move…move ahead!" he ordered everyone, but kept looking about. What would his father do? He wanted to do it the way Lumis would. "Move," he ordered, lowering his voice. His stomach spurted sour heat, his hand shook.

"What should I do, Colwell?" Miles licked his lips, backed out of the stall. He kept his gun on the prisoners, but he couldn't see Colwell. "Where are ya?"

"Back here, near the door, ya idiot!" Colwell shouted, getting to his feet. "The Injin's got my gun! Kill him!"

White Hawk aimed his gun on Colwell and pushed a stunned Peggy out of the light of the doorway and into the shadows of the barn.

Peggy frantically tried to untie the leather strap from around her mouth, but it only grew tighter. She watched in horror as Miles took a step out of the stall and moved in front of his captives, his gun aimed at White Hawk.

Just as Miles was about to fire, Aaron rushed him from behind, tackling his legs.

A surprised Miles careened into the stall before both boys hit the ground. One shot rang out, then a cry of pain.

"Aaron!" Sara screamed, rushing forward to where Aaron and Miles had fallen.

"I'm all right!" Aaron said, rolling off Miles and getting to his feet. He wiped the taste of blood from his lips, as he looked back down at the body. "It was an accident!" Aaron said, stunned. "He fell on his gun." Aaron couldn't quite believe what had happened. He watched as Miles lay twitching, his right arm bent into his body and a slick of blood oozing from under him. Suddenly, the spasms stopped, and his pale gray eyes opened to search the stranger's face. And in a voice no more than a breath, "I did...good...didn't I?"

Sara knelt beside Miles, trying to find a pulse in his neck. Moments later, she looked up and shook her head. "He's dead," she whispered. Sara's eyes filled with tears. "Poor, poor kid. Likely never had a chance to do anything but die."

Aaron frowned at Sara. "Yes, well," he said, his voice clouding with conflicting feelings. "I wouldn't pity him, Sara. He would've killed you."

"I know," Sara agreed, but I don't think he really wanted to. It's so sad." She turned to Peggy. Oh, no! Peggy was bending over, retching and panicking, trying to remove the gag. "Here, let me do it, Peggy! Hold still!"

Finally, Peggy stood still long enough for Sara to remove the gag. Gasping for air, Peggy pointed to where Donald Colwell had been moments ago.

Both White Hawk and Aaron ran to the entrance of the barn. They saw Colwell riding away on a large gray horse.

"He's getting away!" Aaron hollered and glared at White Hawk. "You should have stopped him!" He looked as if he were about to punch White Hawk.

Sara rushed to stand between them. "Stop it, Aaron. Just calm down! It's not White Hawk's fault! He had a gun pointed at him, same as we did."

"He should've used the gun!" Aaron protested.

Molly came forward. "White Hawk was likely afraid he'd shoot you or Peggy." She turned to White Hawk. "Here son, give me the gun."

White Hawk appeared to hesitate.

"Please, White Hawk," Peggy pleaded. "There could be another accident."

White Hawk reluctantly handed Molly the pistol.

Sounds of gunfire and horses riding away echoed nearby.

Molly cautiously glanced outside at the corral. "Colwell's too far away. Likely, the Carey's as well! We'd best stay put till the men come for us."

Peggy's legs suddenly turned liquid-weak and she leaned against a stall, hanging on and taking deep breaths.

Aaron and White Hawk rushed to help.

Aaron reached Peggy first. "I've got her," he said, putting an arm around Peggy. He glared at White Hawk. "Just move out of the way."

White Hawk's chin rose in defiance, but he backed away.

Aaron stood beside Peggy, keeping his arm around her shoulder. "Colwell's gone, he can't hurt you now, Peggy."

Gratefully, Peggy leaned into Aaron's chest, took a jagged breath and let it out slowly.

There were more sounds from outside. Tarney began barking.

"Hush! Hush, ya all!" Molly ordered. She stayed close to the front of the barn. "Someone's come'n. Get out'a sight!" she ordered, stepping to the side.

Just then, Zek appeared at the entrance of the barn. He peered cautiously through the doorway and gingerly rubbed the back of his head. He gave a wide smile when he saw Molly.

"Guess I missed all the action," Zek said, sheepishly.

"What happened to ya?" Molly asked.

"That big ox 'a man hit me with a shovel."

"Mighty happy yer alive." Molly offered. "I'd best take a look at that hard head of yers." She moved to inspect Zek's head. He was shorter than Molly but bent his bald head like a naughty child. "Ya old coot! Ya sure got a bump, big as a stump."

Seconds later, Molly's husband, Jake, bounded through the side barn door. Tarney ran to greet him.

Molly grinned at Jake. "What took ya so long?"

Jake ran to his wife and put his arms around her. "A sight fer sore eyes, ya are, Molly girl!" He beamed, giving her a hearty hug.

Moments later, Tarney dashed forward and jumped up against Cass as he entered the barn. Cass bent to give Tarney a quick pat on the head. "Is everybody all right?" He glanced about in the dim light.

Seeing Cass safe loosened a wave of feeling in Sara. "Cass!" she exclaimed, dashing up to him. Before she thought about it, she flew into his arms. "You're safe!"

Instinctively, Cass held her. "Yes," he said, startled. The feel of Sara against his chest, sent a wallop of emotion smashing through him. He didn't want to let her go.

It was a moment before either of them realized what they had done or where they were.

"Oh--." Sara mumbled, backing out of his embrace. "I'm so glad you're safe." She felt her face flush and saw that Cass's face had reddened as well.

Cass cleared his throat. "Seems, we're all fine!" He frowned and looked about, and then noticed the blanket-covered body lying nearby.

Peggy volunteered, "That's Miles. White Hawk saved our lives." She wanted to give White Hawk credit, for he appeared to linger near the rear of the barn, deliberately keeping his distance. She suspected he felt responsible for letting her stepfather get away.

Sara quickly offered, "Yes, and it was Aaron's brave tackle that saved White Hawk and all of us. He tackled Miles and then Miles fell on his gun, shooting himself."

"Yep, that's how it was," chimed in Molly. "That boy saved us all."

Aaron beamed. "Tarney was a big help, too. She distracted him." Aaron bent down and gave Tarney a grateful hug, then glanced up at Cass. "What happened to the rest of the Careys? How's Orleans? Is he goin' to be all right?"

CHAPTER THIRTY-THREE

"Orleans will be fine. But he'll need to stay here until his leg is better," Cass said, and glanced at Molly and Jake for confirmation.

"What happened to Lumis Carey?" Sara asked.

"I doubt he'll be making trouble for awhile," Cass explained. "Jake shot him in the foot as he rode off. Colwell will likely stay clear, as well. He'd be a fool to hang around here. Seems Lumis wasn't too pleased with Colwell, and blamed him for his son's death." He glanced at Molly and the girls. "I'd appreciate it, Molly, if you took the girls back to the house for a rest. Jake, Aaron and I will see to the burial. Zek and Orleans can stay here and keep watch." He looked at the sky. "It's nearly noon. We might be able to make a few miles on the trail yet."

After the women left, the men stood about deciding where and how to bury Miles Carey.

Jake said, "We'd best get him in the buckboard, haul him out a ways. We'll make a cross out of respect for a young soul gone."

Aaron added, "We could paint a sign to tell his old man that his son's death was an accident, though I doubt he'd believe it."

"Might not be a bad idea, Aaron." Cass agreed.

"Worth a try," Jake agreed. "Might not keep ol man Lumis from seeking revenge, but we'll worry about that later."

Cass turned to Zek. "You'd better stay here for awhile." Rest up. You took quite a hit on your head. I'm afraid the coach might scramble your brains—-what's left of them!"

"Yer right there, Cass. Besides, I'll be right enough to look after Orleans and help Jake and Molly--keep a watch for Lumis Carey." He turned to Aaron. "Think you and Cass can drive the rig till you sign up a new driver?"

Aaron stepped forward. "Don't worry, Cass and I can handle the team."

Sara and Peggy returned to the way station to help clean up the mess and prepare the noon meal. Damage to the way station was not as bad as at first thought, and by noon the clods of missing dirt had been chinked in, the floor swept of debris, but less easy to clear were the memories.

Sara shuddered at the image of Miles being carted away—-a gray blanket covering him. His body might have been anything. But it wasn't just anything. And right now, as she peeled potatoes, he was being laid in the ground. "It's wrong!" She cried, putting down the knife and covering her face. "No! No!" she cried, as other memories assaulted her. She slumped forward, laying her forehead against the table.

"Dear child," Molly said, "you jist stay put. I'll get a cool rag." She rushed to the kitchen sink, dipped a rag into the porcelain basin and came back to Sara. "Here, take this, dear. You've had a mighty big shock. Sure yer fit ta travel?"

Sara sat up, took a deep breath and placed the cloth on her forehead. "Yes, thank you. I'll be better in a few minutes." She saw Peggy's concerned look. "Don't worry, Peggy. I'm fine."

A few minutes later, the terrible images passed, but she was left with one of her headaches. She'd better try to get some rest for she'd be needed later.

Peggy was too restless to sleep or rest. Abruptly getting up from the table, she rushed to the door. "Excuse me, I need some air."

"Well, then. You can take a bowl of stew to White Hawk. He most likely won't come in. But you be careful," Molly suggested. "Zek is in the corral standing guard. But hurry back, young lady." Molly warned as Peggy walked away, bowl in hand.

As Peggy walked towards the corral, she was aware of how sore her body felt and she knew there were probably red marks across her face from where the leather had dug in. She could have been killed—-all of them could have been. They had survived, she reminded herself. Praise God. Yet, a shudder plunged down her back. For how long? Would God protect her next time? In spite of others trying to reassure her, she knew in her heart that Donald Colwell would come after her and her friends. She had put them all in danger. Maybe she should leave them--face Donald on her own. At least that would keep her friends safe. "Please Lord, tell me what to do," she murmured.

Peggy was relieved to see White Hawk standing with in the corral. "I've brought you some food," she said, setting the bowl down on a nearby stool.

White Hawk did not look up. He kept his attention on , gently rubbing handfuls of straw along the pony's brown and white spotted hindquarter.

Peggy stood silently and watched awhile as tossed his neck playfully and then bent to nibble fallen straw on the ground.

Finally, White Hawk turned to face her. "I go!"

"Go? Oh, White Hawk, no!" Peggy cried. "Please don't go…. you're not well, yet. Stay with us a few more days!"

"No! I go, now!" His voice was harsh. He walked through the corral gate and stood next to Peggy. His tone was softer as he looked into her eyes. "I go. You come," he said simply.

His words caught Peggy off guard. "Oh, White Hawk…I….I wish I could," she mumbled, biting down on her lip and avoiding his eyes.

"No! You come with me. My family take care!" Ever so gently, he took his hands and cupped Peggy's face, so that she had to look deep into his eyes, feel his breath upon her skin.

Mesmerized, Peggy's legs grew weak. "I….I can't go. I promised my friends to go to San Francisco. They….they need me!"

Slowly, White Hawk let go of her face. Then he removed the sacred pouch from his neck and carefully placed it over Peggy's head and around her neck. "Keep you safe," he said, stepping back.

"Oh, White Hawk, it's beautiful. I….I don't know what to say…it's so special." Peggy tried not to cry as she fingered the soft leather pouch. "I'll keep it forever."

"Yes," he grinned, "it long time." He turned abruptly, rushed back to WalksThrough, jumped up and rode through the open gate. He did not look back, but raised his arm and fist in the air.

Dazed, Peggy watched her friend ride away. "He's gone," she whispered to herself. She stood numbly watching until the horse and rider were mere specks in the wide landscape.

It seemed a dreamscape. But soon, the harsh sun on her head told her otherwise. Should she have gone with White Hawk, disappeared into the prairie, as well? For a moment, a wild impulse spurred her to say yes. But what did she really feel? Did she want to go? Would that have helped her friends? Would that have stopped her stepfather? No. It would have only involved more people. "White Hawk! Oh, White Hawk, why did you have to leave?" She murmured, shaking her head. He wasn't well. Oh, she would miss him, had never met anyone like him. They seemed to read each other's mind. How strange to think that in such a short time, she'd grown so close. But what did she really feel? She didn't know, except that her chest felt sore as though something had been ripped away.

Peggy held her head. Tears ran down her cheeks. "Oh, why must everyone leave?" she whispered broken-hearted. She noticed the stool and the bowl sitting there. "He left without any food," Peggy murmured, setting the bowl aside. She sat down and put her hands together. "Dear Jesus, please keep White Hawk safe. And keep Sara and Aaron from harm. Please, dear God, help me to go on. Help me, please. Tell me what I should do."

It seemed only a few minutes before Peggy heard Sara calling. She walked back to the way station, to discover that the team had been hitched and everyone was waiting for her.

"White Hawk has gone," Peggy whispered.

Sara saw the forlorn look on Peggy's face and quickly rushed to put her arm about Peggy's shoulder. "He must've been in a hurry to see his family."

"Yes," Peggy murmured.

"Well, he could've said goodbye," Aaron snapped

"Best use the privy, Peggy," Sara gave Peggy a quick squeeze. She ignored Aaron's attitude. "We'll be leaving in a few minutes."

"Oh, yes, of course," Peggy replied. She walked to the outhouse, and was only dimly aware that someone had replaced the ash and straw. After she was through, she found a bucket of fresh water outside, rinsed her hands and face, dried them on a clean flour sack hanging outside on a peg. A little mirror hung on the outside. She glanced at herself. Was that really her? Her hair was wild as a scarecrow; her face showed the red marks. "It doesn't matter," she said, lifting her chin.

Molly stood next to the stagecoach as Peggy came forward. "Here," she said, holding a basket of food. "Take it."

"Thank you so much, everyone," Peggy said, taking the basket and settling inside next to Sara. She glanced out the coach window. "I'll never forget you all." She looked at Orleans, who was leaning on Zek's arm. "Get well soon."

Jake stepped forward, "You take care, young lady. I expect to see you one of these days singing on some fancy stage in San Francisco."

"Yes." Peggy smiled. "Thank you again for everything."

Once the goodbyes had been said, Cass and Aaron took their seats. Aaron gave a loud GEEEEHAAA and the coach and team of six lurched forward. They were off.

Peggy and Sara waved goodbye until the way station was out of sight.

Sara glanced worriedly at Peggy. "Are you alright?"

"Yes," Peggy replied distractedly as she glanced out the window.

"It's only going to get hotter," Sara said. "Fortunately, there's a bit of breeze coming through the windows. This will help." She bent to opened her satchel and took out two small, lace fans. "Here, Peggy."

"Thanks." Peggy nodded, taking the fan and setting it on the seat. "We're so small," she said, her voice soft. "Like a dot of ink on a huge, yellow sheet of parchment."

"Seems so," Sara said thoughtfully. She settled back against the cushions and watched the sun-drenched grass stir beneath a touch of wind. The patterns of gold and russet were so beautiful and ever changing. In the distance, a gathering of high clouds joined to form white ribbons in a blue sky. Close at hand, she heard the rhythmic clip-clop of the horses and felt the surging movement pulse through the coach. How fast they moved, determined as the wind. She reached her arm through the window to catch it.

CHAPTER THIRTY-FOUR

White Hawk followed Donald Colwell for two days. Once he'd gotten close enough to take coup, but the sleeping man stirred. Another time, he'd come near enough to shoot him, but as he took aim, a dark cloud passed across the moon. The shot missed, Colwell rode away shouting, "I'll be back, hunt you down, kill you!" The next day, White hawk followed, but was unable to get close, and Colwell rode into a wagon caravan where he stayed out of sight.

White Hawk knew it was time to return to his village. And as he rode into camp, many children rushed forward, shouting his arrival. His mother, Summer Bird, heard the shouts and came running. When White Hawk saw his mother, he jumped down from Walk Through, clasped his mother in his arms and whirled her about.

"I was so afraid you had been killed. Walking Bear told us what happened." Her teary eyes searched his face as she caught sight of his arm.

"It's healing." White Hawk smiled reassuringly.

Summer Bird said nothing more, but walked arm in arm with her son to their tipi.

His father, Black Coyote, had heard the shouts and came rushing back to his tipi. He could hardly believe his eyes when he saw the wound on White Hawk's arm. "What happened, my son?"

"I will tell you, but first, I need some food."

"Let the boy rest. I'll prepare food," Summer Bird, cautioned her husband.

"Yes! But we must celebrate!" Black Coyote said, motioning for his son to sit. "You shall have a feast!"

His cousin Standing Bear and many others came to see White Hawk that night, and even the next day, while he sat in the family tipi, telling his story and receiving friends. He spoke about Peggy, and the young white brother and sister who saved his life.

It took several days of rest, good food and the comforts of home to revive his strength. On the third evening, he sat in the tipi with his father and Uncle Gray Rain. They had been discussing his skills and readiness to take his place as a man.

"It is time, now," Black Coyote's deep voice clouded with

feeling. His dark, brown eyes searched his son's face as though there might be a question, but then he nodded. "It is time!"

White Hawk knew his father spoke of The Vision Quest. It would be the biggest event of his life, the gift of manhood--his new name, and reveal who he was and what was expected of him. He trembled with excitement and a little fear. He did not want to embarrass his family by failing this test, this honor.

His Father continued, "First, you will enter the Earth Lodge and renew your spirit."

"And then," his uncle, Gray Rain smiled, "you must eat your fill of wholesome food, for you will have three nights and four days to endure the fast."

"I am ready!" White Hawk asserted, a bit more confidently than he felt. But, he reminded himself, I am not a child. I have stood up to a white man, have already endured days without much food. He smiled to himself. He could do this. He was ready.

The next morning, at dawn, he entered the sweat lodge to purify his body. The tipi was already warm with sweet, steamy air. White Hawk took his place next to a circle of steaming rocks. He must continue to pour water over the rocks so that steam filled the tipi, bathing him in pungent mist. Within minutes, he was covered with sweat. He rubbed his body with tuffs of sage. He prayed for strength. Finally, he returned to his tipi for his special feast.

Summer Bird smiled as she presented him with a basket of fresh cooked meat, fish, potatoes, turnips and sweet, red-berry soup.

When he'd finished eating, he thanked his mother and father and announced, "I'm ready." He was growing impatient for the adventure to begin and eager to discover the place that had been prepared for him—-his very own secret place that would challenge him into manhood.

Black Coyote and his Uncle Grey Rain led him from the tipi. His father placed a black cloth over his head. "Do not remove this until I say."

"It smells like WalksThrough," White Hawk said, taking comfort in the scent. He found humor in the fact that they led him by two leather straps, like a horse, only for him, a strap in each hand. Neither his father nor Uncle spoke as they led him along.

It was just as well, White Hawk thought, for he wanted to discover the way through his other senses. But after a couple hours, the trail changed, the air was hot. The ground became rocky as the path turned upward. He stumbled at times. His father and uncle had to help him along, and that annoyed him. He hated being off balance, not being in control. But he said nothing. Sweat poured down his face, stung his eyes. The cloth itched. But he didn't complain.

Finally, they stopped. Black Coyote removed the hood from his son's head and handed him a buffalo robe. "This will keep you warm."

White Hawk looked down. He stood on a narrow rock ledge that jutted out from a cliff. It seemed solid enough, but when he glanced over the edge, he knew with some satisfaction that if he fell, he would fall to his death. Far below, the land looked only vaguely familiar, since he'd never seen it from such an eagle's perch. Good-- a challenge.

Besides giving him a fine new buffalo robe, his father handed him a knife, a small leather pouch of sage and a larger pouch of water and directed him. "Walk along the ledge until you come to an opening. There you will stay. I will come for you on the fourth day."

His father and Uncle left.

White Hawk discovered his seed bed was a disappointing little cave---shallow, only about four feet deep and six feet long, room enough to sit, but not stretch. It was just a dry, dusty place of uneven, hard-packed earth.

White Hawk knelt, took his robe, spread it out and sat facing West, grateful for the rest. He could see the land below, and far, far in the distance hazy mountains. He watched shadows zig-zag cross the land as the sun moved behind him. It would be dark soon. Once the cave darkened, he felt chilled. He wrapped part of the robe about him and sat watching three hawks circling in the sky, and aiming for their evening meal. "My brothers, I too, am hungry. Bring me something to eat." Oh, how he wanted to join the hawks in the easy currents of wind. He imaged he could fly off the ledge and soar in lazy circles above the land. A dangerous thought. If only he could stand up, move about, run. But there was nowhere to go. He felt trapped, like an animal. Angry, he blamed his father. Why couldn't he have found a better place? "Be patient," his inner voice demanded. He sighed. He must expect more of himself. Everything was part of his test and part of his quest. He must resist blaming others, for now he was a man. "It is good--I have a dry, safe place to sleep." However, he thought uneasily, there'd be no fire to keep away animals. No matter, he would hear them, make noise, scare them. And since the cave was hidden from view, a man like Colwell would never find it. Yet sourness rose in his throat as he remembered the man's threats. No, not likely here, White Hawk reminded himself. But a Pawnee---maybe. White Hawk set his knife on the robe beside him.

He tried to stop his legs from twitching. He must learn to stay still as ground. During a hunt, a brave would have to stay still, waiting for hours. He must prove he can do that.

He wondered what his friends and parents were doing. He thought about Peggy. Would he'd ever see her again…probably not. A dark sadness covered him. He thought about his brother. He missed him so much—-so much. Pain fastened across his chest, his heart ached. Once again, he saw his brother's body. "Oh, Great One Above, I am sorry," he cried. "Forgive me, forgive me." Anguish poured from him. His cries echoed from the cave to the sky.

By nightfall, he'd finished crying. He sat watching the stars cover the sky like rippling light on water. Later, he slept. Morning light nudged him awake. He was hungry.

White Hawk remained in his seed chamber for three nights and four days. He sang songs to the Four Corners of the Land. He asked Sweet Medicine for a special spirit song. At night he became afraid and sang many chants for bravery. He had dreams, spoke to his grandfather, who had passed into the spirit world last year. He dedicated his journey to the healing of his Uncle's wife, Stone-At-River, who had fallen ill the day Red Moon, Standing Bear, and he had left camp. He pleaded over and over again for Sweet Medicine or the Great Spirit Above to bring him a vision and reveal the purpose of his quest. Visions of death swirled about him.

Childhood memories tore at him like lizards biting into flesh. He saw his character, his selfishness, his temper, and his childish need to be right. All these were presented to him night and day. He felt the hollow blackness of everything, the unknowing silence. He was afraid--he was terrified. By the third day, he was out of water and his throat ached. His stomach cramped. He floated in darkness. Images of animals whirled about him. He became a wounded buffalo, a baby in his mother's womb, and a grain of sand. He slept.

On the eve of the third day, White Hawk felt warmth surround and pass through him, as if a beam of sunlight found its way into the cave. A moment later, a vision came--a giant, eagle feather lay atop an ancient tree. At its roots were the bodies and blood of many men. The spirit of the Eagle Feather spoke to him. "White Hawk know that in the time to come there will be a great war. The ground and the tree will seem to die. But it will not die. Then there will come a time when the Great Nations of your people will give new life to the tree and show the way of peace for all mankind. The Great Nations will teach others to live in harmony and wisdom. Many tribes will gather to honor the earth wisdom of your ancestors and the unity of the tree. They will show the ways of wisdom and healing. Many new teachers and healers will sit at the root of the Tree, listen to its voice and learn. White Hawk, you will be the first generation, a reminder of things to come. Do not walk with your head down, be patient. Know that there will be ten generations before the time of earth wisdom when all will be reborn through the knowledge of ancestral ways and hear the voice of The Tree. One day, men of many colors will have visions of The Tree of Life and hear its voice."

The vision spoke to him in a voice deep within his own spirit. "White Hawk, your name shall be Eagle Feather in Tree. You will walk with gentle spirit and follow the path of right action, respect all men, and become a maker of peace, even in your generation."

On the morning of the fourth day, Eagle Feather in Tree awoke to hear his Father and Uncle calling. White Hawk crawled from the cave, pulling his buffalo robe behind him. At last, he stood on the rocky ground above the cave. Before greeting his father or uncle, he stretched his arms high, giving thanks to The Great Spirit above, then ran about like a chicken, jumping up and down and racing about. Finally, he accepted Gray Rain's gift, a fresh pouch of water and a handful of berries.

They returned to the village. Several days of storytelling, singing, dancing and feasting were given to honor Eagle Feather in Tree. Even the young chief, Black Kettle, came to honor him and his family.

CHAPTER THIRTY-FIVE

During the week, Cass stopped to rest and gather information at way stations, military posts, as well as wagon trains. Folks were curious about the new coach and often begged for passage. Finally, after turning down a flirtatious, young bride who wanted to escape her "worthless" new husband, Cass decided not to stop at any more wagon trains. Important road conditions and news could be gained at the way stations, at forts or from riders returning from the West.

By the beginning of the second week, Cass hired a new driver, Danny. He didn't appear much older than Aaron, Sara thought, but Danny admitted with a grin that he was passing twenty-five, and was a married man with two children. Though shorter than Aaron, he could handle a team better than men twice his size. His red hair hung down in uneven lava-like layers, and his face had a fan-shaped mass of freckles across his nose. He'd had experience riding for the Pony Express for two months last year, and more recently for the Overland. He signed on till Salt Lake. And that meant that some of the time Aaron or Cass could ride in the stagecoach.

Sara really looked forward to those few hours with Cass. At first, her attraction to him left her tongue-tied, especially when she remembered how he'd held her close at the way station. She knew they'd both felt something. But he'd not said anything and had remained a perfect gentleman. Sometimes, she caught him looking at her, and it unnerved her when their eyes met, or when she stood close to him. But more and more, she'd been feeling guilty. Hadn't she made promises to Mark? But, she countered, she hadn't exactly promised to marry him. Not so fast, her conscience rebuked. You have promised to settle things with Mark. You're not free. Sara sighed. Where would all this lead. At the moment, it was muddling her brain—distracting her, like a silly school girl. No! She'd keep a tight rein on herself--keep her wits about her. After all, she barely knew the man. And…there was still a long way to go. The important thing was getting to San Francisco on time for the court date and helping Uncle Jacob and Clara. Anything else was foolishness.

Her discomfort eased a little when she realized that Cass was deliberately trying to make her blush. She wasn't about to let him get the better of her. She'd give it back to him. This morning, he'd winked at her. Instead of turning away, she'd spoken up. "Why, Mr. Bartlett, I believe you're flirting with me."

His answer was a pitiful sigh, "I just can't seem to help myself!"

Sara shook her finger and slanted her eyes, "I've been warned about the likes of you, Mr. Bartlett."

"I'm delighted and crushed!" he said, offering a wolfish grin. Before long, his teasing, easy manner put Sara at ease, especially when he told her amusing stories about his travels last year in England and France. And she didn't mind when he deliberately drew her out, asking about her and Aaron's early years in Boston, and their more recent move to Omaha, Nebraska. Usually, thinking about her parents was too painful. But talking with Cass seemed to help. Getting to know Cass and learning about the death of his own mother, made Sara feel less alone.

As the days passed, Sara began to be more comfortable around Cass and looked forward to those rare moments in the coach together. Sometimes they'd share stories. Sara told him about attending the theatre in Boston and her education at Mrs. Waverly's School for Young Women. She talked about her time in Omaha working with her father in Mr. Morgan's Hardware store. She confided her hopes that she could try some of her ideas in her family's store in San Francisco. She hoped, as well, Aaron could receive more education.

Just as often, she and Cass would lapse into comfortable silence. Much of the time, Cass needed to catch up on sleep. Sara enjoyed watching him stretch out his long legs, and lean against the side of the coach. She marveled at how he could fall into a soundless, deep sleep, even as the coach bobbed and weaved like a basket on a donkey.

Stopping for the night at way stations offered relief from being cooped up and tossed about all day. There were always interesting folks to meet and stories to share. When they joined in evening festivities at forts and campgrounds, Peggy volunteered to lead the singing, and as the days passed, her confidence grew. It was wonderful to see. Sara thought her friend was amazing. Besides her talent, Peggy was a fun person to be around. In spite of everything that happened to her, Peggy was positive and helpful. Whenever they stopped long enough, and there was light, Peggy would pick up the Bible and read. Sometimes she read aloud. It was interesting, Sara thought, that the verses seemed to say something that had been on her mind. It was a pleasant coincident. Sometimes she wished she had Peggy's unwavering faith, but she didn't. What she did have was her purpose, her promise. Maybe that was all she'd ever have. It was enough for now.

No one mentioned Donald Colwell, though he remained a presence on their minds, and continued to give Peggy nightmares. It was hard for Sara, as well, to block out painful images. She had her own sleepless nights.

If there were a danger from Indians, Cass never mentioned it or let on he was worried. None stopped them. But whenever they saw small groups of Indians in the distance, everyone wondered if it could be White Hawk. Peggy worried about White Hawk. "He'll be fine," Sara reminded her. "White Hawk knows how to survive on the prairie better than we do." And thanks to Cass, they were surviving, as well. That knowledge was a wall against darkness.

Amazingly, Sara hadn't had one of her "spells" all week, and she began to feel more hopeful about getting free of them. The only concern now was for Uncle Jacob's health. Hopefully, there would be a letter waiting for them in Salt Lake, telling about his condition.

She'd write letters to the Davis family, tell them about her and Aaron's good fortune. They'd be so happy and relieved. She wondered how Mr. Davis was doing—-was he healing as expected? And Mark--maybe, by now, he'd understand, but she doubted it. His dream of marrying her was part of his hope for the future. That kind of hope, she knew, was something to cling to in hard times. Had that been on her mind? No! She'd been more self-serving, her conscience argued. But, she countered, had she even known her true feelings at the time? She had, of course, in some part of her. But she'd been a coward. It was too painful to be honest—-to say goodbye forever, to her dear friend. And now? Oh, she sighed, she couldn't think. It was too tiring, confusing. Once they got to San Francisco, it would sort out.

"Looks like a storm ahead," Aaron frowned, pointing to low hanging, purple-black clouds to the west. They'd appeared suddenly, he thought, taking a spy glass from under the seat of the driver's bench. They're coming this way and moving fast."

The prairie was a wide expanse, with no apparent shelter. "Could hit us head-on, likely less than a half hour," Aaron said. "Do you want Danny to take my place?"

"No, you're just as able," Cass said. He glanced down at the map he kept close at hand. "I figure it's no more than five miles to Junction City and there's a stable there. Let's try for it."

Before long, Cass realized they weren't going to outrun the storm. "We'd better stop; get out the India tarp. It's in the boot. I'll try to keep the team steady. But hurry."

Once they reined in the team, Aaron quickly climbed down and ran toward the rear of the coach. "Come on, Danny," he yelled into the coach window. "Hurry!" he shouted as a sharp gust of wind knocked his hat off. He grabbed it back and quickly unstrapped the covering of the boot. "Here, take this sheet to the girls. They can fasten it across the windows inside."

Once India tarps covered the coach inside and out, Danny insisted on taking his place in the driver's set to help Cass with the horses. The team charged ahead, racing against the worst of the storm to come.

Sara, Aaron and Peggy sat huddled together, listening to the wind swirl around them. India sheeting flapped against the wooden sides of the coach like a million bats demanding entry. Sara kept reminding herself that it was only the dreadful sound that made it so frightening.

It grew dark.

Peggy shouted, "It's like being in a cocoon, isn't it? I wonder how a butterfly feels just before it emerges."

"Probably can't wait to get out." Aaron said, hunching down in the seat under a blanket. Tarney sat on the floor. "Don't worry. It's just a little old storm." He covered Tarney with his blanket. Inside the coach there were no clues as to how fast they were moving, but they could sense it as the coach lurched and swayed over uneven ground.

"It's exciting." Aaron grinned as Peggy fell against him.

"No, it's not! It's dangerous." Sara snapped, alarmed. She imagined that at any moment they would overturn.

Thunder roared, streaks of light flashed all around. Shouts from Cass and Danny were drowned out, but a quick turn in direction told the passengers that something was happening.

Within minutes, huge sheets of water rolled across the prairie. Wind struck with terrible force. Rain pummeled the stagecoach. The India tarps loosened, part of the window cover tore away. Rain slanted inside.

Finally the coach slowed.

"We're stopping. Get ready," Aaron warned, poking his head out the window. The coach finally stopped. Aaron quickly opened the door. He heard Cass urging, "Come on!"

Danny and Cass were each leading three horses toward the side of a little hill. "Come on, Peggy, Sara." Aaron grabbed Peggy's hand. "We'll make a run for it."

Huddling under lap blankets, the girls trudged after Aaron as he led them towards a mound-like hill with an opening. Once inside, they learned the cave-like place was really an abandoned sod house.

Aaron couldn't see very far inside, but held tight to Peggy's hand. "Keep your head low," he instructed, having just bumped his against the dirt ceiling. He heard Cass and Danny trying to calm the team. Fortunately, the racket outside was blunted by layers of sod above them. He watched as Cass untied an oil lantern from his belt and lit it.

"Better stay back against the walls," Aaron warned, "away from the horses." Aaron worried that if anyone moved three feet closer to the team, they could easily get crushed or stomped on. The horses were fretful and kept moving about. He hoped there was enough room. Finally, he saw that the space was larger than at first thought—-maybe thirty by fifteen. There were small piles of dirt around the floor where the walls and ceiling had come down. Several charred places on the floor suggested cooking fires. He wondered what stories these walls could tell—-spooky stories, he imaged, as the lantern light threw giant, eerie horse shadows about. Strewn around were bits and pieces of wood that had once been furniture--a stool with one leg, part of a bench, and in the corner, a charred book. Someone knew how to read. Aaron wondered why the occupants had moved. Had they gone on to a better life?

Before long, the storm passed, the wind subsided, and the horses were once again put in their traces and moving at a determined pace. It was slower going, now. Muddy patches along the trail worked against the coach's wheels. And in places, the land looked as though a giant hand had pressed it flat. But they were moving, toward their destination. It had been exciting and scary, all at the same time, Aaron thought. He'd felt more grown up, especially when he took Peggy's hand. He'd wanted to protect her, knew she trusted him, relied on him. It was a good feeling.

An hour later, Cass announced they were approaching Fort

Riley. "We'll stop to change horses, stretch our legs and dry off. But I want to try to make Junction City for the night."

A late afternoon sun appeared, and brought a rainbow across the eastern sky. It was a welcome sight and Sara allowed it to be a symbol. The sun had been obscured by the storm, for a time, but it was still there, and was now making a lovely huge rainbow across the sky.

So much had changed in their lives. She and Aaron had lived through the worst of things: the death of their parents, cholera, Peggy's near drowning, Donald Colwell, the Carey clan and a terrible storm. Yet there was something pulling them forward. And suddenly, in spite of her damp clothes and frizzy hair, she felt hopeful.

She smiled and took a deep breath. They had done the right thing, leaving the wagon train. And in a few more weeks, she'd be in San Francisco. And she would keep her promise. Nothing was going to stop her. Nothing!

CHAPTER THIRTY-SIX

After stopping in Junction City for the night, drying their clothes and having a hot bath, they left refreshed and eager to make up the lost time.

During the next ten days, the many way stations became a tedious blur of smelly little houses, with hard, lumpy beds and poor food. The days were long and hot. It became difficult to keep a positive attitude, though Sara tried. She kept reminding herself that the stagecoach was the fastest and best way to San Francisco. She missed not having time with Cass in the coach, or even in the evening. He was either busy managing the team, or gathering information about the road, and spent a great deal of time going over his maps, making notes. He said the stagecoach line needed as much detail as possible. In the evening, by the time the horses were fed and bedded down for the night, it was too late for much visiting. Sara knew Cass always made an effort to ask everyone how they were, but it was clear, he was tired and merely being civil. She began to wonder if he was deliberately keeping his distance from her.

The landscape slowly began to change as a great plateau rose toward the west.

More and more wagons and folks walking with carts or riding on horses filled the trail. And as a result, the road to Denver was littered with debris of all kinds. There were splintered wheel parts, chairs, split barrels and all kinds of furniture. Old wagon parts lay abandoned next to the bones of oxen or horses. And graves--some so small, Sara knew they were for children. She fought back the urge to cry, fearing that once started, she'd be unable to stop.

Aaron glanced pensively out of the coach window. "Soon we'll be deep in the mountains, Peggy. You'll like that. Cass said there are forests with huge trees, fresh streams you can swim in and great places to camp. We'll have plenty of good water and grazing for the horses, too."

"I wonder what Denver is like," Peggy said, picking up Aaron's enthusiasm. "I can hardly wait to see it. Is it close to the mountains?"

"Cass said no. Denver's on a big open plain with mountains to the west. We'll be there in a few days. He says Denver's a regular little village with about 150 cabins and several new, two-story wood houses. One was built as a way station. About two years ago, they had a gold strike at the confluence of Cherry Creek and the South Platte. We'll go right by there. Maybe even pan for gold."

"I doubt Cass will take the time," Sara said, sounding a little disappointed.

"Right," Aaron agreed. "Probably, not much left, anyway." "Cass says the news of gold brought a lot of folks, but most went back empty handed. But now, there's a new strike in Colorado City, a little farther to the west." Aaron looked pensively out the window. "I bet Rufus would've wanted to go—if he was well." Aaron's voice clouded for a moment. He cleared his throat and added. "I bet he'd agree with Cass that Denver will become a big city because it's one of the last places to get supplies to cross over the mountains."

Several days later, they stopped to camp along Cherry Creek. A beautiful spot, Sara thought. You could see the mountains rising in the far off distance, with white surfaces sparkling in the morning sunshine.

"We'll rest the team and have our noon meal here." Cass nodded, looking about and noting small groups of people gathering along the River's banks. The atmosphere was friendly and hopeful.

They were higher now--the air thinner, and when Sara stepped out of the coach, she suddenly felt woozy and clung to the door a moment.

"Are you alright, Sara? Aaron asked concerned. "Cass says the altitude takes getting used to."

"I guess so," she smiled, taking a deep breath and letting it out slowly. "But the air smells so fresh and sweet."

Aaron frowned. "I'm queasy, too." He held the door open for Peggy. How are you, Peggy?"

"A little light-headed," she admitted.

"Come on, lean on me," he said, giving Peggy his arm, and leading her to where Cass and Danny were setting a blanket on the grassy bank of the river. A picnic basket waited with hardboiled eggs, pickles, apples, and sausage.

Sara, Peggy and Aaron sat down on the blanket and began reaching for food. Sara rolled her shoulders and stretched her arms. It felt good to be able to move freely. She thought that sometimes it was easier to travel with the prairie schooner than the stagecoach. At least in the schooner, she could walk miles every day, not always cooped up and have the dust flying everywhere. "Will we have a bath tonight?"

"I expect so," Cass said. "It's a real two story house, brand new, as I recall coming through last year."

Sara was surprised to hear that Cass had been through the area before. But of course, she reminded herself, he arranged the way stations for the stagecoach line." Did you go all the way to San Francisco?"

"No," he answered, "Just to Salt Lake City." He was busy making sketches in a tablet, but looked up and smiled.

"Oh," she said, once again, feeling the sudden effect of his very blue eyes. She couldn't look away, for a much too long moment, and felt her face flush. Her cheeks must look red as cherries, she thought, and stumbled over words. "I......I...it must surely be nice." She felt lightheaded and flustered.

"Salt Lake?" he asked innocently, but gave a sly grin.

"You are a tease, Cass Bartlett," she said, "but it'll cost you an egg." Sara grabbed a hard-boiled egg just as Cass was about to.

Aaron said, "I hear Salt Lake is a pretty big city."

"Yes," and getting bigger," Cass grinned, his eyes on Sara.

Aaron glanced at Peggy. "The Mormons built it. They can have many wives, and of course, many kids," he said coloring.

"Yep. Very industrious," Cass said.

Danny was eager to join in the conversation. "Some men have thirty or more wives."

"Do you? I mean, are you a Mormon?" Aaron asked.

"No, but I know quite a few. Good folks if you're fair."

"You must be eager to get home," Sara said cheerfully, bluntly ignoring Cass.

"More than eager," I expect, Cass chimed in, grinning.

"Yer right there. Been gone over a month. My wife and babes will be waiting. Guess I'll just have to be patient a couple more weeks."

The hotel in Denver was a real two-story house, with an upstairs that provided four rooms for sleeping, and two spacious, down the hall, bathrooms——one for men and one for women. Most unusual, Sara thought. The food was delicious and soon after supper, she and Peggy headed for a welcomed bath, and a good bed.

The next morning, at the livery, Cass was approached by several folks who offered to pay for passage——some begged to be taken to

Salt Lake City. But Cass refused everyone. He had several reasons, but he hadn't told his young passengers, the main one. And now, as he and Danny went about hitching up the team, his conscience demanded more. He'd better think about the consequences of his impulsive choice. Should he tell them? Would they be safer, if they knew? They'd already been through enough—-were still on edge. Donald Colwell was one thing, but they could be in more danger if they were considered accessories. At Fort Riley, he'd been warned that Southern sympathizers and spies were on the trail, hunting the same information. Some of these men, privateers, sold information to the highest bidder, and would do anything to get their hands on his dispatches and portfolio.

So far, all his sketching and note taking hadn't raised any questions. The youngsters were convinced his only purpose was to scout locations for future way stations—-which was partially true." Cass thrust his fingers through his hair. Damn! He should've thought it through. It didn't feel right, deceiving them, and it was bothering him, more and more. Early on, he'd wanted to help them get away from Colwell. But, his conscience reminded him, he'd readily taken advantage. He'd known they'd be a good cover, but.... Cass bit down on his lip. He'd made them accomplices. Wonder what Sara would say. Cass cringed. Maybe they'd be better off catching the Overland Stage in Salt Lake. He'd think about that.

CHAPTER THIRTY-SEVEN

Later in the week they entered the foothills of the Front Mountains. The air was hot during the day, but cold and windy at night. They could see snow on some peaks up ahead, deeper into the rugged mountains. Most nights they camped outside, usually near a stream or river.

"There's a cabin of sorts up head," Cass announced. "We'll have shelter for the night, at least."

As they approached the small log house, there was no sign of anyone. The house appeared to have been closed up for some time, as the wood shutters were closed over the two front windows and a stained note was nailed to the door. It read: "Gone for Gold."

"The Howards are gone, it seems." Cass frowned and looked down at the ground. "We can't get horses for another twenty or thirty miles, so we'll have to stay over and rest the team. We'll lose a day." He looked very disappointed.

"It's just as well," Sara said, trying to put the best face on it. "The altitude is making everyone tired. I know the horses must feel it worse, since they work so hard. I hear a stream close by. Maybe, I could take time to wash some clothes."

"Probably a good idea," Cass nodded. "But be careful." He smiled. "I wouldn't want to have to wrestle a bear for you."

The image made Sara smile and she felt her face flush. However light-hearted it sounded, she knew there could be some truth to a bear problem. She'd definitely be careful.

After peering inside the cabin, Sara found two beds, a two burner, pot-bellied stove, and a Dutch oven. "This is wonderful!" she exclaimed. "I'll heat water for sponge-baths for everyone and make a hot meal." She turned to Peggy who'd just walked in. "Did you see any wood about?"

"Yes, I saw a whole stack of wood and there's even dry kindling under a tarp at the side of the house."

The girls eagerly set about their chores.

Once the horses had been taken care of, Cass returned to the cabin. "You girls can have the beds. It'll be safer than sleeping in the tents."

"Thanks Cass. Sleeping inside has been suggested." She pointed to a note nailed on the wall near the stove: "Watch yer behin' fer bears, mountain lions, skunks, 'n udder critters."

"He probably wasn't joking," Cass said, raising his eyebrows. We'll build a good campfire, and maybe they'll decide not to join us for a night cap."

Finally, after airing out the cabin, sweeping the floor, and preparing the evening meal of beans, rice and bacon, the day drew to a close. The sun went down early in the mountains and the air cooled quickly. The weary men said their goodnights and expressed gratitude for the luxury of two buckets of hot water and a bowl to wash. They soon bedded down in the tent, near a small campfire. Once the men had retired, Sara and Peggy lit the oil lamp and enjoyed their own sponge bath near the stove.

"That little stove should throw off enough heat to keep us cozy," Sara said, pulling her long flannel nightshirt over her head. "I guess Danny and Aaron are taking first watch." She hoped the campfire was big enough to keep away wild animals. Of course, Tarney would warn them.

"Well, goodnight everyone," Sara said, ducking her head out the cabin door. She was surprised to see Cass approaching.

"May I talk to you a minute, Sara?"

"Oh, of course," she said. "Just a moment." She turned, rushed inside and grabbed the quilt off her bed, and quickly wrapping it about herself, she whispered to Peggy who was already in bed, "I'll only be a moment." She gave a happy little wave as she quietly closed the door and followed Cass.

"Are you going to be warm enough, Sara?" Cass asked, realizing that she was only a little better than half-dressed.

"I'm fine." She assured. "The quilt's plenty warm."

Cass pointed to a fallen log. "Let's sit over there."

Sara's mood plummeted at the sound of his voice and the look on his face. He was upset. The air about her suddenly chilled, and she pulled the quilt closer. Had she done something wrong? Maybe he was just tired. The altitude did that. He must be worried, what with the delay and all. Probably tense. Maybe she could get him to relax.

It was a lovely evening. The sky was a plum color, just turning to indigo. A few clouds drifted across a full moon, which appeared ever so close. There was plenty of moonlight edging the trees and the nearby stream gurgled merrily along. Now and then, an owl hooted.

"My, the moon appears close." Sara said, suddenly feeling stupid. What an obvious thing to say. But she continued, "I feel as though I could reach up and grab a handful of stars, don't you?" She saw Cass looking down at the steam which sparkled in moon light. He looked thoughtful and didn't appear to have heard her.

Sara stood gazing at the water, clutching the blanket tighter. "It's so quiet, except for the stream, and the wind through the trees." She waited for his response. "Nature has its own music, don't you think, Cass?"Why wasn't he talking? Oh, how she so hoped Cass was not angry with her. She just wanted to sit by the stream and enjoy this time alone with him. They'd had so little--just the two of them.

She watched Cass take a hanky from his trouser and wipe a place on the log. He suddenly grinned and made a sweeping gesture. "For you, my lady."

Grateful for a moment of lightness, Sara sat down, settling the blanket about her legs.

"It's a lovely evening," she tried again.

"Yes, it is," Cass agreed, his voice soft. He cleared his throat. "I...I...need to talk to you about something, Sara. I...I haven't been entirely forthcoming--that is... honest with you." He paused, looking down at his hands.

Sara took a deep breath, hoping Cass's hesitancy wasn't bad news. The very nearness of him set her heart racing. "What do you want to tell me?"

This shouldn't be so difficult, Cass thought, feeling his stomach muscles clench. After all, this was Sara. She'd understand, wouldn't she? She looked so young, so trusting--innocent--like some mythical forest creature in the moon light. Moon light brushed across her face and fanned around her hair. That face, those eyes, darkening--pulling him in. He jerked back. "Mosquito," he slapped his wrist. What was he thinking? In another moment he would've kissed her.

Cass shifted his feet, and began again, his heart pounding. "I...I." He looked away. How could he tell her that he had deceived her? She'd hate him. He didn't want that. But, worse, his deception would shatter her trust, break her heart. She was already raw with grief, and he knew she hadn't allowed herself to express it. Poor kid was working hard just to carry on. No, he couldn't add to her grief.

He couldn't hurt her. Yes, he realized he'd been wrong, not telling her about his mission—-not giving them a choice. He knew how important that was for Sara. But now—-no, he'd only worry her. Besides, he countered, he <u>was</u> getting them to San Francisco. That's what they wanted. Maybe that was all she needed to know, for now. Later, he assured himself, with just the slightest prick of conscience, he'd tell her what he'd done. Hopefully, once they were safe in San Francisco, she'd forgive him. She would, wouldn't she?

"You seem upset." Sara took a breath. "Is it something I've done?"

"Oh, no! You've been great. I just wondered if….if you'd …gotten enough to eat…and…and if the bed is…is…OK?"

"Fine. Thanks for asking," she murmured softly, shifting a little closer to him on the log.

Impulsively, Cass jumped off, and expended his hand to help her off.

Sara, suddenly dizzy, stumbled slightly and found herself against Cass's warm chest, his arms encircling her.

Neither of them moved. And before she could think, he was bending down, his lips pressing hers. She sighed and kissed him back. It was the most natural thing in the world, like breathing in sweetness.

Cass pulled away. "I…I…shouldn't have done that. I…I don't know what came over me. I apologize."

"Apologize? Oh, I see," Sara said, turning away. "It's easily explained. I mean, with us being so high up--near the stars and--all that moon light--makes a person dizzy." She turned and rushed for the cabin. Her back was straight as a tree, but her lips remained supple and warm, her whole body trembling.

Nothing more was mentioned about "the kiss," though Sara smiled to herself as, now and then, she'd bring the memory to her lips, like a pressed rose in a diary.

The next two weeks tested everyone's courage and endurance as they traveled deep into the Rocky Mountains. Surrounded by endless mountain peaks as far as the eye could see, the trail wound up majestic heights of over eleven thousand feet and descended into deep canyons. At times fog shrouded the narrow trail, and they were forced to wait till the mist lifted.

The trail snaked around rocky cliffs with drop-offs plunging thousands of feet. A misstep meant certain death.

In the higher elevations, they camped in treeless meadows, near snow covered rocks. Firewood was scarce, but traces of summer grass remained.

The thin air conspired against them. Exhausted by early afternoon, they made camp most days by two o'clock. The heat of the day gave way to cold nights, and at lower elevations they were plagued by swarms of insects.

They crossed Blue River, and then the Continental Divide--a cause for celebration.

There were still many more mountains to cross before they'd reach California. It was taking longer than expected because several way stations had been abandoned, which meant fewer team changes and fewer creature comforts. They had to wait and rest weary teams, and often only two horses were provided.

Cass reassured Sara and Aaron that they'd arrive in time for the court date. Though relieved, Sara couldn't stop worrying about Uncle Jacob, and Clara. Was Uncle Jacob worse? Hopefully, there'd be news waiting for them in Salt Lake. That was still days away. She'd have to be patient.

When they arrived in Salt Lake, their first stop was the postal office. Unfortunately, the hoped for news from Uncle Jacob had not arrived, nor was there word from the Davis Family. That part was expected, Sara thought, as they wouldn't have made it that far. Still, it was disappointing. But she and Aaron would be in Sacramento in a week or so, Sara reminded herself. She'd look forward to that. Maybe she could buy a new dress. After all, she didn't want to arrive in San Francisco looking so hapless. All her dresses were road-worn and faded. A new dress was just the notion to give her thoughts a boost. She must look a fright. Her hands were like leather, her nails all jagged and her hair felt more like a crow's nest. Whatever must Cass think? Maybe he wouldn't want to be seen with such a motley bunch. Could that be the reason he'd become sort of distant? Or maybe she'd said or done something. The more she thought about, the more she realized it had started shortly after "the kiss." Had he been embarrassed? Maybe, he thinks I'm too forward. After all, I did kiss him back.

The thought struck like a mule kick and plunged Sara into a dreadful whirl of feeling. She sat up in the narrow little bed and leaned on her elbow. Had he been deliberately avoiding her? Good

Heavens! Had she pushed Cass away? "Oh, no!"

Peggy rolled over half asleep. "What's wrong?"

"Oh, Peggy, I don't think Cass likes me anymore."

"Nonsense. I see the way he looks at you."

"That might not mean anything...except--."

"Well, I'm sure he likes you. Now get some sleep, Sara. It's too cold to stay awake." Peggy scrunched under the covers.

The next morning, after breaking fast, Cass approached Sara as she washed dishes in a small barrel outside the tent. "It's a nice morning, isn't it, Sara." He smiled down at her. "Thanks for doing so many chores for us."

"I'm more than happy to help out."

"Well, I just want to thank you for being so patient these last weeks, especially. I know I've been a little edgy and preoccupied. I've had a few things on my mind, but I want you to know that I think you're terrific, how you put up with the dirt and heat, never complain. It can't be easy, especially for a girl."

'A girl?' The words tore at Sara's heart. She winced. How old did he think she was? Really! She'd be eighteen in a month. But all she said was, "Thank you, Cass." Raising her chin defiantly, she added, "I think you've been more than patient and kind, yourself, considering your advanced age!" She winked and quickly dashed away. Five minutes later, it occurred to her that Cass Bartlett was conveniently trying to put her into a safe place in his mind. A girl? Well, we'll see about that!

CHAPTER THIRTY-EIGHT

They'd crossed a forty-mile desert, days of being covered in biting dust. Swirls and little columns of stinging sand rose against the stagecoach, rough as sandpaper. They wore kerchiefs over their nose and prayed the horses would endure. And then, more mountains—-the great Sierras.

"It feels like we'll never get out of mountains," Sara sighed, looking out the coach window. Another week along the trail had brought them into California, but still in mountains, the endless mountains. Somehow she had expected California to be different, magical or something, but every day was more a blur of the same heat and stomach jarring trails. And while much of the scenery was beautiful, she'd been unable to appreciate it the way she thought she should. Sleepless nights worrying about Uncle Jacob and a growing uneasiness with Cass had left her edgy and restless. Even now, with Cass sitting beside her, she knew he'd pulled away, raised an invisible wall between them. Maybe it was just as well. She felt too raw, too vulnerable to challenge anyone, let alone her own feelings. Peggy suggested she confide her feelings to God. It seemed a sacrilege, considering her doubts. But she realized she didn't feel quite so angry at God. Something inside her had changed. Perhaps talking about her feelings, confessing the doubts would be helpful. She began to feel a little easing in her spirit, but there were times when it was all she could do to keep her impatience from infecting everyone else.

Within a few miles of Grass Valley, Sara noticed a disturbing change in the land. A huge area of forest had been cut down. Only a few thin trees struggled against a nearly barren landscape.

"What happened?" Sara frowned, turning to Cass.

"Mining," Cass explained. "They've been cutting trees for over ten years in these parts, some for the mines and some for timber."

Peggy looked out her side of the coach window. "Where do the animals go? So many must have lost their homes."

Tarney was curious as well and hung her little face out the window, sniffing the air.

"There's still a lot of forest left." Aaron volunteered.

Sara shook her head. "It will grow back, though."

Cass answered, soberly. "It takes hundreds of years for some kinds of trees. Sometimes the scrub trees take over, and it'll never be the same. Folks talk about replanting."

"Can you replant a whole forest?" Sara wondered.

"Not really. You can replant some trees, but a forest grows naturally, it has different trees, different layers and each with its own set of animals."

Sara hadn't expected to see ruined land in California, and the unhappy sight was the first stain on her picture-book dreams.

It was near dusk when the stagecoach entered the little town and drew up to the main street. Grey weathered, wood storefronts stood quiet and pale in the evening light. Here and there a little breeze pushed against aging signs and churned eddies of dust along the near deserted buildings.

Two men stood talking near the entrance of Ben's Barber Shop, and they turned to stare at the stagecoach.

"Why is it so quiet?" Aaron asked.

"Most mining towns fell on hard times after the 50's."

Sara watched as a few merchants came out of their shops to stare at the strangers in the new stagecoach. Several women walked out of a tavern next to the hotel and waved in a friendly manner when they spotted Cass and Aaron getting out of the coach.

Tarney barked excitedly as Cass tipped his hat and smiled back at the strangers. He winked at Aaron. "I said it was a friendly town."

The coach drew up near the entrance to a two story, gray building with a large wooden sign over its entrance: Grass Valley Inn.

"Is it always like this?" Peggy asked.

"No." Cass grinned. "The town comes alive in the evening."

Sara watched several middle-aged women carry heavy packages of groceries down the dirt street. "They look so very tired," Sara said, more to herself.

Cass nodded. "I expect they are. Many women take in boarders, mostly miners, to help support the family. Mining's slowed and the drought makes it hard on the farmers. There's less work and money to pay for the fundamentals." Cass noticed the disappointment on Sara's face as he opened the door of the stagecoach and stepped out. He offered his hand to help Sara down the two steps to the street. Tarney jumped down first and sat wagging her tail, watching Cass and Sara.

"Thank you," Sara mumbled, stepping down. "Oh," she said, startled by her swift reaction to Cass's touch. A flash of warmth had spiked through their hands. It was most unsettling. Did Cass feel it? Sara knew her face had probably flushed red. "Come on Tarney," Sara insisted, marching up to the hotel.

If Cass felt anything at all, Sara couldn't tell.

"Don't worry, Sara," Cass said, rather business like. "This town knows how to survive. They're going into deep quartz mining and there'll be a boom again, according to the newspapers. I may even invest." Cass smiled as he led everyone through the hotel's large swinging doors. "You'll be comfortable here," he said, taking the luggage from Tom, the driver Cass hired in Salt Lake.

Tom looked red-faced and flustered as he confided to Cass, "If you don't need me, I'll leave ya for the night. I've got a coupl'a friends here, I'm wantin' to meet."

"Go ahead, Tom," Cass nodded his understanding. "We'll see you first thing in the morning." Cass took the luggage and placed it next to the registration counter.

"At daylight, then," Tom said, rather stiffly and bowed to the ladies. "Have a nice evening, Miss Robbins, Miss O'Neil, Aaron."

Before long, Cass had managed to obtain two hotel suites, one with its very own bathtub.

"You girls might as well relax and get a good night's sleep. Aaron and I can use the bath down the hall. We'll take the coach and horses down to the livery before supper. Might take an hour or so, but if you're hungry, don't wait for us. Just go ahead and order what you want. They'll put it on my bill." He stooped down to pet Tarney. "She's the spunkiest little dog I ever did see." He beamed at Sara. "Go ahead and order her a steak on me."

Cass's generosity made Sara uncomfortable. "She'll have some of my supper," Sara said, ignoring Aaron's scowl. It was too bad if Aaron didn't understand. He should realize that they were already far too indebted to Mr. Bartlett.

"Suit yourself, then," Cass said, pleasantly, heading for the door. Apparently, he hadn't taken offense.

"And keep this locked," Aaron ordered, responding to Sara's cool tone. Why did she always act so…so strained-around Cass? The man had gone out of his way for them, and not only that, he was a darn sight more patient with Sara than anybody should be--way more than he would. Aaron glared at Sara before slamming the door behind him. "And stay out of trouble!"

"Stay out of trouble! Indeed!" Sara fumed.

"Aaron's just worried, I think." Peggy commented distractedly. "I'm sure he's fearful about leaving us alone." She was busy looking about the room. It appeared spacious with its large bed and wide window that looked on to the street. There were two chairs with a small wooden table between. A dark, green sheet covered the bed. "The bed's so soft," Peggy said, bouncing on it. Tarney took her cue from Peggy and jumped up and landed at the foot of the bed. Content, she scrunched her head down on the softness and stayed there. "Imagine giving us the room with the bathtub," Peggy said, eyeing the little closed off area with the copper tub. "Mr. Bartlett is the kindest, sweetest man I ever met." She looked for confirmation from Sara, who was busy unpacking.

Sara frowned. "I just hope to pay him back as soon as we get to Uncle Jacob's." Lately, Sara had begun to wonder about the very pleasant and helpful Mr. Cass Bartlett. What exactly were his reasons for helping? "We'll pay him back, everything he spent," she reiterated, pulling a dress from her satchel. "This dress is a fright!" Sara rebuked a wrinkled and musty blue skirt and white blouse. "Everything is dirty!"

Peggy was looking about. "We'll be in Sacramento in a few days--buy a new dress before we get to San Francisco. You'll feel better about everything then!"

"I suppose so," Sara said, doubtfully. She had to agree with Peggy about how nice Cass had been. "I am grateful, of course. Guess I'm just tired. We'd better get our baths over with, and then wash out some undergarments. They'll be dry by morning what with the heat. That's something."

After bathing and preparing for the morrow, Sara felt better, more civilized. However, they were, by now, very hungry and decided to go to the dining room. They left Tarney sleeping at the foot of the bed and tiptoed out the door, went down the staircase and into the hotel dining room. The hotel was nearly empty. Only two other tables were occupied.

"Good evening, ladies," bowed a beaming barrel-chested waiter, as he led Peggy and Sara to a small table. Wiping his hands across a large, white apron, the older man bent cordially and extended menus. "I understand you ladies are traveling with Mr. Bartlett. We'd be pleased to get ya anything ya want."

Peggy smiled up at the waiter. "Mr. Bartlett is most kind. What do you think I should order?"

"I'd recommend the trout dinner, Miss."

"How much is it?"

"Wouldn't trouble yourself over that, Miss."

"Never-the-less, I'd like to know." Sara announced coolly.

"I see," said the waiter, a bit taken aback by the young woman's attitude and looked to Peggy, but she colored with embarrassment and peered down at the white tablecloth. "Well then, perhaps perusing the menu is in order. Let me know when you're ready," he nodded with forced dignity and walked away.

"I wonder what kind of women he thinks we are?" Sara said, stung by the possibilities.

Peggy ventured a mild criticism. "I think he thought we were ladies because we were with Mr. Bartlett. I didn't sense any disrespect--at first."

"Peggy," Sara corrected. "We have to be careful. After all, our reputations may be at stake."

Peggy nodded her head in agreement, though silently wondered how their reputations could be at stake since they knew no one. Besides, there didn't seem much cause for disrespect. Still and all, Sara accounted more about these things than she did.

The girls finally decided on the trout dinner and were delighted by the sweet, fresh tasting fish. They ate heartily, and finished with a dessert of custard topped with whipped cream. It was the most heavenly dessert Peggy had ever tasted.

"I'm too full," Sara said, getting up from the small green, plush chair. "Maybe we can go for a walk. It's not quite dark yet."

Peggy looked doubtful. Maybe we shouldn't go off on our own. Maybe--." She didn't want to say anything, but she felt uneasy about being without escorts. She hadn't liked the looks they'd been getting from some of the men in the restaurant. There seemed to be three times as many men as woman. Several had put their knives down and just stared. Peggy had tried to ignore their looks, but it made her queasy, brought up her fear that her stepfather might catch up with her. She didn't want to worry Sara, so said nothing.

As they left the restaurant and began walking on the boardwalk, several men ambled up to them. One unsavory looking fellow came close, "Are ya offering a good time, ladies? I'm jist yer man!" He attempted to grab Peggy's arm, but Sara had a firm grasp of it. "Leave her alone!" Sara snapped, pulling her away.

"Awe, I jist need a little fun, for the evening," he continued yanking Peggy's arm. "I kin pay ya."

Get away!"Sara stomped her boot heel on the man's foot and then jabbed him in the stomach with her elbow. The half drunken man reeled back and staggered sideways as Sara pulled a stunned Peggy along. Several men laughed and jeered at their friend. "She got the better of ya, Gus!"

The man laughed and continuing to stagger and follow the girls. "There be others," he called, his voice slurring, as Sara rushed Peggy away. A few yards later, they ran into the hotel and up the stairs. Once safely in their room, Peggy and Sara flopped down on the bed, catching their breath. Neither said anything for a few minutes. Finally, Sara's anger erupted. "Blast! What rude behavior. What on earth were those men thinking? They must think we were....or that any unescorted lady is a.... Of all the nerve!" She pounded the pillow beside her. "How dare they! Women ought to be allowed to walk along the street without an escort, without being accosted!"

Peggy bit her lip. "I guess we shouldn't have been alone!"

"Nonsense! We have a perfect right to walk where we want, escorted or not."

Peggy sighed. "I don't think we should tell Aaron or Cass," she offered softly.

"You're probably right, Peggy." Sara's lips pressed to a line. "They'd get all dramatic, try to keep us from ever going out by ourselves. Oh, but it makes me furious. It's so unfair!"

CHAPTER THIRTY-NINE

The roads into Sacramento were dusty and crowded with a variety of carts, wagons and riders as folks converged from all directions. But Sara didn't mind the heat or delays as there was a sense of excitement in the air. She worried about Peggy who appeared listless, not her usual self. She knew that Peggy hadn't slept well, but decided not to comment and understood that last evening's situation had stirred up a number of fears. Hopefully, one day, soon, that would be far behind her. Sara wondered where Donald Colwell was. Had they seen the last of him? Sara vowed she would do anything she could to make her friend feel safe.

As they neared the levee, Sara took several deep breaths, capturing the pungent smells of the Sacramento River and willing the moment to memory. She'd remember this day for ever. Tomorrow this river would carry them all the way to their new home. It seemed a miracle. They'd finally made it, only hours away.

"Just think," Aaron turned excitedly to Peggy, "in two days we'll be in San Francisco and start our new life!"

"I know. I can hardly wait," Peggy said wistfully. "I just hope your Uncle and little Clara like me."

"Of course they will. I'll be sure to tell Uncle Jacob what a great help you've been. He'll find out soon enough how wonderful you are." Aaron hadn't meant to reveal so much.

Sara noticed Aaron's blush and quickly changed the subject. "Sacramento looks more like a New England town than any we've seen so far, don't you think, Aaron?"

"Yes, it does," he heartily agreed. "Nice wide, tree-lined boulevards and bigger buildings. What's that over there?" Aaron turned to Cass and pointed out the window.

"Must be the new capitol building, I heard they're building," Cass replied, glancing at Sara.

"Looks like they're ready to lift those large, granite blocks any day now," Sara said. "What a grand place it's going to be. I hope to see it finished someday."

"I'll make sure you do." Cass smiled warmly.

"That would be nice," Sara muttered, suddenly flustered.

"By the way," Cass said, "I was told that there were shops just a few doors from the Orleans Hotel. You'll have time to buy those new dresses you've been wanting."

"That's wonderful!" Peggy and Sara exclaimed. They pulled up to the Orleans Hotel on Second Street, where they would spend the night. It appeared newer and fancier than any hotel they'd seen so far. The two-story brick building had ten white columns along the front. White lattice trim and white shutters outlined the many windows. A fancy wrought-iron railing framed a balcony along the second story. Dozens of horses and carriages lined up in front of the hotel and throngs of people were leaving or entering.

"I've wired ahead for our arrangements," Cass said. "Aaron, you and the girls can go ahead and I'll take the coach down to the livery and settle up with our driver. I have a message to deliver to…a friend, and I need to make arrangements for the stagecoach and team to remain in Sacramento until Russell Hammond gets here next month. That way we'll have two new ones for the line. I'll be an hour or so. If I'm any later, you go ahead and eat. The hotel has a reputation for good food. Don't wait for me." He paused and glanced down at Tarney. "I bet she'd like to come along, see what's going on at the livery, if that's alright with everyone."

Sara frowned. She didn't like the idea of Tarney being separated from her; especially, in such a hectic place. But she trusted Cass. "I'm sure you're right. She'll enjoy that."

Sara found the hotel lobby noisy and crowded. She heard that two large wedding parties were entertaining and planning to host their weddings on board the Chrysopolis tomorrow. What fun that will be, she thought.

Neither Peggy nor Sara had seen so many elegantly dressed ladies, and it made them aware of just how shabby their own apparel must seem. Most folks appeared well dressed and many women were wearing what Sara supposed was the latest Paris fashions. Some were sporting large, feathered fans and strutting about the lobby like royalty, fanning themselves energetically.

Before long, Aaron had made the room arrangements and given Sara a key. "Better go buy your clothes before the stores close. But don't take too long, everyone's hungry."

He frowned. "Maybe I should go with you. You could get lost!"

"Hardly," Sara admonished. "There's a ladies' dress shop just three doors away, and next to that is the men's haberdashery."

"Well, alright. I did want to nose around, hear what folks are talking about, and read some newspapers."

"Good idea, Aaron. You go ahead," Sara agreed. "And we won't be long."

"And try not to get into any trouble!" Aaron grinned.

"That's no fun!" Sara retorted, abruptly turning away. As Sara and Peggy entered the shop, an attractive, young sales clerk walked forward. "Welcome Ladies," she smiled, delicately daubing a lace hanky over her forehead. She tried to tuck a blond curl behind her ear. "Please," she nodded, making a friendly gesture for them to take a seat and directing them to several plush, red chairs.

"What a pretty little shop." Peggy said, looking about. There were colored drawings of gowns on pink painted walls and one large, gold-framed oil painting of a bucolic scene with ducks and geese around a little pond.

"So glad you like our wee shop. My older sister designs most of the gowns. And Mom and I help with the sewing."

"How wonderful to be doing this with your family," Peggy said, taking a seat.

Sara was in her business mode and remained standing. "Do you have anything ready-made--something suitable for the boat trip to San Francisco?" Sara looked about, not seeing dresses. "Indeed I do," the clerk replied, giving the girls a quick assessment. "I'll be right back," she smiled and rushed behind a dark, green curtain and into another room. In a few moments the clerk returned with several outfits in her arms and placed them on a gilded metal rack. "This will be a start!"

Before long, Sara and Peggy had tried on a number of garments, deemed "most suitable" by the clerk.

Finally, Sara chose a green, redingote day dress, with pink trim. It was shaped small at the waist, over a snug little corset. "Not very comfortable," Sara frowned as Peggy laced it in back. "I'm not used to wearing anything so tight. How on earth am I supposed to breath?"

"Carefully," Peggy grinned, helping Sara step into two long petticoats.

"It is pretty," Sara admitted, turning around and glancing in a long mirror. The dress had a wide-based skirt, down to the ground, and the petticoats added fullness. "How do ladies get in or out of coaches?"

"Very carefully," Peggy grinned. "Oh, but don't you just love the sleeves?"

"I've never seen anything like them." Sara said, turning to the clerk.

"They're in the 'pagoda' style," the clerk offered. "The very latest fashion!" she reassured. "You'll notice that the sleeves fit tight at the shoulders and then flare near the elbow. Don't you just love the cascade of little pearl buttons down the front and have you ever seen such a sweet turned down collar?" The clerk clapped like a happy child. "Oh, but it does look as if it was made for you, and so compliments your red hair."

"It's certainly nice," Sara admitted, twirling around and around. "How much is it?"

"Only fifteen dollars. It's on sale--was twenty-two."

"Oh, Sara, it's perfect!" Peggy exclaimed.

"I'll take it," Sara stated. She also selected a second garment, a dark green, traveling cloak-coat, made of light alpaca and trimmed with a darker, green ribbon. Lovely, Sara thought. "It'll keep me warm on those foggy San Francisco mornings Cass mentioned." Finally, to complete the ensemble, Sara chose a charming white 'spoon' bonnet, decorated with green ribbons, as well as a small, green clutch purse and matching gloves.

Peggy's choice of garment was a soft shade of pink, cut close to the waist over a corset. The skirt funneled out to a wide base with satin borders in darker pink. The sleeves were straight with an opening cut to the wrist, which revealed a chemisette, lawn sleeve underneath. Her collar, unlike Sara's, was not quite as high. She chose a traveling coat of gray wool and her 'spoon' bonnet was dark pink with flowers and feathers adorning the crown.

After several more undergarments and nightgowns were purchased, the girls thanked the clerk and left the shop, each carrying two, large, brown-paper wrapped bundles.

Having decided to wear their new clothes out, Sara and Peggy strolled happily down the boulevard. "I feel so much better," Sara said. But had she made a mistake buying clothes right now. They might need the money at Uncle Jacob's.

No, Peggy was right. They needed proper things to wear, and especially for the court case next week. There might not be time to look for something else. Besides," she reassured, many of the things were on sale!

Peggy smiled. "Just think, Sara, tomorrow at three o'clock we'll be in San Francisco to start our new life! I can hardly wait!" She had not thought about her stepfather in several days. She'd made a vow not think about Donald Colwell or the misery he'd caused her and her mother. She'd picture her Mother, imagine how happy she'd be at this moment. They were going to live in a fine house, and she was going to help Sara and Aaron. Aaron would be with his beloved horse, and everything would be wonderful.

When the girls returned to the hotel room, they found that Cass had ordered ham and cheese sandwiches, along with a pitcher of fresh milk.

"He knew you'd likely be after supper time and hungry as goats," Aaron grinned, "I already ate."

"Where is Cass?" Sara asked, setting the packages down on the bed. She was disappointed at not seeing him.

"He wanted to check the telegraph office. Thought there might be more news about his father. He learned in Grass Valley that his father is home recovering from the grip and not doing well. He's worried."

"I'm so sorry," Sara said. "He didn't say anything. I wish he'd have talked to me about it."

"Why should he? You haven't been exactly friendly."

"Don't be silly, Aaron, I'm his friend."

"You haven't exactly acted like it these last weeks."

"Of all the hurtful things...."

Peggy interrupted, hoping to ease the situation. "I'm sure, he'll tell us more, when he knows. He probably didn't want to worry you."

"Yes, that sounds like Cass," Sara said, feeling only a little relieved. Of course, Aaron was right. She hadn't acted very friendly. "I'm really sorry."

"Cass said something a few days ago," Aaron offered, "I think he's had problems with his father for a long time. He said, he 'wanted to patch things up' and mumbled something about 'The Prodigal' returns." Aaron frowned. "But don't let on you heard it from me. I don't think he wants anyone to know."

"Sometimes I just don't understand men!" Sara shook her head. "Why can't they just say what they feel?"

"Because it's his business," Aaron said impatiently. "And besides, he's sort of private, like me!" Aaron turned, grabbed the packages off the bed. "I'm going back to my room and wait for him. We've already telegraphed Uncle Jacob, said we'll be in at three tomorrow afternoon. Thanks for these," he said, taking his packages. "See you later." He turned in the doorway and smiled at Peggy. "You look like you could do with a good night's sleep." Her frown surprised him and he quickly added, "but you look real nice. I really like that dress." And with that he walked confidently out the door.

"Men!" Both girls exclaimed.

Before long, Sara and Peggy had eaten their supper and prepared for bed. After prayers, Peggy snuggled down into the large bed and promptly fell asleep.

Sara felt a nagging restlessness. She'd waited up, hoping that Cass would knock on her door and say goodnight. But he didn't. Now the air inside the room seemed stifling, oppressive. It was hard to breathe. Sara got up, crossed to the window and opened it wide. Soon cool air flowed into the room. She remained by the window, looking down on the street below. A long row of street lamps stood like soldiers along the boulevard, their pale, yellow light glowed eerily. Close by, steamers sounded their mournful, lonely horns all along the river.

Suddenly, Sara felt as if she were wrapped in a fog of sadness, her body weighed down. Tears began streaming down her face, and she thought it odd, this sadness. Why now, on the eve of their arrival? It was, after all, everything they'd worked for, everything her parents had hoped for. They'd come so far. San Francisco. Was she afraid she might not see Cass again? Yes, that was part of it. But it was more—-much more. Suddenly, her face felt hot, her vision blurred. She staggered as a sharp pain cracked across her chest, unearthing the terrible buried feelings. Grief roared to life, exploding and overcoming her will, forcing her to her knees. Her heart ached near to bursting. "Oh, God! It's so unfair…so horribly unfair. Oh, Momma……Daddy," she cried, placing her arms about her chest, rocking back and forth as waves of tears and grief spilled out. "How could you, God, how could you take them" she cried.

"Sara?" Peggy called, awakened by Sara's cries. She sat up and when she saw her friend hunched over on the carpet, she rushed to her side, knelt beside and pulled her close.

Clinging to Peggy as though her life depended on it, Sara sobbed her heart out.

"It's all right, Sara, go ahead and cry." Peggy whispered,

holding on to Sara. "It's what's needed." Peggy understood the overwhelming surge of feelings. It was Sara's time to grieve.

Peggy knew that all Sara's pain had been pushed down deep inside. But grief, Peggy knew, was like an angry fist, keeping pain in, life out. And Aaron was right. It could make a person sick. Peggy gently brushed Sara's hair off her forehead, as sobs shook through her body.

Finally, Sara's tears subsided, her head lolled back, and she fell fast asleep in Peggy's arms. Ever so gently, Peggy eased Sara down on the carpet and went to gather a pillow and two blankets from the bed. She placed the pillow under Sara's head and tucked the blankets around her. "Sleep here, dear friend. You'll feel better in the morning."

Peggy got back into bed, and folded her hands in prayer, once more. "Thank you, dear Lord," she prayed, "for this amazing day and for your 'Blessed Assurance.' Amen."

CHAPTER FORTY

Sara awoke to find that she was lying on the carpeted floor, the blankets bunched at her feet. Surprisingly, she felt rested, though a little stiff. Then she remembered what happened. She'd sobbed her heart out and fallen asleep in Peggy's arms. Peggy had been so sweet and kind--had taken care of her. She looked at the bed. Peggy was sleeping soundly. That was good. Sara stretched the kinks from her legs and arms. Amazing! She felt really good. Something had changed. She felt lighter, as though a burden had been lifted from her shoulders.

A bit of early morning light came through the pale yellow drapes. What a pretty room this is. The yellow walls had recently been painted and there was a romantic picture of ladies and gentlemen having a picnic near a lake. Sara smiled. She remembered times when, she too, had picnics along the way. How thoughtful of Cass to provide this comfortable, attractive room. She would never be able to thank him enough.

Sara quickly gathered her things and went behind the screen to take a sponge bath. She quietly bathed, combed her hair and put on her new dress. She was ready and excited to go down stairs and see Cass and Aaron.

Soon Peggy awoke and prepared herself for the day. Both girls felt better in their new dresses as they went into the dining room and ordered a breakfast. After, they walked the two blocks to the levee.

The air was refreshing and the excitement along the River was catching. At dawn the levee was already busy. Several large, passenger ships were docked alongside loading ramps at the river's edge. Many smaller stern-wheelers, with flat bottoms, were loading or unloading freight. All sorts of barrels and boxes were being stacked or hauled along the top of the bluff, waiting to be carried down to the river below. A colorfully uniformed brass band entertained passengers as they lined up, waiting to board the largest and most royal looking paddle-wheeler, the Chrystopolis.

Sara and Peggy found Aaron admiring the large ship. "This is the one we'll be taking," Aaron announced. "Come on, Tarney," he urged, pulling on Tarney's rope leash. Tarney balked.

Peggy bent and tenderly stroked Tarney's head. "She's frightened, so many folks rushing about, all the noise and confusion."

"You'll be fine, won't you, girl." Aaron crouched down and lifted Tarney into his arms. "Let's go," he urged Peggy.

"I want to get a good place in line."

"Oh, what a beautiful ship!" Peggy exclaimed, amazed at the sight of the large, two-story white ship. "It looks like one of those pictures of a Southern mansion, all those fancy scrolls and curlicues along the edge of it."

"Yes," Aaron turned to look, but he was watching the many smaller boats maneuvering between larger boats. He wondered if his boat, The Promise, would do that?

"Hey, Cass," Aaron called as Cass and Sara came to stand in the line with him. "Where do all those smaller ones go?" Aaron pointed to the great variety of smaller boats moving in and out along the levee for as far as the eye could see.

"Depends, the smaller, flat-bottom boats can cruise in waters too shallow for larger ones. Some will haul passengers and goods up and down the river, stopping at small farm settlements. Farmers rely on these little steamers to take their crops to market since the roads are often flooded or in ragged condition. Whole towns depend on these river-boats."Oh, look!" Peggy exclaimed, "there's sheep going on a barge."

"You can see all manner of things along the river," Cass said. "It's a life of its own, and can be very profitable--sometimes dangerous."

"Dangerous?" Aaron asked."Not enough docking space. Men compete, overload the boat. It gets over-heated, the boiler explodes and the boat sinks."

Sara shook her head. "That's just greed!"

Cass smiled. "I agree."

"Any big steamships ever explode?" Aaron asked eagerly.

Cass nodded. "In '55 the Pearl blew up and seventy-five people were killed, and all because the captain wanted to make the best time and have 'a competitive edge,' he'd claimed."

"That's terrible," Sara said heatedly. "There should be some sort of law or control!"

Cass nodded, pleased by Sara's fervent reaction. "Unfortunately, these days greed can easily overtake common sense. Folks don't like government restrictions. But they're necessary for safety."

"Oh, look!" Aaron pointed to a man urging a fine looking stallion on to a barge. "Reminds me of Rebel. I told you about him."

"Yes, you did. He's waiting for you in San Francisco."

"My father sent him around The Horn, over three and a half years ago. He was just a yearling."

"Where is he now?"

"Boarded out." Aaron sighed. "There's a dispute about who really owns him. But we do. Mr. Locke, a crooked lawyer is trying to claim him." A strong current of emotion caught Aaron by surprise and he quickly pushed it down, and looked away. "What's in those sacks over there?

Cass explained. "That's wheat. Some farmers have started growing wheat in the last few years. Seems the area can grow almost anything. Could make a difference if there's a war."

"Do you really think there'll be a war?" Sara frowned.

"I think it's possible," Cass said, but quickly turned to Aaron. "You mentioned your boat. What's it like?"

"I haven't seen it yet. Uncle Jacob wrote that The Promise is 40 feet long, flat-bottomed and has a two foot draft and goes 15 knots."

"Sounds like it'll be ideal for hauling goods. Hope to see it."

"Oh, you will! Do you think I can talk to a captain about my ship, find out how to get started in the business?"

"Aaron," Sara cautioned, "We should wait and discuss this with Uncle Jacob, first." She didn't want to spoil Aaron's excitement, but they still had to prove their claim on The Promise and Rebel, as well.

"Well," Aaron said excitedly, "it doesn't hurt to talk to people, get all kinds of ideas."

Cass nodded. "You can talk to Norman C. Marcus. He knows everything about the shipping business. I'll introduce you."

"That'll be great! Won't it, Sara?" Aaron's mood lightened as he thought about what he could do with The Promise.

"Yes, of course," she said. "I'm sure we'd appreciate any help."

"I'd hoped you would," he offered, raising his eyebrows and flashing a mischievous smile.

"Oh," Sara's breath caught, as a current surged through her body. Her face flushed. She quickly turned to Aaron, "I'll--I'll hold Tarney, now."

"She's a bit wiggly, but sure, if you want to." Aaron handed Tarney to her.

Finally, they were in line, going down steep steps to board the Chrystopolis along with what appeared to be several hundred people, some with pets. One man had a monkey on a leash and a heavy-set man carried a parrot on his shoulder.

Sara saw two English bulldogs eyeing Tarney. She turned to Aaron. "I guess you'd better carry Tarney. I'm not sure I can hold her still." Sara had never seen so many people in her life. She recognized some faces from the Hotel wedding party of last evening. They were still in a jovial mood and kept blowing on little reedy noisemakers.

"Oh, isn't this fun!" Peggy said, entering the gangplank. She had a moment of panic and clung to the rail. Could her stepfather be among the crowd? No! She scolded herself. She was not going to let him spoil this experience. She held her head high and took a breath.

"Here," Aaron quickly offered his arm.

The party mood on board was catching as they strolled towards the dining room lounge. Peggy could hardly contain herself. "Just look at those chandeliers. Oh, do let's go exploring. I want to see everything!"

"You go ahead," Cass encouraged, heading for a red, leather chair in the corner. I need to catch up on the San Francisco papers. We can meet back here for breakfast, later."

"Me too, and I'll keep Tarney with me." Aaron quickly sat down next to Cass. He liked the idea of getting a head start on things. Maybe he'd pick up some useful information. He glanced briefly at Sara. "Just don't get lost!"

"Aaron, that's silly. I hardly think we'll get lost on board a ship. Besides I'm a grown woman," she emphasized, glancing at Cass. She hadn't appreciated his "pretty girl" remark and was hoping he'd offer to show her about the ship. But apparently he was more interested in looking at a newspaper. "Well, then," Sara lifted her chin and turned swiftly, "we'll explore the ship!"

Aaron shook his head as he watched his sister and Peggy leave. "Women! I don't understand them sometimes. They want you to be concerned and protective, but then when you are, they get mad!"

Cass nodded, "I know what you mean. I can't always judge their moods. Sara was unusually quiet this morning. Did she say anything to you?"

Aaron shook his head.

Cass thought that sometimes Sara was too proud for her own good. Of course, she was used to handling everything since her parents died. And she deserved to be proud of her ability to do so. Cass sighed, and shook his head. He certainly wasn't going to undermine that. But still, he wished she'd just tell him how she felt. If something was bothering her, he'd try to help. Most likely Sara was worried about her Uncle and young cousin. Not knowing what she'd find must be hard on her. He just hoped she knew that he'd help her any way he could.

Cass put his newspaper down and watched Sara as she wound her way through the dining room and ambled toward the deck. Her loose, red hair bounced with each determined step. He smiled to himself. Sara was an unusual young woman. It was going to be amusing, watching Sara Robbins navigate San Francisco society. He wouldn't want to miss that!

Peggy and Sara strolled about the ship. "Oh, Sara, isn't this the most elegant ship. And look at all the people. I've never seen so many beautiful men and women and such fancy clothes. Oh, just look at how the brass railings gleam in the morning light--like bands of gold. Wouldn't you just love to have a house like this?"

"It's pretty, but I keep thinking of all the people it must take to keep it polished."

As Sara and Peggy continued to the upper deck, the

promenade level, they saw people waving goodbye to friends above on the cliff. Many stood listening to the brass band, which had just boarded.

Suddenly the ship's engines roared to life. Two huge side-wheels churned forward, whipping dark water into a foamy green. A musical calliope played a galloping kind of tune, and two sharp blasts of a horn echoed along the levee as the engines continued beating their rhythmic way into the River.

"We're on our way!" exclaimed Peggy, and I'm hungry!"

Peggy and Sara came back to the dining room and joined Cass and Aaron at a rather elegant table that was covered with a white damask cloth. Fine crystal goblets and silver flatware were set for four. In the center, a crystal vase held a single yellow rose.

"This is like a palace!" Peggy said, admiring the room.

The dining room was larger and more elegant than any she'd seen. Suspended from the ceiling were ten crystal chandeliers, casting soft shadows and a romantic glow over everything. Red-velvet loveseats lined russet-colored walls, and in the middle of the room were three, long serving tables filled with platters of fresh fruits, meats and cheeses. At one end, silver tea pots held steaming, hot chocolate, tea and coffee. Large trays of fancy breads and succulent pastries were placed on a separate table. Several children were eagerly grabbing handfuls. Peggy smiled. Their parents obviously weren't watching. People appeared to be parading about or visiting in small groups. So many folks knew each other. What a perfect place to host a wedding party.

Cass put the menu down. "Suppose you all let me order a fine breakfast--seeing as how this will be the last meal we'll have together--maybe for some time."

'The last meal.' The words plunged into Sara's heart. A lump as big as a bone wedged in her throat and tears welled up. She turned her face away.

"Are you all right, Sara?" Cass asked concerned, as he saw Sara fumble for a hanky. Cass rose to offer his. "Is there something I can do?"

"No," she mumbled, too close to tears to speak. It seemed now that the "flood gates" had been open, she was unusually sensitive, and tears more easily bidden. Quickly, Sara got up from the table and started across the crowded dining room, weaving her way awkwardly through busy tables.

"Sara?" Cass called, caught off guard by her sudden departure. "Sara! Wait!" When he saw Peggy was about to run after her, he said, "That's all right, Peggy. I'll see to it. You stay and have breakfast. I'll be right back." Cass headed towards the exit as Sara rushed through.

Aaron's eyes followed Cass as he disappeared into the crowd by the exit. "Maybe I should go help."

"No, we best stay put," Peggy offered softly, placing her hand on Aaron's arm. "I think Sara needs to be alone with Cass. They have some things to talk about."

"What things? What happened just now?" Aaron didn't understand, but sat back down.

Peggy's eyes followed the pair as they left the room. "I think Sara is unhappy about saying goodbye to Cass. I think she found out that she cares for him more than she knew."

Aaron didn't agree. "Naw. They get on each other's nerves. She doesn't like him half the time. I mean, they're always getting on each other's nerves."

"Maybe."

Aaron was still looking toward the exit. "I don't know. She's been awful jumpy lately, keeping to herself. It's hard to know what she's really thinking."

"I suppose. But you're both so proud. Sometimes it's hard for either of you to tell people what you're thinking."

"You're probably right." Aaron admitted. "I don't know, Sara's been kind of difficult. I think she misses Mark. I told Cass that Sara was engaged and was probably missing her fiancé."

"You told him that?" Peggy gasped.

"I did! I had to because sometimes Sara was so darn grumpy and ungrateful. I knew Cass wondered what was wrong with her. So, I told him that Mark Davis asked Sara to marry him, and that she's probably missing him."

"Oh, no!" Peggy groaned, shaking her head. "What did he say?" Peggy was almost afraid to ask.

"He said, 'She's too young!' And he was pretty stern about it, too."

Oh, dear, Peggy thought. Sara wouldn't like that at all. "Aaron, I think we shouldn't say anything to Sara. It'll only upset her."

"I guess. Though I don't know why. She *is* too young. I told Cass I agreed."

"Oh."

CHAPTER FORTY-ONE

"Sara!" Cass called, hurrying up the stairway to the promenade deck. "Sara, wait!" But when she didn't stop, he assumed she couldn't hear him through the churning of the paddle wheels and the throng of people. And when he caught up with her, she turned her back and stood clutching the ship's railing. "Sara? What's wrong? Are you ill?"

"No. I'm…I'm fine." She avoided looking at him as he came near. "I just needed some fresh air and to…to think."

"I understand. You have a lot on your mind."

"Yes, but," she hesitated, "we all have." Then she took a deep breath and slowly turned to face him. "I'm afraid I've been very self-absorbed. Please forgive me."

"Of course, but you've been a great sport, wonderful help." Cass waited for Sara to say something, but when she didn't, he asked, "Is there anything I can do?"

"No, but thank you." When Sara saw the concern in his eyes, it made her feel very tender. "I was sorry to hear about your father."

Cass glanced away. "I'm sure things will get better now that I'm home."

"I'm sure they will," Sara encouraged.

Cass turned to face her. "I…I've been meaning to thank you. Thank you for coming along with me. You've all been great company--a real help. I know it hasn't been easy. Not many girls would be such a good sport."

Sara's expression barely changed as she listened to Cass. "Not many girls." Once again those words stung. She glanced down fleetingly and then back at him, waiting to see if he understood what he'd done. Her eyes fastened on him, challenging him to see her as a woman.

Cass was suddenly uncomfortable. He tried to ignore those hazel eyes--so green, reflecting the water like a dark current, challenging. He took a deep breath and cleared his throat. "I told Aaron to get in touch with Judge Marshall. He's honest and an old family friend. He'll help. But promise me you'll never let your ownership papers out of sight. Don't give them to anyone, even for a day. And don't sign anything, unless I've taken a look at it. Promise me, Sara."

Sara nodded, barely moving.

He wished she would say something, anything. His thoughts blurred. Those green eyes...so trusting...so open. "Sara, you've got to be careful. This city is full of ruthless people--men and women who'll do anything for gain."

As Sara moved a little closer, Cass' muscles tensed. "There are men who'll tell you they're doctors or lawyers, but they aren't...never trained." Cass felt his blood quicken. "Quacks of all kinds." He thought she looked beautiful standing there with the morning light shimmering through her hair. "It's a town where any woman is--" He felt her warmth move into his chest, her eyes a magnet. Her lips demanded his, her breath so sweet and close. Slowly, he bent---.

"Well, if it ain't Cass Bartlett, big as life!" A deep voice boomed across the promenade. The man sauntered up, cocky as a rooster. He appeared to enjoy interrupting a romantic moment, and grinned suggestively. "Thought you was still back East, hobnobbing with the Hoy-poloy." He moved a step closer to peer at Sara. "Seems you brought us back a prime specimen." The man's wide, square face loomed even closer, unabashedly looking Sara up and down. "Yep! Prime filly, I'd say. She's a credit to ya, Cass."

"This is Miss Robbins," Cass said, stiffly, and backed Sara away. "She's with me," he said, nearly knocking the man over as he took Sara's arm.

"Miss Robbins!" the man bowed, grinning malevolently, "I expect we'll meet again. Soon, I hope!"

Sara automatically nodded, but was glad Cass was hurrying her away from the boorish, ill-mannered man.

"Who was that?" Sara asked.

"His name is Johnny Bufford. No one for you to know," Cass said, sternly moving her along. "He's the sort I was warning you about. Now do you understand?"

"Yes, I…" Sara said startled. She'd never heard Cass use that tone before.

They were about to walk back to the dining room when another person called out to Cass. An attractive, well dressed man in his mid twenties, Sara supposed, came rushing forward with a pretty, petite brunette on his arm.

"Cass, it is you. Marilee was right. She thought she saw you and this lovely young lady a few minutes ago. What a pleasant surprise! Didn't know you were back. Uncle Chuck said you were on your way." He eagerly extended his arm, and the two men shook hands. "Thought maybe you'd joined the Union army back East, or would it be the Confederate?" he teased. "Thought maybe your three months in New Orleans would have persuaded you in the value of Southern Culture."

"My experience with Southern culture is strictly cuisine, cousin."

"If you say so. And with that in mind, would you and the lovely young lady join us for some aperitif?" Sloan smiled at Sara and tipped his hat.

Turning first to Sara, Cass began the introductions, "Miss Robbins, this is Miss Marilee Brenner, who is engaged, I understand, to this ne'er-do-well cousin of mine, Sloan Bartlett."

"How do you do," Sara replied, hoping her eyes were not still red or her face quite so flushed from the near kiss.

"Where are you from, Miss Robbins?" Marilee asked in a friendly manner as she immediately took Sara by the arm and began walking beside her.

Taken by surprise, Sara quickly replied. "I'm from Boston, originally, most recently Nebraska."

"Are you visiting or staying?" Marilee interrupted.

"Oh, I'm staying!" Sara answered enthusiastically.

"Wonderful!" I know all there is to know about this city, all the wicked gossip that's worth knowing." Marilee scrunched up her shoulders and added in a conspiratorial manner, "You can ask me anything."

Uncertain how to respond, Sara asked, "How long have you lived in San Francisco?"

"Since `48. My father, God rest his soul, came out in first gold rush, but he wasn't one of the lucky ones. Of course, as it turned out, he was." Marilee's big, brown eyes sparkled with mischief. "Daddy opened a restaurant, bought some land, and made a fortune. I actually have a very nice dowry. Oh, but we nearly lost it all in the depression a few years ago...'55, I think it was. After Daddy died, Sloan here helped to straighten the finances, so mother and I manage quite well. It allows my mother to travel. Right now she's visiting her sister in London. But she'll be back for the wedding."

Sara noticed Marilee turn around to look lovingly at Sloan who walked a few paces behind her. "Isn't he the best looking man in all of San Francisco?"

Marilee changed the subject, before Sara could respond. "I like to know about business, do you, Sara? I make Sloan explain everything, so I can help make decisions. Some people criticize, of course, but folks in San Francisco are not so hide-bound as they are in the East--fortunately, for me." Marilee giggled. "Sloan says I'm bit of a rare bird. I am," she concluded enthusiastically. But he loves me. I enjoy working. I believe a woman can do nearly anything a man can. Do you think that's disgraceful?"

"Not at all!" Sara quickly agreed. Sara thought Marilee talked faster than any two women, but it was refreshing, and Sara offered, "Things are changing. Even in the East. Lots of women are working now in factories. But I hear it's really hard work, because you have to sit or stand for 15 hours a day. And you can't go outside or see the sun or anything."

"Sounds perfectly horrid," Marilee frowned. "But I warrant it's different when you own your own. My friend, Maybelle Turner, lives in Georgia, and her father's gone a lot, so she manages the plantation--oversees everything and has since she was sixteen. She's nearly twenty, same as me. Do you work, Sara?"

"No," Sara answered, "but I plan to!"

"How delightful. I'm sure we'll be great friends!"

Sara appreciated Marilee's frankness, and the fact that she liked business was a point in her favor. "I plan to be working in the family hardware store."

"Hardware! Why I'll come and buy everything I need from you. What fun! Are you engaged to Cass?"

"Marilee!" Sloan chastised, having overheard. He looked embarrassed as he walked up to her. "Sometimes you go too far!"

"Oh, nonsense, Sloan!" Marilee retorted. "Sara and I are just getting to know each other."

Sara's face stung with embarrassment. She didn't like being the object of a quarrel. But she couldn't help noticing that Cass appeared amused.

Ignoring Sloan, Marilee rushed Sara forward out of Sloan's hearing and continued talking in a sprightly manner. "I saw the way Cass was looking at you. I think he's sweet on you. Do you love him?"

Sara felt a flash of heat as the words shot through her like lightning. "Goodness!" she exclaimed and settled for a small denial, "we've only known each other a few weeks."

"Bother!" Marilee grinned. That's plenty of time!"

Sara laughed, and then leaned forward and whispered, "Well, I do like him a lot."

"Good!" Marilee said, grinning knowingly. She saw Sara turn red. "Oh, don't worry. I won't say anything, for now. But you should know that things happen very quickly here in San Francisco. People fall in love and don't waste any time. That's because there's a male population of seventy percent. Women are grabbed up pretty fast, I can tell you. However, in Cass' situation," she paused a moment for emphasis, "there's a number of young ladies who'd love to be in your position. You best do something about that or Miss Pricilla Mathews will snap him up. She's been after him for years. I can't abide her myself." Marilee took on the look of a true conspirator. "We should make some plans, Sara."

"Marilee," Sara began in a firm manner, "I do appreciate your interest, but I can't make any plans just now. I have far too many things to take care of." Sara didn't like the feeling of being manipulated by Marilee, however well meaning. She needed to set some boundaries.

"As you wish," Marilee agreed good-naturedly. She liked Sara's directness. "There'll be time," she said sweetly. "I have just the thing. I'm having a soiree in two Saturdays. Will you come? You don't have to bring Cass unless you want to. They'll be plenty of young men. You can bring anyone you wish. I'm having some musicians and three local poets. I hope you like poetry readings?"

Sara relaxed a bit. "I like poetry. But I've never been to a reading. I'd like to bring my brother and my friend, Peggy O'Neil. She's a singer and I'm sure she'd love to be included."

"Wonderful! Do you think she'd want to sing for us?"

"I don't know. She's kind of shy, but I could ask."

CHAPTER FORTY-TWO

Marilee Brenner spent the rest of the morning giving a lively report to anyone who would listen about the latest goings-on in San Francisco.

As they began crossing the bay and heading for port, Marilee pointed out some of the city's historical landmarks. "Over there was Happy Valley," she pointed to an area on the beachfront. "When my family and I first arrived in '48, it was nothing but an old, wet, stink hole, without sanitation, just a miner's tent city, for down and outers. Everyone had terrible dysentery most of the time from the bad water. Imagine, we lived there through one summer and fall, and all the time it was cold and damp and stank something fierce. Now there are delightful houses, even a church and school. Of course, we've had lots of fires, but folks always rebuild. "That's how things are in San Francisco. Last year's catastrophe is this year's promise."

They stood at the railing, watching the city as it rushed towards them. And when the ship's horn blasted three loud hoots, Sara felt a thrill of excitement.

Soon Aaron appeared on deck with Tarney. Tarney spotted another dog and began barking. Aaron pulled on her rope to restrain her as a large, black bulldog rushed up and stood eyeing her.

"You'd better hang on to Tarney," Sara cautioned, not liking the way the bulldog was sniffing around Tarney.

"I know, I know!" Aaron retorted, picking up Tarney and holding her.

As people began crowding against the railing, Cass came and stood next to Sara. He bent down and whispered. "Better stay close."

Sara's face flushed as she felt his breath upon her cheek, and her legs suddenly went weak. It was embarrassing, Sara thought, not daring to look into his eyes. She suspected Cass knew exactly the effect he had on her. She tried to steady her voice. "I hope this won't take long."

"Long can be good if it's all part of the excitement of the moment." Cass grinned suggestively.

Sara burst out laughing. She couldn't help herself. "Oh, you are a rogue and a devil, Cass Bartlett. I think a "gentleman" recently warned me about the likes of you."

"Well, then, consider yourself forewarned."

Sara couldn't hear his whispered reply because they were caught in a noisy mash of people waiting to leave the ship.

Cass glanced up at the San Francisco skyline. "It's good to be home." He sighed, then raised his voice and pointed to an expanse of wharves along the waterfront. "In '51 we had eleven wharves, but there was a huge fire--demolished every one and most of the ships, too. Over a hundred ships."

Aaron exchanged a look with Sara. "Good thing The Promise wasn't there then. What happened to all the ships that were docked?"

Sloan continued, "The ships were mostly charred hulls, so they left them, added fill and built over. In some cases there are buildings today that have rotting old ship parts as their basements. In the old days, the whole city kept burning down, so they finally passed an ordinance and now brick buildings are required.

Marilee added, "People are always starting over. It's what gives the town its energy, I think."

Sloan suddenly pointed to a cliff about a hundred feet tall. "That's Rincon Hill. Uncle Chuck, Cass's father, has a big house there." He grinned at Cass. "Been a while since you've seen it yourself, hasn't it?"

Cass nodded and glanced at Sara. He noticed her listening to Sloan, but she appeared more interested in watching the ship dock. What was she thinking? Moments ago, he'd felt her pulling away, distancing herself.

Cass frowned at the idea, impatiently working his knuckles against his forehead. He cracked his neck trying to relieve tension, and watched folks shove their way to the railing. He heard the captain's "Everyone please stand back." Suddenly, a young couple rushed into each other's arms and embraced. The crowd cheered.

How lucky they were, Cass thought. If only things were different, not so unsettled; especially the situation with his father and the possibility of war, maybe months away. He shook his head, took a deep breath, and inhaled the familiar salty air.

No, he reminded himself, this was not the time to pursue the charming Miss Sara. Besides, she had her own 'interests' to sort out. Still, Cass smiled ruefully; time will tell.

He stood at the railing, watching the ship move into place. Wood pressed and groaned against the pier, like a reluctant bull forced in a slot.

"Well, you're home, Cass!" Sloan cried, clapping Cass on the shoulder.

"Yes," Cass winced.

Finally, the wheels stilled, a heavy anchor plunged, and a final guttural blast of the ship's horn echoed along the wharf.

Happy shouts rose as passengers rushed towards the gangplank where the captain and his crew stood in line to bid adieu.

Down on the wharf, a brass band played a rousing march, and an out-of-tune tuba made a mournful sound, but no one seemed to care.

Peggy clutched at Sara's arm. "I'm so excited. I can't believe we're really here."

"I know," said Sara, suddenly in awe. "It's amazing--hard to believe. Whoops!" She felt herself being rushed along in the crowd, "Hold on, Peggy!" she called, trying to reach her hand out.

Fortunately, Cass was at her side, and took hold of her arm and then reached for Peggy's. "I've got you. Hang on. It won't be long now!" They quickly stepped down the gangplank to the dock below. "Stay close to me," Cass warned.

All along the wharf, people were getting off or on ships. Dockworkers pulled small carts of merchandise to the many smaller boats hugging the docks. There was a sense of urgency as men carted wagons loaded with wood to the larger ship's furnaces.

Men selling fresh fish lined up in stalls along the wharf, while "callers" shouted out the names of hotels, trying to entice customers. Chinese men carried baskets filled with yellow streamers or bird-like kites, and women in black dresses sold bouquets of flowers. Adding to the confusion were a dozen soldiers on horses prancing about, showing off their new, dark blue uniforms.

"It's always like this. Isn't it fun?" Marilee grinned, "I sometimes come down here to buy fish just for the excitement."

Sara did not think getting mashed in the crowd was all that 'exciting.' However, she didn't want to be a wet blanket. "It's certainly colorful!" She glanced anxiously at the long line of carriages and coaches waiting for passengers. "Hope Uncle Jacob got the message," she muttered to Aaron who was standing next to her, holding a squirming Tarney. She frowned. "Aaron, please hold her tight. If she got loose, she'd surely get trampled."

"I know. I know." He gave Sara a look as if to say, "don't nag."

He put his head next to Tarney. "You're just as eager to be home as everybody, aren't ya, girl. Don't worry! Uncle Jacob will be here soon. And he's going to see that you're about the best dog in the whole world! Soon, now, we'll be home! Home! That was the best word in the whole world.

A half hour later, they stood on the wharf, still waiting. Most of the passengers from the Chrystopolis had disembarked, and the carnival atmosphere dispersed, leaving only a few carriages at the end of the dock. Marilee and Sloan had waited a while, but finally said their goodbyes.

There was no sign of Uncle Jacob.

Aaron frowned. "Sure hope he got the message. I said we'd be looking for the 'Robbins' sign."

Sara turned to Cass, "Please don't feel you have to wait." Sara scanned the remaining coaches. Two appeared for hire. "I'm sure we can manage on our own."

"I'm sure. Nevertheless, I'd feel a whole lot better knowing you were safely at your uncle's. We'll wait a bit longer. There's my driver now." He waved at a portly groomsman, who sat atop a large, shiny, mahogany colored carriage, holding the reins of a pair of black horses. "Mr. Sandavol, over here."

The older man maneuvered the coach closer and scowled down at Cass. "The only thing I mind," he said, scratching his bald head, "is being called Mr. Sandavol. Is it yer so high and mighty now, ya can't call me Flynn?"

"Flynn," Cass bowed, very formally. "May I present Miss Sara Robbins and her brother, Master Aaron, and, of course, Miss Peggy O'Neil."

"Howdy." Flynn grinned, as he observed the way Cass looked at Sara. Special friends of Charles jr. are fine with me." He winked at Cass.

Sara was surprised to hear Cass being called "Charles," and she couldn't help but wonder at Cass's sudden rush of color. Was it a blush? She quickly turned to Mr. Sandavol.

Cass quickly explained. "The Robbin's coach should be here soon. We'll wait until it comes."

Flynn grinned. "That's fine with me."

Sara frowned. "It's very kind of you to offer to wait, sir, but I'm sure you must be in a hurry, what with Mr. Bartlett senior ill and waiting.

"Not to worry, Miss. Mr. Bartlett Sr. is rightly improved with the news his son come home. A wee wait is no fuss at all."

And wait they did, for over an hour. And when Uncle Jacob's coach failed to arrive, Cass's determination to see them home proved stronger than Sara's resistance.

After everyone, including an eager Tarney, settle into the comfortable six-seater, the coach pulled away from the wharf area and they were on their way.

Mr. Sandavol sat up in the coachman's seat, aiming a steady stream of encouragement at the horses. He turned to Cass sitting next to him in the driver's seat. "So Cass, you haven't mentioned anything about the new coach. How does it compare to the one you left in Sacramento? Your father ordered this as a surprise for you."

"Well, I am surprised. It's beautiful. It's even grander than the one we took across the country." He hadn't expected his father to order a new coach—-make such an extravagant gift. Usually, his father required him to earn everything.

Sara thought the carriage was spotless inside and out, and the blue-velvet swabs were as luxurious as any armchair.

Fortunately, the black, leather top was rolled back, so they had an excellent view of the waterfront as they headed along a bumpy, dusty road parallel to the Bay.

Peggy was enjoying the view and could barely contain herself. "Isn't this beautiful, Aaron?"

"Yes," Aaron smiled, taking a deep breath of the salt-tangy air. He watched Peggy. He loved watching her, seeing her enthusiasm. Sometimes he had to force himself not to stare. She looked real pretty in her new dress. He'd have to remember to tell her that. He was very proud of her, the way she'd grown up since they'd met three months ago. She'd changed; didn't look so scared or unsure. That was something, considering what she's been through. He'd do anything to keep her safe. He wished he could take away her nightmares. He'd heard her cry out at night, but they hadn't seen Colwell in almost a month. Hopefully, he was gone from their lives. Peggy deserved a good life. She was wonderful--so sweet and beautiful! He was sure Uncle Jacob would think so. "Won't be long, now, Peggy," he beamed and reached to give Tarney a pat. "What do you think of things, girl? We're just about home."

Tarney sat contentedly beside Aaron, her tongue hanging out, her right paw touching Aaron's lap.

No one seemed to mind the occasional lurching of the coach as it rumbled over ruts. They were used to that. And besides, they were almost home.

CHAPTER FORTY-THREE

Sara sat back against the comfortable upholstery, trying to enjoy the many new smells and sights. Home! How wonderful that sounded. If only she could relax. Part of her was excited, and another part was growing more anxious as she mulled over things Clara had mentioned in her letter.

"What's wrong, Sara?" Aaron leaned forward for a closer look. "You're as restless as a jumping bean."

"I'm fine!" she snapped, shaking her head. She didn't mean to sound so cross. "Sorry, Aaron. I'm just worried about Uncle Jacob. Our last news was in June when we first came into Leavenworth. That was over three months ago. I've been mulling over what Clara said about her father's friend, Jessica, leaving and about the new housekeepers. Remember, she said that the lawyer Locke had hired them."

"Isn't that the same man who's trying to get your property?" Cass frowned.

"Yes," both Sara and Aaron replied.

"I have all the papers to prove our claim, but he's a---"

"A thief!" Aaron interjected. "But he won't get away with it!" Aaron added vehemently.

"I just hope he hasn't done anything to hurt Uncle Jacob or Clara," Sara said, biting her lip.

"Well," Cass offered, "I suspect that if the situation had worsened, you'd likely have gotten a message, since we stopped at all the post offices and message boards."

"You're probably right," Sara said, taking a deep breath, and settling back against the seat. She smiled as she glanced out at the harbor. How like Cass to try and calm her anxiety. How many times had he done that for all of them---like the captain of a ship. She smiled as she watched Cass observing the many ships leaving on the late afternoon tide. Such a distinguished profile, Sara thought. There was a trace of afternoon beard and it seemed so--so masculine. He looked very handsome in his beige, linen day jacket. His thick, dark hair, which he'd allowed to grow longer, was tied back with a thin strip of leather. It suited him.

As if sensing her watching, he smiled. "It's beautiful, isn't it?"

"Yes," she answered, suddenly aware she was staring at his lips. Unintentionally, she touched her lips at the memory of their kiss. Would he ever kiss her again? Would he lose interest, now that he was home? Sara felt her face grow warm. Was it flushed? Oh, no! Did he notice? Tears threatened. Quickly taking a hanky from her sleeve, she daubed at her cheeks. I must get hold of myself, take a firm hand over these feelings. She'd be too busy to--. She took a deep breath, reminded herself she had a purpose that was more important than anything else. Besides, it wasn't as if she'd never see Cass again. He'd promised to help them with their case, and she knew he would. She'd still see Cass, just not every day. Maybe in time, she could be a help to him, show him she wanted to be a true friend. She sat up straighter and put the hanky back in her sleeve. "After everything is settled, Cass, I hope you'll allow me to visit your father. Perhaps I can suggest some healing herbs."

"I'm sure it would be appreciated."

Aaron beamed in pride. "Sara's very good about such things."

Cass smiled. "I'm not surprised."

"She doesn't like to brag, but she's really good."

"I don't doubt that for a minute." Cass said, seriously, smiling at her.

Sara felt shy, and turned her head away. "My isn't the sea air invigorating." Sara bit her lip. What a stupid thing to say. She turned back to face him. "I...I...want to thank you again, Cass, for all your help. She looked directly at his eyes. A spurt of excitement surged through her as their eyes met and held. There it was--that thrilling pulse between them. But now, she didn't look away.

Cass said, "Yes, it's all very <u>invigorating</u>." And as he held her eyes, a sweet understanding passed between them and settled somewhere deep inside.

For several seconds everything seemed to stop. Nothing existed but the two of them, wrapped in that magical moment.

Suddenly, the carriage slowed.

"Whoa!" Flynn said, reining the horses to a stop.

"Wonder why we're stopping here," Sara looked about. There weren't any buildings or houses, just fields. A shiver of apprehension moved up her spine.

Aaron and Cass quickly opened the coach door and stepped out, meeting Flynn as he came around.

"What's the problem, Flynn?" Cass asked, concerned.
"Midnight's favoring his left hoof. He may have taken a stone. I'll check it. It won't take but a few minutes." He nodded to his passengers. "Sorry for the delay."

"I'll help," Aaron said, following Flynn. "Sara, you and Peggy can stay in the carriage or stretch your legs. This isn't going to take long."

Sara and Peggy decided to stretch their legs. Besides, the view over the cliff provided a breath-taking panorama of the Bay.

"Sara," Peggy began cautiously, "there's something I've been meaning to tell you, but I--"

"Peggy, you know you can tell me anything."

"Let's walk over there," Peggy pointed to a large rock jutting out from the hillside. It looked far enough away. "Come on, Sara," she said, grabbing her arm. "I don't want anyone to hear us."

"Goodness, Peggy, you sound so serious."

"It's about something Aaron told Cass."

"Better tell me. I can see it's important."

Peggy took a deep breath and whispered, "Aaron told Cass you were engaged."

"What? Oh, no!" Anger exploded. "How could he? Oh, rats!"

Anger gave way to embarrassment. "Heavens, what must he think of me? I nearly kissed him! I've practically thrown myself at him." Sara began pacing. "I...I don't know what to say...or...or do. Oh this is terrible." She covered her face with her hands. "Terrible!"

"I'm sure you'll be able to explain later, Sara. Please don't take on so. Do you want me to tell him the truth?"

"No! Oh, Peggy, I'm so embarrassed." But the more she thought it, the more troubling it became. What kind of man would try to kiss her if he thought she was engaged? Oh, this is awful. I don't think I can look at him."

"Now you're being a silly goose. He likes you. Believe me, he's your friend. He'll understand. Maybe I shouldn't have told you."

"No, no, Peggy. I'm glad you did--but that brother of mine. Just wait till I get my hands on him!"

The stone in Midnight's horseshoe was simple enough to fix. Aaron was given the honors of removing the tiny pebble, and he reassured everyone. "He'll be a bit sore, but if we take it easy, he won't be too unhappy."

A few minutes later, they were on their way.

Sara kept her face turned away from Cass and glared at the passing scene in stony silence, still fuming with cross currents of indignation and embarrassment. Apparently, others took little notice of the change in her mood.

"Oh, look over there, Sara." Aaron pointed to two dozen blue uniformed soldiers marching on a nearby field.

Aaron turned to Cass. "If there's a war, I'll be joining them."

"Yes," Cass nodded, "I expect you will."

"Aaron Robbins you most certainly will not!"

"I will, if I want to, Sara! And you can't stop me!" Aaron glared. "Besides, I'll be sixteen in less than a month and it's my duty to fight!"

Cass knew how upsetting the idea was for Sara. He wanted to calm her fears. "If there's a war, the West will not get the worst of it, likely. But Aaron's right, it would be our duty."

"But Aaron's too young!" she protested.

"That may be, but many fifteen-year-olds have done their part before. But, as I said, I wouldn't worry about that now. We'll just have to wait and see." He tried a reassuring smile.

The idea that Aaron would leave and join the army, or God forbid, become wounded, dissolved Sara's anger in a vat of dread. What would she do if anything ever happened to Aaron, and what would Uncle Jacob and Clara do? And Cass! Oh, no! Of course, he would join, as well. No!

Peggy noticed the stricken look on Sara's face. "Sara, please don't worry, we've been through the very worst of things. You know we have. And we're here! We've made it. Please, dear friend," she reached for Sara's hand. "Remember God has brought us this far, and we have each other." Peggy reached for Aaron's hand. "Nothing will ever come between us." She smiled.

Less than a half hour from the dock area, Cass' carriage pulled up to Uncle Jacob's. "We're here," Cass announced, eagerly stepping out of the coach and turning back to help Peggy and Sara down the two steps. "May I present your new home." He made a gallant bow. But the courtly flourish quickly died as he glanced up at the large two-story house. What once might have been an elegant and stately home looked run down and faded. A wide veranda extended around the side, but most of the scrollwork was missing and the porch leaned slightly. The front steps tilted in, as though the house were falling into itself.

Aaron's reaction said what everyone else was thinking. "Could this really be Uncle Jacob's?" He turned to Sara.

"Somebody seems to be visiting." He nodded at the two-seater carriage with its small, gray horse tied to the fence in front. Aaron shook his head. Things did not look good. Glancing about, he saw a dilapidated carriage at the side of the house and next to that, a small buckboard, and neither looked like they'd been used in a while.

"This appears to be the place," Sara frowned, noticing the barn-like shed about twenty feet off to the side of the house. A faded, barely readable, sign hung crooked across the barn door: Robbins Hardware and Sundries. This was not at all what she expected. "At least we're here." Sara didn't want to show her deep disappointment, nor make Cass concerned. The house certainly didn't look the way it had in the tintype Uncle Jacob sent a few years ago. Ever since then, she'd dreamed of a beautiful, two-story white-framed house with lovely bay windows. It had been such a part of her dreams about San Francisco, and her Mother's, as well. This was to be the family home, big enough for two families. Her mother had looked forward to planting a fine flower garden around the front and a big vegetable garden in back. Sara had always imagined her mother tending to things, making everything beautiful. For a moment, Sara imagined her mother standing on the porch, a bunch of newly cut flowers in her hand. The image of her mother seemed so real, and even appeared to smile and speak, "It will be all right, my dear daughter." Transfixed, Sara stood, not daring to move. All too soon, the image disappeared.

"It's really lovely," Peggy volunteered. "I've seen old houses like this. When my daddy bought our old farmhouse, it looked worse than this. We fixed it up real fine and it was very pretty. All this wants," she said sweeping her arms to include the barn, "is someone to take care. I'll help."

"Thank you, Peggy," Sara said, snapping out of her daze, I know you'll be a big help." Sara turned to Cass and extended her hand. "I can never thank you enough. You saved our lives. I'm sure Uncle Jacob will want to thank you personally."

Cass stepped forward. It was hard to hear Sara's words and not feel guilty. Hopefully, she'll understand some day and forgive him the deception. He owed the youngsters more than he could say. He cleared his throat. "I'll see you through the door, but I think it's best to wait until your Uncle's feeling better."

Cass held Sara's hand, cupping his over it. "Don't worry, Sara, everything will get sorted out." He smiled and gently let go. "I promise!"

Cass paused as though he might have more to say, but instead, bent down and gave Tarney a scratch behind her ears. "I'll miss you, young lady." He stood up and added, "Don't forget, Aaron, send for me, any time, for any reason. You know where. And, I'll see you in a week for the court date, just as we discussed."

CHAPTER FORTY-FOUR

"Thank you, sir!" Aaron gave Cass a salute and walked with Tarney and the girls along the overgrown path to the porch. Tarney bounded up the three steps and waited by the big oak door. As Aaron knocked, the youngsters turned and waved to Cass.

The heavy door squeaked opened.

"What do you want?" A middle-aged woman opened the door a crack and peered at three young people. "Well," she said, "speak up! I don't have all day!" The woman stood stiff-necked in her black uniform and held the door as if it were a shield against the devil himself.

Unaccustomed to such rude behavior, Sara hesitated. She stood comparing the envelope and tintype in her hand to the numbers on the oak door. "My name is Sara Robbins, and I'm...is this Jacob Robbins' residence?" She glanced at Aaron for confirmation. "Maybe this isn't the right place."

"Maybe it ain't," the woman sneered, still refusing to open the door more than an inch.

"My name is Sara Robbins," she began assertively, "and this is my brother Aaron, and our friend, Miss Peggy O'Neil. "Who are you?"

"I'm Edwina Smedley, the housekeeper," she answered, a bit surprised at Sara's impertinence.

"Well," Sara began, "this is the last known address of the Mr. Jacob Robbins. We're Jacob Robbins' niece and nephew. I believe he's expecting us."

"Have any proof? Person can't be too careful." She put a hanky to her long nose. "All the riff-raff around these days."

"You say he's expecting you?" Edwina looked at them as if they were selling fleas. She scowled at Tarney. "Dogs a Sara   presented the tintype of Uncle Jacob and her father taken four years ago. "That's our father," she pointed.

"Aren't allowed."

"Who's there?" questioned another voice from behind the door. A pleasant looking woman stepped forward and ignoring Edwina's efforts to wedge her out, opened the door wide. "Oh, please do come in!"

"They can't come in here!" Edwina protested. "Nonsense, Mrs. Smedley. Jacob's been expecting them. I'm Jessica Banner, a friend of your Uncle's." She smiled warmly at the youngsters, and turned to Mrs. Smedley. "You may go about your business, Mrs. Smedley. I'll see to this."

"Well! I never!" Edwina spun around and marched through the parlor to the kitchen.

Sara turned in the doorway, nodded at Cass who stood at the gate and gave a parting wave. Momentarily, her eyes misted as she watched his carriage move away. She turned back to face the kind looking woman with vibrant red hair piled high on her head.

"I'm Jacob Robbins' niece Sara and----"

"Land's sake! Of course you are! Come in. Come in!" Jessica exclaimed. "Jacob will be so happy to know you're here safe and sound. Unfortunately, he's sleeping now. I'm afraid he hasn't been well."

"We know," Aaron said, entering the large parlor. "We heard he broke his arm last winter and got a bad cold this last spring. We were awful worried. But now we're here to help!"

"Bless your hearts. You're just the tonic he needs. But you must be exhausted," Jessica said, escorting them into the room and motioning them towards a large circular green-velvet sofa. "Please do sit down."

Aaron spotted Tarney sniffing under the sofa and then running to the grandfather clock in the hall way. "Come here, Tarney. Behave!"

"Oh, let her be," Jessica said. "She needs to look over her new home. By the way, I'll bet she's hungry. Have any of you had anything to eat?"

"Not since breakfast, on the Chrystopolis," Aaron admitted. "This is our friend, Miss Peggy O'Neil. She's come all the way with us."

"I'm so delighted you're here, Miss O'Neil. Are your parents here, as well?"

"No, ma'm. I'm an orphan, now." Peggy answered in a near whisper.

"We're her family now," Aaron asserted.

Jessica's warm, brown eyes nodded in understanding. "I'm sure Jacob will welcome you, Miss O'Neil." She turned to Sara, "I'd say the first order of business is making sure you all have something to eat, and I bet your pretty little dog could use a nice, juicy bone." She bent down and gave Tarney a pat.

"Thank you. We'd be grateful!"

"Well, you just rest here in the parlor while I get some tea ready and see what else I can round up. I just got back to San Francisco, myself yesterday. Been gone several months, I'm sorry to say. I expect your Uncle wouldn't have gotten so ill, if I'd been here. At least, that's what I like to think," she smiled. "So glad you young folks are here." She glanced toward the staircase. "There's another who'll be excited to see you. It's all Clara could talk about since I arrived this afternoon." She stood at the bottom of the stairs and called. "Clara, dear, they're here!" Jessica turned and headed for the kitchen.

"Clara!" Sara called excitedly, but paused as she saw her cousin standing shyly at the top of the stairs.

Clara clutched the mahogany banister, unsure if she should come down. Cousin Sara?" Clara's voice was soft. Hesitating briefly, she came slowly down the stairs. "I wasn't sure you'd come."

Sara rushed forward, put her arms around Clara and gave her a sturdy hug. "We're really here. Everything's going to be all right, now!"

"Oh, Sara, I was so scared," her voice wavered, but was soon replaced with excitement. "Now Daddy will get better!" She suddenly caught sight of Tarney. "Is that your dog?"

"Yes," Aaron spoke up. "Don't be afraid of her. She'll just kiss you, is all."

Clara's fear melted as Tarney ran up to her and kept licking her hand. "She likes me! What's her name?"

"Tarney," Aaron said, beaming with pride. "And she really likes you. She doesn't like just anybody, either."

"She's very pretty." Clara smiled up at Aaron. "Can I feed her?"

"Sure!" Aaron smiled. "Say, do you remember the little wood doll I made you just before you left Boston five years ago?"

"I still have it. It's my favorite."

"Good," Aaron said, beaming. He saw Clara staring at Peggy. "I want you to meet a special friend, Peggy O'Neil. She came all the way with us. She wants to help at the hardware store and then go on the stage and be a singer."

"I'm happy to meet you, Miss O'Neil," Clara curtsied.

"Nice to meet you, too. I've heard so much about you."

"Really?" Clara said, glancing at Sara. "Oh, I'm glad you're here. Daddy will be so happy."

"When can we see him?" Sara asked.

Clara shook her head doubtfully. "I don't know; he's awful sick."

"What does the doctor say?"

"He won't tell me anything. Just says I should stay away and be quiet. I don't like him. He's not our doctor."

Sara glanced at Aaron. "We'd better have a look."

"I'm not sure Mrs. Smedley will let you. She's awful strict about that."

"Well, I can be strict, too." Sara said, determinedly.

Just then Jessica came into the parlor, carrying a black lacquered tray and set it down on a round, oak side table. "I've found some scones and strawberry tarts. Tea and cocoa will be ready in a moment. I brought a little ham for supper so we can eat in an hour or so. But I expect you want to see your Uncle soon as you can."

"Yes, that would be wonderful." Sara looked thoughtfully at Aaron. "Maybe it'd be better if you and Peggy waited until I see how he is. Too much excitement might--"

"Ok," Aaron reluctantly agreed. "But holler if you need me!"

Sara started up the stairs, and noticed Clara's reticence. "Don't worry, I'll be very quiet," she assured and held out her hand.

Clara hesitated only a moment, and then eagerly grabbed Sara's hand, leading her up the stairs. Jacob's room was the first door on the left.

They entered quietly. The room was dark and Sara could barely make out the sleeping man in the large four-postured bed. He was breathing evenly, but the air was stale and heavy. Sara bent and felt his forehead. It was cool and a little clammy. His pulse was weak and his face had an unhealthy pallor to it.

Sara turned to Clara. "Has the doctor been here recently?"

"Yes, but Mrs. Smedley made him have a new doctor. I don't think he's helping." She glanced worriedly at her father. He's not like our regular doctor."

"What's the name of his regular doctor?"

"Dr. Cutler. He's a nice man. You can tell he likes Daddy, and Daddy was getting better after his pneumonia. But then Mrs. Smedley said Doctor Cutler couldn't come any more and we had to use Dr. Bonner."

"I see," Sara said, thoughtfully. Something was definitely not right about the situation. She'd get to the bottom of it, first thing, tomorrow. "Right now, I think your daddy could use some fresh air," Sara walked to the window where heavy, green drapes were pulled tight to shut out the light. She quickly drew back the drapes, and was surprised to find a large bay window. Unfortunately, all three sections of the window were dirty and two were nailed shut. She opened the one a little and was pleased to feel fresh air enter the room.

Glancing about, it was obvious that the whole room, so crammed with heavy furniture, hadn't been cleaned thoroughly in ages. That was something she could take care of very soon. Perhaps later, Uncle Jacob would let her rearrange the furniture to make it less oppressive.

Sara noticed Clara anxiously watching her, and she smiled confidently. "I won't do anything to disturb him."

Clara moved to the bed. "Daddy? Sara is here to see you." Clara touched her father's damp forehead, but he didn't stir.

"When was the doctor here?"

"Last week. He brought more medicine, I think. But he only talks to Mrs. Smedley."

"I see. I wonder where she keeps the medicine." Sara had seen people on the wagon train who had the same pallor

They'd been given too much laudanum, and she knew that could be deadly.

Sara glanced at the nightstand next to the bed, and pulled out the drawer. "Is this it?" she asked, holding a small vial.

"Yes, that's what Mrs. Smedley gives him in the morning and at night."

Sara opened the vial and smelt the liquid. "It's laudanum, just as I thought." Sara frowned, clutching the vial in her hand. She stood up and stretched her back. "I think we'll let your father sleep for now, Clara. But I need to talk to Aaron, so would you please ask him to come up and then give us a few moments alone?"

Clara nodded, but paused at the door.

"Don't worry," Sara reassured. Everything's fine."

Clara quickly went down stairs and it wasn't long before Aaron appeared at the door and entered quietly.

"Whew! It stinks in here," he whispered, walking to the bed and looking down at Jacob. Aaron didn't say it, but Jacob appeared like folks on the wagon train before they died.

"Aaron," Sara kept her voice low. "Mrs. Smedley's been giving him Laudanum and it's poisoning him."

"Do you think it's on purpose?" Aaron whispered.

"I don't know. But we've got to find out. And soon!"

CHAPTER FORTY-FIVE

Soon after Jessica left to fetch Dr. Cutler, Sara resolved to confront Mrs. Smedley about her care of Uncle Jacob. It might not be easy to get the culprits to admit anything, but Sara was determined that if it were to be a cat and mouse game, she would be the cat. She needed to prove that the Smedleys were in cahoots with Locke, as she suspected, and she knew that Aaron might get too angry and ruin their chances of getting that information.

Fortunately, she convinced Aaron, Peggy and Clara to wait on the landing upstairs, but within hearing of the parlor meeting.

The Smedleys had taken to their room next to the kitchen and stayed there the first hour that Sara, Aaron and Peggy had been in the house.

The news that Sara wished to speak to her, threw Mrs. Smedley into a temper. The woman raised her voice so that the youngsters could hear her rant from the parlor.

"That young lady, who does she think she is? I'm in charge! Besides, it's against Dr. Bonner's orders," she huffed.

"Careful, my darling, Edwina," her husband cautioned, lowering his voice. "If Jacob dies we don't want to appear culpable. Right now, we can blame any mishap on Dr. Bonner or Locke, or maybe his kin." He smiled and patted his beloved on the arm. "Dear heart, you're always trying to be helpful."

"You're right, as always, Ralph," she simpered. "Just remember all the sorting of barrels, listing things. Oh, I've worked my fingers to the bone. And to no thanks!" Edwina stomped about whipping herself into a froth of indignation.

"Take it easy, dear heart," Ralph insisted, looking concerned. He knew his wife's temper might tinder to a roar.

Edwina rushed out of the room, followed by Ralph and marched to the parlor.

Sara stood waiting. It was obvious that Edwina was ready for a fight. Ralph, however, appeared cautious. He frowned, sat and cleared his throat several times as he waited for Sara to speak.

"You wanted to see us?" Ralph asked quietly.

"Wants to see us! What nonsense!" Edwina glared at Sara. "I

don't have time for this! And I'll not answer to you—-a mere child!" Edwina's gray eyes darted like knives about the room. "What lies has that child been telling?"

"Please," Sara nodded at Mrs. Smedley, gesturing to a green patterned chair. "I'd like to ask a few questions about my Uncle's health. I need just a moment of your time." She deliberately appeared respectful. Her voice fairly purred. "Would you please take a seat? I know you must be weary, working so hard all day! This won't take long."

"Well, I never!" Edwina slightly mollified, flounced into the seat. They sat opposite Sara.

Sara cleared her throat. "First of all, though I appear young, I wish to reassure you--relieve your "concerns," and explain that I have quite a bit of experience nursing patients who've taken laudanum." She paused briefly then shook her head sadly. "I know how difficult it must be for you working with someone so ill and demanding all the care." She waited to see if Edwina had taken the sympathy bait.

Edwina took it, bowed her head. "No one knows how much. Lord knows, I've worked my fingers to the bone." Edwina pulled a hanky and sniffed, "I've tried my best, is all I can say."

"I'm sure," Sara nodded pleasantly, though her emotions pushed at her throat like a fist. Oh, how she'd love to punch that arrogant, self-serving look off Edwina's face. "You did your best, and now I need to know how much laudanum you've been giving Uncle Jacob."

Edwina glanced at Ralph. "Only as prescribed. It's on the vial. Anyone can see," she frowned.

"Did you give him any extra, at times?" Sara tried to keep from sounding suspicious.

"I gave a little to calm him down," Ralph added, "the extra, I mean--only in the last week. Seems he's worried about a court date. Of course," he cleared his throat. "Don't know about that, do we, love?" Ralph glanced anxiously at his wife. Had he said too much? He withdrew a hanky from his pocket and wiped his forehead.

"I see. And who ordered the laudanum?" Sara continued blandly.

"Why Dr. Bonner, of course," Edwina replied, cagily.

Sara's voice remained even, "And it was Mr. Locke that suggested Dr. Bonner, I believe."

"Naturally!" Ralph spoke up.

Edwina gave him a scowl. "We ah--"

Sara stood up, the meeting at an end. "Thank you for your time. Since Aaron and I are meeting with Mr. Locke in a few days, we can discuss your "service" with him, at that time. Until then, your help is no longer needed."

"What do you mean?" Edwina looked to Ralph. "She can't do that, can she?"

"Do not concern your selves," Sara offered calmly. "Aaron and I will be taking care of Mr. Robbins. Besides, Dr. Cutler is on his way here, now. He'll be evaluating Uncle Jacob--perhaps recommend a change in the prescription."

Sara lifted her chin determinedly. "You are both free to go, immediately. Be sure to tell Mr. Locke, that I insisted."

Edwina's jaw dropped and Ralph paled. They were shocked beyond words. Edwina sputtered and couldn't quite get her words out. "This is highly—highly--wrong and –and--." She rose from the seat, and then sat back. "I—I don't—"

"Never-the-less I insist you leave immediately!" Sara turned and walked calmly into the kitchen.

Edwina and Ralph followed behind Sara.

Edwina's scowled her fury, raising her fist. "You haven't seen the last of us, young lady. You'll be sorry, I promise you that! If Jacob dies, it'll be on your head. Mark my words, you won't get away with this--this robbery! Come Ralph. Just wait until Locke hears about this!"

With the Smedleys out of the way, everyone became very busy putting Uncle Jacob's room in order. Aaron soon had the bedroom windows pried open, and Peggy and Sara washed them to a sparkle. Then Aaron rolled his uncle first on one side than the other, so that the bedding could be removed and clean linen replaced. Uncle Jacob barely stirred even when he was moved.

They worked quickly and quietly to remove clutter and to straighten the tops of bureaus. Soon the room took on a new personality. Aaron found an oriental screen folded against the wall, pulled it open, and placed it around part of the bed. Now he was able to give Uncle Jacob a private and much needed sponge bath. After the bath, he dressed him in a clean nightshirt.

Though Jacob remained listless, by the time Aaron finished, there was a slight change in Jacob's color.

"He looks better," Sara said, bending over him. She laid her fingers against his wrist. "His pulse is stronger."

"Daddy," Clara said, gently touching his forehead. "We're all here--Sara, Aaron and even their friend, Peggy. Oh, please, please wake up, Daddy."

A sigh escaped the pale lips.

"He hears us, Sara. He hears!" Clara repeated excitedly.

"We better let him rest," Aaron suggested. "Tomorrow I'll give him a shave."

Having finished making Uncle Jacob more comfortable, they went downstairs to wait for Doctor Cutler and to make sure the Smedleys left.

They stood on the veranda watching the Smedleys leave. "And don't come back," Aaron hollered, as the couple charged through the gate, suitcases in hand, bristling with indignation. They looked angry as badgers, Aaron thought.

Tarney followed the couple to the gate, barking and pacing along the fence.

Infuriated, the Smedleys hurried down the road, stopping a couple of times, setting their large suitcases down, and glaring back at the youngsters. Edwina shook her fists and hurled invectives. "You haven't seen the end of us. You'll be sorry!"

Sara noticed Clara shudder. "You don't have to worry about them, anymore!" She put her arm about the girl.

"But what if Aunt Jessica couldn't find Doctor Cutler?"

Aaron quickly offered. "I'm sure she'll find him--perhaps not until tomorrow, but he'll come. We'll just have to be patient. Besides, your daddy is already better. Right, Sara?"

Sara nodded and smiled confidently. "Maybe you should heat some of that beefy broth, you mentioned. He might take some, now."

"Oh, yes! I will!" Clara said, bounding inside.

Aaron glanced at the side of the house. "Think I'll go look at the barn--see if it's suitable for Rebel," Aaron said. "Jessica mentioned that I could use her lorry tomorrow to go to the Johnson Stables. She drew me a map and everything. I can hardly wait to see Rebel. Hope he'll remember me. I have to make sure everything is ready when he comes home." Aaron glanced at the horizon. "It'll be dark in an hour or so." He turned to Peggy. "Be sure to call me if the doctor comes! Come on Tarney, we have work to do!" Aaron jumped down from the porch and ran around the side of the house.

A half hour later, Doctor Cutler arrived. Sara quickly ushered the pleasant looking, gray haired man upstairs. He soon confirmed their suspicions.

"You youngsters have saved Jacob's life. Another week of this," he held up the vial, "would have killed him."

It wasn't long before the doctor finished his examination and came downstairs to the kitchen.

Aaron had come in a few moments earlier and sat impatiently at the kitchen table. He jumped up when the doctor entered the kitchen. He thought the doctor looked very serious. "Well, how is he?"

"In time, better," Doctor Cutler said.

There were sighs of relief.

Doctor Cutler continued, "I believe we've caught this in time. However, the release of the addiction will take awhile. You'll have to be patient and stout-hearted—-and don't be frightened."

"What do you mean, doctor?" Clara's brown eyes grew wide.

"He'll be plagued with fearsome nightmares--be sick to his stomach, have chills and fevers, but in a few weeks he should work free of it. Just be sure to move him often--keep his blood moving and see that he doesn't get bedsores.

"Oh, we will," everyone assured.

"And," the doctor continued, "as soon as possible, get him to exercise, make sure he eats hearty food. He'll need to build strength."

Doctor Cutler sat at the kitchen table and accepted a cup of tea from Clara. "Thank you, young lady." He turned to Sara. "I've suggested the withdrawal schedule—-nothing too abrupt. I believe he'll be himself eventually."

"But probably not in time for the court hearing?" Sara suggested.

"No, I'm afraid any stress will set him back."

"Don't worry, Sara," Aaron quickly inserted. "We have everything we need for the judgment date, and don't forget, Cass will be there to help."

"Sounds like you youngsters have everything under control. Just let me know if I can help in any way. I consider myself an old friend. Just come get me, if need be."

CHAPTER FORTY-SIX

After Doctor Cutler left, everyone felt like celebrating. Relieved and excited about the good news, no one could settle down. There were suddenly so many new things to think about.

Aaron had some ideas for the barn. "I think I can make two stalls by moving over the tack area. And I looked closely at the carriage," Aaron said, enthusiastically. "It's been neglected and the seats need new stuffing, but the body doesn't need much repair. I can do it. But we're going to need a good, sturdy horse to pull it. Maybe when I visit Rebel at the Johnson Stables, they'll have a horse for sale. We certainly can't use Rebel to pull a carriage or wagon." He paused and scowled at Sara. "Do we have enough money left?"

"We do!" Sara answered. "You can spend sixty dollars." But then she remembered something. "You'll need to buy feed most likely. We have five acres, according to the deed, but it hardly appears to be enough to support one horse, let alone two. Better ask at the stables what we should do about feed. It's probably different from what we're used to."

"I hadn't thought of that," Aaron said soberly.

"Don't forget, I have money, too," Peggy offered. "If you could get the carriage ready before next week, then I could go to town, buy a sewing machine and some fabric. I can make us all some new clothes, maybe even in time for Marilee's party."

"I don't see why not, Peggy!" Aaron beamed. "I could go with you and help. We could see the sights, as well!"

"That would be wonderful!" Peggy turned to Clara. "I noticed a piano in the parlor. Do you suppose your daddy would let me play it, just enough to practice my singing for Marilee's party?"

"Daddy loves music. I'm sure he'll be happy to have you sing and play."

Aaron thought it a great idea. "Probably help him get better!" Aaron said, smiling at Peggy.

"You're so sweet, Aaron," Peggy returned, a bit shyly.

Clara suddenly remembered, "We also have a sewing machine. It's old, but it works. Mrs. Smedley wouldn't let me use it, but I know how. I could show you—-for your new dresses. There's even some fabric Momma put away in the cedar chest in my bedroom. And if we had two sewing machines, I could help make the new dresses."

"That's wonderful! Oh, Clara, what fun we're going to have! There may be more fabric in the basement, too."

"I just remember something," Aaron said, heading for the basement door. The basement--one place he hadn't investigated. "What's down there, Clara?"

Clara looked uneasy. "I don't know. Mr. and Mrs. Smedley wouldn't let me go down there. They said it was too dirty and dusty. But they were always there."

"Hmmmmm. Wonder what kept them so busy," Aaron said, suspiciously. He wouldn't put it past the Smedleys to do something spiteful before they left. "Clara do you have a lantern?"

Clara shook her head in alarm. "We do, but please don't go down there. Mrs. Smedley said there were spiders and rats."

Aaron scowled. "Rats or no, I'm going to see what's there! Bring me a lantern, Clara!"

After Clara returned with the lantern, Aaron instructed everyone. "Stay in the kitchen, and don't let Tarney come down. I'll holler if I need help." Aaron held the lantern in front of him as he cautiously descended the basement stairs.

Before long, there was a loud crash and an "Ouch!"

"Aaron! Are you all right?" Sara yelled, heading down the stairs. "Oh, dear!" She found her brother sitting on a barrel, rubbing his right leg.

"You're hurt!" She knelt to inspect the wound.

"I'm fine!" he snapped, pushing her hand away. "Just hit my shin on the corner of that stupid wood box."

"Well, be careful!" Sara warned, lifting her skirt and standing. "It's awful dark and creepy—-probably rats and who knows what else!"

Aaron picked up the lantern and moved it about. "Sure a lot of stuff down here--looks like small crates and barrels that haven't been opened yet. Look over there, Sara." He swung the lantern toward a nearby corner where a half dozen pickaxes and shovels leaned against the stone wall of the basement. "Hand me one of those pickaxes. I want to see what's in this small barrel."

Aaron used the end of the axe to pry open several slats. "Wow! Look at these brand new hammers!" Aaron exclaimed, handling one and testing the weight. "Nice!" he said, setting it back into the barrel. "I can hardly wait to see what else is here. I guess not everything was burnt up in the store fire."

"Maybe there wasn't even a fire!" Sara said, glancing about. "Wonder if Uncle Jacob knows!" She suddenly frowned. "But why would the Smedleys claim everything was destroyed?"

Sara and Aaron looked at one another, eyes wide and said, "They planned to steal it!

"Those blooming thieves—-keeping Uncle Jacob sedated so they could come back and take everything. This stuff's worth a lot of money." Aaron glanced about. "Maybe there's something in that little desk over there." Aaron pulled on a narrow drawer and suddenly it popped open and nearly fell to the floor. Inside were a few pieces of parchment. Aaron glanced at them. "Look, Sara!" There's a receipt from a company, Farnworth Drydock Yard in Sacramento."

"What does it say?" Sara asked coming to look.

"Says the boat called The Promise is in drydock yard B7 and ready for final delivery. Wow!"

"Want until Uncle Jacob hears this. The boat didn't get burnt up—at least as of two weeks ago. That's fantastic news. I wonder what else we'll find," Sara said, glancing about.

"Right!" Aaron agreed. "But we better keep a sharp eye out, and make sure the Smedleys can't get in. I noticed small windows here and there. I can't tell how many. They seem kind of small to crawl through, but I wouldn't put it past those crooks to try. For now, we'll barricade the outside door of the basement, and tomorrow, when there's light, we can look at the windows. Sara, do you have your Derringer handy?"

"It's in a compartment of my satchel, upstairs."

"Good! Keep it handy! I put Rufus's colt at the top of the hall closet. Those crooks don't know who they're dealing with!"

Upstairs, the news about the hardware goods and The Promise was greeted with great excitement.

Clara was sure it would make her father get well faster. "I can hardly wait to tell him. He'll be so happy. Can I do it?"

"Let's let him rest. Tomorrow will be time enough," Sara suggested.

"Now all we need," Aaron said, "is to find the right space to rent and Robbins Hardware store will be back in business!"

"Let's celebrate!" Peggy suggested.

It was past twelve when they went upstairs to their new bedrooms.

"I put fresh linens on every bed," Clara announced as she led everyone and Tarney upstairs. "Aaron, you might like this room best." She opened the door next to her father's room. "It's very ah--horsey."

Aaron was surprised to see a spacious, wood paneled room with a tall bookcase along one wall and colorful horse prints on the others. "It's perfect!" he exclaimed, running to the bed and bouncing on it. "Comfortable, too! Come on up, Tarney," he patted the bed and then remembered. "Is that okay?"

"It's up to you, Aaron," Clara grinned. "It's your house and your bed, now."

"Wow! My very own house. My very own bed." Aaron shook his head, hardly able to believe it. "This is great! Well, good night, everyone. See you in the morning. Come on, Tarney! You'll sleep here with me. It's your home, too."

Across the hall, Clara opened the door to a large room with a huge four-poster bed. "This is my room," she said shyly. "The bed is big enough for three."

"It certainly is!" Sara smiled, catching the underlying hope in Clara's words. "You know, Clara, I'd feel so much better, if Peggy and I could sleep here with you--just for tonight."

"Oh, Sara, yes, of course. That would be wonderful!" Clara turned to Peggy. "Do you mind?"

"It'll be fun!" Peggy said. "And what a beautiful room you have!"

Clara quickly ran and got Sara's satchel from the hall closet where she'd stashed it earlier, and then hurried back.

"Thank you, Clara," Sara said, taking her satchel. She set it on a cedar chest at the foot of the bed and opened it. Everything was there: her important papers, the Derringer and assorted clothing. "Good!" Sara said, stifling a yawn.

"What a pretty, feminine room," Peggy said, twirling about. She didn't feel at all sleepy. "I've never seen anything quite like it! And what a lovely idea, Clara—-having just two walls with the climbing rose wallpaper, and the others painted a soft green." Peggy walked to see what was behind the pink and white striped screen. "May I?"

"Of course, Peggy," Clara grinned.

"Oh, Sara, look--a copper tub and privy commode!"

"I see." Sara nodded, yawning.

"A room fit for a princess, which you are, of course, Clara."

Clara beamed.

How cheerful and comforting everything appeared, Peggy thought. The whole room was bathed with a warm glow from a crystal oil lamp on the bureau. "It's perfect, Clara."

"Here's your nightgown, Peggy." Sara pulled it from the satchel and shook it.

"This hardly seems fitting for such a fine room."

"I have an idea," Clara said. "If you don't want the nighty any more, it could become part of a story quilt. That's what my momma did." She pointed to a large quilt carefully folded at the foot of the bed. "When Momma came west, she saved all the different scraps of clothes and bits of fabric to make a quilt, so she could remember and tell me all about her adventures getting to San Francisco."

"That's a wonderful idea! Just imagine, I could do that for my daughter someday!" Peggy smiled, and impulsively rushed to give Sara and Clara a big hug. "I'm so grateful and happy to be here with you," she said softly.

"Well, you're part of our family, now, Peggy!" Clara declared, eagerly clasping her arms about Peggy. Finally, they were ready for bed and knelt to say their prayers. Each offered prayers of gratitude for what God had done to bring them through the hard and dangerous journey, and there were special prayers for those still on their way.

Sara knelt in gratitude. Gone was the familiar tightness, the resistance to prayers. Gone was the bitterness. She needed God. And that, she knew, was His gift. "Thank you Lord God," she said, "for finding me again." She didn't understand it all, but felt as if a stone had been lifted from heart. And as she thought about it, an image formed. She saw the heavy stone being cleared from Jesus' tomb. "Yes, new life," she murmured, feeling as if the image had come from outside of herself and been given with humor. "Yes, I understand. Thank you, Lord. A special warmth enveloped her. This must be what others have called 'The Blessed Assurance.' The warmth seemed to move around and through her. It was as real as a blanket and light as a touch. "Thank you, Lord," she said, humbly, her heart full of awe and wonder.

Down the hall, in his bedroom, Aaron lay back in bed, an arm around Tarney. "You're a fine dog, Tarney—-my very best friend," he whispered, giving Tarney an affectionate scratch behind her ears. "And tomorrow, we've lots of work to do, but we can do it, can't we? We can do together."

Aaron remained thoughtful, marveling at what they'd come through and what he'd learned. So many folks had helped him. Good folks who were willing to teach. There were so many things he knew and could do now. He'd learned to repair wagons and harnesses, build camp sites, read the weather and the flow of river currents. So much more. He'd even learned more about people--how you had to give them a chance, even if they were very different. He thought about White Hawk--how they were alike in some ways. He hoped White Hawk had made it back to his family. He thought about his own Mom and Dad. He knew they'd be proud of him. He was sure they'd love Peggy. Oh, how he wished they could have really known her better. Peggy was so sweet and she'd brought something special to the journey. She made him think about some things, and he liked listening to her read from the Bible—especially, Psalms. Maybe his parents would've thought she'd make him a good wife some day. On that happy thought, Aaron and Tarney closed their eyes and went to sleep.

CHAPTER FORTY-SEVEN

The next week was a busy one. Uncle Jacob was improving daily and Aaron visited Rebel at the Johnson Stables every other day. But he knew he'd have to leave Rebel there until Uncle Jacob's barn was properly repaired and made ready for two horses. Early every morning Aaron was hard at work on the barn.

Sara stood along the wood-pole fence watching Aaron nail fresh boards on the side of the weathered old barn. "It's looking great, Aaron, but you should come in for breakfast now and be ready when Cass comes."

Aaron merely nodded. "Sure hope Rebel likes his new stall. I can hardly wait to get him home. Uncle Jacob says we have all the papers to prove our case, so it shouldn't be long now. And Mr. Johnson says he thinks he's found a draft horse for us to buy to haul goods."

Sara smiled. Aaron appeared excited--in his element. All week long he'd worked ten or more hours sorting through things for the hardware store and building the barn.

"I'm not finished yet." He glanced worriedly at Sara. "We'll still need more lumber and money for the second horse."

"We'll have what you need soon, now," Sara offered cheerfully. "As soon as the case is settled, we should be able to sell things." She turned away from the fence. "Better come and get dressed. We'll need to look our best and Cass should be here any minute."

It was as if Aaron hadn't heard, for he replied, "I want to meet with Mr. Johnson and set up a training program for Rebel. Mr. Johnson thinks we could enter him in the quarter-horse races next spring. "Of course, that will take more money."

"Don't worry. We'll be able to soon—-maybe even at the end of today. You're doing a great job, Aaron. And...I've been meaning to tell you that...that I think you're just about the best brother anyone could have."

Aaron grinned. "Only 'just about'?"

"We'll see. There's still time," Sara teased, but suddenly felt close to tears. "You really were wonderful on the trail---so grown up and amazing...and...and I love you so much." Sara wiped her eyes and turned to rush back to the house. "Better hurry and get washed and dressed," she called as she entered the back door. "We don't want to keep Cass waiting."

As Sara entered the house, she reminded herself that most everything was being put in order, and without problems. However, her feelings still felt raw and on edge and had for several days. Besides worrying about the meeting with Locke, there'd been her unexpected feelings for Cass. She hadn't thought she'd miss him so much. Not being able to see or be with him every day felt awful, as if a part of her had been misplaced. Her chest ached. The memory of his face and voice haunted her days and dreams. And now, as she thought about him, and was about to face him, she felt all jittery and weak kneed. Would she act like a silly chit? Heavens! That would only reinforce his idea of her as a school girl. She just had to settle down. If only she could keep her pulse from racing, and her mind from cramming into a jumble. She took a deep breath, reminding herself, that this was the most important day of her life.

An hour later, Aaron was placing kindling in Uncle Jacob's bedroom fireplace. He bent carefully, setting each piece and making sure to keep the cuffs of his new brown suit from touching the grate. He asked his Uncle. "Do you think the suit looks right?" He turned around to offer a second view.

Jacob glanced thoughtfully from his rocker by the window. "I'd say you look very prosperous—-a regular young business man."

"Thanks. Cass helped pick it out three days ago. I didn't have time for tailoring. It's a little large," Aaron looked down at the cuffs. "But that way I save some money, when I grow into it. There's plenty of give in the leg, too. Cass said it might only last one season, the rate I'm growing." He saw his Uncle smile.

Aaron quickly changed the subject. "Sure is good to see you up, sir." Aaron glanced thoughtfully at his uncle. Though Jacob looked pale, he's green eyes seemed clearer, as he sat in the old rocker by the bay window. "You're getting better every day." Aaron quickly walked over to the bed, took a green, wool throw blanket off the end and brought it to Jacob. "Here," he placed it around Jacob's legs. "Jessica said to keep this around you when you were out of bed."

"Thanks." Jacob shook his head and raised his shoulders. "Jessica worries too much."

"Sara, too. And she gets awful bossy about it."

"It's the mother hen in them."

"I guess," Aaron said, getting an image of a chicken squawking, gathering chicks and pecking at the ground.

Jacob smiled. "They mean well, of course." He slowly lifted himself out of the rocker and walked to his bureau. "I rummaged through a few drawers yesterday. Good thing Mrs. Smedley was a poor housekeeper. Found some papers--purchase orders on Locke's stationary and signed by the Smedley's--after the fire." He handed a brown envelope to Aaron. "Don't worry about anything." He winked. "You and Sara have everything you need and are more than capable. I'm very proud of you, son, as I'm sure your Mother and Father would be."

"Thank you, sir," Aaron's voice clouded. "You get some rest now." Aaron watched his uncle get slowly into bed and lay back against a stack of fresh, white pillows. Soon his eyes were closed, and his breath came in easy little puffs.

Aaron turned, walked quietly to the door. Doctor Cutler was right. He said the worst of the laudanum withdrawal would be over at week's end. It seemed so. But Doctor Cutler also warned that Jacob would be more susceptible to disease. They had to be extra careful.

During the last week, everyone had taken turns staying up at night with Uncle Jacob. They'd watched him suffer terrible spasms, sweats and awful stomach pains, which seemed even worse at night. He'd had night terrors. Aaron knew a little about that. But last night was different--Uncle Jacob had slept through. That was a good sign, but they'd still keep an eye out for chills.

Aaron flattened his hands against his hair, settling down his cowlick as he came down stairs and walked into the kitchen. He noticed Sara and Peggy sitting at the table, Sara with her nose in a stack of papers.

"Hey, thanks, Peggy, for washing and ironing my shirt. Do I look all right?"

"Oh, Aaron you look so handsome--a perfect business man!"

"Thanks. Uncle Jacob thought so, too." Aaron's face flushed.

Sara looked up. "How'd you sleep?" she asked abruptly. "You don't look like you feel very well."

"Gee thanks. I'll try not to get by on my looks."

Sara calmly replied, "We need to have our wits about us, especially this morning."

"Well, too bad they're not handing out any more <u>wits</u>." "Aaron, please, I'm just concerned."

"Well, I'm not, so stop nagging!"

"Fine!" Sara snapped and poured a glass of milk and set it firmly in front of him. "You need your strength!"

"What we need is to win our case! And we need more money!" Aaron blurted.

"But you have mine!" Peggy piped up. "I told you, the two hundred and fifty is yours."

"We can't take that!" Aaron sounded insulted.

The budding argument was diverted by a loud knock at the front parlor door.

"I'll get it, Aaron. Eat your ham and eggs. It's probably Jessica. She said she'd be here early, before we left." Sara bolted from the table and rushed to the parlor door.

CHAPTER FORTY-EIGHT

Sara opened the door to a grinning Cass Bartlett.

"Good morning Sara." He said, recovering from her surprised expression. "Did you think I'd forget? I said I'd go with you to meet Mr. Locke."

"Yes…no, no of course, not," she said, flustered. "I knew you'd keep your word."

"You look…very… nice," Cass offered, smiling and noticing Sara's green-striped skirt and fitted forest-green jacket. "That outfit becomes you."

"Oh," Sara said, a bit distractedly.

Cass watched Sara fuss with her hair. Obviously, she hadn't quite finished dressing. Her hair hung loose, untamed. A most delightful look, he had to admit. And her hazel-green eyes appeared as though she'd just awakened. "You look very …fetching, Miss Robbins." He handed her his hat, which she took and put on the peg by the door and turned quickly from him, into the parlor. "I know I'm early," he offered, wondering at her cool reception. "Your Uncle, how is he?"

"Getting well, thank you." She stopped abruptly and turned to look at him. "I…I…do want to thank you, Cass for helping us. We are very grateful."

"Sorry if I'm too early. I'd hoped to have time to go over the papers."

"Oh yes, of course," Sara answered, feeling her face flush. She quickly poked her white-shirt back into her waist-band, and shoved a lock of hair off her forehead. I must look a fright, she thought, staring into those amazing blue eyes that had, once again, plunged her into a whirl of feeling. Her face warmed, and a sudden jolt pressed down the length of her, leaving her weak in the knees. She shook her head. "What did you say?" Did he say anything?

Cass paused, raised his brows. "I said I'll wait in my carriage, if you prefer." He pointed to his mahogany colored coach waiting near the gate.

"Oh, no! I mean…that's not necessary. We're ready." She stepped towards the kitchen. "Aaron," she called. "Cass is here!

Please have a seat in the parlor," Sara gestured. "I'll get Aaron."

Cass nodded and sat down on the green-velvet settee.

Peggy came bounding out of the kitchen. "Oh, Cass, how good to see you," she rushed up, stood on tip-toes and planted a kiss on his cheek.

Surprised, Cass stepped back to look at her. "You look wonderful, Peggy. San Francisco agrees with you."

"Yes, it does. I'm very happy here. How is your father?"

"Much better, I'm pleased to say. We've been very busy. But he's hoping to meet you all very soon."

"I can hardly wait!" She turned to Sara. "Won't that be wonderful--to finally meet Mr. Bartlett, Sr.?"

"Yes, it will," Sara said, recovering her sea-legs. "I'm really looking forward to that." She truly was.

Cass returned her smile.

In spite of feeling unsettled, Sara couldn't help noticing how handsome and distinguished Cass looked this morning. She could hardly take her eyes off him. He wore a charcoal-gray suit, with a light gray vest. It made his eyes even more vivid. And his great-coat of fine black wool emphasized his wide shoulders.

Aaron came bounding into the parlor. "Hi Cass!" He turned impatiently to Sara. "Thought you'd be ready. Your hair isn't done. Better hurry; don't want to keep Cass waiting."

"She was…ah, entertaining me." Cass smiled.

"I was not entertaining…I was just--." Sara bit her lip. "Never mind, I'll only be a minute." Sara rushed to the stairs and without glancing back, lifted her skirt and sprinted up, two at a time.

Before long, Cass, Aaron and Sara were on the road heading to town and their meeting. The encouraging voice of Cass' driver, Flynn Sandoval, talking to the two grays, and their comforting clip-clop helped eased Sara's nerves. Having Cass beside her, his quiet assurance, meant a great deal. It all came down to this day, and to the decisions of men she didn't know.

A half hour later, Cass' sleek carriage arrived on Montgomery Street. Flynn brought the horses to an easy stop, and let the passengers out. Cass quickly instructed his driver when and where to pick them up.

Sara glanced up at the beautiful, three-story brick building. Tall white columns flanked the front, and pretty white and black marble tiles lined the spacious entry and extended inside, in to a wide lobby.

"Oh, good, there's Judge Marshall now, Cass stepped forward to greet a sandy-haired, middle-aged man. The two shook hands. "Hope you haven't been waiting long, Clive."

"Not at all," he smiled pleasantly.

"This is Miss Sara Robbins and Master Aaron."

"Master Robbins, Miss Sara, I'm delighted to meet you." He bowed respectfully.

Sara smiled, relieved to finally meet Judge Marshall. Cass had mentioned him and assured Sara that he was a very honest and knowledgeable man. He appeared to be a pleasant, intelligent man, about the same age as Uncle Jacob, though not as tall. His forthright manner gave her confidence, while his grey eyes radiated good humor.

Judge Marshall stood perusing the papers Cass offered. But after only what seemed like two minutes, he returned them to Cass. Sara felt her stomach drop. Could he have had time to know and understand what was in them? He'd barely glanced at some of them. A jolt of fear pressed down her spine. She had to remain calm.

"Are you all right, Sara?" Cass asked.

"Yes," she nodded and continued walking. Their steps clicked loudly against the glossy, hard surface of black and white marble. The sounds mirrored the thumping of her heart.

Sara took another deep breath as they paused at a solid oak door. Across the door, written in gold, was the dreaded name--A.E.Locke, Esq. Law.

Sara glanced at her brother. His face had that determined thrust of chin—-so like their Dad, she thought. "We can do this," she said, pressing her lips.

Cass appeared relaxed. And when he saw her looking up at him, he winked and said, "Here we go!"

He rapped firmly against the paneled door. They waited only a moment before Mr. Locke opened the door. Apparently surprised to see four people, he frowned, and his eyes narrowed at the sight of Judge Marshall. "Well, Judge Marshall--Clive, I...I didn't expect to see you." Locke brushed aside strands of thin white hair from his forehead. "Come in, come in."

Cass held the door open. "The Robbins' family expressed a desire to have an impartial witness to this meeting," Judge Marshall explained, as he walked in. "I'm acting as their legal consultant.

"Ah, yes, good, good." Locke cleared his throat and walked to his desk. He turned, settled a pair of small round glasses on the thin bridge of his nose, and motioned everyone to take chairs.

There were six large, red, leather chairs around an oversized mahogany desk. "You might wish to sit over there, Miss Robbins," he pointed to a red velvet settee across the room. "It's more comfortable," he smiled indulgently.

"I prefer here," she said, standing behind a chair directly in front of the desk.

"Of course, my dear." He smiled and waited until she and the rest were seated.

Locke's thin-lipped smile and watery gray eyes made Sara think of a lizard."We're here to discuss our...." Sara began.Mr. Locke cut her off. "You must have had quite an

exciting journey, Master Aaron. I'm glad to see you made it safely." He did not look at Sara.

Cass interjected. "We haven't met. Cass Bartlett's the name." Cass did not stand or offer his hand. "I'm representing the family."

"The son of Charles Bartlett?"

"Yes, now I suggest we get to the business at hand. Judge Marshall has limited time."

"Of course," Locke said, scowling down at his desk, and glanced up with a quick smile. "Most kind of you to show interest. I'm sure this won't take long at all." He nodded cordially at Judge Marshall and reached for a folder in front of him. As if to ease his discomfort, he shook his head, "Such a shame about your Uncle. He's quite ill, I understand,"

"You understand incorrectly, sir!" Sara snapped. "He's quite well, no thanks to the Smedleys who poisoned him."

"Really!?" Mr. Locke was caught off guard. "Young lady, you mustn't slander people. It's against the law." He glared at Cass, as if to suggest he should control his client.

"It's true!" Sara continued, her anger rising. "We have a doctor's report."

Judge Marshall turned to Sara. "Good heaven's young lady, that's quite an accusation."

Mr. Locke's face tightened. "I must remind you not to exaggerate in business dealings, Miss Robbins. Never-the-less, I will overlook this outburst,...ah...statement for we have considerable business to attend."

Aaron and Sara glanced at each other.

"If I may be allowed," Judge Clive Marshall cleared his throat. "I'd like a moment to look over your papers, Stanley."

"I think you'll find everything in order," Locke said with a righteous air.

They waited as Judge Marshall looked at each document on the desk, comparing it with those Cass handed him from Sara and Aaron's folder. Before long, Judge Marshall handed back the two sets of folders.

"Well, Stanley, I have looked over the ownership papers. They are intact and duly notarized. "It's clear that Sara and Aaron Robbins, as well as Jacob Robbins, are the sole owners of the horse known as Rebel and the boat known as the Promise. All debts for storage and maintenance have been paid, according to these records," he nodded at Sara's folder. "The Hardware store and all redeemable contents are the rightful property of the Robbins estate. I believe this is provable in any court."

Stanley Locke drew in a breath, paused, and pursed his lips thoughtfully. "I will, of course, be very happy to find your proof of ownership in good order, Miss Robbins. No one is trying to cheat you or your Uncle. I was merely trying to help Jacob when I lent him the money for repairs on the boat, which unfortunately, was burnt and sank near Sacramento." He turned and glanced out of the window in back of him, then turned again to them. "Also, the warehouse had a fire, as you've likely heard, and since Jacob had not paid for <u>all</u> the merchandise, I took a note out on his property. Naturally, I felt it was only right he and his daughter be allowed to remain there--at least until you arrived." He smiled and leaned over the desk. "I have not foreclosed, as I might have, seeing as how the mortgage has not been paid. And to further show my good intentions, I allowed a horse, Rebel, I believe its name was, to be used as collateral, a highly unusual piece of guarantee, I might add. Then, as you know, the horse has been boarded and costing money every day. But I insisted it be cared for by the best. Now, I think you'll all agree, that I have been more than kind…or shall I say, helpful to your family."

Sara rose from her seat. "Helpful? I'll tell you--." Aaron gave her a warning jab with his boot. She turned to glare at him, but shut up and sat back down. Aaron was right. They needed to know more. "Perhaps, you'd better explain," Sara said, regaining control.

Locke droned on. "I'm the one who's been holding the "cart," so to speak, and I'm pleased that you have proper ownership papers, so that I may transfer them to my name and have the foreclosure proceedings begin immediately. And to show my good will, I shall negotiate some recompense to you and your family. I realize this situation has been most unpleasant for you."

Aaron turned to Judge Marshall. "I'd like to say something, sir. I don't know much about law. However, I over- heard Mr. and Mrs. Smedley mention the 'merchandise' is stored." He turned to Locke, "and by you. Perhaps," he challenged, "you can explain how something can be stored at one place and be burnt up at another."

Mr. Locke rose from his chair. "The impudence! How dare you accuse me!"

"In fact," Aaron continued, "I believe nothing was burnt up, not even The Promise!"

Furious, Mr. Locke removed his glasses and slapped them down in front of him. "This is too much! You must control your client!"

"He's doing just fine." Cass said evenly.

Locke looked imploringly at Judge Marshall, then suddenly changed his manner and sat down again. "I didn't say everything was destroyed, as you must recall!"

Aaron insisted, "There was no fire, and all the merchandise is safely stored--part in our basement and part in a warehouse near China Town." Aaron pushed three pieces of paper onto the desk.

Mr. Locke refused to go on the defensive. "I've a good mind to sue your client, Mr. Bartlett for wrongful accusation."

Judge Marshall, in a much slower tempo, brought the meeting to a close. "I think I'll have a look at the contents of the valuables in storage and compare the bills of lading." He turned a cordial face to Locke. "That way, there won't be any dispute as to what remains of the estate."

Judge Marshall turned to Aaron. "Mr. Robbins will you be able to show me proof of the merchandise tomorrow? Then I'll make a recommendation to the court as to whom or how much is owed. In addition," he looked directly at Locke. "I will consider bringing charges of criminal wrong doing to any of the parties, if I find it." Judge Marshall turned to Cass and smiled at Sara and Aaron. "I think this concludes our meeting for today. We'll meet again tomorrow at eleven in my chambers."

Locke appeared grim: his lips drew a hard line. "Tomorrow then!" He nodded coldly and walked to the door and opened it.

They hurried from Locke's office and out of the building. Traffic in front was a whirl of activity. People were rushing in and out of the building and across the street as buggy and coaches pulled alongside the walkway.

"Ah, there's my carriage, now." Judge Marshall said, waving it in. "I'll look forward to seeing you tomorrow. Should be quite a show," he chuckled, stepping into his coach.

"Thank you," Aaron and Sara waved. "We'll be ready." Judge Marshall tipped his hat as his carriage pulled away.

As soon as his coach left, others came forward, jockeying for space. Sara saw a familiar looking phaeton.

"It's Jessica's," Sara said surprised. "I see Mr. Hwang, my uncle's former store manager. He came to the house several times, asking after Uncle Jacob, but he was told by the Smedleys 'to stay away and not to bother the sick man.' Jessica, of course, welcomed Mr. Hwang." She looked concerned. "I wonder what he's doing with her coach? I hope nothing's wrong with Uncle Jacob."

Cass and Aaron looked at each other. "I think you'd better tell her," Cass said, with a cagey look.

CHAPTER FORTY-NINE

"Tell me what?" Sara demanded. She wasn't in the mood to be left out of anything, nor have her brother conspire with Cass. The very idea!

"Okay, I'll tell you, but you have to promise to cooperate."

"Cooperate?" Sara huffed. "What does that mean?" She glared at Cass.

Cass frowned. "We're setting a little trap for Mr. Locke. He thinks Aaron knows where the merchandise is stored."

Aaron butted in, "I have a hunch, but I'm not exactly sure which warehouse. Mr. Hwang showed us last week, what he thought might be the place. Now Cass thinks Locke will try to have the goods removed this afternoon. We're going to follow him and catch him moving it."

"And just when were you thinking of telling me."

Cass tried to defuse the situation. "Mr. Hwang will take you home," he said calmly. "No need for you to worry. It's all been planned. We can handle it."

"I see," Sara said tightly, and then suddenly brightened. "Fine! I'll come along, too."

"That's not a good idea, Sara," Cass explained. "It could be dangerous—-the docks are no place for a girl."

"I'm coming! Whether I'm with you or not!"

Aaron shook his head. "We'll be standing around in the cold. You may have to wait all day. You'd hate that."

"But did you ever think he might not go where you think? Maybe someone else will do it for him."

"Sara has a point, Aaron. Do you have any ideas?"

Sara noticed Mr. Hwang coming towards them. "I think we should ask Mr. Hwang. He knows the waterfront better."

"Good idea." Aaron rushed over to Mr. Hwang, pulled him aside and explained the situation.

Mr. Hwang grinned from ear to ear and repeated something in Chinese.

"I have idea," Hwang began excitedly. "If goods in same place, I stay at dock there, put up kite. You see from b'ock way--maybe two.

I let kite go high--special red dragon. It mean Smed'ey or Mr. 'ocke there. I see them before. No prob'em."

"What if they go to another warehouse?" Aaron frowned.

"No prob'em, you chase. I stay make money. But no sel' dragon kite." He grinned. "I see you later at Mr. Jacob's."

"I'll go with Mr. Hwang," Sara stated. "I can help with the kites."

"Maybe," Mr. Hwang grinned, "I put her on end of kite string and f'y her home."

Just then Cass' driver, pulled up in front.

"Before I leave, I want you safely home, Sara. This is dangerous business, and I don't want to have to worry about you." Cass gave her a stern look. "I don't want anything to happen to you."

"Cass is right, Sara. Please...just go home."

"All right," she said, raising her chin. "You two go ahead. I'll stay out of trouble."

Sara was glad not to be cooped up in a carriage for the afternoon. Besides, she had another idea of how to help.

When Sara returned home with Mr. Hwang, she found Jessica in the kitchen preparing vegetables for a pot roast. The room was warm and smelled deliciously of roasted meat and vanilla sugar cookies. Peggy and Clara were rolling out the cookie dough and cutting them with tin circle shapes. They were eager to hear about what happened in Mr. Lock's office.

"Thank you for bringing Sara home," Jessica smiled. "Won't you stay for a cup of tea, to warm you, Mr. Hwang?"

"No time, I go now...maybe catch fish on a pole. Maybe catch big crook fish."

Sara was ready to put her plan into action. "Jessica, maybe Mr. Hwang could give me a ride to the grocers on his way. We need some fresh fruit and vegetables for tomorrow. Besides I feel awful hemmed in and restless. I need to get out, do something."

"I understand," Jessica said kindly. "It's been a difficult morning." She turned to Lin Hwang, "Would you mind dropping Sara off at Freddie Fays and making sure she hires a carriage back?"

"I'd like to go too," Peggy said.

"Well, I guess it's safer for you to be together. But don't dawdle. Be back in a couple hours. I've had enough excitement for a week. Mr Hwang, please make sure they get a reliable coach." She turned to Sara and Peggy. "And don't even think about walking back."

Jessica wiped her hands on her checked apron. "I've a list of things you can pick up."

Sara exchanged a smile with Peggy. "We'll be quick as we can."

"I'll get my cape, Sara," Peggy said, and a shawl for you." She darted for the stairs.

"Wait for me at the gate, Peggy. I need to get something in the basement." She turned to Mr. Hwang. "I'll be right back." She saw Jessica's questioning look. "There's a perfect little basket for fruit and such downstairs."

"You hurry back, young lady."

"Don't worry, Jessica. Peggy and I've come across a whole continent. A few civilized city streets won't be any problem."

"I wouldn't count on them being too civilized, either!"

Before Jessica could change her mind, Sara bolted for the back stairway. Besides the basket, she knew just what she wanted from the basement. It would be a perfect disguise.

Mr. Hwang sat impatiently waiting in the coach with Peggy. "She better hurry! Wind for kite no wait!" Mr. Hwang frowned at the sky and shook his head. "I take you market...no time lose. Kite need plenty winds. I no 'ikee sky."

"Here she comes now," Peggy said, as Sara rushed through the gate, carrying fishing poles, a basket and two, large Chinese hats? What in the world did Sara intend to do?

"You no makee trouble." He looked suspiciously at Sara "You go <u>shopping</u>!" he insisted, stubbornly refusing to get up in the coachman's position. He glanced back at the house not sure whether to leave.

"Hurry, Mr. Hwang. We've no time to lose," Sara insisted, handing Peggy the poles as she climbed into the coach, and settled the basket on the seat beside her.

Lin Hwang shook his head, taking his place at the reins, and giving Lily her go ahead. He kept mumbling, "This girl makee trouble for me!"

The two young women settled back into the coach. Sara quickly whispered her plan to Peggy. "Think I've got everything we'll need." She flipped open the wicker basket's top to show Peggy. Inside were all kinds of fish hooks, sinkers, a rolled line of catgut and a knife.

"I've never gone fishing before," Peggy grinned.

"Oh, you'll love it. I'll show you how. But now we'd best concentrate on the streets and remember them, so we can find our way home."

The closer they came to their destination, the more uneasy Mr. Hwang appeared. He glanced about, rather anxiously, Sara thought. Of course, she reminded herself, the narrow streets were very crowded--so many horses and carriages vying for places to stop.

Before long, they pulled up to a small shop that had rows of boxes with neatly displayed vegetables and fruits in front. "This Freddie Fay. You shop, go home."

"Mr. Hwang," Sara began, "how far away will you be? Maybe Peggy and I could drop you off at the dock and we could drive Lily and the coach home."

Lin Hwang stiffened. "I follow order from 'ady Jessica."

"Of course," Sara said, "but--" she was about to mount an argument.

"You no go there. Bad place. I not far, maybe six blocks," he scowled. "You go home. I go meet Cass. He tell police come. You stay here. I tell Freddie get coach. You no makee trouble. I have wife in China. Jacob no help me...you make problem."

"We won't cause any trouble, I promise."

"I wait. You go Freddie Fay. Say Lin Hwang out front."

Sara and Peggy grabbed the hats, fishing poles and basket, stepped out of the coach, and entered the shop.

Soon an older man with a slight limp and a long, white goatee came out and limped over to Lin Hwang. He bowed and said something in Chinese.

After Hwang made arrangements for the girls, he left in Jessica's coach and headed for the docks.

Sara was delighted with the idea of renting another coach. "I have an idea." She grinned at Peggy as she confidently strolled between colorful bins and boxes of fruits and vegetables. She picked out green bell-peppers and six potatoes. "Look, Peggy! They have boxes of oranges and lemons! We must get some. What a treat!" She placed one under Peggy's nose. "We'll have one at the dock later."

After they'd made their selection and paid, Mr. Fay placed everything in a jute string bag and escorted the girls outside to a waiting carriage.

Mr. Fay helped them in, bowed deeply, gave directions to the driver, Billy Chang and waved them on.

They'd gone less than a half a block when Sara tapped the driver on his back. "Please, sir, would you mind going by way of the docks?" She smiled demurely.

The grey-haired driver frowned.

Sara added, "Of course, I'll pay extra. You see my brother is most likely down near where Mr. Hwang is selling kites. I want to give him a ride home."

Sara thought the driver could use the money. He was a frail looking man, with hair as fine as mist and shabbily dressed. Poor man. Whatever warmth his brown coat once offered, was of little use now. She saw him shiver and look hungrily at the coin, and was relieved when he nodded and turned his horse about.

When they were in a few blocks from the dock area, they spotted kites flying over the roof of a warehouse.

"That must be Mr. Hwang's," Sara said.

"Maybe others are selling kites, too." Peggy suggested anxiously.

"Most will be selling over there." Sara pointed to a long series of carts and booths that lined a street across from the wharf. "Better let us off over there," she told the surprised driver. "We'll walk the rest of the way. And if you'll wait until we return, I'll pay you two dollars more." The fee, Sara had been told for taking them to the dock was fifty cents. The extra would likely convince him. "I'll just leave my sack of groceries in your coach," she said, grabbing two oranges and putting them into her basket.

The coachman shook his head. "I'll wait Miss, till the afternoon tide comes in." He glanced down at his pocket watch and quickly returned it to his vest. "Then you're on your own."

The girls clambered out of the coach with Sara clutching the basket and Peggy carrying the poles and hats.

Before walking onto the dock, Sara paused and took one of the stiff, wide-brimmed straw hats and put it on Peggy. It was shaped like a kettle cover and would easily hide their hair and faces. "Here," Sara grinned, tying the hat under Peggy's chin. "You look a regular little Chinese person, except, of course for your green day dress. Oh, well. We'll stay out of sight," Sara emphasized, placing the other hat on her head. "Come on!"

"I don't suppose we look much like fishermen," Peggy said, trying to keep up with Sara's brisk stride.

"Just don't catch anyone's eye. We'll be fine, soon as we get down on the little boat landing. We can hide behind one of the rowboats."

As they rounded a corner of the warehouse, they saw Mr. Hwang. He was busily setting up more kites and had his back toward them. He was bending over a wooden box where he had a number of kites packed together.

"Keep your head down and hurry," Sara said rushing down a ramp just left of the dock. They were finally on the lower level where a platform moored smaller boats. "Let's sit over there." She pointed to an old, peeling, white rowboat which had been taken out of the water and left on the platform. "We can sit behind that and watch the dock above. Keep your pole up and drop the line into the water. Best not talk above a whisper and don't look up at the dock. You keep an eye out for Cass in case he comes by water. I'll glance up, now and then."

Peggy looked doubtful. "You better tuck your hair up. It's like a red flag."

They soon settled themselves on the platform, next to the rowboat and dutifully held their fishing poles in the water.

"If nothing happens soon, we'll go home. I don't want to worry Jessica," Sara concluded. She wondered if Cass was able to get the police to come."

Sara watched the kites Mr. Hwang put in the air. Some looked like fish swooping down to the edge of water, while others soared high in the sky, bright red and blue birds. "They're pretty, aren't they? Sure wish I could fly like that. Who knows? Maybe, someday. A long time ago, an Italian painter and inventor thought people might be able to fly. He drew it."

"That would be nice." Peggy shivered as a gust of wind raised her lidded hat. "This wind cuts through my bones and seems to be coming from all directions." She glanced up at the sky. It looks to be about three. Maybe Locke will wait until nightfall."

"I don't think so. Cass thinks he'll move stuff during the day-- make it look like regular business." Sara hunched her shoulders up and down to relieve the tension. She could see Peggy shivering. "You're cold. Maybe we should go."

"I'm feeling a little seasick, too," Peggy admitted. "The dock is rocking more." She eyed the water gushing over the platform, a few feet away.

"Must be the tide coming in. It's later than I thought," Sara said, suddenly concerned. "Let's gather our stuff and go." As Sara got to her feet, she nearly lost her balance as a wave struck the platform, rolling her against the side of the rowboat. "Better hang on to the boat, Peggy. I'll carry the basket, if you'll carry the poles. And watch your step. It's slippery now."

"Look," Peggy cried, motioning to the top of the dock. "Something's happening. Mr. Hwang is trying to get the dragon kite up, but it's tangled."

Just then, several large men walked toward Mr. Hwang. One stood towering above him, pointing to the street. "You Chink, you belong over there!" But when Lin Hwang shook his head and pointed to the kites, the burly man raised his arm and brought it down on Mr Hwang's back. Lin Hwang fell to his knees. The two men snorted a laugh, briefly glanced about, and then entered the warehouse.

"Oh, poor Mr. Hwang. We have to help him, Sara."

"Wait. Mr. Hwang is getting to his feet. He appears all right. Now he's getting the dragon kite up. Oh, no, it's not catching the wind right. It won't be a signal if it doesn't rise higher, above the warehouse roof. "Oh, rats! There's Locke walking toward the warehouse. He's got some mean looking men with him. Don't look up, Peggy, he might see us." Sara hunkered down lower. "Oh, dear, where are Cass and Aaron?"

CHAPTER FIFTY

"The Smedleys!" Sara's hand stifled a cry as she watched Edwina and Ralph walk along the dock near the rear of the warehouse, yards from Lin Hwang. "They'll recognize him. And there's Locke following." Sara pointed to the tall, thin man, followed by the two men who'd attacked Mr. Hwang. "We have to stay calm, think." Oh, where were Cass and Aaron?

"What should we do, Sara?"

"I'm not sure. But keep low. We'll inch along this platform, use the rowboats for cover, and head up the ramp to the dock. Once they go inside the warehouse, we can hide behind those barrels on the dock. But keep that hat over your face, and be ready to duck behind one of the rowboats if anyone looks in this direction. Drat!" Sara saw Ralph Smedley glancing over the side of the dock at the water. He was looking down at the lower platform, near where they were. "Quick! Scrunch down behind here," Sara said, grabbing Peggy's arm and pulling her down next to a rowboat. Sara peered gingerly around the front of the boat, and when she glanced up, she saw that Mr. Hwang was standing about 50 feet away from the Smedleys.

"What's Mr. Hwang doing?" Peggy whispered, not daring to raise her head."

"I'm not sure, but it looks like he's talking to himself and dancing around like he's a little crazy. He's pretending to be tangled up in his kite string. That's clever. The two men who shoved Mr. Hwang earlier, just shrugged at the sight of him. Now, they're going inside the warehouse. Oh, no! Mrs. Smedley is walking up to Mr. Hwang." Sara held her breath.

"What's happening?" Peggy asked fearfully.

"Mr. Hwang is putting the kite across his face and whirling about. Mrs. Smedley must've ordered him to move because he's covering his face with the kite and backing away. But Locke is glaring at him, motioning him away from the entrance. Good, Locke and the others are entering the warehouse. And Mr. Hwang is running toward the other side of the dock. Come on Peggy!" Sara picked up her skirt and the basket. "Hurry! Take the poles." Sara darted ahead, scrambling up the ramp and onto the dock with Peggy dashing after.

They ran across the front of the dock. Rounding the corner, Sara and Peggy nearly bumped into a very startled Lin Hwang. He was preoccupied in trying to get the dragon kite up and over the top of the building. He motioned for them to stay behind him.

Sara knew that however much Lin Hwang might want to help, he could offer no real protection. He kept shaking his head, but wisely remained silent and pointed to the walls of the warehouse. Sara nodded and put her finger over her lips. She knew that the thin walls would carry any sound, and put her ear against the wall, hoping to hear what was going on inside.

Within minutes, Mr. Hwang had the Dragon kite flying over the top of the warehouse. If Cass was anywhere near, he would surely see it.

"Look over here, Sara," Peggy whispered, pointing to a small window high up along the warehouse wall. Peggy turned to Mr. Hwang. "Can we use your little kite box?"

Lin Hwang nodded and placed his box under the window. He was about to climb up.

"Let me," Sara insisted. "I'm the tallest." Sara lifted her skirt and gingerly stepped up. "I can't quite see; it's so dark in there." She strained to inch taller. "I can almost see, but the window's too dirty."

"Here," Lin Hwang handed Sara a scrap of cloth. It was part of a tail to one of his kites.

"That's better." Sara rubbed away some sludge. Standing on her toes, she cautiously looked inside. She saw Mr. Locke in the middle of the warehouse, holding a lantern and giving orders. She heard Locke say, "All right, now roll those barrels over here. Ralph, you have the numbers?" he gave Mr. Smedley a shove. "Don't just stand there! Edwina, bring me those papers and I'll check them off, myself. You," he motioned to the two bearded men, "get those sacks of rice and put 'em here, in this cart." Sara saw Locke and the two men wheel several large carts already loaded toward the door. "Oh, no! They're almost finished."

"What shall we do?" Peggy looked about frantically.

"I'm thinking," Sara said. Her first idea was to create a scene-- delay them. But if they were almost finished, the only sensible thing would be to follow them, see where they were taking everything.

"Look!" Peggy pointed to two large rowboats moving quickly towards the dock.

"Thank God!" Sara murmured as she saw Cass and her brother manning one of the boats. She jumped from the box and rushed forward, hoping to warn them not to make any noise.

Police!" Hwang whispered, excitedly as he saw the other oarsmen pulling the boat up to the lower platform. "We hurry now," he said, reigning in the dragon kite. Peggy began putting the other kites into the box.

Just then, the door of the warehouse opened, and Mr. Locke stuck his head outside, looked cautiously about, but when he saw the boat pulling up with Cass and the other men, he swore and quickly ducked back inside.

"They're trying to get away," Sara cried. "Come on!" she shouted to Peggy and Hwang, not waiting as she ran ahead towards the warehouse door.

"That girl be death of me!" Lin Hwang shook his head, not sure which way to turn. He was very grateful to see Cass coming up the ramp.

"Lin Hwang, wait!" Cass called as he bounded up onto the dock. He was closely followed by two policemen, who immediately rushed to the warehouse door and stood ready, guns in hand. Cass motioned for everyone to stay back and wait. He stood listening.

"Sara's inside!" Peggy wailed.

Cass quickly pulled a colt .45 from the holster at his belt and with his other hand motioned the two officers to roll aside the heavy double-door.

Inside, the warehouse was dark. Muted daylight filtered in from several high windows, and it took a minute for Sara's eyes to adjust. No one was about, but then she heard shuffling noises coming from the smaller storeroom. What should she do? Maybe if she confronted them, it would act as a distraction until Cass and the police could get there``.

Suddenly, Cass came bounding through the door and rushed to her. "What do you think you're doing?" His voice, more snarl than whisper. "Stay back! Over there."

Shocked, Sara backed away, but tripped over a sack of rice and landed on her knees. Sara struggled to right herself. Once on her feet, she stood still, watching Cass point his gun toward a dark area.

"Give it up, Locke! You're surrounded," Cass hollered.

A burly policeman rushed forward and stood next to Cass. "Locke, come on out. You'll have a chance to talk. Resist and you'll go to jail!"

A grim-faced Locke swaggered forward, an insolent smirk on his face. "I don't know what all the fuss is about." He brushed himself off. "I was just doing a little business with my clients here, the Smedleys."

Edwina and Ralph stepped from behind large sack and glared at Sara and Aaron. "Those brats are behind this. Let me tell you, you'll be hearing from my solicitor." Edwina turned imperiously to the officer in charge. "What is your name, officer?"

"Sergeant Gillman," the officer replied easily.

 Mr. Locke asserted himself as the person in charge. "Don't be duped by these young people or their representatives." He shook his finger and jabbed it, pointing. "They're breaking the law, interfering with commerce and..."

"We aim too," Aaron rushed forward. "This man's a

thief, Sergeant Gillman. And we can prove it." He moved to stand next to Peggy.

"This is an outrage!" Edwina screamed, rushing forward. "I'm a lady. I won't be treated like a… a… common criminal."

Just then, three other policemen appeared. Two of them rounded up the loudly protesting Smedleys and the other officer hand-cupped Locke's men. They were all pushed into the main room of the warehouse.

Edwina resisted, twisting and turning, against the officer's grip. "Let me go this instant, you bully!" She tried stamping his boot, but he quickly side-stepped.

"Everybody just stay put!" Officer Gillman ordered calmly, giving Edwina a critical look. "I'll take those papers, Mum."

"Ralph do something!" Edwina sputtered in anger.

Ralph glared at his wife. "Shut up!" he said spitefully.

Locke surged against the officer cuffing him, trying to throw him off balance. "You fool! Don't you know who I am? I'm A. E. Locke, and I refuse to be hand-cuffed."

"You'll have your chance to prove anything you want in court. Now," he turned to one of the officers, "see if the paddy wagon has arrived. Then take them down town."

"You'll hear from my lawyer," Edwina shouted, but stopped abruptly as she looked at Locke and realized he was her lawyer. The group was herded outside and into a waiting horse-drawn wagon which had a little caged area.

"You won't get away with this!" Locke fumed, spewing invectives even as he was led to the wagon.

"You'll pay for this! You….you…Riffraff!" Edwina's shrill voice struck like a serpent's tongue! "You'll be sorry! I'll get you for this!"

Still resisting, Locke and the Smedleys were hauled into the paddy wagon and soon on their way to jail.

CHAPTER FIFTY-ONE

During the next week, Judge Marshall reviewed the documents, compared the merchandise at the warehouse and in Uncle Jacobs' basement. He was accompanied by two police officers of the court, so that everything was objectively done and legal. When that was finished, Judge Marshall presented his findings to the court appointed judge.

The court found in favor of the Robbins and gave the go-ahead for Sara and Aaron to take possession of their goods. In addition, criminal proceedings were started against Locke and the Smedleys; however, they were released on bail with warnings to stay clear of the warehouse and the Robbins.

Once legal approval was granted, Sara and Aaron, along with Peggy and Lin Hwang, spent a very busy week at the warehouse going through hundreds of barrels and boxes and itemizing every item. It meant long hours, but with rewarding surprises, as well, almost like opening Christmas presents. They discovered boxes and barrels of all sorts of things. It was especially exciting when the girls found fabric. Peggy lifted a bolt of pale-blue, silk brocade.

"Oh, Sara, look at this! Just think of all the beautiful dresses someone could make!" Peggy rubbed the fabric against her cheek.

Sara nodded thoughtfully. "Yes, but it should be displayed just right. She held up a bolt of red and white check print. "These would make beautiful curtains." She set the bolt back in an unused barrel. "Maybe I should paint the barrel, make it more appealing to put things in."

Aaron frowned. "Don't waste precious paint just to make things pretty. There goes the profit!"

"That remains to be seen," Sara countered. "You have to suggest ideas to people, too, you know. Besides, pretty things will appeal to women." Sara danced about waving a bolt of green muslin.

"Maybe," Aaron countered, but we have to be practical, Sara. You should ask Cass. He always has good ideas."

Sara abruptly stopped. "That won't be necessary," she answered sharply. We'll manage just fine on our own!"

Several times during the week, Cass stopped at the warehouse to discuss things with Aaron when Sara wasn't there. Decisions had been made, and Sara felt left out.

"It's obvious that Cass Bartlett doesn't know me or my ability. He needs to realize," Sara lifted her chin, "that I have just as much say in running the business as you and Uncle Jacob. And," she emphasized, "he knows by now that I'm not some simpering, silly chit!"

"Yes, yes, Cass knows that," Aaron said impatiently.

"It's a matter of respect," Sara insisted.

Aaron was getting very annoyed with Sara's touchy attitude around Cass. "I don't know what you want. He likes you a lot. I see the way he smiles at you."

Sara flushed. "It's not the same thing at all. "I certainly can't respect a man who doesn't respect me--all that I am!"

"Sara, the way you act, I'm surprised he even talks to you!" Aaron accused. "And if I were Cass, I'd stay clear of you. Look what he's done for us. He's offered to help us rent a space downtown and gave us money to lease it with."

Sara stiffened. "There! You see. He didn't bother to discuss it with me!"

"He couldn't," snapped Aaron. "You and Peggy had gone to the market. We can have a space tomorrow if we want."

"A space downtown?"

"Yes, thanks to Cass. It's only 50 by 200 feet, but in six months we can get another 50 feet next to it. He'll even co-sign the lease if we want."

"I'll think about it," Sara stated mulishly. "It's just that...well, I don't like being so indebted to Cass."

"Indebted?" Aaron shook his head impatiently. "He's being a friend, is all. He wants to help us!"

"Aaron, we don't really know him all that well. I mean, as a business person."

"Sara!" Aaron looked about to explode. "What's wrong with you? The man helped us escape Colwell, got us across the country, got us a lawyer and now he's offered to help us get set. What does he have to do to prove himself?"

Sara opened her mouth, but Aaron interrupted. "You're impossible, Sara!" He stalked away and flopped down on a large sack of rice. "Peggy, maybe you can talk some sense into her."

Peggy hesitated. She hated it when Aaron and Sara were angry with each other. And every day now, there seemed to be some situation. "Maybe," she began slowly, carefully repairing a rip in a large gunnysack, "maybe it might be wise to have an agreement where you pay him back--."

"Yes!" Sara said, enthusiastically. "That's it. We'll sign a legal agreement--itemize everything--pay back with interest." She suddenly frowned. "But we can't give him any part of the business or Rebel or The Promise!"

It was at that moment that Cass appeared at the warehouse door. He'd obviously heard the exchange.

Sara tried to recover composure, but she was embarrassed, and pressed her hand over her apron. "My brother and I were just wondering how to repay you," she said a bit haughtily.

"I see," Cass said, grinning and doffing his hat.

"Interesting," he said with a provocative tilt of his head and walking up to Sara. "And good day to you, too!"

"This is serious business," Sara retorted, wishing Cass wouldn't stand so close. "It's our whole life and there are other people involved." Sara held on to her best schoolmarm expression.

Cass cleared his throat. "Sorry, I'm..."

Aaron interrupted. "Sara's worried about paying you back, is all. We appreciate all your help very much, don't we, Sara?" he asked pointedly.

"Well, of course!" she said testily and then caught herself. "We are greatly indebted to you."

Cass winced at her words, but returned a civil manner. "There is something you can do for me. My father heard me talk about our journey. He'd like to meet all of you. It would mean a great deal if you would come and have tea with him." He saw Sara hesitate. "Of course, if you're too busy." Cass looked at Aaron. "I know you're in the middle of setting up." He glanced about at all the boxes and barrels. "I don't want to impose."

"Heck!" Aaron's face lit. "We'd be happy to come--anytime, Cass!"

Cass smiled at Peggy. "That includes you, of course, and Uncle Jacob, Mrs. Banner and of course, Clara."

"That's very thoughtful," Sara acknowledged." She pushed a few damp strands of hair off her forehead. Goodness, she'd been sweating, and moved a foot farther from Cass. "I've looked forward to meeting your father."

Cass beamed. "Will next Saturday do? I've taken the liberty of inviting my cousin, Sloan and Marilee, as well---you met them on The Chrystopolis. Around tea time?"

Sara nodded, "Yes, four o'clock Saturday would be fine." Sara was thinking that since it was Monday, she would have time to prepare.

"Your father must be feeling much better to have visitors," Peggy volunteered.

"Yes. It's amazing how fast he's improving. I guess it helped to have me home." Cass smiled and shook his head, as if just realizing that.

"You're very lucky to have your father," Peggy offered wistfully, "and I'm sure he feels the same way about you."

"Hope so," Cass said. "Well, now, about our tea, I'll pick you up at three o'clock." He turned to leave. "And about the other thing--paying me back. I could use some professional guidance." He motioned to a few bolts of fabric. "I'll be needing new drapes for my office." He grinned at Sara, "Something cheerful. I'll trust your taste."

Sara brightened. "Well, that's wonderful. I'd be happy to see what I could do. It's one of my favorite things--putting ideas and fabric together. In fact, it's one of the services we plan to offer our customers--taking things to people's homes." She ignored Aaron's scowl. "I'll bring some samples on Saturday," she concluded happily.

CHAPTER FIFTY-TWO

Since rental space was at a premium, Sara, Aaron and Uncle Jacob made a quick decision to rent the new space. And thanks to Cass, they were able to secure a ten year lease. Planning and preparing the store would take several weeks, but they quickly hired a carpenter to help build shelves and partitions.

Sara was satisfied that she had her say about the general layout of the store, but she left many decisions to Aaron. He and the carpenter had good ideas about the placement of goods and flow of things. Lin Hwang found two tall, used glass cabinets that had been in a Chinese shop. The price was excellent, and Sara and Peggy had all kinds of ideas on how to utilize them.

"It feels like Christmas, doesn't it?" Peggy said bending over a barrel, sorting through straw. "Look at these ladles, tin cups and five wash boards." Peggy held one up and pretended to be scrubbing something. "We had one just like this on the farm. I sure wish Momma were here." Peggy shook her head and brushed the dust off her apron. She took a deep breath and glanced about. "Just think, Sara, by next week, all this will have some order, and you will have a real store. Just like your Momma and Daddy wanted."

"Yes," Sara agreed softly, if nothing else happens. They were nearly out of money and credit, but she didn't want to worry Aaron or Peggy, so had not mentioned it. She was glad that Peggy hadn't mentioned her stepfather all week. It had, however, crossed Sara's mind that the store's name, The Robbin's Hardware Store might attract Colwell. Would he remembered their name? Sara sighed. She couldn't worry about everything now. They'd have to keep an eye out and do the best they could. In any case, she took her Derringer to work with her.

In a few days, the store took shape. The partitions were in, and most of the boxes and barrels had been brought over from the warehouse and Uncle Jacob's basement.

Uncle Jacob had improved enough so that each evening he held a meeting in his bedroom to help plan the next day's work. Soon, he assured them, he'd be able to come to the store.

"Yesterday," Sara said, sitting in Uncle Jacob's rocker, "Jessica and I looked at some of the other stores, to check prices and see what they carried. I think we have a unique look, with plenty of variety. We should have a big grand opening, offer a prize or something to bring people. Lin Hwang suggested we could hang kites outside. Peggy and I can make fliers and put them around." Sara's eyes were bright. "Maybe have something for children. Parents would most likely come if they could bring their kids. Clara could hand out candies or something."

"I swear, you two are born merchants." Uncle Jacob nodded. "Take after your Daddy," he smiled.

"I didn't know my father was interested in such things."

"Well, he was. It was his idea to have a family day, at the hardware store."

"I never knew that," Sara said, thoughtfully.

"You're father was a very smart man. But he was quite a handful growing up—-according to our father."

Aaron who sat at the end of the bed, was suddenly all attention.

"Really, he was? What kinds of things did he do?"

Jacob smiled. "That'll have to wait for another day. Now, it's time for bed."

On Wednesday, Marilee Brenner came to see the new 'enterprise.' "Cass said I should drop by. I hope you don't mind?" Her dark curls bounced as she strolled towards Sara, carrying a small basket. "Here are some fresh bran muffins and a jar of strawberry jam. My cook, Martha, made them. They're wonderful! Just smell them!" Marilee pulled back a white damask napkin.

"Oh, thank you, Marilee, they smell delicious. How thoughtful," she smiled, took the basket and set it on a barrel. "I'm so glad you stopped by."

Marilee glanced about. "My, what an interesting assortment. You seem to be in the middle of things. If you have an apron, I'll lend a hand."

"Oh, no. You'll get all dirty, but thank you," Sara said, admiring Marilee's small, saucer-shaped hat. It had a green and gold feather lashed across one side. "That's so pretty."

"You can have it, if you like." Marilee started unpinning it.

"Heavens, no!" Sara protested.

Marilee shrugged and strolled up to a shelf where tin tea pots were set side by side. "Cass told me about the tea his father is giving this Saturday. Has he mentioned who's coming?"

"No, and it's really not my—-"

"Well," Marilee interrupted coyly, gingerly picking up and inspecting an iron skillet. "It seems a certain young lady has inveigled an invitation. Apparently, she's been visiting Cass' father." Marilee rolled her brown eyes. "To see how he's recovering--of course, now that Cass is home. Hmmph. Just be prepared my dear, to go a "round" or two with Miss Priscilla Mathews. Remember I told you, she has 'plans' for Cass," if you know that I mean."

"Oh." Sara felt her stomach turn flip-flops. "Marilee, I don't quite know what to say. It's up to Cass and his father."

"Oh, balderdash!" Marilee fumed. "Just look your best. I'll do the rest."

"Really, Marilee, I'm sure that--".

"Enough said on that subject." Marilee waved her hand. "I must say, these goods are more interesting and exotic than what one finds in other hardware stores. This part's a kind of ladies haberdashery. I shall tell all my friends to come and buy things from you. Husbands and wives together--what fun!" Marilee turned to face the back of the building. A partition separated it from the front where she stood. "Who is that singing?"

"That's my friend Peggy--the one I told you about when we met."

"Oh, yes! What a lovely voice. I asked if she'd sing. Has she agreed?" Marilee was listening very attentively.

"Well," Sara hesitated. "She said she would, but it'd help if you asked her personally."

Sara and Marilee strolled to the back of the warehouse. "Peggy, I'd like you to meet Cass's soon to be cousin-in-law, Marilee Brenner."

Marilee put her gloved hand out to Peggy. "You have a lovely voice. I'm so happy you agreed to sing at my soiree." She beamed and bent forward as if sharing a special secret. It's a very special occasion. "I'll be announcing my engagement! Your singing will be a special gift to Sloan and me."

Peggy frowned.

"Oh, please, it would mean so much. And I have a friend, a pianist, who I'm sure would be happy to play for you. He can play anything."

Peggy looked helplessly at Sara. "I haven't practiced." .

"Oh, you'll love Karl," Marilee interrupted. "The two of you can practice at my house before hand, every day, if you like. I have a wonderful grand piano, and a perfect little stage area."

Marilee watched Peggy fuss uneasily with her blue shirt and white shirt. She guessed Peggy was thinking about what to wear.

"As far as a performance gown," Marilee eyed Peggy's figure like an experienced modiste. "I have just the thing. I bought it last season, but haven't worn it. It might be a tad big." She walked around Peggy. "But that won't be a problem. I have the best dressmaker in San Francisco. There's nothing Madame Florencia can't do with a piece of fabric." She noticed Peggy's hesitancy. "Naturally, I shall pay for it! After all, an artist should be properly compensated, and that can be part of the payment." Marilee's excitement increased. "Don't you think that's perfect?" Marilee clapped her hands. And the very best thing--oh, tell her, Sara.'"

Sara shrugged, slightly confused.

"You know," Marilee insisted, "how we planned to announce to everybody about the new store. My soiree would be a perfect time-- all those people, in a happy mood--get them interested." She waved her wrist to emphasize. "Some have plenty of money, I can tell you. They'd love to spend it at your store, I'm sure! Oh, Peggy, you'll help Sara make the store a big success."

Sara and Peggy burst out laughing. Marilee was irrepressible.

Nothing was to be left undone, once Marilee had begun a project. She had a perfect plan for every detail. "Oh, this will be such fun!" She rushed to hug both girls. "I'll pick you up tomorrow so you can meet Karl. We'd best get started."

After Marilee left, Peggy panicked. "I can't do it!"

"Peggy, calm down. It'll be fine. You have a couple weeks to practice."

"But," Peggy protested. "All those people in fancy clothes. I don't want to embarrass you or Aaron or Cass either. Do you think they'll be dancing and everything?"

"Dancing?" Sara pondered the idea. For a moment she allowed a picture of herself in Cass' arms. "Oh, dear! What'll I wear?"

"It's two weeks away, as you said," Peggy offered. "No, I mean, this Saturday's tea to meet Mr. Bartlett, senior." The idea of meeting Cass' father and Priscilla Mathews, all at the same time, suddenly loomed as a huge event and one she wasn't remotely ready for. Maybe she shouldn't go. No, she reminded herself, that wouldn't be respectful to Cass or his father. She had to go, ready or not.

CHAPTER FIFTY-THREE

"Now I see why women always want a bigger carriage." Aaron critically surveyed the three young women sitting opposite him. "Your dresses and all that frill stuff sure takes a lot of room."

Marilee leaned forward and smiled coquettishly. "It's called fashion! And we always hope to make you men delighted by it."

Marilee's referring to him as "men" caught Aaron off guard, but it pleased him. He felt his face flush. "I think that red dress is nice on you, Marilee." He turned to Peggy. "That blue dress looks very pretty on you, Peggy." He noticed the neck-line was lower than usual. While he liked the way it looked on Peggy, he wasn't sure he'd want other men gaping.

"Well, I hope it's not too low cut." Peggy said, fingering the lace about her neck.

"Naw, it's…it's just right," Aaron assured.

"What do you think, Sara?" Peggy frowned.

"What?" Sara answered distractedly. She'd been mesmerized by the slow rhythmic clip-clop of the two horses. "I'm sure it's fine," she offered, and remained looking out the window. She tried adjusting the lace around her bodice. The whole dress was too snug. She liked the pale peach color, but it wasn't very comfortable. Still, it'd be worth it, if Cass liked it.

Sara had been thinking about Cass, tracing the changes in their relationship, remembering moments, bits of evidence that would assure her he felt as she did. She sighed. Just when she thought they'd come closer, he'd pull away. Is it because he thinks I'm too young? Doesn't he know I'll be eighteen in two weeks? Would that make a difference? Was it because of Mark? Did he really believe she was engaged? A stab of guilt burrowed into her conscience. She'd been disloyal to Mark, hadn't she? Maybe Cass would find that a terrible fault. She hadn't had time to explain about Mark. Oh, why was falling in love so complicated?

"That dress makes you look much older, Sara." Marilee smiled, as if reading Sara's thoughts. "And that soft peach and pale lace around your bodice suits you very well."

"Thank you," Sara said.

"You look very nice, Aaron." Peggy turned to smile at Aaron. "That brown suit is new, isn't it? And I like the camel-colored vest."

"Well, Cass sort of picked it out. I went to his tailor." Aaron usually didn't like being the center of attention or talking about such things, but it felt good to have Peggy like the way he looked.

Marilee turned to nod and wave at a passing coach. "We're nearly there. It's a rather formal looking house from the outside," Marilee continued, "with its huge Grecian pillars and marble steps in front. It's not so formal or stuffy inside; but it does need a women's touch--someone like you, Sara." Marilee smiled to see the effect of her words. "Someone with innate taste. You did bring the samples, didn't you?"

"Yes, they're in my satchel, up front with the driver," "I'm sure Cass and his father will be impressed."

"I'm looking forward to helping Cass decorate his new office."

Peggy and Marilee exchanged knowing looks.

They passed several large coaches on the way up the hill. Aaron was impressed. "Wow! Look at those horses. I think they're Morgans, like Danny and Reeves. I sure wish we could've kept them." Aaron shook his head. "I miss them, don't you Sara?"

"Yes, I do, Aaron," Sara said sympathetically.

"At least we have Rebel."

Sara gave Aaron a gentle smile. She knew how important Danny and Reeves had been to Aaron, and how sad he'd been to give them up. She was very proud of him—-the grown up way he acted. Letting go of things one loved was painful, but a necessary part of growing up.

A long circular drive, large enough to turn a coach and four horses, brought them to the entrance of the Bartlett home. It was, as Marilee described, a very grand two story house with several large pillars in front and a rather formidable entrance with the tallest doors Sara had ever seen.

"Sure is a big place. Even bigger than yours, Marilee," Peggy said, as the coach stopped.

The carved doors of the house opened and a middle-aged man rushed down the steps to the carriage. Sara wondered if it was Mr. Bartlett Sr.

"So good to see you again, Miss Brenner."

"Sylvester, it's good to see you too," Marilee said, allowing the man to take her hand and help her out of the carriage. "These are my friends...the ones who crossed the continent with Cass. May I introduce Mistress Sara

Robbins, Mistress Peggy O'Neil and Master Aaron Robbins."

Sylvester gave a formal bow and smiled warmly. "Pleased to meet you. I've heard Cass mention you. A remarkable trip, I understand." Sylvester's round face and sturdy build radiated energy and good humor.

Sylvester turned to Flynn. "Good to see you too, Flynn. Soon as I see the guests inside, I'll come back and guide you and the horses to the carriage house. We've been rebuilding it, so I'll need to show you the way."

"Right, as you say, Sly. I'll wait here."

Marilee picked up her green-satin skirt and rushed up the steps, and then waited at the door as Sylvester opened it with a flourish and escorted them in.

The entry was a large, two-story, semicircular room with a curved, dark wood stairway off to the right. Sara noticed the marble floor with its round patterns in pinks and browns offset with a honey-white star in the middle. In the center of the room was a large ornate table with a crystal vase filled with roses of all colors--roses this time of year. Most unusual, Sara thought. But, she reminded herself, this is California.

As a long, paneled door slid open, happy voices echoed into the hallway. A tall man walked towards them. Smiling broadly, he walked up to Aaron and extended his hand. "You must be Aaron."

Aaron eagerly shook the man's hand. "I can guess who you are, sir," Aaron said, looking up into grey-blue eyes.

"You look just like Cass!"

"I'll take that as a compliment, though I always considered that he favored his mother. But thank you! And this is Miss Sara, of the 'fiery-red hair and sea-green eyes.' So pleased to meet you." He smiled heartily. "And this is Peggy, the young woman who has such a pretty voice,' and I might add, such a pretty face." He turned towards Marilee. "I hope you're not too grown up to give your old "uncle" a hug, especially since you're going to have to put up with me as your real uncle soon. That is, if you are still set on marrying my nephew?" The mischievous grin was a duplicate of Cass's.

"You heard! Shame on Sloan or was it Cass who said? Spoilt my surprise! Naughty boys!" Marilee feigned a pout and stood on tip toe, lifted her lace fan and gave a quick tap on Mr. Bartlett's nose. "I could hardly wait forever for you." She twirled about. "You can see I'm not getting any younger."

"But certainly more beautiful! Guess Bartlett men are a little slow about some things." He winked at Aaron. "It isn't good for a young man to wait too long." He turned his smile to include Sara and Peggy and seemed to linger for a moment on Sara, but then he remembered. "I've taken the liberty of inviting a few of your young friends, Marilee."

"Oh? And who might that be?"

"Why, Priscilla Mathews. She couldn't wait to be one of the first to congratulate you."

Marilee glanced quickly at Sara. "I'm sure. Well, that was very thoughtful of you, Uncle Charles."

As though reacting to Marilee's little frown, Mr. Bartlett cleared his throat. "You undoubtedly need to freshen up. Marilee, why don't you show Sara and Peggy where the powder room is, and I'll take Aaron with me. We'll meet you in the morning room in a few minutes. Take your time."

"Come along Sara, Peggy." Marilee turned quickly and rushed ahead to a door partially hidden beneath the stairway. "Wait until you see the powder room."

Sara followed Marilee, but paused to glance back at Mr. Bartlett and Aaron as they disappeared through large paneled doors. Sara's heart was pounding. Had Mr. Bartlett seen her color at the mention of Priscilla? Did he see how she felt? Oh, she was so embarrassed. If only she didn't show all her feelings with the flush of her cheeks. What a curse that was. She would never be sophisticated like other girls.

The powder room was indeed elegant. Gold faucets, pink marble on the walls, and a pedestal basin sat beneath a gilded mirror. There was even a separate area for the commode.

"A person could live in here!" Peggy exclaimed.

"Wait until you see the rest of the house!" Marilee washed her hands and took a small, hand embroidered towel to dab at her face. San Francisco is so dusty!" She tucked up a few strands of dark hair. "Feel free to use the towels or whatever you need."

Peggy was fingering small, sweet-smelling soaps in a dish. "I've never seen so many at one time. This one smells like lilacs." Peggy cupped the soap to her nose. "The Bartletts must be very rich."

"Yes. Mr. Bartlett and his brother, Thomas, came out in 1850, after the Mexican war. They did very well with a number of enterprises. Tragically, Thomas was drowned in a boating accident."

"How sad for Sloan," Peggy said, watching Marilee in the mirror.

"Yes, it was. But Uncle Charles was very good to Sloan. Raised him like his own son. Made sure he and his mother had everything. Mr. Bartlett helped my family, too. I adore him and would do anything in the world for him."

"You know Cass pretty well, then, I guess," Sara said, thoughtfully.

"Yes, I've known Cass and Sloan since I was twelve."

"I wonder why Cass feels his father is so..."

"Distant?"

"I guess," Sara sighed.

"After Cass's mother, Loretta, died, Mr. Bartlett wasn't himself for a long time. He was heartbroken. Cass was only fourteen. He began making friends with a rough crowd and getting into fights. Uncle Charles tried everything, gave him plenty of opportunities, but Cass was very resentful. Quite a handful. So, Uncle Charles sent him back east to live with a cousin and go to school. I don't think Uncle Charles had planned it to be so long. But it turned out that he didn't see Cass for several years. Then Cass went to college and after that he traveled a bit."

Sara shook her head. It seemed so sad. "They haven't had much time together."

"I know. And I think Uncle Charles realized it too late. I know he begged Cass to come back before going off to college. But Cass was stubborn. Now there's a big wall between them. But I sense a change."

Just then there was a knock on the powder-room door.

"Come in!" Marilee called.

"Oh, I didn't know anyone was in here?" Priscilla smiled, entering.

"You didn't?" Marilee said, coolly. "Then why did you knock!"

"Well, excuse me," Priscilla huffed. "I was taught to knock before entering a closed door."

"How very right of you Priscilla."

Priscilla opened her fan defensively, "Why I..."Oh," she

fumbled for a smile, "Marilee, you are such a tease. I swear, I always forget," she simpered.

"I might as well introduce you to my friends," Sara Robbins and Peggy O'Neil. This is Miss Priscilla Mathews."

"How nice to finally meet you, both." Priscilla eyed Sara in obvious appraisal. "Cass has told me so much about you." She offered a sugary smile. "You're much better looking than I thought."

Marilee turned to the mirror and deliberately reworked an errant curl. "Cass is not one to gush, is he?"

Ignoring Marilee's comment, Priscilla put her lace gloved hand to her head and tinkered with several dark curls. "I heard that congratulations might be in store for you and Sloan."

Marilee frowned. "When you hear it from me, then you'll know for sure, Priscilla."

"I'd be happy to hear it." She turned to face Sara and Peggy. "Are you ladies finished in here?"

"Oh, yes. Excuse us!" Peggy moved a few steps, eager to be gone from the obvious tension.

As Peggy and Marilee left, Priscilla grabbed Sara's arm. "Would you mind staying, Sara, and helping me with my gown?"

Sara, caught half in and half out of the powder room, turned back inside. "Oh, sure, I'd be glad to help." Sara motioned to Marilee. "You and Peggy go on. We'll be along soon."

Marilee shook her head in disgust. "Are you sure?" Marilee did not feel right about leaving Sara.

"You go ahead." She waved them on.

Priscilla smiled helplessly. "You're most kind. I think a hook on my outer petticoat came undone. I'd hate to trip and fall."

"Of course, I know what you mean. I can take a look."

"Dear me, I can't seem to do the least common thing for myself. I don't know what I'd do without my maid, Serifina. Do you have a maid, Sara?"

She made it sound like an innocent question, though Sara knew the petite, dark haired girl was fishing for information. She couldn't resist, "No, I have my friend, Peggy, to help me!"

"Of course," Priscilla said, her mouth drawn in seeming pleasure. "Friends are so important. I do look forward to gaining Marilee's friendship. Alas, we don't see nearly enough of each other. But that's going to change. Being on good terms with ones in-laws is the basis of family life, don't you think, Sara?"

Sara had lifted the dress up high on Priscilla's back.

"Can you see the culprit? Careful!" Priscilla moved aside a clutch of jet-black curls that hung half-ways down her back."

Sara searched and found a loose hook. "I think I see the culprit. There's one missing. Oh, dear, and one is broken." Sara frowned, concentrating, but something Priscilla had said, made her pause. "You mentioned Marilee's friendship and...."

"And in-laws. Yes," Priscilla smiled, "Could you reach into that little drawer there and find me a straight pin? There are usually some there."

As Sara pinned the fabric together, she felt short of breath. Her hand flew to her throat. "I need some air."

Priscilla was looking into the large gold mirror over the sink. "I don't suppose anyone will notice the flaw underneath." She settled a flounce of lace on the low bodice, and then gazed with satisfaction into the mirror. "Isn't this sumptuous? Mama ordered it especially for this tea." She leaned closer to the mirror and pursed her lips, then rubbed them to gain color. "I recollect that this dress is Cass' favorite color. He just loves this shade of green."

Sara took several shallow breaths. The girl had as much sensitivity as a potato. "Fortunately," she said tartly, "tastes change, don't they, Priscilla?"

Priscilla smiled sheepishly. "I think I know Cass's tastes." Giving a coy side glance, she moved closer. "I guess you can be one of the first to know."

"Know what!" Sara's heart thundered.

"Momma says she and Mr. Bartlett Sr. have come to an understanding. It's all been arranged."

"Arranged?"

Priscilla lowered her eyes demurely, and spoke softly, "So Cass and I can be engaged by Christmas."

Stunned, Sara leaned against the sink.

"Careful! You'll get your dress wet."

"I...I.." Sara struggled.

"Mercy, Sara! Are you all right? You look white as snow. You're not going to be sick, are you?" Priscilla stepped back.

"No! Of course not!" Sara glanced up to see Priscilla's pursed-lip smile reflected in the mirror. Suddenly furious, Sara raised her voice. "Really, I'm perfectly fine! I'll just need a moment! Please leave!"

"Good heavens!" Priscilla said, astonished by Sara's tone. She turned and smiled sweetly, as though forgiving the outburst of a child. "Of course, Sara. Thank you so much for helping. Are you sure you don't want me to loosen your corset?"

"No!"

"Well, if you're sure?" Priscilla raised her eyebrows. "You do seem very pale. I so hope you're not ill." Priscilla thought Sara looked about to vomit. "Oh, dear!" Priscilla quickly rushed to the door, but paused long enough to give what good manner's dictated. "Pity you're not yet used to our climate and food. It can cause any number of problems, and I do hear there's a dreadful ague going about."

"So I hear. There seems to be any number of nasty things going around."

"Yes, well," Pricilla said, not entirely sure of Sara's meaning. Quickly leaving, Priscilla called out. "Hope you feel better."

Immediately after Priscilla left, Sara raised her fists. She'd like to strike the marble sink--smash the mirror--anything. No! She leaned over the sink, her stomach churning. No! She would not throw up--she would not! A tide of anger threatened. It wouldn't do! She cupped her hand under the faucet and bent to drink a few sips.

Sara glanced at the mirror and took a breath. I've never looked better, she acknowledged--pale or not. She quickly rubbed her cheeks, fashioning a blush of color. But would it matter? Would Cass even notice? Was Priscilla telling the truth? Was Cass engaged? There was only one way to find out!

During the afternoon tea, Sara developed a dreadful headache. Her forehead felt tight and she knew she was probably squinting. Fortunately, no one mentioned it, and she gratefully sipped the warm tea and let others carry the conversational burden. Her first instinct had been to punch Priscilla in the face or spill hot tea down her bodice. But of course, she didn't and gradually gained a measure of civilized control as the afternoon wore on. She watched Aaron tell Mr. Bartlett Sr. about their adventures crossing the plains, and was happy to hear Cass give Aaron so much credit. The older gentleman was impressed with Aaron's ability to handle a wagon. "Of course, Sara did it, too," Aaron admitted.

"That pioneer spirit is just what San Francisco always appreciates," Mr. Bartlett said, smiling at Sara.

As the afternoon worn on, the conversation remained lively and ranged from the latest news from back east to current theatrical events, along with a rather forced discussion on fashion from Priscilla. There was, as yet, no indication of anything special between Cass and Priscilla. Sara watched a smiling Priscilla lean into Cass and daintily placed her hand on his sleeve. Cass appeared cordial, but not overtly friendly, but he didn't exactly move away, either. Is Priscilla more the kind of girl he wants? Sara felt a chill down her back. Perhaps, she didn't really know Cass Bartlett, after all.

CHAPTER FIFTY-FOUR

The next week kept everyone busy preparing for the grand opening of the hardware store. Uncle Jacob came several times to oversee the progress and offer advice. He was very pleased with the way Sara and Aaron had taken charge. Supplies were itemized and arranged on shelves, merchandize ordered, and newspaper ads and flyers placed.

The days seemed to speed by and there was still so much to do. Sara grew more concerned that they might not be ready for the opening as advertised, but Uncle Jacob assured her they would.

Thursday afternoon Cass stopped by, but Sara was on an errand and missed him.

"Well," she questioned Aaron. "What did he say?"

"Nothing much, just 'The store looks great.'"

"Did he say anything about me?"

"Nope."

"Did he seem disappointed that I wasn't here?"

"Couldn't tell. I asked if he saw Peggy at Marilee's. He said he hadn't, but that he saw a picture of Peggy in the Alta, announcing her debut. Both of us thought that was a bad idea."

"I agree, but I doubt Colwell would be around here," Sara said. "When Marilee stopped by Wednesday, she said she'd hired guards. So I think they're prepared."

"Let's hope so."

Finally, the evening of the soiree arrived.

At seven, the first guests began to arrive. Mr. Flan, the butler, met the Robbins family at the door and escorted them into the large entryway where their coats and scarves were taken by two servants in dark, green uniforms with gold braids on their shoulders.

"Beautiful evening for a soiree, isn't it?" Marilee beamed as she and Sloan came forward to greet them.

Clara let go of her father's hand and rushed up to Marilee. "Oh Marilee everything looks so beautiful, like in a fairy tale castle."

"And aren't you just as pretty as a princess!" Marilee put her arm around Clara for a hug. "I'm very glad you all came early. I know Peggy will be relieved to know you've arrived. She's upstairs putting finishing touches on their hair and should be down momentarily to join us."

Aaron stepped forward, frowning and glancing about. Not more than a half dozen folks had arrived as yet, but he knew Peggy would be worried that her stepfather might sneak in. "If you see Peggy, tell her I'll stand guard at the door till everyone gets in. I know what Colwell looks like."

"I'm sure she'll appreciate that. But I wouldn't worry about his getting in. Even if he tried, we have two big burly guards, and Peggy gave a description. We're all on alert."

Sara hugged Marilee. "You look lovely," she said, and Sloan-- you look very happy."

"Oh, I am." He placed his arm around Marilee and stepped forward, extending his hand to Jacob. "So glad you could come."

Uncle Jacob returned a hardy shake. "May I present Jessica Banner, my good friend and my daughter, Clara."

"So pleased to meet you," Jessica said.

Clara curtsied, and looked up at Sloan. "You're even taller than Marilee said."

Sloan laughed.

Clara stared at Sloan. "You have blue eyes same as Cass."

"Yes, he does," Marilee answered. "And don't you love that handsome white jacket?" She beamed up at him.

Jessica stepped back to study Marilee. "I declare, something's different, about you, my dear!"

"You can blame him!" Marilee said, putting out her hand to show a diamond engagement ring.

"Oh, Marilee!" Sara exclaimed. "It's lovely."

"Sloan out did himself!"

"Congratulations!" Everyone said, gathering around. Aaron shook Sloan's hand.

Sara bent forward for a closer look at the ring, then stood back to observe Marilee. "Marilee you are positively radiant. And that royal-blue gown is exquisite. Very Parisian."

"Thank you, Sara. As a matter of fact, I ordered it from Paris last spring. Only it took so long to arrive that it's out of fashion."

"Ah," began Sloan with an elegant flourish, 'Thy eternal summer shall not fade, nor lose possession of that fair thou owest!'"

"How very Shakespearean of you, my darling!" Marilee teased, her fan at his chin and returned, "'Nor time a dandy's tune to play.'"

Aaron wasn't too sure about the Shakespeare part, and his stomach was having a tug of war. Being at Marilee's, seeing her huge house, unsettled him. Maybe two guards weren't enough. He wondered if Sara had thought to bring her Derringer. Clara was saying something to him.

"Doesn't Marilee look beautiful?" Clara asked.

"Oh, yes, especially her hair." Aaron flushed and turned away. He glanced worriedly into the arched doorway of the next room where a number of large, round tables, covered in white table cloths, were set about the room. "Seems like you're expecting a lot of people."

"Actually, only about 100 people." Marilee said, turning to wave at a couple entering.

"You know everybody?" Aaron frowned.

"Oh, yes!"

Sloan shook his head. "Remember last spring?"

Marilee winced. "I nearly forgot. We had five unexpected "guests." Let's hope that doesn't happen tonight. I've only food and seating for 100 or so. Everyone's been hand-picked for Peggy. I'd hoped to build anticipation for the 'mystery artist.'" She sighed. "The picture and her name weren't to be used until after the debut." She noticed Aaron searching the faces of the folks thronging into the entryway. "Flan knows most everyone, and besides, he has the invitation list."

"Is there anything I can do?" Sara asked, feeling a little restless. Seemed like there was a swarm of folks coming through the door all at once. "Perhaps I could help take coats or something."

"No, you just enjoy yourself, Sara," Marilee said quickly, a bit distracted.

"I bet Peggy's scared," Aaron said. "Maybe I should go up stairs--reassure her."

"No," Marilee said gently, "she asked to be left alone. But she'll be down and join us at the table for awhile, before her performance."

"All right, I'll stand at the front door."

"Introduce yourself to Mr. Markum, the front door guard."

Aaron nodded and left.

Marilee and Sloan accompanied the Robbins' party into a large, elegantly decorated room. Its high arched ceilings held four sparkling, crystal chandeliers. Candelabras on the two long serving tables reflected golden light on the silver serving trays. Fine china was stacked at one end, and two other tables in the center of the room, held all kinds of food. A white uniformed chef stood at one end, waiting to cut a roast beef, leg of lamb or baked ham. Two servers waited alongside.

Clara was amazed. "Look at all the food, Daddy!"

"Quite a party," Jacob said, taking Jessica's arm.

Jessica smiled. "The room looks lovely." She glanced about. The room was the size of a hotel ballroom. Ten tables had white damasked table cloths, and silver finger-bowls with gardenias that scented the room.

Marilee returned. "Oh, there you are." She motioned them forward, waving her white-gloved hand. "Please do go ahead and start eating. I want everyone to be splendidly satisfied before the concert."

"Can I have whatever I like?" Clara whispered to Marilee.

"Of course," Marilee encouraged. "My caterer, Peter Jobs, would be insulted if you didn't. When you finish filling your plates, take them to the front table. You'll find your name there." She pointed to a table next to a small stage at the far end of the room. "You'll be sitting with Sloan and me at the first table near the stage." She nodded at Jacob. "That way I can introduce you to people, business people." She tipped her fan over her mouth to cover the small conspiracy.

"Marilee loves putting people together." Sloan added proudly.

Marilee winked at Clara. "I've trained Sloan to think of me as an intrepid impresario rather than a meddlesome female. Now we shall work on the rest of the male population," She smiled at Jessica. "Sara has me convinced to become a Suffragette."

Jessica raised her eyebrows at Jacob. "That will be quite a force," she said and laughed when Jacob raised his.

"Speaking of impresarios," Marilee continued. "I've invited one this evening. He's agreed to represent Peggy if all goes well. Of course, I didn't tell Peggy; thought it might make her more nervous." Marilee smiled. "Oh, excuse me," she said, noticing a group of people enter the dining room, "Sloan and I must see to the other guests. But we'll join you soon."

After Marilee and Sloan left, the Robbins party began filling their plates and then walked to the table where their name was printed. A few feet away, on a raised blue carpeted platform, a string quartet played a lively Viennese waltz.

Aaron returned in a few minutes and came into the dining room. He'd put food on his plate, but when he sat down to eat, he wasn't hungry. Barely touching the food, he kept his eyes on the crowd. Where was Cass, he wondered.

Before long the tables were filled with happy, noisy folks. Looks like everyone wore their Sunday best, Aaron thought, watching Marilee and Sloan stroll about to chat at each table.

"You're scowling, Aaron." Clara said, shaking her head in disbelief. "Don't you like the roast beef and creamed potatoes?"

"I'm not hungry," Aaron answered distractedly.

For the next hour, excited conversation mingled with the rattle of silverware, growing louder as the glasses of wine were filled several times. The noise overpowered the latest musicians, two Spanish guitarists.

Jacob looked up and smiled as he noticed Cass enter the room. "There's our young friend, now." He waved and saw Cass smile and acknowledge the Robbins' table.

"It's about time!" Aaron said, standing, ready to join him. But when he noticed Cass stopping at a number of tables, he decided to sit back down and wait. So many people wanted to talk to Cass, it seemed.

Cass walked about the tables greeting friends; some he obviously hadn't seen in years. An older gentleman, reached for Cass's arm roughly detaining him.

"I hear you got yourself engaged to that Mathews gal."

Cass' expression barely changed. "Where did you hear that?"

"Well, the source was none other than the little lady herself." The man raised his chin boxer like, "isn't that right, Betty dear?"

The gray-haired matron replied, "Horace and I are very happy for you. I declare, you couldn't do better than Priscilla Matthews. Good family. I'd say you were a lucky young man!" She beamed, putting up a magnifying glass.

"Priscilla told you?"

"Yes, she and her mother and I had tea, don't you know… the other day...she says--," she was about to expound.

"Excuse me," Cass interrupted, "my party waits." Bowing slightly, he quickly left and weaved his way across the room, not stopping for those who called to him.

CHAPTER FIFTY-FIVE

"I want to talk to Cass," Aaron said, rising from his chair and heading for him. But he saw Cass walk briskly to his father's table and whisper something in Priscilla's ear. The young woman scowled, abruptly excused herself and hurriedly followed Cass through the maze of tables out of the room. Aaron wondered where they were going in such a hurry.

"Oh good, here's Peggy," Aaron said, relieved at seeing her rush toward their table. "It's about time!" he said, feeling strangely unnerved. His stomach was jerking around inside like a Mexican bean. "How are you feeling, Peggy? Everybody is excited. Are you scared?"

"I'm fine," she said, taking a seat. "Don't worry. I've been practicing all week. I think I'm ready." She smiled and placed her hand on top of his.

"You look wonderful, Peggy," Sara said, watching people stare at their table and point to Peggy.

Sara glanced briefly at Cass's table and nodded cordially to Mr. Bartlett Sr. "I thought I saw Cass earlier."

"Yep," Aaron answered his eyes on the stage area, where the pianist Karl was putting candelabra on the gleaming black, grand piano. "I saw Cass leave with Priscilla."

"Oh," Sara murmured. Her heart plummeted like an anchor A hush fell across the room as Marilee walked up on the stage, smiled at the audience and waited graciously for the room to quiet. She motioned for Sloan to join her.

"As you know," Marilee began, "this evening's entertainment is two-fold. Not only are we honoring the fine talents of our artists, we are also honoring the return of a dear friend, Cass Bartlett." She glanced about the room and pointed to him as he was making his way back to his table, followed by a pale but stoic looking Priscilla.

Aware that she and Cass were singled out, Priscilla kept her chin high, offered a firm smile as she sat stiffly beside her mother and Mr. Bartlett sr.

Few would have guessed that moments ago Cass make it clear he had no intention of marrying her. But Mrs. Mathew knew. Her daughter's face, the knotting of her hanky, and the pursing of her lips, spoke disaster. Never-the-less, both women sat poised and resolute as they stared at the stage.

Marilee smiled at her guests. "Dear friends, it is now my distinct pleasure to introduce you to our special artist this evening, Miss Peggy O'Neil, and her accompanist, Karl Forman. I'm proud to say this is her debut performance in San Francisco. Miss O'Neil has traveled the continent to be with us this evening." She gestured at Karl and left the stage to sit at the Robbins's table.

An excited hush fell over the audience as Peggy and Karl took their places.

"She doesn't look nervous at all," Aaron whispered to Sara and Uncle Jacob. "She's beautiful!" He watched Peggy smile at the audience and include everyone with a sweep of her arm and then unfurl a large black, lace fan which she held against her red, satin bodice.

"I've never seen her lovelier!" Jessica whispered, winking at Aaron.

Aaron felt his face color, but couldn't take his eyes off the change in Peggy. She looked like an angel, all shimmering in candle light. Her pale hair, pulled up on one side had two large white flowers next to her ear. The whole picture reminded him of that afternoon when he'd seen Peggy standing in the river with the sun all soft and misty against her back. She'd looked like an angel then, too.

So many things had happened to them since then—-just a little over a month ago, but it seemed ages. It was like he'd known Peggy forever. A sharp pain seared across his heart, forcing him to take a breath. Peggy's life was changing--probably, forever. Would he lose her?

As Peggy gave a final smile down at the Robbins's table, she caught Aaron's eye. It was but a moment, but for Aaron, a moment without beginning or end. And he knew in the bottom of his soul, that he loved Peggy-- and always would.

Polite applause drew to a close as Peggy nodded to Karl to begin the piano introduction. The first piece was "Greensleeves," which Peggy sang to Cass, as though he had jilted her. Cass chuckled as everyone applauded her amusing interpretation, everyone except Priscilla, who sat rigid as a soldier. Peggy sang "Drink to Me Only" and strolled about, flirting with several young men in the audience. When the song was over, Peggy curtseyed and walked off stage.

Next came Karl's solo part of the program. He played two piano selections and then Peggy appeared again to sing two more songs. As she approached the stage area, the audience roared their approval.

Concluding the program, she sang "When Irish Eyes Are Smiling," and encouraged the audience to join the last chorus. Someone requested, "Johnny's Gone for a Soldier." It was a sad and moving song from the Revolutionary War. Now it had a whole new meaning. The room grew quiet. Karl didn't know the song, so Peggy began alone and sang what was in everyone's heart. When the song ended, there was a long silence, and then the applause began and rose to a crescendo.

Marilee walked on to the stage, applauding. "Isn't she wonderful?" Again the audience stomped its approval. Peggy bowed once more and exited the stage and took her place at the Robbins table.

Marilee smiled and drew Sloan on the stage with her. She looked lovingly at him. "I have another surprise. It concern's the honorable Cass Bartlett, my soon to be cousin." Marilee grinned mischievously, and took Sloan's hand in hers. It took a moment for the crowd to realize what she was saying.

"Yes," Marilee smiled, "Cass will become my cousin-in-law, willingly or not. However, he has done something for all of us, very willingly. Today Cass has officially joined the Army. And because he is too modest, he won't tell you what a hero he is, I will. He traveled across the country as a "special courier" for the Army." She looked down at him. "Apparently, and--it's all still very hush, hush-- he was scouting military locations—I believe you call it and looking out for Southern spies." There was a strong reaction from the audience, some hooting approval, other's booing. Marilee looked nonplused. "He is a real American hero."

Cass, embarrassed, shook his head, as if to say "she exaggerates." Stunned at the news, Sara nearly fell off her chair. "Why didn't you tell me, Aaron?" she whispered.

"Honestly, I didn't know."

"Please stand up Cass," Marilee insisted, waving her arm at him.

Cass stood, shook his head at Marilee and his finger at Sloan. A brief scowled flashed across his face, but he accepted the audience's hearty approval. This was not supposed to be public knowledge, and he'd wanted to tell Sara and Aaron in his own time. He looked over at the Robbins' table and noticed Sara's crestfallen expression. She looked away as he caught her eye. Aaron was grinning and gave a-thumbs up.

Sara watched as Cass's father placed his hand on Cass's sleeve and heard him say. "Well done, son."

Sara's chest went cold. She felt dizzy, grabbed the back of her chair. The room spun. Confusion--icy reality dashed over her. Her journey—her time with Cass--a lie—-deliberate lie. Oh, no! Dear Lord, what was happening? Everything seemed unreal. She had to get away—-leave. She rushed from the table and headed for the powder room, but a tall woman stood up suddenly and blocked her way. Next, she heard loud voices coming from the front entryway.

Everyone turned at the sound of a deep throated roar from the back of the room.

"That's her! That's my daughter!"

CHAPTER FIFTY-SIX

Peggy froze in place. Unable to move, she watched Donald Colwell enter the back of the room, brandishing a gun in one hand and a bowie knife in the other.

Sara turned back to see her Peggy's stepfather. Good Lord, how had Colwell gotten past the guards? He looked different, that was why. He'd been mistaken for a gentleman in his grey dress suit and shaved beard. But there was no mistaking his crazed, murderous intention as he weaved through the room waving his knife.

Shocked guests rose to get out of his way, chairs fell, drinks spilled. Colwell's huge bulky body thrust further into the room, his face a mask of hatred, his voice radiated fury, "Where's that sniveling pup who stole her? She's mine...belongs to me!" He roared. "I'll kill anyone who comes near her! Ya hear!" He pushed through tables and chairs, forcing folks aside as his arm thrust his bowie knife forward.

"Here now!" Several men shouted, rising to stop him. But he brushed them aside, and knifing one in the arm, drawing blood. Shocked and frightened, people scrambled out of his reach.

"Stop him! What's he doing?"

Two men grabbed for him, tried to hold him, but were thrown aside.

A panic stirred the room; people began fleeing through the doorways.

Colwell shouted back at them."She's a slut, I tell ya. I 'otta know! I'm her pa!"

Mortified, Peggy barely heard Cass and Uncle Jacob pulling her. "Come on!" Before she realized it, Peggy felt two strong arms grab her from behind, and thrust her up and over a shoulder.

"Don't worry," Cass said, "I've got you." He motioned to Jacob. "Get the women out back." Carrying Peggy over his right shoulder like a sack of grain, Cass rushed her from the ballroom, following Sloan and Marilee down the hall towards the library.

Cass' father, Priscilla and her mother, as well as Jacob, Clara and Jessica and Sara rushed behind him.

"Everybody---in there," Marilee ordered, pushing them through the library door. "It's a metal door. No one can get through, even Colwell. You'll all be safe there."

Once inside, Cass eased Peggy off his shoulders and down on a blue velvet love seat. "You stay here," he looked at Sara. "Stay with Peggy and the others." His voice left no doubt that he expected to be obeyed. "Where's Aaron?"

"I thought he was following." Sara glanced at the closed door. "I've got to go find him. Donald will kill him!" She bolted for the door.

"No! Stay put!" Cass grabbed her.

"Let me go" Sara struggled against Cass's grip.

"No! Sloan and I will get him."

Grim faced, Sara stood glaring at the door.

Cass turned to Sloan. "Anyone have a gun?"

"Marilee," Sloan said, "Your father's old 45?"

"It's up there." Marilee pointed to a leather box on a book shelf about three feet off the floor. "It's inside, clean and ready. We keep it in case of robbers."

"Good!" Cass reached up, took the box down and carefully removed the gun. He checked it, then nodded for Sloan to open the door.

CHAPTER FIFTY-SEVEN

Cautiously, Cass and Sloan entered the hallway leading to the ballroom room and glanced about. It was deserted, except for two carts with dishes stacked, waiting to be moved into the kitchen. A noise sounded on the other side of the kitchen door. Sloan wheeled about, pointing the .45.

"It's only me, sir!" A very frightened Flan came through the kitchen door. "Oh, Mr. Bartlett," he whispered breathlessly, "Ya scared the very Divil outta me."

"Where's Aaron?"

Flynn leaned against the wall, as though catching his breath. "Don't know. I thought the boy was with you."

"Where are the two men I hired?" Sloan asked.

"Haven't seen'm," Flynn scowled, "but Karl went for the police."

"Colwell?"

Flynn pointed to the dining room.

"Get some rope, Flynn," Sloan ordered.

"Yes, sir. It's in the pantry. I'll get it! Should I bring a butcher knife?"

"Yes!"

Flynn paled. "I just remembered. All the big knives are in the dining room."

"Better hurry with that rope."

As Flan rushed into the kitchen, Cass and Sloan inched along the hall wall. They stepped into the ballroom and saw Aaron and Colwell at the right side of the room near a wall of windows. Colwell held the bowie knife in one hand, his gun in the other. He was only a few feet from Aaron and backing him towards the windows. "One way or the other, I'll kill ya."

"Put the knife down!" Cass hollered, running into the room.

"Stay outta this, Bartlett!"

"Put the knife down or I'll shoot!" Sloan yelled.

"Come closer and I'll kill the pup." Colwell's knife flashed over Aaron's head. "He stole Peggy. He's gonna pay!"

"If you want to fight, fight me. I was the one who stole her!"

Cass taunted, edging closer and off to the side. He had to draw Colwell left, so Sloan could get a shot without hitting Aaron.

Suddenly, Colwell wheeled around. "I'll kill the lot of ya!" He fired his gun; it clicked, but didn't fire! "Damn! useless thing!" He threw it aside.

The distraction gave Aaron a chance to reach up, grab hold of the heavy drape next to him. He yanked it with all his might. The rod gave and cracked.

"What the?" Colwell scowled up at the jagged half of a drapery rod, hanging over his head, like a broken cross. He watched stupefied as a massive column of fabric fell slowly toward him. Colwell dropped the knife. "I'll kill ya, with my bare hands." He flung himself at Aaron, but his right boot tangled in fabric. He tripped and fell to one knee, pulling heavy brocade down on himself.

Before Colwell had time to think, Aaron stepped away from the drape, scooped up the rest and tossed it over Colwell's head.

"I'll kill ya!" Colwell's bellow was muted by the fabric as he flailed about like a trapped animal.

Just then, Flynn rushed into the room carrying a coil of heavy rope. He quickly handed it to Sloan.

"This will cinch him," Sloan said, glancing down at the writhing form. "Puts me in mind of a mad dog."

"That's what he is," Cass said, winding the rope about Colwell's ankles.

Sloan got the rope about the man's neck, but Colwell resisted, bucking and rearing.

"Man's strong as an ox," Sloan said, gritting his teeth.

Aaron ran to one of the banquet tables, grabbed hold of a silver candelabra and rushed back to see that Colwell had managed to free one arm. Without waiting, Aaron raised the candelabra, brought it down on Colwell's head. The blow stunned Colwell. He went limp.

They quickly bound Colwell, trussing him like a steer.

A few moments later, Colwell came to, rolled like a stuffed sausage from side to side. "I'm suffocating! Can't breathe!"

"Hold still," Cass ordered. "I'll cut you a slit to breath."

Colwell's body lay motionless, but his voice rose in defiance. "You're all so high and mighty. You won't stop me! I'll get that lying whore if it's the last thing I do!"

"Shut up or I'll crack your head open!" Aaron shouted in fury, lunging forward with the candelabra.

"Aaron!" Cass called. "Enough! Aaron!" Cass's voice demanded. "Go tell the others it's safe. We got Colwell."

But Aaron just stood there, white knuckles clutching the candelabra.

"I said," Cass repeated firmly, "tell the others. And stay till I come for you."

Aaron took a deep breath, set the candelabra down and then ran to the library door.

"Oh Aaron," Peggy rushed to him as he entered the library. She threw her arms about his neck. "Thank God you're okay!" She hugged him.

Aaron grinned at Peggy. "We got him. Nearly killed us, but his gun misfired." He looked at everyone's shocked face. "I guess you were sort of worried."

"Of course we were worried!" Sara rushed to his side. "What happened?"

"We got Colwell tied up. Now we're waiting for the police. Sloan's already sent for them."

"Cass?" Sara's hand was at her throat.

"Oh he's fine." Aaron beamed, turning to reassure Marilee. "They saved my life."

For the next few minutes everyone gathered about Aaron querying him about the details of the "capture." Aaron eagerly gave them a blow by blow description.

"You're a very brave young man," Mr. Bartlett Sr. said, coming forward to shake Aaron's hand.

"It was your son who did it, sir." He glanced over at Marilee, "and your nephew."

"I'm mighty proud of you, Aaron," Uncle Jacob said, coming forward to put his arm around him.

"We were all so worried," Jessica said, as Clara came and gave Aaron a hug.

Priscilla, however, sat stiffly on the couch, not taking any interest in the capture tale. Now that her ordeal was over, she rose from her seat, nodded to her mother. "It's rather late," she said, in a resigned tone. "Perhaps, now that the excitement is over, Mr. Bartlett will be good enough to see us home."

"Yes, of course," he replied kindly. "As soon as I see to Cass and make sure the police get here. He noticed the distaste on Priscilla's face, the shrug of annoyance.

They didn't have long to wait for Cass.

"Everything's under control," he reassured as he bounded into the room. "Sloan and Flynn have Colwell in hand, and Karl returned to say the police wagon is on its way." He smiled at his father.

Mr. Bartlett Sr. took that as a cue to step forward.

Relieved and proud, he put his arm about his son. "Good job, Cass." His voice was full of feeling. "For a minute there, I was kind of worried."

"For a whole minute?" Cass teased.

"Naw, you're a Bartlett---thirty second's worth."

"That's better." Cass nodded, seeing the respect in his father's eyes. "Good," he repeated softly to himself, and then he winked, adding, "Sloan's a Bartlett, too, don't forget."

"A good team, I'd say." Charles Bartlett smiled.

Cass turned to Peggy, made an elegant and rather elaborate bow, "We Bartlett men promise that you'll never have to worry about Colwell, again. He'll be tried for attempted murder. Sadly, we found one of the guards injured. He's still out cold, but it looks like he'll be fine."

Peggy covered her hands over her face. "It's all my fault!"

"No, it wasn't your fault, Cass said, "but now the crisis is over, and you don't have to worry any more".

Peggy looked stricken. "I...I...don't know what to say."

"Nothing to say," Cass reassured. He glanced at Sara and seemed about to say something, but didn't.

A half-hour later, Colwell was carted off in a Paddy-wagon, two armed policemen sitting beside him.

Everyone stood outside watching the wagon leave and waiting for their coaches to be brought from the carriage barn. Mr. Bartlett Sr. noticed Peggy holding her head down. "That was a very frightening experience for you. But I expect the lasting impression will be of your performance. You were splendid! I imagine you'll be besieged with requests to perform."

Peggy looked up at him with her large blue eyes. "Thank you sir, but I doubt anyone will want to come and see me."

"Nonsense!" Marilee spoke up. "I know Mr. MacGuire was very impressed. I imagine that your "dramatic" debut will become the talk of the town. People love a good melodrama. Mr. MacGuire is a showman; he'll take advantage of the public curiosity." Marilee seemed very certain.

Priscilla, standing impatiently sneered, "Sounds a rather prurient interest!"

"Quite!" Marilee agreed. "But, it will launch Peggy's career."

"What is the world coming to!" Priscilla huffed.

"We'll just have to wait and see, won't we, Priscilla!" Marilee offered cheerfully.

"Really!" Priscilla sneered, pressing her lips as she busied herself with her cape, making a display of shielding herself from the cool night air.

Soon the Bartlett coach arrived. Mr. Bartlett Sr. helped Priscilla and her mother into the coach, and then turned to Cass. "Are you coming, Son?"

"No, Sloan and I are going down to the police station to make our statements. Sloan can bring me home later."

"I see." Mr. Bartlett smiled. "Good idea." He turned before getting into the coach. "Jacob, I'll be paying you a call. I hope to see that new store of yours--sounds like it's quite a new version of things." He smiled at Aaron. "And I'm especially eager to see that fine horse of yours—-Rebel, is it?"

"Yes, sir." Aaron announced proudly.

Jacob stepped forward. "You have a fine son, Mr. Bartlett. I'll be eternally grateful."

"Yes, he is a good son, a good man," Chuck Bartlett said, thoughtfully. He quickly entered the coach and closed its door.

"Good night, sir." Cass stuck his head into the coach window. He smiled at his father and nodded to the two women. "Goodnight Mrs. Matthews, Priscilla."

"Good evening," the two offered. Priscilla stared straight ahead, her back pressed against the leather seat as the coachman signaled the horses away.

Next, the Robbins's coach pulled forward.

"Are you coming home, Peggy?" Aaron asked hopefully.

"Yes, I want to be with my family." She glanced at Marilee. "I hope you don't mind."

"Of course not. I understand."

"Thank you!" Peggy said, relaeved. "I'll send Mr. Hwang with a message in a day or two and we can make plans." Peggy quickly hugged Marilee. "I can never thank you enough."

"Goodnight, then." Marilee smiled. "Just remember, the evening was a great success. You'll be the toast of San Francisco before you

303

know it, Peggy!"

Even before Peggy had settled in the coach, Aaron turned to her. "You were really wonderful tonight!"

Peggy reached out for Aaron's hand and gave it a squeeze and then leaned to kiss his check.

Surprised, Aaron touched his cheek and grinned.

Cass held the door of the coach open for Sara, but when she was about to step in, he put his hand out. "I need to talk to you. Can we have lunch tomorrow?"

"Yes, of course," she said, suddenly concerned by his serious tone.

"I'll look forward to it." Cass took her hand and held it for a moment, allowing a warm current to pass between them. "Till tomorrow then."

Even when they returned home and were ready for bed, the full impact of the evening had yet to be absorbed, but they were too weary to talk. Aaron said a hurried "goodnight," and went to his room. Peggy barely said two words. She seemed to be in a daze as she prepared for bed.

"I know you're exhausted, Peggy and upset, but you were wonderful tonight," Sara said. "Just remember that." She watched Peggy shake her head, crawl under the covers and turn her face away. Sara sighed. If only there was something she could say or do to make it better--perhaps if she prayed.

Sara quietly knelt at the side of the bed and put her hands together. "Dear Lord, part of me still feels like a hypocrite about praying, because I'm not sure if it's just my need for a God or something more---more real, even if I can't see or touch it. And it feels sinful to pray and not be sure--disrespectful. But I don't mean to be."

Sara paused, took a deep breath and let it out slowly. "Guess I'm still angry about Mom and Dad." Sara shook her head. "It makes me crazy when folks excuse things and say, 'God has his reasons,' or 'it's not for us to question.' I hate that. It…it seems so lacking…so weak minded…so giving up when really we need to fight things…things like disease or bad people. Cholera is a sickness that people can do something about. And I don't want these same folks inventing Your reasons, or trying to convince me you're real. I need to know for myself." Sara sighed. "Is that too 'uppity?' I know I am sometimes, and I'm sorry if I ask too much, but please--if you're real, please hear my prayer for Peggy and help her. I know she's hurting and can't even give voice to it all. She feels ashamed and humiliated by what her stepfather said, and she blames herself. Please let her understand---give her strength to overcome what others might say or do. Show her that she can rise above that. Keep her safe. And thank you, Lord, for keeping Aaron and me safe, and letting us keep our promise to Mom and Dad. I admit, Lord, my faith is more desire than real, but I do sense a presence, a kind of guidance that's here for us. I hope it's true. So thank you. Thank you for what I sense and especially for showing me how good it is to talk to you. I know I have a long ways to go, but please help me to see and know more about you and what you wish from me. Yours, Sara…Amen"

CHAPTER FIFTY-EIGHT

"You're up early, young lady," Jessica said as she came into the kitchen. "See you're dressed and ready for your date with Cass."

"I'm not sure it's a date," Sara said softly, slicing pieces of bread. "Thought I'd make French toast and ham." She bent to give Tarney a small piece of ham. "She's been such a good girl, haven't you sweet Tarney?"

Tarney wagged her tail and eagerly took the treat.

"Oh, by the way," Jessica said, setting the table. "Mr. Hwang picked up the mail for us late yesterday--seems you have a letter."

"Oh?" Sara quickly wiped her hands on her apron and rushed to the parlor. She found the letter on the small sideboard. "It's from Mark," she announced excitedly, rushing back to the kitchen. "I've been waiting for this." She took a deep breath. I hope everything is all right."

Jessica nodded. "Mark and his family were very close to you."

"Oh, yes. Mark's like a brother. His whole family is like family," Sara said, eagerly opening the letter.

It read:

Dear Sara,

I expect you are at your Uncle's now. Hope he is better and that you and Aaron are well. My Dad is getting better and Mom is much happier. I guess because of my news.

I'm not sure how you'll feel about this and I know we talked about my coming down there to discuss our plans. I got to thinking and I realized you weren't keen on marrying a farmer. I can understand. But I did meet a nice girl, Martha, and she took a shine to me and wants to be a farmer's wife. So we got married in Salt Lake City. I hope you will forgive me. You will always be a part of our family.

Yours, Mark

p.s. best to Aaron and everybody.

"Oh!" Sara plunked down on a kitchen chair. "Mark's married!" She slammed the letter on the table. "Married! I can't believe it!"

Covering her face with hands, she kept shaking her head and saying, "He's married." Sara stood up and began pacing. "He was supposed to come here!"

Tarney followed close at her heels.

"Tarney get out of the way!" Sara snapped, nearly tripping.

The little dog dashed under the table and stayed.

"Sara, you're white as a sheet. Better sit down. I'll you a glass of water."

"No, no!" Sara shook her head as tears streamed down her cheeks. She pulled her hanky from her apron and wiped them away.

"It must be quite a shock for you."

"Yes! I can hardly believe it. Married! It's ironic really. He was always so set on marrying me, but I….I……was the one who…oh, dear." She blew her nose and sat. It was a minute before she could say anything. "I'm sorry, Tarney. I didn't mean to be so cross." She bent to pet the top of Taney's head. "I'm not sure whether to laugh or cry. I feel sort of strange, like I'm all a jumble." She clenched her fists.

Jessica ran to the water pitcher. "I'm so sorry, dear. Here's a glass of water. I'll put the kettle on for tea."

"Oh, Jessica, it's so confusing. I feel angry and relieved, yes relieved, all at the same time." She put her hand over her forehead and took a breath. "More relieved, than angry, actually. I've been so worried about disappointing Mark, hurting him because of everything he's been through. I felt so guilty because of Cass." She stood again and began pacing. "Here I've been losing sleep, dreading telling Mark I couldn't marry him. I'm relieved, but I feel as though someone punched me in the stomach." Sara grabbed the letter, read it again, and sat down, staring at the piece of paper. "All this time, I was feeling so awful, so guilty for having to tell Mark how much Cass means to me." She took a sip of water, set it down and jumped up. "Oh, Jessica, I'm so happy!" She twirled about and threw the letter in the air.

Tarney began barking and running about the kitchen.

"It's all right, Tarney."

"Well," Jessica said, "I'm glad you're taking it so well."

"Don't you see, I'm free. That awful weight has been lifted." She rushed to throw her arms about her friend. "Oh, Jessica, I'm truly happy, and I'm happy for Mark!"

"What's all the commotion?" Peggy asked, sleepily entering the kitchen.

"Mark's married!" Sara said.

"Oh?" Peggy looked confused.

"Isn't that wonderful?" Sara rushed to show Peggy the letter.

For the next few hours, Sara was able to share the news with her family. And while she didn't say it aloud, she knew deep inside that it was for the best.

Shortly before noon, Cass arrived. As he knocked on the door, Aaron hollered from the kitchen. "I'll get it!" Aaron dashed to the parlor door. "I knew it was you," he said opening it wide.

Thought you'd be gone by now," Cass smiled. "You were going to see Rebel, right?"

"I decided to wait until after Sara tells you her news. I want to see your face."

"News?" Cass looked up to see Sara coming down the stairs, a frown on her face as she walked up to her brother.

"What did you say, Aaron?"

"Nothing, Sara, honest." Aaron raised his shoulders in exaggerated innocence.

Sara shook her head. "Please come in Cass," she said, nervously pressing a curl behind her ear.

"Hope I'm not too early," he said, sitting down.

"No, no, I'm ready to leave. Aaron don't you have something to do?"

"It'll keep."

Cass nodded to Aaron. "I need to speak to Sara, alone, Aaron."

"Oh, all right," Aaron said grudgingly. "I'll be back by the barn, if you need me." He glanced between Sara and Cass and grinned. "See you later," he said dashing away.

"That brother of mine can be so…so obtuse, sometimes."

"I suspect he's more aware than he lets on. Typical brother—wants to annoy you." Cass looked thoughtful. "It must be hard for him, all he went through—having to grow up so fast." It kind of reminded Cass of a phase he went through himself a long time ago. He smiled. "Maybe acting childish at times, allows him to retain some innocence." Cass shook his head. "But what do I know?"

"More than I do, it seems. You understand him better, these days, and he certainly listens to you."

"He's smart. Very talented," Cass said and paused for a moment, looking more closely at Sara. "Is everything all right?

Aaron mentioned some news."

Sara sat down on the chair opposite Cass, but avoided looking directly at him. "I've received a letter from Mark. He got married in Salt Lake City."

"That's wonderful news!" Cass exclaimed and then realized it might not be Sara's reaction.

"I suppose," Sara said, soberly.

"You're disappointed?" Cass frowned.

Sara took a deep breath. "Not really. It was just a shock."

"Sara, look at me. Do you still love Mark? Did you want to marry him?"

"No!" Sara shook her head. "I don't think I can marry anyone." She looked about to cry and turned her face away.

"Why is that?" Cass held a stern, penetrating look.

"I want to be able to work, to take care of my family, be a suffragette, do things, discover things about myself, my abilities--things I couldn't do as a wife."

"Is that all?"

"Well," Sara said, anger flashing, "it may not seem like much to you. I know how men think. Most men, anyway."

"You do, do you?"

"Yes! And I don't appreciate your smug tone."

"Sara, my dear, Sara." He shook his head. "I'm a man and I'm telling you that I think you should be yourself, do all the things that you love, things that make you so much of who you are--the woman I love and the woman I hope to make my wife."

"What?" Sara sat back, stunned. "What did you say?"

Cass got up from the settee and kneeled before her. "Sara Robbins, you are the woman I love. Will you be my wife?"

"Oh, my---oh!" Her hand flew to her mouth.

Cass reached into his vest pocket and pulled out a little blue, velvet box and opened it. "This is for you, if you want it." He took out a small gold ring with a ruby stone set between two small diamonds. "It belonged to my mother. My father knew I was going to do this and insisted I offer it to you."

"I...I...don't know what to say."

"Say what's in your heart."

"Oh, Cass, I do love you. Yes, yes," she cried, tears streaming down her cheeks. "Yes, I will marry you." But as soon as she said it, she realized something. "Oh, but you know I need to work at the hardware store. Are you sure it's all right, with you?"

"Yes, of course. I know you need to do that."

"But before you totally agree, Sara, you need to know something." He took her hands and helped her stand. "I'm going to be an officer in the Army. I want to help preserve the Union. You know now that I was a currier for the Army. I wanted to tell you when I first took you with me. But it had to be a secret. I wasn't supposed to disclose the mission. I apologize. In truth, I used you and Aaron. Can you forgive me?"

Sara frowned. "At first I was angry when I learned. But then, I realized you couldn't tell me. I'm proud that Aaron and I could help. You certainly saved our lives. We'd have been at the mercy of the Carey brothers. That's for sure."

"I'm glad you feel that way. The thing is, while I expect to be in this area for now, if war comes, I might have to leave San Francisco. I could be gone awhile. Folks think it'll be over in six months, but no one can be sure. Are you willing to risk that?"

Sara looked into his eyes. "Yes, Cass, I am," she said softly. "I believe, like you, we need to keep the country together, build something wonderful for all kinds of people. It's worth fighting for."

"Thank you, Sara." Cass kissed her and she eagerly kissed him back.

EPILOGUE

The news of Sara and Cass's engagement was greeted joyfully, but tempered by the political climate of the city and the upcoming election, a month and a half away. The Democratic Party was split into several fractions. Many elected officials were Southern men of pro slavery persuasion and threatened to push California for secession if Lincoln were elected. Others wanted to divide California into two states--some hoping to take a portion for a new slavery state. Others claimed "California gold will pay for the war."

The sense of foreboding grew as November 6th approached. Cass felt that the dissolution of the States might happen even before a president took office in the spring. There was even talk of England and France supporting a war between the North and South, especially over the cotton issue. And if the country came into turmoil, there might be a grab for land from foreign governments.

Aaron wanted to join the army, but Cass talked him out of it, explaining that he would be needed on "the home front." The hardware store could help in the war effort, and his boat The Promise might serve as an important supply link for the army along the Sacramento River.

Sloan joined the Army, as well. He and Marilee happily upped their wedding date to join Cass and Sara, so a double wedding was held on November 30th on the stage of Marilee's home. Peggy was Maid of Honor for both Marilee and Sara. Clara and Jessica were Brides' Maids; Aaron and Tarney walked down the aisle together. Gone was the stigma of Colwell, replaced with the love and beauty of the occasion. Peggy, once again, proudly sang for the brides and grooms and a hundred happy guests.

How did the Civil War affect California, seemingly so far from the fields of battle? Perhaps our young protagonists will show you in my next novel.

Rebel and The Promise is Delores Dahl's debut novel. A second novel, in progress, *Billy Frankenstein,* has recently been optioned by Noble House Entertainment, Inc. In addition to her work as a writer, Ms Dahl is a professional actress, photographer, teacher and an accomplished painter. She lives in Bothell, Washington and loves spending time with her three daughters and their families. Ms Dahl can be reached at: rebelandthepromise@gmail.com

Made in the USA
San Bernardino, CA
04 November 2014